Confessions
in B-Flat

Confessions
in B-Flat

ESSENCE BESTSELLING AUTHOR
DONNA HILL

Entangled Publishing, LLC
10940 S Parker Road
Suite 327
Parker, CO 80134
rights@entangledpublishing.com

Edited by Stacy Abrams and Jen Bouvier
Cover design by Bree Archer
Cover images by
isaxar/GettyImages,
PeopleImages/GettyImages, and
Denissova/Depositphotos
Interior design by Toni Kerr

HC ISBN 978-1-64063-829-7
TP IBN 978-1-64063-899-0
Ebook ISBN 978-1-64063-830-3

Manufactured in the United States of America

First Edition November 2020

10 9 8 7 6 5 4 3 2 1

Also by Donna Hill

When I began this project several years ago, my intention was to tell a story that was centered on a seminal moment in American history—the civil rights movement. I wanted a story that spotlighted two sides of that era and also showcased the beauty, rhythm, and vibrancy of Black culture during that tumultuous time. My characters Jason and Anita emerged to represent the two sides of the movement, and throughout the ups and downs of their relationship, they rub elbows and work with some of the historic figures of that period.

While many layers of this novel are born out of real events, I have taken a bit of creative license with dialogue for these historic characters. I also want to acknowledge that though no one civil rights leader was perfect or adhered 100 percent to only their approach, the ultimate message of this novel is that it is through understanding each other that we gain insight into the ways we can work together to achieve peace.

So many of these turbulent times are etched in my memory: the riots in Brooklyn and the aftermath—it took decades to recover—the March on Washington, the rhythm of old Harlem, the assassination of President Kennedy—they sent us all home from school that day—and of course Motown, the soundtrack of my life, among so many other memories. All these experiences, direct and indirect, are infused in every line of this novel.

What I didn't know when I began Confessions in B-Flat *was that a new movement of the time would arise, Black Lives Matter, and that we would see a worldwide resurgence in the demand for justice. Neither did I know that by the time I submitted this manuscript for the final edits, the world would lose the last of the civil rights icons, John Lewis, who in this novel inspires my character Jason to pick up the torch.*

In that vein, I dedicate this novel to the great John Lewis, and to all the voices and freedom fighters who he inspired to rise up to demand justice and equality and make "good trouble."

Donna Hill

Chapter One

September 1963

J ason Tanner loosened his tie as soon as he walked out of Paschal's Restaurant, still caught in the spell of the past two hours. This was the first time he'd been invited to literally sit at the table with the major leaders of Dr. King's nonviolent movement. The meeting at Paschal's had been set up as a wind-down and debriefing following the success of the March on Washington the prior week.

The impact of witnessing and being part of the march for equality still pulsed in his veins. More than 200,000 protesters had descended upon Washington under the blaze of an August sun in what news outlets were calling the largest civil rights gathering in US history. Dr. King's rousing speech about his dream for a better world, which was already being touted as one of the most powerful oratories in history, still made the hairs on his arms rise.

Flatware had clicked against china while voices rose and fell between mouths full of golden fried chicken and deep swallows of sweet tea. Dr. King—surrounded by John Lewis, the twenty-three-year-old wunderkind and rising star in the Student Nonviolent Coordinating Committee, who'd given a stirring speech during the march; Baynard Ruskin, the architect of the march; Jesse Jackson; and Andrew Young—

had insisted that now was not the time to sit back. "There's no room to turn back now. We have to keep pushing ahead while we have the momentum," he'd said, and that had only reaffirmed the commitment in Jason's belly.

He'd had his first up-close taste of the magnetism of Dr. King and his message of brotherhood and equality when Dr. King had come to preach at his local church, Mt. Zion, six months earlier. Jason had been enthralled as much by the message as the man. Dr. King was young, not much older than he was, yet the reverend was on a path to change the world. "Every step toward the goal of justice requires sacrifice, suffering, and struggle," Dr. King had said that Sunday morning. It made Jason rethink the value of punching a time card as the company bookkeeper for DeKalb County's big furniture company. *A respectable job for a young Black man*, his father had insisted. But after that Sunday sermon, he'd begun to question his own worth.

What would his contribution be?

Jason had worked hard at not acting as overwhelmed as he felt by the pure power that sat around the table at Paschal's that day. The restaurant was owned by brothers James and Robert Paschal, but beyond being restaurateurs, the brothers were staunch supporters of the movement. They often posted bond for jailed protesters, served complimentary meals, and extended their hours of operation to accommodate families who needed to reconnect with their loved ones released from jail. Paschal's served as a gathering hub for Dr. King and the supporters of his nonviolent resistance movement, who came together as much to plan next steps as to decompress from an event or just relax with good food and better friends, which was what had brought Jason to Paschal's on a Friday afternoon.

Dr. King was certain that if they kept the pressure up,

President Johnson would have no choice but to sign the civil rights bill into law. Dissenting voices around the table raised the reality of countermovements up North led by Malcolm X, who'd never hidden his skepticism about the path that Dr. King chose. Malcolm's philosophy challenged the nonviolent pursuit of integration. His position and message to his followers was to defend themselves against "the white devils" with the mindset of "by any means necessary," which Dr. King could never support.

The young firebrand insisted that Negroes must rise up and stop turning the other cheek. His message was spreading across the North and filtering down South, an issue that was discussed at length around the table.

"I respect Brother Malcolm's passion," Dr. King had intoned. "However, it is counter to our message and could very well damage any chance we have of getting the bill on the president's desk signed."

"The only way to make any dents in his rhetoric is to have a presence up North," Ralph Abernathy said. "A *strong* presence. Fine what we are doing here in the southern states, but if we are going to succeed, we need our brothers and sisters in the North to fully embrace the cause."

"Grassroots is the way to go. Set up a main office. Get volunteers. Organize," Baynard said. "Same way we did here."

They'd agreed that they must expand and strengthen their message in the North, but to do that, they needed someone to lay the groundwork, and no one from the committee could be spared.

"I could do it. I'll go to New York and set up a headquarters," Jason had said, the words out of his mouth and into the laps of those at the table before he could blink. His heart thudded when all eyes had turned on him.

Then the men broke into a half-hour debate on the merits

of Jason Tanner starting up an office in New York. It was actually John who'd given the most impassioned words of support, reminding all the skeptics that at one point, each of them had been Jason Tanner. Ultimately, Dr. King agreed, which made Jason's heart swell with pride, and plans would immediately get underway. The meeting had ended on a high note, touting the success of the march and Jason's relocation to New York. They all shook his hand and clapped him heartily on the back, each intoning how important his work in New York would be. The group finally dispersed with plans to meet the following week.

Now, out from under the heavy gaze of men set on changing the world, he considered what he had just committed to do. His throat grew dry, and the nerve under his right eye began to tick. The first time he'd ever been out of the state of Georgia was for the march. He'd read about New York, seen the news, heard the stories about the "fast life," and, up until this afternoon, it had not been a place he'd ever wanted to visit. Now he was on the cusp of packing up his life and leaving his family and everything he knew. What had he been thinking? That was just it. He *hadn't* been thinking.

He'd been swayed by the collective power that surrounded him.

He took a handkerchief out of his pants pocket and wiped his brow. It was barely three, but the streets of Atlanta were relatively empty. The air hung heavy with humidity. He looked upward. Gray clouds hovered in the distance. A storm was coming.

He undid the top button of his winter-white shirt, starched to within an inch of its life just the way he'd been taught since he was old enough to handle the heavy iron without dropping it on his foot. He draped his jacket over one arm and tucked the thick folder under the other.

Jason strolled down Hunter Street, trying not to think about the fifteen-minute walk in the sweltering heat, when a beautiful sky-blue Cadillac Eldorado, with chrome rims polished until they gleamed, glided by. Its owner was dressed to the nines: tan wide-brimmed hat with a suit to match. The driver stopped at the corner as the prettiest black-on-black Lincoln Continental convertible that Jason'd ever laid eyes on crossed the intersection. He licked his lips.

One of these days, I'mma be behind the wheel of one of them beauties.

A dribble of sweat slid down the length of his spine, returning him to his reality. Throwing his hat in the ring among the men at the table who understood deep in their souls the importance of their mission was one thing. But it would be a different story to announce to his family that he was leaving home to live in a city "of sin," as his mother would say.

He knew that his folks' negative response would be born out of fear for him and the work ahead. They'd watched the dogs, the hoses, the violent arrests in horror. But the North was different, he would argue. He had a calling, he would insist.

Everyone had to do *something* if change was ever going to be had for the Negro.

This was his time. This was his duty.

He turned onto Stone Road for two long blocks. The tree-lined street did little to stave off the humidity that wrapped around him like cellophane, sucking the air out of his lungs. He could feel his shirt sticking to his back.

A flash of light cut through the sky. He picked up his pace and turned onto Elderts Lane. Friday was family night at the Tanner house, and tonight they would be joined by thunder and lightning.

"Hey there, Jason!"

Jason waved at Mrs. Crawford, who had to be 150 if she

was a day. She'd been his family's neighbor since before he was born, and she was old back then.

Mrs. Crawford had been like a second mom to him when he was a kid. There were many afternoons he'd sit at her wobbly kitchen table after school with a peanut butter and jelly sandwich while she quizzed him about his day, what he'd learned, and talked about her garden and her bad knee and how she expected him to be somebody special. *Yes, ma'am*, he'd always agree.

He wondered now if this trip to New York would fulfill that prophecy.

"How you doin', Mrs. C.?"

"Well as can be expected. Knee acting up," she said from her perch on the porch.

Jason hid his smile. Mrs. C.'s knees had been *acting up* for as far back as he could remember. The refrain fell from her lips as easily as "good morning." She was probably the fittest seventy-year-old woman he knew. "Sorry to hear that. Storm coming. You should get inside."

She waved her thin hand in dismissal. "Storm's always coming." She laughed. "Tell your mama I fixed up my peach cobbler and to come over for a piece."

"Sure will. Save me a slice."

"When you gonna settle down with a good woman? Handsome boy like you."

Jason grinned. "One of these days, Mrs. C. Promise."

She waved off his response and pouted.

Jason pushed open the white wooden gate that creaked and rocked on its hinges, announcing his arrival the same way it had when he was a teen and tried to sneak in after his curfew. He walked down the short path to the house, and just like when he was sixteen, the front door opened. But instead of his dad, Ralph, with his thick, calloused hands shoved into the pockets of his blue work pants and a scowl painted on his brick-brown face, it was his mother who greeted him.

"I thought I heard someone coming." Mama beamed at him.

Jason jogged up the three steps. He leaned down and planted a full kiss on his mother's smooth cheek that made her giggle like a schoolgirl. His mother was sitting squarely in her late fifties but didn't look a day over thirty. Her full head of jet-black shoulder-length hair—which she kept pressed until it hollered and curled in the latest fashion, courtesy of Miss Hazel's Beauty Salon every Saturday the Lord sent—was her crowning glory. His mother always said, "God ain't seen fit to give me height or money, but I got me a head fulla beautiful hair and a brain to go with it."

"Hey there, Clara," she called out to Mrs. Crawford. "I'll be by later after supper." She slid her arm around Jason's waist and glanced upward. "Storm's comin'."

"Sure is. How's Dad?" he asked as he closed the door behind them.

"Good spirits, all things considered. Won't see the doctor. Stubborn as a mule. He's in the living room, watching the game."

Jason approached the entrance to the living room and stopped in his tracks as he watched his dad slowly lower himself into his favorite chair. The strain tightened the veins in his neck while his knotted hands gripped the arms of the chair for support. The years of working the docks and driving a truck for hours and weeks on end had eventually taken a toll on Ralph Tanner. The arthritis in his knees and hips made it difficult to get around and, on bad days, more like impossible. Doctors had recommended hip surgery, but his father wouldn't hear of it. Nobody was gonna cut him open and put metal inside, not if he had a say. A few aspirin and he'd be fine, he insisted.

Jason and his mother walked into the living room. Jason dropped his jacket and the folder on the couch and headed over to his father, who was reclining in the chair designated for his use only. A pillow was propped under his knees.

"Hey, Dad." He bent down and hugged him.

"Good game. Knicks and Celtics. Knicks losing at the moment, but it's close." Dad glanced up at him. "You coulda played professional ball," he said for the zillionth time. It didn't matter that Jason didn't have an athletic bone in his body. Just the fact that he was a six-foot-three Negro male was enough for his father.

Jason patted his father's shoulder. "Mm-hmm." He plopped down in the paisley club chair, whose fabric had seen better days, but it sure was comfortable.

"Dinner will be ready about five thirty. Patrice is on her way from work, and Mason is upstairs doing who knows what," Mama said from the arch of the living room door. She wiped her hands on a blue-and-white hand towel.

"I'm glad everyone'll be here," Jason said. But now he wished he'd had more time to plan his words. His thoughts were spinning in his head so fast that his stomach knotted.

Too late to turn back. He'd up and volunteered to go to New York without really thinking. Then, to his delight and ultimate alarm, he'd gotten the membership's blessing. The enormity of what he'd signed on for was slowly sinking in.

And the table of world changers at Paschal's was no match for Ralph and Mae Ellen Tanner.

He ran his finger around the collar of his shirt. As a team, his mother and father always presented a united front, one that he and his siblings, friends, and family found difficult, if not impossible, to break. They were a formidable pair, and they were in unison about their support of Dr. King's nonviolent movement, but they only cautiously tolerated Jason's participation as long as it was confined to attending meetings.

When he'd announced that he was going to Washington, it had taken nearly two months to convince them that he would be all right. He didn't have that kind of time now. Dr. King wanted him in New York as soon as possible.

Thunder rumbled in the background.

Dad looked over the top of his glasses at his son. "Why's that?"

"I have some news that I want to tell everyone at once."

"Why *you*?" his mother asked, clearly distraught. Lines deepened around her eyes.

"Mama, I've been preparing for this for more than a year. I've organized and trained hundreds right here in Atlanta. Dr. King believes I can do good work in New York."

"I don't like it one damn bit," his dad said, taking a swallow from his sweet tea and then slamming the glass on the table. "Nothing but trouble up North. Fast life." He shook his head. "I don't like it one bit."

"I think it's great," Patrice, his baby sister, said and flashed a dimpled smile at him as she ladled mashed potatoes onto her plate. "Jason has the chance to do something really important, be part of changing the world and the way the world sees colored people. You should be proud. Dr. King is something special, and he thinks Jason is special, too. That means a lot."

"I watched that march on TV," Mason said. "That was something. Wish I was there. Proud of you, big brother." He waved a leg of fried chicken at Jason.

Jason smiled and patted his brother's back. "Thanks, Mase."

"How long you gonna be gone?" Mama asked.

He looked his mother in the eyes, saw the love and the worry hovering there. He wished he could say that everything would be fine and there was nothing to worry about, but he'd likely be lying. Although the work they did was based on nonviolent resistance, their adversaries didn't always feel the same way.

The chances of being beaten with billy clubs, water hosed, attacked by dogs, or simply "made to disappear" were all part of his reality—and the reality of everyone committed to the movement.

"I'm not really sure. As long as it takes."

His mother muffled a cry.

Dad cleared his throat. "I don't like it, not one bit," he repeated, "but I...I understand."

Jason blinked in surprise. His mother inhaled a gasp.

Dad slowly shook his head as he spoke. "My daddy and my mama was born slaves. All they knew was how hard life could be. By the time I came along, they were just beginning to understand what freedom meant." He drew in a long breath, looked off into the distance. "Even though they said we was free, it didn't mean nothing to some folks. Can't count the times the night riders sat out in front of the house in those damn white robes." His expression tightened into a series of hard lines, and he paused for a long moment before speaking again. "There ain't no feeling to compare to having to cut your own daddy down from a tree and watch your mother fade away from heartbreak. I couldn't stop none of that, but...I can now."

The Tanner siblings sat frozen in silence. Tears glistened in Patrice's eyes. Mason's long fingers curled into fists. The power of the images that Ralph had shared with his family for the first time held them.

Jason's nostrils flared as he sucked in air, his shoulders curved under the weight of his father's words. He had known that he'd be met with resistance, resistance of the here and now, but not with a past so powerful that decades later still held them all in its grip. The terror that his father had endured was one he didn't want visited upon his son or his family ever again. Jason understood that. But his father couldn't protect him forever. They *both* knew it.

Rain slapped against the window, each pelt felt like a stab to his heart, as he knew what he must do and how his decision would affect his family.

His father's dark eyes, which had witnessed too much, passed from one to the next at the dinner table. Mama took her husband's hand.

Jason watched as his father painfully rose to his feet, gave him a somber look, and slowly ambled away.

He wanted both his parents' blessings, but he would leave without them if he had to. The challenge ahead was bigger than one man's dark and painful past or even a woman's broken heart.

Violence was what this country was built on, but it could not be the way it survived.

He came from a legacy of men and women who had endured the unspeakable. It ran in his blood. And his father had to know that. For as much as he railed against him going North, Jason believed deep in his soul that his father saw the possibility of the Negro people embodied in his son.

It was his calling.

He had to answer.

• • •

More than two weeks had gone by since that Friday night dinner. He'd endured the one-word answers and painful stares until his father came to him after another Friday night dinner. He asked Jason to walk with him out on the porch.

They sat side by side on the swing, quiet, contemplative, looking out to the purple sky as the sun began to sink.

"I know what you doing is important work, son. I admire that. We not gonna stop worrying about you and we not gonna stop ya." He placed his hand on Jason's shoulder. "If you gotta go to try to make things better, then you gotta go," he finally said. "For your grandmother. And for your grandfather."

Jason clasped his father's thigh. His throat clenched. "I will make things better. I promise."

Leaders of the March on Washington for Jobs and Freedom meet with Senator Everett Dirksen (R- IL) at the Capitol Building. Left to right: Whitney Young, National Urban League; Dr. Martin Luther King, Jr., Southern Christian Leadership Conference; Roy Wilkins, NAACP; Walter Reuther, UAW; Senator Everett Dirksen; John Lewis, Student Non-Violent Coordinating Committee. 1963-08-28. (25417)

(c) Walter P. Reuther Library, Archives of Labor and Urban Affairs, Wayne State University.

Chapter Two

U nder an umbrella of September heat and haze, the crowd had swelled into the hundreds on the corner of 125th Street and Lenox Avenue. Police, dressed in riot gear, stood along the fringes, itching for something to spring them into action.

Anita Hopkins squeezed among sweaty bodies handing out flyers for the next community meeting the following week. "Hope to see you there. Hope to see you there. Bring a friend," she shouted to everyone who took the flyer. With each gathering, whether on a street corner or in the local office, the crowds grew and the message spread, confirming her belief in the messenger.

Brother Malcolm voiced all the things she felt about what was happening to her people.

Up on the makeshift platform, Brother Malcolm stirred the crowd, challenging them to band together and stop looking for acceptance from the white man who held no goodwill toward the Negro. "Nobody can give you freedom. Nobody can give you equality or justice or *anything*," he intoned. "If you're a man, you take it."

"Take it!" The crowd roared its approval.

"Yes! We take it!" Anita shouted, pumping her fist in the air.

"You don't have a peaceful revolution. You don't have a turn-the-cheek revolution. There's no such thing as a nonviolent revolution... The goal of Dr. Martin Luther King is to give Negroes a chance to sit in a segregated restaurant beside the same white man who has brutalized them for four hundred years."

Anita joined in the applause, energized by the words that she internalized. She was tired, tired of seeing her colored brothers and sisters with their heads bowed and shoulders slumped under the weight of racism. She was tired of watching the news only to see men, women, and children beaten in the streets, dragged and kicked by the very people sworn to protect and serve.

There had to be better. There had to be more.

Here in Harlem, where she'd made her home, she was surrounded by the culture and vitality of her people, from the mom-and-pop shops, jazz clubs, and street vendors to the vibrant attire and bold Afros that defined them. She embraced her naturalness, proud of her hair, which rose like a halo around her face. But beyond the boundaries of Harlem was a harsh, ugly world that still viewed anyone who looked like her—with her brown skin, big hair, and full lips—as less than.

Brother Malcolm was right. If the Negro people wanted true freedom, they had to take it.

On her way back to her fourth-floor walk-up apartment, she gave out the last of her flyers to folks she passed on the street, encouraging them to attend the community meeting. Everyone could do something, she believed, even if it was making sandwiches for the meetings, typing up notices, or bringing a friend. She volunteered a few hours a week at the

Action Network, a growing community-based organization that kept the locals involved in developments from voting to garbage pickup to political rallies.

Her other more personal contributions were the messages in her poetry.

As an only child, she had found her best friends in books. She could spend hours sitting in the library or curled up in bed with a novel. As she grew older and tried her hand at writing, she eventually accepted the fact that she would never be a novelist, but she did have a way with poetry.

She studied the poetry of Phyllis Wheatley, Paul Laurence Dunbar, Claude McKay, Countee Cullen, and Gwendolyn Brooks. She had recently stumbled upon a new poet by the name of Nikki Giovanni, whose words and turns of phrase she totally fell in love with. And of course there was Langston Hughes, who viewed poetry as a representation of a people and the power words could wield.

Anita believed that as well, and as she slowly came to discover and hone her own poetic voice, she understood when Hughes opined that poetry could be as delightful as it was disturbing. It could make you slip away or make you think. That's what she wanted to do every time she crafted a poem, every time she stood in front of a crowd and poured out the words from her soul—she wanted her audience to *think*.

There was power in words. Clearly orators like Brother Malcolm understood that. She understood it, too.

She tossed her trusty tote bag on the plaid couch and dropped down beside it. When she stretched her denim-clad legs out in front of her, she noticed a mustard stain on her gray T-shirt and wondered how that had happened. She crossed her sneakered feet, released a deep sigh, and rested her head against the back of the couch, closing her eyes.

All she needed was twenty minutes. Just twenty minutes

before she had to get ready for work. Once there, she would be on her feet for at least six hours before the last of the customers finally shut the door behind them. On any given night, especially weekends, the B-Flat Lounge was at or near capacity. The live music, inexpensive food, and stiff drinks were a major draw, and there were never enough waitresses to keep up with the demands of the clientele. On some nights it was standing room at the bar and an hour wait on a table. She hoped tonight wouldn't be one of those.

The phone rang, and Anita groaned. In order to answer it, she would actually have to get up. Her mind said *go*, but her body resisted. The phone continued to shrill, seeming to get louder with every ring.

Anita pushed to her feet and crossed the small space to the tiny kitchen. She plucked the canary-yellow phone from the wall.

"Hello?"

It was her manager, Henry. One of the waitresses had called out sick, and he knew that Anita understood how busy it was on a Friday night, so could she get there right away? He was willing to pay double.

The dangling carrot of double pay was the shot of adrenaline she needed. "Give me a half hour."

J ust like Henry said, the B-Flat Lounge was bustling with the Friday-night crowd, and it was barely eight. She suspected that most of them flocked to B-Flat to find refuge from the heat as much as for the food, drink, and entertainment. The wide ceiling fans, placed throughout the space, lowered the temperature by at least ten degrees. The lounge had air conditioning, but Henry was a cheap bastard when it came to paying the cost of utilities, and he turned on the air only under duress.

She was in for a long night.

"I'm here," she said, coming up behind Henry, who looked like he'd been forced to wait tables.

Martha and the Vandellases' "Heat Wave" was playing while the live band took a break, and the song had fingers popping and feet tapping.

He glanced over his shoulder, and his relief was palpable. She almost felt sorry for him. Almost.

"Thank God. You can take the other side."

"Going back to put down my things." She leaned in close. "If you'd hire more help, you wouldn't be in this predicament." She flashed a snarky smile and started to sashay away, then turned back. "And I want ten minutes tonight."

By eleven, Anita swore she was seeing double. Her back ached, her feet were screaming, and she still had three more hours to go. From the moment she'd come out of the back room, it had been nonstop. Folks sure were hungry and thirsty. The upside was double time and the generous tips, which would pay off more than a couple of her mounting bills. She'd already been to the back room twice to empty her pouch. It was a good night.

Around midnight, Henry came to the small stage and tapped on the mic to quiet the crowd.

"Ladies and gents, I hope you're having a good time tonight," he shouted to a round of applause. "As always on Friday nights, we take a break from the music and bring it down a notch with another kind of soul stirring. Tonight, please put your hands together for our very own Anita Hopkins."

To a chorus of stomping and clapping, Anita wound her way around the tables and chairs and walked up onstage. She gave Henry a wink, then adjusted the mic stand to her diminutive height. "Evenin', y'all!"

"Evenin'!" they shouted back.

"Tonight I have something special. A little something I been working on. Hope you will enjoy."

She turned to the band trio and signaled them to begin. The sax man blew out a plaintive note.

Anita dragged in a breath and cradled the mic in her palm. Her voice floated along with musical notes across the hushed space.

> *"Beyond my window*
> *I see a place new and bright;*
> *Beyond the billy clubs, fear, and riot gear,*
> *I see tomorrow.*
> *Beyond my window*
> *Is a hope that is possible,*
> *Possible for me to be*
> *More than they say I am,*
> *What I know I can.*
> *Beyond my window*
> *The brothers hold their heads high;*
> *The sisters swing their hips in jubilation.*
> *Gone is the pain of the past*
> *Open is the door, closed no more.*
> *For me. For you.*
> *Beyond my window*
> *I see what could be,*
> *A place where we are free.*
> *All comes at a price,*
> *This free that I see*

Still waiting for it to be
Here somehow. Right now.
The wait must be over,
Long overdue and patience lost,
The singing draws to an end.
The other cheek will no longer turn
Away from what must be done
To see what must be seen from my window."

She opened her eyes and gazed out into the semidarkened room that filled with finger snaps and shouts of "More!" Adrenaline pumped through her veins, made her heart race and her soul soar. Her fingertips tingled. She beamed with delight and obliged her adoring audience with two more poems before leaving the stage to thundering applause and the smooth sounds of Smokey and the Miracles' "You Really Got a Hold on Me."

Anita carried her shoes in her hands as she all but crawled up the four flights of stairs. She needed to get in at least a few hours of sleep; tomorrow was another big day. She was on duty at the Action Network from noon until four, then her shift at B-Flat. At least she had Sunday to look forward to and dinner with her folks.

She flopped across her twin bed and pulled the pouch with her tips in it toward her. It was filled to near bursting. She laid out the singles and fives, then the loose change, and meticulously counted each bill. Forty dollars and ninety-seven cents. She never could understand how people tipped in nickels and pennies.

She rolled onto her back. Not bad. Not bad at all when she added it to her pay for the night and the extra for covering. There was enough for the light bill and to put some food in the fridge and maybe even to treat herself to a new outfit.

She threw her arm over her eyes. She would donate some of her money to the Action Network to help with the next rally and still have enough to cover her bus trip to DC. She'd volunteered to visit the field office that was launching a new job-training program in the community. On her way back, she planned to stop in Philly to see her cousin Gwen.

Yeah, it had been a good day after all.

...

September 15, 1963

Jason lifted his short-brimmed hat off his eyes and peered out of the rain-splattered window of the Greyhound bus. The wide-open land and green grass were long behind him. It had been only hours since his whole family had waited with him at the depot, waved frantically as the bus pulled out of the station. It already felt like days.

He touched his cheek where his mother had kissed him and left it wet with her tears. He could still feel the solid embrace of his father's arms wrapped around his as if it was his last chance to ward off any harm coming to his son.

"Proud of you," his brother had said, clapping him on the back.

"Gonna miss you, Jase," his sister had said, fighting back tears.

He'd fought back his own tears of misgiving, needing to be strong and resolute for them. But everything that was familiar and the security that came with it was disappearing into the distance, and he worried, as he had silently for weeks, whether he'd made the right decision. The life he'd lived in Georgia was familiar. He knew how to read the faces of white folks and hear between the words they spoke. He ain't never had no dealings with northern whites and didn't know what to expect or how he would be received.

Like Pastor Bishop always said, *Better the devil you know than the devil you don't know.*

He pressed his face closer to the window. Towering buildings etched themselves into the gray horizon, resembling images from the gothic novels the teachers forced them to read in high school. The tropes of castles on hilltops, feisty damsels, and arranged marriages were about as much of his reality as him going to the moon. True, he'd always heard about the promise of the North, that things were better there for the Negro. But how much different would his life really be in New York? Would his skin suddenly no longer matter? How would he fit in with the "fast life" of the big city?

"Thought you was gonna sleep straight through, young man."

Jason turned his stiff neck toward his seatmate and was met with a smile set between full cheeks. "Hope I wasn't snoring."

"I'm used to it. My late husband could lead a chorus when it came to snoring. Twenty-five years, you can handle most anything."

Jason felt his face heat. "Sorry, ma'am."

She laughed, sounding almost childlike, which didn't sit with the light streaks of gray in her hair and the wisdom in her dark deep-set eyes. She patted his arm with a thick hand. "No need to apologize. You missed the last rest stop. Hungry?"

It was his grumbling stomach that had actually woken

him, and he wondered if she'd heard that, too. "I appreciate you asking, ma'am, but I can hold out till we get to New York. Thank you, though."

She tipped her head a bit to the side, sizing him up. Jason shifted in his seat, tried to flatten the wrinkles in his pants.

"First time traveling to New York?"

"Yes, ma'am."

"You really don't have to call me ma'am, not after having spent the last fifteen hours together. Edith Hall." She stuck out her hand, which was as soft as cotton.

"Jason Tanner."

Her round cheeks and perfect marcel waves streaked with threads of silver reminded him of his aunt Faye. She was the only one in the family beside his sister and brother who had stood by him right away when he announced that he was leaving Atlanta. She was his father's eldest sister and the only one of six siblings who had ever been out of the state of Georgia. Jason believed it was Aunt Faye who finally helped his father see the light.

What his father failed to realize was that he'd gotten his stubborn streak honestly. He was no more than eight or nine when he'd watched his father sit on the porch night after night with a shotgun across his lap while the black pickup trucks filled with rowdy Klan members threatened to set the house on fire if he didn't sell his land.

His mother had begged him to just sell, but his father refused. It could have cost him his life—all their lives—but he'd done it anyway. *A man gotta stand for what's right*, his father had said, *and defend what's his*.

Jason knew his moment to do what was right had arrived. He couldn't sit still any longer. And once he'd gotten his father's blessing, he knew it was because his father not only believed but accepted that his son had to do what a man was called to do, just as he'd once done.

"Sure you won't have some?"

Jason blinked Edith back into focus—on her lap was a Tupperware bowl. She snapped open the blue plastic cover, and the mouthwatering aroma of fried chicken drifted up his nostrils and set his stomach to howling.

Edith chuckled. "Your mouth may be sayin' no, but your belly is sayin' yes." She lifted the bowl toward him. "Go on now, don't be shy. Help yourself."

Jason licked his lips. The chicken was a perfect golden brown, and he instinctively knew that it was seasoned just right. "If you insist. My mama always told me to accept blessings when they're offered."

"Sounds like a wise woman." She pulled some paper napkins out of her purse and handed them to him.

Jason sank his teeth into the golden meat. The skin crunched just right, the juice and seasoning bursting in his mouth. His lids fluttered closed, and he hummed in appreciation.

She dug in her bag and pulled out a thermos. "Lemonade?"

"Yes, ma'am. Ms. Edith." He wiped his mouth with the napkin and gratefully took the cup of lemonade. "You have family in New York?"

"Some. Most of them are still in Birmingham. I moved to Atlanta about five years ago. But when my husband passed last year, and with all the mess down South…" Her expression pinched. "I figured it was time for me to finally pull up stakes and come north. Just went back home for my cousin's wedding. What about you?"

"No, ma'am. Everybody's back in Atlanta."

"Hmm. Big move, coming up here alone. New York is not like anything you ever seen before, I can tell you that." She laughed. "More chicken?"

"I think I will. Thank you." He chewed with pleasure. It reminded him of what his mother always said…something about the kindness of strangers.

"Got some place to stay?"

"Uh, yes. As a matter of fact…" He wiped his mouth and hands with the napkin, then dug inside the pocket of his suit jacket and pulled out a folded sheet of paper. "My aunt Faye has a friend who runs a rooming house in Harlem." He opened the paper.

Edith took a peek and mouthed the address: 188 126th Street at Amsterdam Avenue. "Pretty decent over there." She bobbed her head in approval. "You should be fine. Clean streets, mostly. Plenty of places to eat. Folks are respectable."

He wasn't quite sure why he was willing to take the word of an almost stranger. He supposed there was that "Aunt Faye" thing about Edith that made him feel everything would be just fine. Her assurances eased the rope of tension that tightened in his gut. Jason refolded the paper and put it back in his pocket. "That's good to know."

"Well, son, I'm going to take a little nap. Wake me when we get to New Jersey."

"New Jersey? I thought you were going to New York."

Edith smiled. "Eventually. I plan on visiting a 'friend,' if you get my meaning." She winked.

"Oh…"

She returned the Tupperware and thermos to her purse, adjusted her hips in the seat, leaned her head back, and shut her eyes.

Now that he was wide-awake and his belly was full, he wished he did have someone to talk to. He stole a glance at Edith. Her mouth had dropped open, and her full lips fluttered ever so slightly when she exhaled.

Back home, his day job kept him busy during the week,

then Sunday dinners were spent with his family. But there was always Friday and Saturday night to get loose with his buddies, Herb and Floyd. They were regulars at all the weekend house parties and often double or triple dated in Herb's Cadillac for nights at the drive-in. They'd all been friends since grade school.

Herb and Floyd were tight like brothers, much like he and his other friend Jeff had been. Jason's mother used to say they were so close, she almost couldn't tell them apart: *Never see one without the other* was her favorite line. With Jeff gone, he often felt like a third wheel, but Herb and Floyd were dedicated to finding and having a good time and wouldn't take any of Jason's nos for an answer.

He smiled. He'd had a solid life in Georgia: steady job, family, friends, good times. Everyone who was important to him, he'd known all or most of his life. Soon he would be alone, in a strange city without comfort of family or the camaraderie of friends, and the prospect suddenly unnerved him.

Jason turned back toward the window. It would be dark soon, but at least the rain that had followed them all the way from Atlanta had finally stopped. By the time he reached New York, it would be close to ten. Then he would still have to find his way to Harlem.

He'd heard about Harlem in some way or other for as far back as he could remember. Back home, Harlem was touted as some kind of mecca for Negroes. It was a lot like the South—*just fancy and fast*, his aunt had warned. He'd find out soon enough.

The bus banged and bumped along for at least another hour, and Jason wondered who really led the chorus in Edith's house, because she had certainly struck up the band. He caught the eye of a young woman in the opposite aisle two seats ahead of him, who smiled at him in sympathy and mouthed the word *Sorry*, then went back to whatever was on her lap.

Jason craned his neck around the seats to get a better look. The woman was busy writing in a notebook. He leaned back. One thing was certain—she had the biggest Afro he'd ever witnessed on a real person. He'd only seen them on actors or models or revolutionaries in the magazines, newspapers, or on television. Her halo of hair rose above the headrest like a crown.

What was most arresting, though, were her eyes and skin that were all the same amber hue as her voluminous hair. It was as if she'd been painted by an artist who loved only one color. Her big gold hoop earrings gleamed against the sepia palette. He knew from reading the papers and watching television that there was a major movement for big 'fros, as they were called, up North.

Back home, all the women still pressed and greased their hair until it shone like new money and was as straight as a ruler. Saturday afternoons, there was rarely a woman or girl to be found outdoors. Every man and boy knew from a young age that Saturday was as close to a religious holiday as one recognized on a calendar: Saturday was press-and-curl day.

Every beauty shop in town was filled from opening to closing for those who could afford the service. For others, grandma's or auntie's kitchen with hot comb, curling iron, and plenty of Dixie Peach fit the bill. Seemed like the whole town smelled like sizzling hair and pomade on Saturday afternoons, and if a woman couldn't get to the beauty salon, she pulled out her wigs, like Mrs. C., which made her look like an older version of the actress Dianne Carroll or one of the Supremes.

The young woman sitting ahead of him was definitely not from the South.

The bus eased to the right, followed traffic, and took the exit ramp.

"Last rest stop before New York City," the driver announced. "Get out and stretch your legs, use the facilities, but be back here in fifteen minutes."

Jason lightly tapped Edith's shoulder. Her bottom lip clamped to the top, and her shoulders shook as if she was wet while her eyes inched open.

"We're in Philadelphia. Last rest stop before New York," he said with the authority of one who had taken this trip many times before.

"Is that right." She covered her mouth and yawned. "Guess I should stretch my legs. At least two more hours to go." She pushed to her feet, adjusted her pillbox hat, and smoothed her skirt, which screamed for mercy across her hips. Then she reached above her head to the rack and retrieved her suit jacket and light overcoat, put both on, and made her way down the aisle. She stopped halfway and looked over her shoulder. "Coming?"

"I think I'll stay."

She shrugged, then walked off the bus.

Everyone got off except for the woman with all the hair. The low murmur of static-sounding voices drifted back toward him, then the beat of something familiar that he realized was a radio.

"That the Four Tops?" he called out.

She glanced over the edge of the seat. Smiled. "Yep. One of my favorites. Saw them once at the Apollo. James Brown, too."

His eyes widened. "Really? You been to the Apollo?"

She turned fully around and rose up on her knees, draped her arms over the back of the seat. "Sure! Everybody goes to the Apollo."

Her intense gaze unsettled him. He felt as if she could see things in him that even he couldn't understand. "I s'pose."

She chuckled. "Where are you coming from?"

"Atlanta."

She nodded as if appraising him. "Is it nice there?" She tilted her head to the side, her eyes still cinched from her smile.

"Yeah, lived there all my life. Good people. Decent way of life."

"Where you headed?" She rested her chin on her folded arms.

"New York."

"Be sure to visit the Apollo!" She winked and giggled, but he didn't feel that she was laughing at him but laughing to share the joy that seemed to dance inside her.

He chuckled. "I'll keep that in mind." He lifted his chin. "Saw you doing a lot of scribbling in that notebook. You a writer?"

Her entire expression lit up from beneath her skin. "I'm a poet," she proudly proclaimed.

"A poet. Hmm, never met a real live poet before. You have any of your poetry published?"

Her full lips pouted. "No. Not yet. But one day I will."

For reasons he couldn't explain, he actually believed her.

"I do some performing at a club in New York." She offered a crooked smile. "I work there, too. Helps in building my audience."

Her unwavering stare made his insides soften and his thoughts grow fuzzy. She started to turn away, but he felt like he needed to keep her talking. "My name is Jason, by the way," he said, stalling her retreat.

"Anita."

The finger-popping beat of "Quicksand" by Martha and the Vandellas cut them off, and Anita raised her hands over her head, closed her eyes, and rocked her hips to the beat. "Quicksand, quicksand…sinking me deeeepeeerr in love with yoooouuu," she harmonized, putting her fist in front of her mouth like a microphone.

Jason was instantly drawn to her impromptu performance and felt a childlike kind of joy. She followed "Quicksand" with "Baby I Need Your Loving" by the Four Tops. "…Baaaaby I need your loving *got* to have all your loving…" He tossed his head back and laughed, snapping his fingers to the beat until she'd finished her "set," then applauded her performance. She opened her eyes, and when their gazes locked, he was hit with a lightning bolt dead in the center of his chest. He dragged in a breath.

Anita did a mock bow, and her smile lit up the dull confines of the bus.

"A writer *and* a singer," he said with a smile. He swallowed over the tightness in his throat.

"Never have all your eggs in one carton or something," she said, laughing. She turned back around and settled in her seat.

Jason sat back. *Anita.*

He peered out the bus window. The passengers were slowly heading back to board the bus. Another few hours on the road and he'd be in New York.

"Oh my God!"

Jason's head snapped up.

"Bastards. Oh my God."

He jumped to his feet and hurried toward Anita. "What is it? What happened?"

When she turned to look at him, her liquid-fire eyes were filled with tears, and his insides shifted, ready to fix whatever was wrong.

Her nostrils flared as she tried to suck in air. "They blew up a church in Birmingham. Four girls were killed. Little girls!"

Her balled fist pounded the seat in front of her.

What she was saying wasn't registering. His brow knitted in confused disbelief. "What? Who?"

Her head whipped back in his direction. Seconds earlier, her expression had been one of utter sadness, but now it was coated in a sheen of fury. She shook the radio in his face. "Who do you think? We didn't blow up our own damn church!"

The ferocity of her words shoved him in the chest. Gone was the congenial poet and fun-loving would-be singer, transformed instead into a ball of rage that lit her eyes and tightened the skin around her high cheekbones. He dropped down in the seat opposite her, envisioning the night riders driving past his home and threatening his family, the echoing stories of folk who had just gone missing one day playing in his head.

This was different, though. This was something deeper than evil.

"This is why we must rise up," she said, pointing vehemently at some unseen enemy. "Because until we do, they'll keep killing us."

"Dr. King teaches us to turn the other cheek, that passive resistance is the way forward. The only way," he said, feeling that he needed to defend himself—against what, he wasn't quite sure.

He sensed her petite body tighten. She snorted a laugh. "So you're one of those do-gooders, huh?" She twisted her body in the seat so she could face him.

An electric shock zapped his chest when those eyes zeroed in on him—accused him. She crossed her bell-bottomed legs one over the other and rocked her red-and-white Converse-sneakered foot back and forth.

She rolled her eyes. "Where has all the marching and praying and begging gotten us? Tell me that, do-gooder."

She crossed her arms.

"Change takes time."

"Four hundred years ain't long enough?" she challenged, even as the light of defiance left her gaze only to be replaced by something akin to amusement. "What's your answer, then?"

She was baiting him, soothing herself with his discomforting lack of a comeback. He was silent.

"It's like Brother Malcolm said, 'By any means necessary.' I chose my voice." She picked up a black-and-white notebook and waved it over her head like Reverend Samuels did with the bible during Sunday service.

He was pretty sure that the Good Book was the last thing on her mind, and he wondered what the folks back home would think of this fiery young woman with revolution for hair and flames for eyes.

"No offense to your beliefs, but Malcolm X preaches violence. That's not the way. We can't bring ourselves down to the level of our enemy."

She smirked and leaned forward. She was inches from his face, and he could see the specks of gold in her eyes, smell the mint on her breath. "You're just like the rest of the idealists: you don't understand the message. It's not about violence. It's about not backing down in the face of the enemy."

With the power of her gaze, she held him immobile. He wanted to look away, but he couldn't.

Or maybe he didn't want to.

The passengers began to return, and the spell was broken.

They filed on the bus, one by one, their expressions reflecting the devastating news they'd surely heard. A pall of despair came with them, spreading, flooding the metal container, washing over everyone and everything until the bodies were limp from trying to fight against a tidal wave they could not change.

Anita jumped up from her seat. "Now is not the time for tears, brothers and sisters," she shouted. "Now is the time to rise up against our oppressors."

The Negro passengers, many probably old enough to have seen and lived through what she could only have read about, indulged her with patronizing smiles as they shuffled to their seats. A young man, no more than eighteen, slowed for a moment and took up her clarion call as he made his way to his seat in the middle of the bus.

"Who's next?" he shouted. "Me, you?" He scoured the passengers with a look of defiance, as if daring them to challenge the truth of what he said. The three white patrons, a middle-aged couple with their young son, were red-faced. They kept their eyes lowered and seemed to shrink into their seats as if the nearly packed bus might suddenly turn on them in their outrage and pain.

Jason watched the fire in Anita's eyes dim, then extinguish. She threw him a look of disgust, shook her head, and flopped back into her seat. "This is why we can't overcome. They won't let us." She slid to the seat near the window and turned her back on him.

Jason opened his mouth to protest, but a passenger returning for his seat cut him off. He slid out of the way just as Edith climbed on board. Her eyes were puffy, and her hat was askew. He took a last look at the young woman and back at Edith and knew where his loyalty rested. He took Edith's arm and ushered her to their seats.

"Are you all right, Ms. Edith?" He helped her sit, then squeezed by her to slide into his seat.

She shook her head. "Lordhavemercy," she muttered. "My church. I grew up in that church." She turned tear-filled eyes on Jason. "One of those babies could be my childhood friend's grandchild."

"I'm terribly sorry, Ms. Edith." Jason took her soft hand in his. "Is there anything I can do?"

She pressed her lips into a tight line, locking any words behind her teeth, leaned back, and closed her eyes.

The trip from Philadelphia to New Jersey was eerily quiet. Even the noisy engine and bumps in the road seemed to realize and take pause.

"New Jersey," the driver finally announced and eased into one of the bus lanes at the depot.

Edith turned to Jason. "You take care of yourself up in New York. World could use more good men like you." She patted his shoulder.

"I plan to. And I'm real sorry for any loss of yours—and the others of course."

Her smile didn't reach her eyes, but it was no less sincere, he knew. She gave a short nod, gathered her things, and followed the somber procession off the bus.

Once the aisle cleared, Jason craned his neck above the seats, hoping, for reasons he couldn't quite explain, that the girl with the giant hair and fireflies for eyes would be sitting alone.

But she was gone.

A familiar disappointment pooled in his chest. It was the same feeling he'd had the day he saw Brenda walking home hand in hand with David Hopper, the captain of the basketball team. He'd spent weeks building up the nerve to ask her to the senior dance. He'd helped her with her math project and even loaned her his shoulder to cry on when her dog ran off. But none of that had mattered. He was the "nice guy," the good friend. David was "the man," the one who got the girl.

He settled back in his seat. The events of the last hour played in his head. He'd become enthralled with the sepia beauty. Her appetite for joy was contagious, and he'd caught it. In an instant, she'd turned from the infectious writer-poet-songstress belting out a Four Tops hit to embodying the very tactics he was fighting against.

Malcolm. He pushed out a resigned breath. No point in even thinking about her any further. They were on opposite sides of the coin. He pulled his hat down over his eyes, determined to put the stunning rebel out of his mind, but from behind his closed lids, she smiled at him.

Congress of Racial Equality conducts march in memory of Negro youngsters killed in Birmingham bombings, All Souls Church, 16th Street, Washington, D.C., September 23, 1963.
(c) Thomas J. O'Halloran/Alamy

• • •

Two weeks later; Harlem, NY

Anita was on the hunt for her oversize tote that she'd gotten for a steal from a local street vendor on 125th Street. The vendor, of Nigerian descent, swore on the souls of his ancestors that the bag was made by hand by a woman from his tribe. Anita had serious doubts, but she'd bought it anyway.

She slowly scouted out her overcrowded apartment, lifting throw pillows, discarded jeans, empty plates. Every available space—which wasn't much—was covered with black-and-white notebooks, pens, writing pads, and crates of albums. Tied with her passion for writing was her passion for music. Once a month, she would take the A train from Harlem all the way to Nostrand Avenue in Brooklyn and visit Birdel's Record Shop.

Birdel's was a hub for true music lovers and not only for rare and current 33s and 45s. They also were the first ones to get tickets for all the shows at the Lowes Theater. Any R&B artist worth their salt appeared at the Lowes, and Anita made it a point to sit front and center every chance she could. And if you were having a party, Tommy, who'd been around since the shop opened, would put together made-to-order cassette tapes of all the hits past and present. Her place was definitely too small for any kind of party, but she had stacks of cassettes, which she'd contributed to many house parties. One of these days, those cassettes would be worth something.

She pushed a pile of clothes out of the way and promised herself that she was going to clean up and get her space into some kind of livable condition. Her mother would be appalled, which was one reason why she never invited her over. Instead, she trekked out to Bedford-Stuyvesant, Brooklyn, every single solitary Sunday to have dinner with her parents.

Her parents lived in the same four-story brownstone in which she was born and raised. But her favorite room in the house was the one on the top floor that was lined from wall to wall with books. Many of them were first editions and some in different languages, courtesy of her mom, a librarian by profession but a lover of reading as a lifestyle.

Growing up, for Anita, that room was a place of fantasy, wonder, and possibility. In there, she could be whoever she wanted to be. She could disappear in between the pages of a novel, become the subject in a biography, or mentally debate the theories of philosophers for hours on end while in the room next door, her father relaxed with his cigarettes and record player, spinning the blues. It was on that top floor, from preteen to adult, that she formed her vision of the world and all the possible ways she could live in it. She grew up where ten-foot ceilings, parquet floors, claw-foot tubs, chandeliers, and stained glass windows were ordinary.

Now her entire apartment could fit into her mother's kitchen.

So the visits served a couple of purposes. They eased her conscience about keeping her parents away and the reasons why she left in the first place—her vision and purpose had outgrown the confines of that space. The visits also reaffirmed to them that her job as a waitress kept a roof over her head and allowed her to pursue her poetry, and that her politics hadn't gotten her locked up or worse.

Now where was that tote?

She had a set later that night at B-Flat and planned to try out some new material. She'd written three poems about the four little girls, but the one she'd worked on for weeks was all about the man she'd met on the bus ride the one from Atlanta.

Where was it? A feeling like panic began to rise in her belly, that sensation she got when she couldn't find the light switch in a dark room or when she walked home alone at night—her spooky-movie phobia. Everybody knew the Black kid always got killed first.

Where is it, damn it? It was just a notebook, but it was the only record she had of him.

He wasn't even her type, but she hadn't been able to stop

thinking about him. She heard the soothing timbre of his voice in her dreams or when she was trying to pay attention to a customer's order. A few times she'd thought she saw him walking along Lenox or Amsterdam Avenue in that same tan suit he'd worn on the bus. But it was never him.

She wasn't sure why she couldn't shake him off like she did most do-gooders. Maybe it was because there was a part of her that felt as if their conversation needed to be continued, like a poem without an ending.

She hated leaving things unsaid.

In the meantime, she needed to find that tote with her notebook inside, then head over to the job she tolerated because it paid the bills and gave her the flexibility she needed, so she held her nose and bit her tongue.

She got down on her hands and knees and looked under the pullout couch. Dust, a random slipper—and her tote. She reached under and pulled it toward her, feeling the panic ease. She pulled the notebook out of the bag, flipped to the pages about him, as if to assure herself that the words remained. *Silly*.

She shut the book, stuck it in her bag, then took a last look in the mirror and fluffed her 'fro over her hairline to cover the thin scar. Then she grabbed her jacket and keys and headed out. She had a new piece she wanted to spit tonight, about him. He'd never know it, though, because they'd never see each other again.

It was better that way anyhow.

Chapter Three

The rooming house was comfortable and clean enough, but Jason couldn't get used to having to share a bathroom with anyone other than family or having to eat out for every meal since there were no kitchen privileges. He needed a job, as he was quickly running out of money, and the stipend sent by the movement didn't go nearly as far up North as it did in the South.

There was a total of six male tenants: three on each floor, with one bathroom per floor. The owner, Horace Miller, who lived on the ground floor apartment, had strict house rules: no drinking, smoking, coming in after midnight, or overnight guests.

For Jason, the rules were easy enough to live by. After all, he'd lived with his parents for twenty-two of his twenty-four years.

He grabbed his towel and the bath caddy that held his toiletries and walked down the narrow pea-green hallway to the community bathroom. With any luck, Lawrence and Randolph were done for the morning.

Lawrence Pratt did odd jobs around town and always seemed to be busy, and when he wasn't doing those, he was driving a cab. He left early and came in late. Randolph Howell, on the other hand, worked only on school days as a driver for those yellow school buses. He was generally gone by seven and back by ten a.m.

Jason knocked lightly on the closed bathroom door. No answer. He turned the knob and pushed the door open, instinctively sniffing the air. Breathable. He locked the door behind him and got down to business.

Since he'd arrived in New York, sleeping at night had been challenging at best. The scream of sirens, rumble of trucks, and yells of late-night partygoers kept him awake most nights. Gone were the simple sounds of cicadas or the occasional hoot owl.

Back in his room, he dressed and prepared for the day. He had to meet up with Michael Irving, the young man who had been assigned to help him set up shop. They'd already found a location—a storefront on Amsterdam—not too far from his aunt Faye. The rent was reasonable, and the movement had arranged to wire the funds for the first three months' rent. After that, he wasn't sure what would happen once the office was up and operational. He'd probably have to find a job if he decided to stay in this noisy, hectic city. It would take a lot of getting used to, and he wondered if "the cause" would be enough to keep him here.

Jason stepped out into the surprisingly cool September morning. He stopped on Lenox Avenue at the newsstand and paid for a copy of the *Amsterdam News*.

He scanned the cover, whose headlines still carried the church bombing in Birmingham. According to the article, the president had ordered in the National Guard to keep the peace while the FBI continued its investigation.

The second headline was about President Kennedy and his impending meeting with Dr. King. Sources close to Dr. King and the White House strongly believed that an agreement on civil rights was close at hand, following the president's first formal address to the American people that took place back on June 11.

He remembered coming in late from work that Tuesday to find his mom and dad zeroed in on the television, barely noticing his arrival. When he came around to see what they were watching, the somber face of President Kennedy, seated at his desk in the Oval Office, looked back at them from the screen. Jason was always intrigued by the curve of the man's vowels when he spoke, a combination of regional dialect and private schooling. He sat down next to his mother, bussed her cheek with a kiss. The president talked about how the pursuit of racial equality was a righteous and just cause, raising eyebrows in the Tanner household, as Kennedy's position had been tepid at best, as he clearly did not want to alienate the legislators in the still-segregated South.

It's a start, he'd mused. At least it gave the movement hope that finally the weight of the White House was behind them, and hopefully, with continued peaceful protests, a civil rights bill would be passed.

President Kennedy reports to the American people on civil rights.
(c) Abbie Rowe, National Park Service / John F. Kennedy Presidential Library and Museum

. . .

Fortunately, Jason could walk from the rooming house to the storefront office, which saved him from the worry of transportation costs. He dragged in a breath and looked across Lenox and 121st Street. Yellow cabs zigged and zagged, bus horns blared, folks on their way to and from work hurried down the concrete streets, others descended underground for the subway—one thing he had yet to try. Shop owners lifted their metal gates, signaling they were open for business.

Life moved on.

His jaw tightened. He folded the paper in half and tucked it under his arm, tipped his head to the newsstand worker, and walked on, merging with the flow of bodies far removed from Birmingham, Alabama, and Washington, DC, but he firmly believed that he was destined to bring the message that in order to succeed, the cause must move beyond the land of Dixie.

In the meantime, though, getting used to the rush, the bumping of bodies, the noise that never seemed to rest, the buildings that blocked out the sunshine, the miles of tar and concrete, was more difficult to do than just thinking about it. Or, as his mother would say, "More than a notion."

He turned onto 125th Street, literally entering a whole other world. Street vendors offering everything from foot creams to books to African fabric to cooked food lined the avenue, hawking their wares, entreating passersby to "take a look" at the "best deal on the avenue" if they'd "just try." The aroma of burning incense teased the nostrils, competing with hot dog and salted pretzel vendors and car exhaust. It was overwhelming, to say the least.

And the people! There were *so* many people.

Up ahead was the Apollo Theater. He'd read about the famed venue for years and, like most of Black America, watched *Amateur Night at the Apollo* on Saturday nights. A flash of Anita's sparkling amber eyes and flashbulb smile bloomed in front of him, and her passionate insistence that he had to visit the Apollo echoed in his head.

He glanced up at the marquee, and something akin to excited pride filled him. He was standing on the threshold where some of the biggest stars had performed or been discovered. He'd add this to his list of things to check out as soon as he had some free time and someone to go with. As busy as he was preparing to open the office, he didn't have much opportunity to forge friendships — at least not like the kind he'd had with Jeff back home.

He and Jeff had grown up next door to each other, attended the same schools, worked side by side at the local supermarket packing bags and stocking shelves, waited tables at Jack's Barbecue, and they even double-dated in Jeff's father's Oldsmobile. Throughout their youth and into young manhood, they'd been inseparable. So inseparable that friends and family referred to them as "JJ," as if they were one person.

When Jeff had been killed on I-95 coming back home from a weekend visit with his cousins in Florida, Jason didn't believe that anything could hurt as much. The loss was all the more devastating because Jason was supposed to have gone with Jeff so that he wouldn't have to make the drive alone. Instead, he opted to stay in town and work some extra hours. He was saving for a car of his own. Guilt, like a shadow, followed him. Maybe if he'd been there, he could have told Jeff to slow down, or watch that truck, or pull over. Something. He could have protected his friend from those men in the pickup.

All the "what ifs" and "should haves" haunted him.

He never did get that car, didn't have one to this day, and

he'd turned his drive for work to something that actually mattered. In a way, he was trying to make amends. And maybe, if he was lucky, one day he'd have another friend like Jeff.

He continued on his walk. The storefront, sandwiched between an abandoned shoeshine parlor and a locksmith, had been secured for the local office on 126th Street and Lenox. He was set to meet Michael Irving, his on-the-ground contact.

Mike, as he preferred to be called, seemed like a pretty decent guy—hardworking, dedicated to the cause. Beyond the fact that Mike was a devout advocate for Dr. King, Jason didn't know much else about him. He'd talked with him only twice.

Michael was out front when Jason came down the block, dressed in a bright-white shirt, suit, and tie. He reminded Jason of a young Adam Clayton Powell. A "redbone," as the folks back home would say. Mixed race.

"Morning," Jason greeted and extended his hand.

"Morning. Walked again?" he asked with a grin that crinkled his dark-brown eyes.

Jason took a handkerchief from the pocket of his jacket and dabbed at his damp forehead. "How could you tell?"

"You *can* take the bus, you know." He took the keys out of his pocket and opened the door.

"I'm working up to it."

Michael laughed, pushed the door open, and flipped on the light. An odor of disuse greeted them.

The "office" was not much more than an oversize storage room. Well-worn plank floors that had long ago lost their luster creaked beneath their feet. In the back, off to the side, were a toilet and sink that had both seen better days but were serviceable. There was a back door that opened onto an alley that led to the next street over.

They'd managed to salvage two metal desks and a file cabinet. Stacked on top of the desks were cardboard boxes filled with informational flyers, posters, and paperwork and two black telephones. Jason picked up the handset. Listened. No dial tone.

"Phone company is due to come before noon and get the phones working," Michael said.

Jason nodded. "That will make things a bit easier." He dropped the handle back onto the cradle. "Our first order of business is to get this place looking a bit more inviting. I'll go down the street and pick up some cleaning supplies from the five-and-ten: mop, broom, sponges, cleaner, bucket. Anything else you think we need?"

"Probably some paper towels and tissue for the bathroom."

"Got it. Be back in a few."

When Jason returned with the supplies, he and Michael got to work. Jason ditched his shirt, tie, and jacket; filled a bucket with hot, sudsy water; and began washing the storefront windows until the sun bounced off them like a new penny on a hard mattress.

While he worked, he took the opportunity to watch the comings and goings on the street, sharing greetings with the array of folks who came and went. There were parents pushing baby carriages, delivery men, toddlers with grandparents, students on their way to Columbia University—not too far away—and a cluster of young men who hung on the corner, smoking cigarettes and swapping stories about their sports heroes' latest feats. He smiled. How many corners had he and Jeff hung out on, just shooting the breeze and enjoying life?

He wiped the perspiration from his head with his forearm, gathered up his cleaning supplies, and was heading back inside when he glanced up and stopped short. His heart raced.

She was coming across the street.

He'd only seen her once, but he'd know that halo of hair and that face anywhere.

As she drew closer, he watched as her expression changed from determination to shock. She tipped her head a bit to the side, squinted with a half smile on her face.

Anita stopped in front of him, adjusted her tote higher up on her shoulder, and stuck her hands in the back pockets of her capri pants. "Do-gooder! I'll be damned."

She was shorter than he'd thought she was on the bus, came somewhere under his chin, but she was still larger than life. Vibrant energy flowed from her.

"Fancy seeing you here," he said and knew he sounded ridiculous.

"Not really. I live around here." Her smile showcased the tiny dimple in her right cheek. "Fancy seeing *you* here, though." She adjusted her weight to her right leg, jutting out a round hip.

Jason grinned and nodded sheepishly. "So do I. Well, not right here exactly, but close."

She lifted her chin in the direction of the storefront. "What's going on here?"

He cleared his throat, remembering her heated remarks on the bus. "Actually, I'm opening a local office for Dr. King."

Her brown eyes widened, raising her thick brows in the process. "Really?"

"Yep."

"So what are y'all gonna be doing exactly?" She squinted at him.

"Training. Recruiting volunteers. Spreading information…"

"Hmm. Well, good luck with that."

"Thank you, I think."

"Look, do-gooder, I admire what you're trying to do. But look around you." She waved her hand. "These people need more than platitudes and marches. They want respect, dignity of work, to be treated like a human being and not by bowing their heads, turning cheeks, and accepting what 'they' decide they want to give us."

"Dr. King wants the same thing," Jason insisted. "But violence is not the way to get what we want."

"Guess we gonna have to agree to disagree, do-gooder."

He tucked in a smile at the barb, which he'd gladly wear as a mantle. "It's Jason, by the way. Jason Tanner." He wiped his hand on his pants leg and extended it to her.

She pursed her lips, paused, then accepted the olive branch. "Anita Hopkins."

"Nice to meet you—*again*, Anita. Looks like we keep meeting under strained circumstances." That seemed to let some of the steam out of her. Her slender body visibly relaxed, even as a shadow of something he couldn't define passed across her eyes.

She shifted her weight again. "How long you been in the city?"

"Couple of weeks."

"How long you staying?"

"As long as it takes." He watched her throat work.

"Guess you haven't had a chance to see much of Harlem."

He wasn't sure if that was a question or a statement. "Uh, not really. Takes a bit of getting used to."

She licked her bottom lip, then dug in her tote and pulled out a stack of papers. She peeled one off and handed it to him.

"Friday nights at B-Flat Lounge." Her eyes picked up the light, turning them a brighter shade of brown. She shrugged slightly. "You might like it. Give you a real feel for Harlem." She smiled.

He took the flyer. "Thanks." He paused. "Will you be there?"

She shoved the papers back in her tote. "Guess you'll have to stop by and find out. Take care, do-gooder." She breezed by him and started off down the street.

Jason turned to watch her departure and wondered if she always swayed her hips like a metronome or if it was purely for his benefit.

She turned the corner and was gone.

He took a look at the flyer. *B-Flat Lounge. Hmm. Maybe.*

Shit. She was actually shaking inside. What were the chances of running into him like that? Zip. Zero. But he'd been like a note that lingered after the song had ended. It stayed with you, compelled you to replay the melody.

That was what she'd found herself doing. More times than she was willing to admit—even to her best friend, Liza—the do-gooder had found his way into her dreams and poured out on paper. She pressed her tote against her side, assuring herself that her notebook was there. What the hell was it about him that had clung to her?

She walked faster, ignoring Winston's and Smokey's whistles. She gave them both the finger—much to their delight—told them they betta be at B-Flat on Friday, and kept going.

This Jason Tanner wasn't even her type. She frowned. *Country bumpkin.* He didn't have the slick polish of the guys she was used to. Besides, their politics were as far apart as the North and South Pole.

She pushed open the door to Action Network headquarters and marched through the cramped but busy office to her tiny desk way in the back, waving and nodding to her coworkers. The office was awash in competing voices and ringing phones.

She'd been working with the network for almost two years, deciding to volunteer after attending a meeting where Brother Malcolm spoke. She'd never been so mesmerized by listening to the words of someone else in her life. It was as much about his delivery as what he said. There was a magnetism about him, a charisma that was disarming. He understood that the power of words—placed just right, with the right inflection—could change minds. Could change *hearts*.

From the moment when she walked out of that community hall, she knew that she wanted to be part of *his* dream for the people. He espoused a society where the Negro was self-sufficient, owning their businesses, their homes, and running their schools without waiting on the permission and handouts of white America. She wholly believed in the message and the man and had committed herself to the cause through her community organizing and her poetry that echoed the messages of empowerment.

Anita sat at her desk and checked the yellow pad that she always kept on top with her list of things to take care of. Today she needed to read all the newspapers and cut out any clips that were in some way related to Brother Malcolm. The organization had subscriptions to newspapers from across the country. They were already stacked in a box next to her desk. Mondays were always the most time consuming to go through, as the papers were larger over the weekend. She meticulously filed away any articles she'd come across, and then she needed to get to the copy shop and pick up the box of flyers.

It was after noon by the time she returned with the flyers. She stacked handfuls on each desk and spent the next half hour out front, passing them to anyone who went by.

She hadn't eaten breakfast and was getting a bit light-headed from standing outside in the sun. She wondered if Liza was ready for lunch.

Liza Daniels was the program director for Mission of Promise, a nonprofit organization that worked with local schools and day-care centers to provide support and resources to struggling families, which was pretty much every family in the area.

She went back inside, took a few of the flyers, and stuck them in her tote.

"I'm outta here, Brother Quincy."

Quincy lifted his head, covered as always with a white kufi. His somber gray-green eyes set in a sandy-brown face settled on her in the way that a teacher assesses a student to determine if they are trying to get away with something. He ran the office, doled out assignments, and monitored the comings and goings to ensure that the headquarters was never short-staffed.

"Good work today, Sister Anita. Thank you."

"Not a problem. I'll be back in on Wednesday or Thursday. Cool?"

He smiled benevolently. "Cool."

She finger-waved to her coworkers and sauntered out, made a right at the corner. She had a mind to take a little detour and see if do-gooder Jason was still up on 126th but then thought better of it. No reason to get *him* thinking that *she* was thinking about him one way or the other.

She stopped in the corner store and placed some flyers on the counter. "Let the brothers know that we're having a meeting on Thursday—Brother Malcolm is going to speak. They need to get involved. You need to be there, too, Mr. W.," Anita prodded.

Charles Winslow had owned the corner store for more

than a decade and his father had before him. He was the eyes and ears of the neighborhood and made the best hero sandwiches in all of Harlem.

He waved a hand. "You young people can do all that marching and protesting. I'm fine just where I am."

"Well, you can do your part for the cause by making sure that everybody who buys a hero gets a flyer. Deal?"

He grinned, flashing a gold front tooth. "You run a hard bargain, girl."

"That's the point, Mr. W." For good measure, she placed more flyers on the counter. "Now don't forget—hero, flyer." She winked.

He chuckled as she walked out, the bell over the door chiming behind her.

Anita took a step outside. Stopped. Thought about it, then mentally put a line through the idea and kept walking in the direction of Liza's office.

A nita crossed the intersection. Liza's building was up ahead. Mission of Promise was in an unassuming three-story brownstone building on a block lined with other brownstones. The founder, Clara Matthews, and her husband, Floyd, lived on the top floor and used the bottom two floors, backyard, and the finished basement to run the program. They opened for service at six thirty a.m. and closed at eight—there were many days when Liza pulled the entire six thirty to eight p.m. shift. She spent her days managing help for needy families, from providing access to food, getting them to clinics, helping with eviction notices, offering resources to childcare and intervention services for families in danger of losing their children, and even making legal referrals.

It was ambitious work, and her friend relished every minute of it.

Anita stepped onto the concrete front yard, then walked to the ground floor entrance and rang the bell. Helen, a college intern who always wore her thick hair in two perfect Afro puffs, answered the door.

"Hey, Miss Anita," she greeted and unlocked the iron entrance gate.

"Girl, you know when you call me 'Miss,' it makes me feel ancient. I'm about five minutes older than you."

They both laughed.

"Sorry. Habit." She stepped aside to let Anita pass. "How's the work coming at the network?"

"Good. Busy as always. You should come to one of the meetings."

"Hmm, maybe," she said, sounding noncommittal.

Anita waved a finger. "Like Harriet Tubman said, 'I freed a thousand slaves. I could have freed a thousand more if they knew they were slaves.'"

Helen twisted her lips to the side to keep from grinning. "Yes, ma'am."

"'Ma'am!' Now I'm done." She squeezed Helen's shoulder. "Liza down here or upstairs?"

"She's in the back. I'll let her know you're here. She's in with a parent."

"Thanks."

Helen continued down the hallway to the back, and Anita walked into the front room that had been converted into a waiting area. All the original detailing that made the brownstones so unique still remained, from the heavy wood-carved sliding doors, massive mantelpieces, and parquet floors to the stained glass banners at the tops of the floor-to-ceiling windows. A crystal chandelier anchored the room that was simply decorated with two antique lavender velvet couches, which always reminded Anita of some French boudoir. They looked like they could be in a museum, but they were incredibly comfortable.

This one room was nearly as big as Anita's entire apartment. Every time she came to visit with Liza, she imagined herself living in one of these grand abodes again, just like the one she'd grown up in with her family in Brooklyn.

The muffled sound of children's laughter drifted into the room from the backyard.

Anita picked up one of the pamphlets on planning a healthy meal just as the other sliding door that separated the front waiting area from the office opened.

Liza beamed. "Hey, girl. Sorry you had to wait." She *click-clicked* across the room. That was the biggest difference between her and Liza: she and heels did not get along, whereas Liza loved them. They were dissimilar in other ways as well. Liza pressed her hair until it hung ironing board straight, while Anita flaunted her natural tendrils as a badge of honor. Liza was five foot seven in her bare feet. Anita, five six in shoes. Anita was fiery, stubborn, and opinionated. Liza was thoughtful, patient, and willing to compromise—all the qualities that made them thick as thieves since they were kids running up and down Putnam Avenue in Brooklyn.

The friends hugged.

"You have lunch yet?" Anita asked.

"Nope. Wanna go over to Harry's?" Harry's was their go-to diner for some of the best burgers in Harlem.

"Perfect." She hooked her arm through Liza's. "You will never guess who I ran into today…"

"Tell, tell."

"As soon as we sit down."

Brownstone in Harlem, New York.
(c) Lisa-Blue / E+ / Getty Images

Anita and Liza entered Harry's, bypassed the long lunch counter, and grabbed a cracked red leather booth near the grimy window that looked out onto Eighth Avenue — definitely the best seat in the house. The decor of Harry's was straight out of a B mob movie, from the worn leather booths, scratched tables that incessantly wobbled, and dull metal flatware to the lousy lighting and noisy ceiling fans. But the food was worth the eyesore. The apple pies, red velvet cake, and lemon meringue on display beneath glass tops were truly the Eighth Wonders of the World. And whatever Harry put in his burgers needed to be bottled and patented.

"Hello, ladies. What are you having today?" The waitress placed a glass of water in front of each of them.

"Hey, Gloria. Our usual. Burgers and fries," Anita said.

"Throw some cheese on mine," Liza said. "Lettuce and

tomato on the side."

Gloria painstakingly wrote down every word on the little green-and-white pad. Anita and Liza often joked that Gloria had been working at Harry's before Harry's was even opened.

"Anything to drink?"

"Coke," they chorused.

Gloria pursed her red-tinted lips that had smudged beyond the outline of her mouth. "Coming right up." She shuffled away, her steps silenced by her thick-soled white shoes.

Liza leaned in, lowered her voice. "How old do you think she is?"

"Very," Anita answered. She reached for her glass of water and pulled the little dish of sliced lemons toward herself. She squeezed one in.

"Okay, we're sitting down," Liza said. "Who'd you see?"

"Him."

Liza frowned. "Him who?"

"Him, the guy from the bus. The one I told you about."

"What! Get out. Where?"

Anita relayed what had happened earlier that morning. She caught a glimpse of Liza's grin, though she was trying to hide it. Anita wanted to bust out smiling, too, but she played it cool and rambled on about the unexpected meeting.

"You know you sound like you got a thing for this guy, right?"

Anita's neck jerked back. "Girl, please. He's a real square. Not my type." She brought the glass to her lips.

"Hmm. Okay."

"Don't say '*okay*' like that. He's not my type."

"Why did you invite him to B-Flat?"

Anita's response hung for a second. "The more the merrier. That's it."

"Hmm. Okay."

"See, there you go again."

"Is he cute?"

He was more than cute in that "country" way of his. Was it the soft brown hue of his eyes that seemed to penetrate beyond her walls or the way the curve of his lips kind of puckered before he spoke? Maybe it was the close cut dark black waves of his hair that she imagined running her hands across. Anita licked her lips. "Not bad."

Gloria returned with their food. The off-white plates overflowed with fries, and their burgers were laid out ready to be photographed for *Food Digest*. They both moaned with anticipation.

"Thanks, Gloria," Anita said for them both.

"Lemon meringue is extra good today," she said before shuffling away.

They made quick work of fixing up their burgers and slathering their fries in ketchup. Gloria returned with a small bowl of pickles. They hummed their appreciation and chewed with gusto.

"So for real, you don't want to see him again?" Liza asked.

Anita put down her burger and wiped the corner of her mouth with the paper napkin. "I don't know," she admitted. It was hard for her to wrap her mind around why Jason threw her off her game. She hadn't felt vulnerable or unsteady around a man since she was a naive teenager, but this one, without really trying, had pried open the door that she'd—with good reason—sealed shut.

"There isn't anything I know of that you don't have an opinion on, an experience with, some words of wisdom or whatever to offer up." She tipped her head to the side and looked at her friend. "So what's the deal? If you can't tell yourself…" She leaned in. "You better tell me."

Anita laughed. "Man, I don't know, I don't know. It's bizarre. He got on my last nerve the first time I met him. He's this corny, suit-and-tie-wearing 'Kumbaya' brother." She slowly shook her head. "We're too different."

"Kinda like you and me, and we're best friends," Liza said with a lift of her brow to emphasize her point.

"So what are you sayin'?"

"I'm saying"—she shrugged her left shoulder—"give him a chance. He clearly made an impression. Don't you owe it to *me* to find out where it could go?"

Anita sputtered a laugh. "Yeah, okay, girl." She pushed out a breath. "Maybe I will. For *you*."

"Yeah, right," Liza said with a chuckle.

"Anyway, enough about me and my nonexistent love life. What's happening with you and Dave?" She lifted her burger to her mouth and took a bite.

Liza sighed. "I think I'm going to have to let that one go."

"Why? I thought things were good between you."

Liza shrugged her right shoulder. "Dave is nice. I mean really nice. Has a good job, easy on the eyes, treats me well…"

"Annnnd?"

Liza leaned forward, lowered her voice. "No skills."

Anita frowned for a moment, then her eyes widened in understanding. "Oh, really? Wow."

"Yeah and it's a shame. Everything else, he's close to perfect."

"He seems like your type, though. You know, stand-up guy, no fluff, no muss. Maybe you can…show him what you need."

Liza sighed. "If only it was that simple. It's not that. I… He just doesn't turn me on," she said on a whisper. "There's no excitement, no thrill."

"Hmm. That's a problem."

"Yeah."

"So what are you going to do? You can't string him along if you're sure it's not going to work."

"I know." She pushed a fry around in a pool of ketchup on her plate. "You know what I want, Nita?" she said in a faraway voice. "I want a man who, when he walks into the room, my heart starts to race. A man I don't want to be without even on our worst days. A man who knows my body and how to make it happy. A man who wants me to be as much a part of his life as I want him in mine." Her gaze landed on her friend. "Asking a lot, right?"

"Our day is coming, girl," she offered, as images of Jason danced around in her head.

Chapter Four

Jason climbed the three flights of stairs, unlocked the door to his room, and shut it behind him. He tossed his jacket on the one chair by the single window and placed his bag of food on the small table. He'd stopped at a rib joint on his way home knowing that once he was home, he would be in for the night.

He and Mike had worked for hours scrubbing floors and walls, emptying trash, bagging the debris from the back alley, and putting it out for pickup. By the time they'd finished, his muscles burned, and his lower back ached. His body begged for rest, but his mind wouldn't slow down. After running into Anita like that…

Anita. A slow smile slid across his mouth.

He turned on the little transistor radio next to his bed to WWRL. Frankie "the Rocker" Crocker, a radio host he was really digging, was signing off for the evening with his satin-smooth voice: "Reach for the moon. Even if you fall short, you will be among the stars. May you live as long as you want, never want as long as you live; may you live to be one hundred, and me one hundred but minus a day, so I'll never know nice people like you have passed away."

Jason grinned, bobbed his head in agreement as the

signature signoff song, "Moody's Mood for Love," began to play, and he tried to sing along. "There I go, there I go, theeeeerrree I go, pretty baby, you are the soul who snaps my control…"

He plopped down on the side of his single bed, stretched out, and tucked his hands behind his head as the song played on. The image of Anita looking up at him with that unflinching determination in her bewitching eyes emerged before him. His stomach tightened.

What was it about her? He blew out a long breath. Then he sat up, reached for his jacket, and took the flyer out of the inside pocket. He unfolded it and smoothed the edges against his thigh.

B-Flat Lounge. 1207 Seventh Avenue.

Doors open at 7 p.m.
Food. Drink.
Live Entertainment Every Friday Night.
No Cover

Friday was only four days away—something to think about. He placed the flyer on the small table. In the meantime, he needed a shower and some food. He grabbed his bath caddy and towel and hoped the bathroom was free.

It was finally Friday. Now that the phones were on in the office, and he was in closer contact with the folks back home, he'd gone full steam ahead in getting the office up, running, and relevant. He had posters made and hung them in the windows. Each morning, he and Michael took turns talking to the folks in the neighborhood about Dr. King's vision and how they could be part of the change. So far, they'd signed up only ten people willing to come to a meeting. Clearly there was much more work to do.

Jason peered closely into the murky bathroom mirror that had long lost its ability to reflect. He ran his hand across the close-cropped waves of hair, glad that he'd stopped for a cut on his way home.

While he'd waited for his turn in the chair, he had been transported back home to Joe's Cut and Trim, listening to the raucous banter about everything from Jackie Robinson and Muhammad Ali to James Brown coming to the Apollo, from wives and girlfriends, to the president.

Even here in the North, there was a divide between Black nationalism and nonviolent resistance. At times the debate grew so heated, Jason thought it might come to blows. But much like every barbershop he'd been in since he was old enough to sit in a chair, these hallowed places were akin to a church service. You laid down your troubles, raised your voice, hoped for clarity and absolution, danced in jubilation, and returned home—changed.

The barbershop was a short reprieve from the pace of the big city. Sitting there listening to the men play the dozens had reminded him how much more alike folks were than they were different.

He checked for his watch, a twenty-first birthday gift from his dad. His chest tightened, remembering that he had no idea where it was. He'd looked everywhere for his watch since he'd arrived in New York. He'd even called home and asked his sister to look for it. No luck. *Every well-dressed man wears a good watch*, his father had told him. He pulled in a breath, adjusted his tie.

Tonight was definitely a night for the well-dressed man.

His suit and tie would have to do the trick.

He returned to his room and put on his jacket. It had been a long time since he'd felt this anxious about seeing a woman. He could count on one hand his relationships of consequence. There'd only been one who had made an impact. After his young heart had been bruised in high school by Brenda Smalls, he'd been cautious about letting attraction get ahead of reason. That mantra had held fast until he'd met Cynthia Bennett.

She was a beauty in every sense of the word: tall, shapely, long silky hair that never frizzed in bad weather, and skin that looked like sunshine. Beyond her good looks, Cynthia met all the qualities that he believed were important: regular churchgoer, similar friends and values, strong family ties, and a firm belief in marriage first, then children.

They rarely argued about anything more pressing than what movie to see on a Saturday night. Cynthia was even-tempered, never raised her voice, didn't challenge any of his ideas, and a cuss word wouldn't dare cross her lips. They were good together, but they were only that—good. Never great, never thrilling. As much as he'd cared for Cynthia, he never felt that electricity when she walked into a room or spent hours thinking of her when they were apart.

Both their families had looked forward to and expected a wedding, but the more they were pressed, and the more he and Cynthia spent time together and talked about the future, the more they agreed that they were in "deep like" but not love.

Jason adjusted his tan short-brimmed hat, which sat in cool contrast to the chocolate-brown suit, the look of a man who married a woman like Cynthia. What was the look of a man who married a woman like Anita? *Wow. Where did that come from?*

He straightened his tie. He would never be city slick or a charismatic revolutionary. He could never be an Anita Hopkins kind of man, and he wasn't sure how he felt about that. He turned off the single overhead light and walked out.

Maybe tonight, he would see things a bit clearer.

Michael was leaning against a sky-blue Oldsmobile, smoking a cigarette, when Jason came outside. He flicked his cigarette away and squeezed out the flame with the point of his alligator shoe.

"Hey, my man. Ready?" Michael greeted with a wide grin.

Jason didn't know quite what to make of him. This Michael was a far cry from the one he'd worked side by side with for the past couple of weeks. In place of the buttoned-down, preppy young man at the office stood a slick, very dapper Michael Irving in front of him, from the tilt of his wide-brimmed fedora to the cut of his navy pin-striped suit and the fancy ride that idled behind him.

Jason gave both Michael and the car the once-over. "Yeah. This yours?"

"Yep. Only bring her out for special occasions." He tapped the roof. "Hop in." He opened the passenger door for Jason, then walked around and got in behind the wheel.

They pulled off, and it was akin to riding on a cloud. The car took the ditches and bumps in the road as if they didn't exist, gliding over them like a skater on ice. The drive was barely five minutes but well worth the experience. The only downside was that they had to park a block away, which left too much time for Jason's level of anxiousness to ratchet up.

"Here we are," Michael said, and pulled open the door.

Mary Wells' "The One Who Really Loves You" pumped from six-foot speakers. Several couples were on the floor doing The Jerk. More than half the tables were already filled.

"You'll really dig it," Michael said above the din. He bopped in and waited.

A hostess approached. "Table or bar?"

"Table," Michael answered for them both.

"Right this way."

"Anything up front?" Jason asked.

The waitress looked at him over her shoulder and smiled. "Sure. I think so." She seated them in the center of the room with a good view of the stage. "Can I get you guys something from the bar?"

"Rum and Coke," Michael said.

"And for you?"

"Coke. Hold the rum."

She looked at him askance, then hurried off.

"Gonna start off easy, huh?" Michael said while bobbing his head to James Brown's "Think."

"Yeah." He swept his hat from his head and placed it on the empty seat beside him.

"Hey, I'll be right back. See some folks I know." He hopped up before Jason had a chance to react.

Absently, he drummed his fingers on the tabletop while he subtly scanned the dimly lit space for any sign of Anita. By now all the tables were full, and bodies were lined up at the bar. He spotted Michael chatting it up with two other men and a woman who was wrapped around one of the men like a scarf.

"Is the rum and Coke for you, do-gooder?"

His heart jumped. He turned to his left, and there she

was, standing above him with that almost-smug grin on her face and a tray in her hand. She set the drinks down on the table.

"Actually, it's for a friend."

Her brow arched. She looked around. "Female friend?"

He leaned back a bit, narrowed his eyes. "Would it matter?" he asked, the question almost a challenge.

She jutted her hip to the side. "No."

Jason licked his lips, surprisingly pleased that she even cared enough to ask. "Michael. We work together."

Her polished red lips curved. "Two do-gooders," she taunted.

"Do you even remember my name?" he playfully volleyed.

"Would it matter?" she said, tossing his own question at him.

Jason leaned back and laughed, folding his hands down on his lap. "Are you always so tough?"

Her lids lowered ever so slightly. "You ain't seen tough, do-gooder." She turned, then back over her shoulder, she said, "Jason." She winked and sashayed away.

Jason rocked his jaw and tried to keep an eye on Anita's movements. He watched her smile, chat, touch a shoulder, buss a cheek as she moved from table to table. She reminded him of the women back home who moved through the world with an authority, never stepping aside or lowering their eyes. The kind of woman his mother would *tsk, tsk* at when she passed one on the street, swinging her hips with a cigarette tucked between red lips, and warn Patrice that she "betta nevah."

He lifted the glass of Coke to his lips and took a thoughtful swallow. How tough was this Anita anyway?

Michael came back totally hyped, laughing and joking with two friends he'd brought along with him.

"Joe, Frank, this is Jason Tanner. We work together. He's

new to town—first time here," he shouted over the din. He pulled out a chair and sat.

The two men extended their hands in turn, which Jason shook.

"Sit down, sit down," Michael said.

"Where you from?" Joe asked. He turned the chair backward and straddled it, then sipped his drink.

"Atlanta."

"Yeah? Have some family down there, but I never been. Heard it's pretty nice, though," Frank said. He tilted his bottle of beer to his lips.

"Not bad," Jason said with a half smile.

"First time in New York?"

"Yep. Takes a bit of getting used to," Jason admitted.

"Keep hanging out with this guy, and you'll be a real regular in no time," Joe said and tipped his glass toward Michael.

Michael chuckled. "Givin' my man here the wrong idea about me," he said over his smile.

"Hope y'all aren't trying to corrupt him with your wicked ways."

Jason's breath hitched for an instant. He felt her standing behind him, then at his side. Her hip brushed his shoulder—intentionally or by accident, he didn't know.

Anita grinned down at him.

"Not at all, pretty lady. But I sure would like to corrupt you," Frank said.

Jason flexed, made a move, but felt her hand on his shoulder.

"I can be corrupt all by myself, baby. No need for any help. But I tell you what, you order some food to go with that drink if you're really concerned about my well-being."

Jason's heart was bumping in his chest. Her fingers pressed

down into his shoulder with more authority than he would have expected.

Frank looked from Anita to Jason, then back again. He shrugged. "Sure. We have a table on the other side," he said with a lift of his chin and got up from his seat. Joe followed suit.

"Then I'll see you on the other side." She turned her attention to Jason. "Ready to order?"

When she looked at him like that, with those long lashes lowered over those sultry eyes, he could easily imagine anything but food. He cleared his throat. "Sure." He picked up the menu. "Burger, well done."

"What about you?" she said to Michael.

"Same."

Anita smiled. "I'll get those orders started." She walked away.

Michael leaned in. "Hey, I'm sorry about all that. They just had too much to drink. But what's up with you and her?" he said, jerking his head in Anita's direction.

"Nothing. I didn't like how your friend spoke to her, that's all."

"Seems like she did a good job of taking care of herself. But there's definitely something there." He lightly shoved Jason's arm while flicking his eyebrows up and down.

Jason laughed. "It's not like that, not really. I barely know her."

"What's '*barely*'?" He finished off his drink.

Jason took a breath, looked around. "I met her a few weeks ago on the bus…" Jason recounted their meeting the night of the church explosion, then running into her again on the street. "She's definitely not my usual type of woman, but there's something about her." Jason let his gaze drift off.

"Humph. Damn, man. That's some story. You need to

make a move."

It occurred to him that she might already be involved with someone. "Do you know if she's seeing somebody?"

Michael shrugged and shook his head simultaneously. "Naw. I mean, I've seen her around the neighborhood, seen her in here, but not with anybody in particular. Don't mean that she don't have somebody tucked away, though." He grinned.

Jason nodded slowly. What did it matter? The idea of them being anything more than ideological sparring partners was kind of out there. He was logical, rational, which flew in the face of why he was really sitting there, acting as if the reason why he was at the B-Flat was for the food and entertainment and not the eyes, the mouth, the voice that had wooed him there.

"Hey, I'll be right back. See a lady I wanna holler at." Mike winked and sauntered off.

Jason leaned back in his seat. The crowd at B-Flat was in full effect. Chubby Checker's "Let's Do the Twist" pulled couples out of their seats and onto the small dance floor. Others stood by their seats or at the bar, twisting their hips, arms, and feet. He bobbed his head to the music, took in the packed tables, the boisterous gaiety, and flashy clothes not much different from those at the bigger clubs back home but a far cry from those at the house parties that he'd frequented.

Anita returned with their plates of food. "Where's your friend?" She put the plates on the table.

"Went to see someone," he shouted.

She planted a hand on her hip. "Well, what do you think so far?"

Was she asking about herself or the club? "So far, pretty cool. Seems like a nice crowd. Hip music." His gaze dragged up and down her body.

"Told ya. Enjoy your meal." She started to walk away, then stopped. "I can take care of myself, you know." Her lips pursed for a moment. "But thanks."

"Hey," he called as she started to go.

She turned back halfway. "Yeah?"

"What time does this place close?" he asked instead of what time she got off.

"One. Maybe two. Past your bedtime, do-gooder?"

He angled his head to the side, offered up an amused grin. "Not the last time I checked."

He watched her slender throat work.

She ran her tongue along her bottom lip. "Maybe I'll look for you."

"You do that."

She studied him for a moment, as if she were thinking about saying something, but then walked away instead.

He bit into his burger, chewed slowly. Like everything else so far at B-Flat, it was pretty darn good.

Michael returned, clearly buzzed, and began rambling about the woman he'd been talking to, but Jason wasn't really listening. His mind was still on Anita Hopkins—how she looked, the things she had said, the spark in her eyes, the way she walked, the way she teased. Every now and again, she'd briefly look in his direction, toss a smile, and keep working the crowd. Maybe it was all a part she needed to play to cajole customers and boost her tips. He had no idea.

"Good evening!" a voice boomed from the mic.

Jason and Michael angled their chairs to better see as the live band set up onstage.

"Tonight, as on every Friday night, B-Flat is here to entertain you. Everybody having a good time?"

Shouts and the pounding of fists on tables reverberated in the air.

The man at the mic laughed. "That's what I like to hear. So without further ado, put your hands together for the B-Flat Combo."

The band played a series of original pieces and standard Friday night R&B for about an hour. Michael made it a point to introduce Jason to friends who came and went while the band played. It seemed that Michael knew pretty much everyone in the place either directly or indirectly. No way Jason could keep all the names straight or, for that matter, actually hear what the names were over the music and loud conversations, but he appreciated the effort.

And then the world stopped spinning when he turned his attention to the stage and saw Anita standing in the spotlight. He sat straight up in his seat. "What's going on?"

"Oh yeah, she's a badass poet. Thought you knew that."

Jason swallowed. "No, I didn't. I mean, I sorta did, but—"

Anita stepped closer to the mic, cupped it between her palms. "Good evening."

"Good evening," the audience shouted back.

"I have a little something to share tonight. It's called 'Fate.'" She adjusted her stance and signaled the band.

> *"Musta been fate that September day;*
> *Came out of nowhere,*
> *Didn't care that*
> *Fate turned my head*
> *In the wrong direction of you;*
> *Couldn't turn back now if I wanted to*
> *Forget that*
> *Fate put us on the same lane*
> *In different rows,*
> *Who knows*
> *Why fate chose us to be on that bus."*

Jason froze. His mouth opened.

> *"For that moment, when bombs*
> *Blew away lives, and the cries*
> *Didn't separate the way hate*
> *Was meant to do,*
> *I looked at you and knew*
> *That no matter the stop we took together,*
> *You knew it, too."*

Anita looked out into the audience. Jason could hardly breathe.

"Thank you."

The audience erupted into applause. She made her exit, and the band went back to playing their set.

"Told you she was a bad sister," Michael said.

Jason didn't know what to say or think. Was she actually talking about them, or was he only wishing that she were? The shock of seeing her up onstage in the first place had thrown him off balance to begin with, so maybe he was just projecting.

"Didn't you say y'all met on a bus?"

Jason blinked Michael into focus. "Yeah."

"Well?" Michael threw him a raised brow.

"Well what?"

"You can't see she was spitting about you and her?"

Jason waved him off, not quite ready for his own suspicions to be confirmed. "Naw, man, there's no way. Like I said, I barely know her."

Michael glanced at him over the rim of his glass. "Not for long," he said. He lifted his chin.

Anita came alongside Jason. "How was the burger?"

He angled his body to look up at her. "Excellent. And you were really good up there."

"Thanks." She pulled her order pad from the pouch that hung around her waist and tore off one ticket to give to Michael. The second one she placed facedown in front of Jason. "Hope you gentlemen enjoyed your night. Come back again."

"Plan to," Michael called out to her receding back.

Jason picked up his bill and turned it over. His brows drew together.

Beneath the total was a phone number and the words: "Call me sometime, do-gooder."

Chapter Five

Anita wasn't on shift at B-Flat until eight, and she didn't do weekends at the network unless a major event was happening. Today was her day to do what she wanted without anyone else's expectations. She took her bowl of Cap'n Crunch cereal and walked to the window.

Liza always teased her that her cereal choice was for kids, but Anita didn't care. She loved the sweetness and the crunch and that every kernel floated no matter how much milk she poured over them. What did that do-gooder eat for breakfast? Humph. Probably grits and eggs with cheese and two perfect slices of bacon. An adult breakfast.

She snickered. *Wonder if he'll call.*

She scooped a spoonful into her mouth and chewed slowly while she watched Saturday morning come alive on the street below.

The sound of metal gates clanged and grated as they were dragged and raised over doorways and windows. Shouts of morning greetings by the brothers who habitually hung on the corners merged with the growing chorus of car horns and music thumping from open windows.

Anita leaned against the frame of the window. These were her people, beautiful in all their combinations, from the bodega shop owners to the African hair braiders, the mom-and-pop eateries and the vendors hawking incense and body oils, mix tapes, and paperback books. They came in all sizes and colors, a human rainbow of awesomeness, able to consistently make something out of nothing and do it with flair against every bit of adversity thrown at them.

She took her last spoonful of cereal. Today was a day to be out and about among her people.

Dressed in her favorite bell bottom jeans, her Black Power T-shirt, and white Converse sneakers, she filled her tote with her notebook, pens, a light sweatshirt hoodie, a rolled towel, two apples, her wallet and keys, and headed out.

She started walking toward 125th Street and stopped on Seventh at a street vendor. He was selling a variety of jewelry laid out on an oblong kente cloth along a portable table and hung from a makeshift jewelry tree. Bangles, rings, chains, and earrings gleamed in the morning light, all with the claim of being "100 percent sterling silver and fourteen-carat gold, my beautiful sister."

Anita bit back her grin. She knew better.

She fingered a pair of oversize hoop earrings in faux sterling silver. A little bit of clear nail polish would keep them serviceable for a while before they eventually turned. It was a trick she'd learned from her mother years ago.

"How much for these?" She held up the earrings.

"Four dollars, my sister. Perfect for you."

"Naw. Not at that price." She put them back down.

"How 'bout two? Two good?"

She pursed her lips. "How 'bout two pairs for three?" She propped her hand on her hip.

He pressed his hand to his dashiki-covered chest. "How you gonna do me like that? Brother gotta make a living."

She shrugged. "And a sister gotta eat."

He chuckled. "For you, two for three."

She picked up the hoops and a second pair that were long and teardrop shaped.

He put the earrings into a small black plastic bag. Anita dug in her purse and took out her wallet. She handed over the five-dollar bill, and he handed her the black bag and her change.

"Pleasure doing business with you, pretty lady."

Anita smiled. "Have a good day." She started off with an extra sway in her hips.

He called out to her. "What's your name, sister? Come by anytime."

She waved and kept walking, steering clear of dog walkers with their pit bulls and German shepherds. She slowed to look in shop windows and stopped to pick up a salted pretzel from the hot dog cart along the way. When she reached 128th Street, she turned and headed east toward St. Nicholas Avenue.

The entrance to St. Nicholas Park was ahead. It was one of her favorite spots to hang out and chill and a major source of inspiration for her poetry. Although the sprawling park — with its rolling grassy hills, bike paths, lovers nooks, and miles of shaded trees — was surrounded by the elevated train and towering tenements, it remained an urban oasis.

Anita hiked up a short path and turned off toward a cove of trees far enough away from the main path but close enough to chronicle the comings and goings.

She secured her spot beneath a towering tree, then took her towel out of her tote, spread it on the ground, and sat with her back resting against the trunk.

A row of cyclists breezed by in formation. On the opposite rise were several families who had set up for a Saturday picnic as summer rapidly drew to a close. It was one of the things she had looked forward to as a kid growing up in Brooklyn.

Brooklynites' go-to spot was Prospect Park, which was complete with a zoo and merry-go-round, a bandstand for concerts, lakes for rowing, miles of grass and trees, and, in the winter, an ice-skating rink.

Her mom, her aunt June, and her cousins Denise and Brenda would pack up her dad's Cadillac with blankets; a cooler full of juices, fruit, and sandwiches; a change of clothes for all the kids; and of course hula hoops, jump ropes, and roller skates. Her dad and her uncle Will had their separate cooler filled with cans of Budweiser. They played hard — running, jumping, skating. They had treasure hunts and eating contests, and as exhausted as they were by the time the sun began to set, they would still beg to stay a little longer.

She smiled at the memories while she watched the kids chase one another with water guns and sticks, screaming and laughing in delight. They would sleep well. A hot bath after a long day in the park was always a prelude to some of the best sleep she'd ever had.

But it was the park on Decatur Street where all the real happenings in the neighborhood went down. It was where she'd met *him,* and her life had changed forever. She lit a cigarette, inhaled deeply, and blew a puff of smoke into the late-summer air while she stared out beyond the rise of Harlem's jagged skyline from her resting spot against the tree trunk.

She plucked the butt of the cigarette from between her thumb and middle finger and sent it into a short sparkling arc that flickered against the green grass and warm brown earth before fizzling out on the concrete. She watched its rise and fall and half smiled, remembering when she'd first learned that little trick.

It had been summertime in Brooklyn, and all the kids from the neighborhood were sitting on the cool concrete of the empty handball court of PS 35. It wasn't quite dark yet. More of that special time when the sun still hangs in the sky and everything becomes urgent and important.

They had been sipping warm sodas and wiping sweat and grime from young foreheads after a hard game of handball when Leon, one of the older boys who lived on Chauncey Street—a block they were told to stay away from—approached with two of his friends. One carried a boom box on his shoulder, blasting Al Green. Leon seemed to glide to the beat.

Leon had an assurance that the other boys she knew didn't have. It was tucked in the corners of his mouth, in the perfect roundness of his curly Afro, the cut of his eyes as they swept across the ragtag group, the way he held his shoulders just so inside the bright-white T-shirt, in the flex of the muscles that were starting to grow in his arms. How his dark jeans draped long teenaged legs and thighs and covered the slight bulge that drew her eyes.

He took a pack of Kool cigarettes out of his pants pocket, asked if anyone had a light. They all looked from one to the other, shook their heads, and muttered a chorus of nos. He turned to his friends and started to laugh. They laughed with him. But it was only Leon's laugh that she heard. It was so full, full of something she couldn't put her finger on, like he had a secret that no one else knew.

She wanted to know what he knew. She needed to know, and that yearning for knowledge that felt like warm water beginning to boil in her stomach and flow through her veins became more important than the parental warnings. More important than punishment, more important than getting home before the streetlights came on.

So when Leon's dark-brown eyes settled not on Cynthia or Tricia but on her and the corners of his mouth curved like a finger of invitation, she took his hand when he extended it to help her to her feet. She walked with him to a quiet corner of the park where the shadows were deeper and told him her name. He said he never knew a girl named Anita, but he wanted to get to know her. He made her feel special, womanly. He made her body yearn for something out of reach. Something that girls whispered about and the boys bragged or lied about to themselves and their friends.

Leon taught her what she wanted to know with soft kisses behind her ears and warm young fingers on tender blooming breasts. She learned things. She learned that her body could make a young man weep, that it could shudder and writhe and she could do nothing to stop it. She learned how to smoke when it was over and how to flick a cigarette away when she was done.

Wednesdays after school became their day. It was a half day for the Catholic high school she attended, and Leon would be waiting for her when she crossed the protective black gates of the school.

Cynthia and Tricia would giggle and whisper as they watched her and Leon walk away from the sanctity of the schoolyard, wondering if the secrets that she shared with them were true. What did it feel like? Did it hurt? How many times had they "done it"? She'd answered their questions with a worldly nonchalance that came with experience and enjoyed their open-mouthed, wide-eyed expressions.

Yes, that year with Leon had changed her. She scrawled "Leon and Anita" on the notebooks that she kept hidden from her parents.

She was fourteen.

She'd already had her period and knew she was a woman, woman enough for a man-child who was seventeen going on eighteen. It didn't matter that her mother told her differently and her father still treated her like a baby. All the girls knew that once "your thing" came down, you were a woman. Her body looked and felt different that year. She would tingle in places she'd never tingled before. She had hair in places she didn't have before. Her mother had to take her to the lingerie shop to get a real bra to cover her breasts that were blooming like summer fruit and constantly needed to be massaged.

She glanced down at her very full breasts. Yeah, that was a while ago. She almost laughed. Almost.

Funny how things change sometimes without you even noticing.

Or maybe she had noticed but didn't want to admit it, because if she did, she'd have to admit to all the other signs she'd tried to ignore back then—the late hours; the new friends; the eyes that wouldn't meet hers; the sullenness; the scent of different that lingered on his clothes, on his face, and in his hair; and the fear that came with waiting.

Waiting like she waited for Leon that last Wednesday at school. He wasn't waiting for her on the other side of the protective black gates. Not that Wednesday or the Wednesday after. It took a while, but she found out that his family had moved away. He was gone without a word, leaving her with a hole in her young heart and a thirst between firm young thighs that she went in a constant pursuit of quenching.

There were others, but never another Leon. She searched for him for three long years in all the Afros, white T-shirts, long young legs, and knowing corners of sweet mouths.

Then one day there he was again, standing on the corner of Halsey Street, drinking a beer out of a brown paper bag, leaning against the wall of the corner store.

She stood still, halted by the years that now stood between them. Three years had changed him into full grown. It was in the set of his jaw that was outlined with the shadow of a beard and not the waning sunlight, the expanse of his chest beneath the worn black leather jacket and the knot between his legs that was larger than she remembered. He turned toward her. The knowing mouth curved ever so slightly before he looked away without a flicker of recognition in his eyes.

Did her knees weaken, or did she trip over the break in the gray concrete? She never knew as she hugged the bag of groceries tighter to her chest to keep her heart from breaking open, blinked away the sting in her eyes, and walked on, fighting the urge to run when her name, more like a question, reached out and caught her right behind her ear before she was out of reach.

"Anita?"

She'd turned, and he was coming toward her, the familiar swagger, the invitation of his mouth dragging her back through time, and he was peeling off her clothes in the tight, hot one-room apartment that he'd rented on that block she should have never been on.

It didn't matter where he'd been, how long he'd been gone, or what he'd done, only that he was back and she was wrapped around him, beneath him, under his skin—which is what she told him, but he said he couldn't take it anymore. He couldn't breathe, he couldn't move or think with her all over him. *What have I done?* she'd pleaded with him. *What have I done but whatever you wanted? What have I done but love you since I was fourteen years old?*

He'd looked at her. *You're smothering me*, he'd said in a voice she didn't recognize. His wide shoulders dropped by inches with each of the damning words that he'd uttered.

His words made no sense. How could her living and loving only for him be the reason why he didn't want her, want what they'd made?

She should have listened to her father, who warned her

about the boys on Chauncey Street, and her mother, who told her she wasn't a woman yet. She should have listened. But it was too late. They'd created something between them that couldn't go away with words.

That was so many other days ago—back then, back there, that other time—but it still felt like right now: that tug, that magnetic pull toward someone who wasn't for you. Like Jason.

She took her notebook and pen out of her bag and spread it open on her lap. Her visits to the park were her opportunities to step outside herself and be one with something other than a cause. Here she could just *be*—quiet, introspective, or not. Here there was no reason to put on her armor, to fight injustice with justice, to do battle against the perpetrators who lined up daily to dictate who could do what, where, and when.

Here—under the glory of the sun, shaded by the veil of trees, cocooned by the laughter and music and nature at its finest—she could just *be*.

Her intention was to write a new piece for a performance, but what she found herself doing was writing a very long diary entry all about how she'd been thinking and feeling since she met Jason and if he would ever call her. Was she being too bold? Too northern for the square country boy?

By the time her pen stopped moving across the page, the scents of burning charcoal and sizzling burgers were carried by the slightly cooling air. The families on the opposite rise had fired up the grill. Her stomach rumbled. She checked her watch. It was after noon, and all she'd had was some cereal and an apple.

She looked over the pages she'd written, surprised that her words had veered off in this direction. Her memory was foggy at best in trying to recall writing down her feelings about a man. Soft and fuzzy was so not her MO. But she could not deny that Jason Tanner sat quietly along the fringes of her consciousness, waiting for opportunities to slip past her defenses and tap her on the shoulder.

She closed her notebook and stuck it back in her bag. Slowly she got to her feet, arched her back, and rotated her neck. She took a last look around. If she left now, she could grab a quick train ride into Brooklyn, stop by Birdel's Record Shop, and maybe check on her folks, which would free her up to sleep in on Sunday.

She hurried out of the park with the intention of taking the A train on 125th and Eighth Avenue. With any luck she would be in Brooklyn before two. She wasn't sure if it was fate or footwork that took her down 126th Street. She hitched her tote higher up on her shoulder and tried to slow the speeding beat of her heart as Jason's storefront office grew closer.

Would she appear casual if she ran into him, or would she look desperate? There was still time to turn the corner and miss his office altogether. Besides, she didn't have time to stop and chat. Her steps slowed. The office was open, and she could see movement beyond the plate glass window. She tried to act as if she wasn't attempting to get a look inside when the door swung open.

There he is. She would have tripped if she hadn't been standing still.

"Hey," she greeted with as much nonchalance as she could summon. "Working on a Saturday, I see."

The corner of Jason's mouth curved slightly. He took a handkerchief from his back pocket and mopped his damp forehead. "Yeah. Six-days-a-week job. How are you?"

"Good. Can't complain." She lifted her chin toward the office. "What are you working on?" Her heart was beating so hard, her words wobbled in her ears.

"Setting up a schedule for training."

Her brows tightened. "Training for what?"

"For what to do if…when you are arrested or assaulted by the police."

The sun heightened the flash of heat in her eyes. "Oh, you mean, lay down and take it?"

Jason pushed out a breath. "You really think that the nonviolent, nonresistant approach is wrong, flawed?" He locked the door and drew down the metal gate.

"I believe," she said, pointing a finger at his chest, "that allowing your body to be dragged, hosed, and beaten and *not* resisting, *not* standing up, *not* declaring that a human being cannot be treated like an animal is cowardly. As long as we continue to lay down, they will keep walking all over us."

She could feel her pulse thump in her temples and knew that she was sounding shrill rather than staunch. She didn't want him thinking of her as some hysterical woman but rather as a person of strong conviction.

But why did it matter what he thought about her anyway?

He slid the keys in his pocket. "Are you working tonight?" he asked, totally knocking her off the soapbox she'd climbed up on.

She blinked. "Yes."

"Maybe I'll see you later. And maybe we can have a real conversation when you're done."

"So you *do* like the B-Flat atmosphere," she said, regaining her footing.

"I like quite a few things."

She swallowed and felt her cheeks flame. "Whatever that means," she lobbed.

Jason lowered his head and slowly shook it, then looked at her. "Where are you headed?"

"Train station. Going to Brooklyn to my fave record shop."

"How far is that from here?"

"Hmm, about forty-five minutes. The A train is express."

"Long way to go for some music."

She leaned on her left leg, jutted her hip. "Birdel's is the one and only spot for all the latest hits. Plus, they have the best mix tapes. And if you're into music like I am, the trip downtown is worth it." She paused a beat. "You should come with me." The words tumbled out of her mouth before she could stop them—now it was too late to take them back. But she didn't think she really wanted to. Her stomach fluttered.

Jason frowned. "To Brooklyn?"

"You don't have to make it sound like that. It'll be fun." She laughed as she tilted her head to the side. "Y'all have subways in Georgia?"

"No."

"You been on the subway since you got here?"

"No."

"So what else you got to do?"

"Maybe I'm busy. Ever think of that?"

"Are you?" she challenged.

"Maybe."

She pursed her lips. "No you're not." She looped her arm through his. "Come on, do-gooder, we're going on an adventure."

"How much is this train ride?" Jason said as they descended the stairs into the 125th Street station. He crinkled his nose as the underground aroma wafted upward.

Anita slid a look in his direction and giggled. "Fifteen

cents. You need a token."

"A what?"

"Token. In place of money. You put the token in the turnstile." She dug her purse from her bag and took out two tokens that were no bigger than dimes. She handed one to him. "Don't say I never gave you nothing," she added with a wink and a grin. "Come on." She jerked her head in the direction of the turnstile. She dropped her token in the slot and pushed the revolving spindles, Jason following.

"We need to be up front." She began walking down the gray concrete platform, passing several worn wooden benches lined with waiting travelers and others who leaned against walls or stood in small clusters.

The stale, murky environment was something right out of the noir murder movies that he watched with his father on Saturday nights. Pale-yellow light bulbs, housed in wire cages, flickered above their heads. The black-and-white tiled walls were splattered with graffiti, and the yellow warning line that ran the length of the platform had seen better days. Discarded paper cups and heaven only knew what else cluttered the tracks, perfect fodder for the rats that scurried between the iron rails.

Anita walked to the edge of the platform, leaned over, and peered down the dark tunnel. "Train's coming," she announced. She stepped back and turned to him.

Jason hoped that his expression didn't reflect the discomfort he felt in being underground and all the "make your skin crawl" sights and sounds that went with it. If it wasn't for the idea that he would spend some time with Anita, the subway was the last place on his list of sites to check out.

"You'll get used to it," she said, as if reading his mind.

He murmured his doubts deep in his throat.

The breeze from the approaching train swirled the loose

debris, and the thundering rumble and squeal of the iron brakes pierced his ears.

The train screeched to a grinding halt. Bodies moved in unison toward the doors that slid open to pour out their human cargo, only to be replaced.

Jason was still getting used to the huge numbers of people who trolled the streets of Harlem day and night. However, the mass of humanity contained in these huge metal boxes gave him pause. It was a little beyond midday on a Saturday, and practically every seat was taken. Other riders held on for dear life to cloth straps that hung from horizontal poles. The inside of the train was a small reflection of the station it just tore out of. The blue-and-gray subway car doors and walls were riddled with etchings ranging from "Lola loves Mark" to street names and cartoon characters splashed on windows with brilliant spray paint colors.

"There're two seats at the end," Anita said.

"I'll stand."

"Hmm. Okay." She shrugged. "But it's going to take a while." She walked toward a few empty seats. Jason reluctantly followed and watched her sit down without a care.

The train jerked violently to a stop, nearly throwing Jason off his feet. He grabbed a pole just in time to keep from going face-first onto the sticky subway floor.

"You probably should sit down," she counseled, her brows rising toward her halo of hair.

The heavy metal doors slid open, and humanity poured in and out. Jason squeezed in next to Anita, caught a whiff of her soft scent.

"Don't look so…*country*," she teased. "Nothing's going to bite you."

He half smiled. "You sure about that?"

Anita giggled. "Welllll, maybe. But I'll protect you, do-gooder. Don't worry," she added, her voice taking on a jazz singer's timbre.

She stared at him in a way that tightened his belly and flooded him with heat. First it was the note on his bill with her number on it, and now *this*—whatever *this* was. He couldn't peg her.

One minute she acted like she could toss him out with the trash, and the next it was like she wanted something more while at the same time being a combination of friendly and adversarial. He looked around and still wasn't sure how she'd managed to corral him onto the subway. One thing he was learning about her was that she was determined.

And determination looked real good on Anita Hopkins.

"See, it's not so bad," she shouted over the conductor's crackled announcement that Fifty-Ninth Street was the next stop.

"Do you do this often?"

"Do what?" She crossed her legs and looked him right in the eye. "Go to Brooklyn or ride the subway?"

He swallowed. "Go to Brooklyn."

She tilted her head to the side. "Hmm, about twice a month. Sometimes more. Mostly more." She laughed, and the tiny dimple in her cheek winked at him. "My parents live in Brooklyn in a big old brownstone on Putnam Avenue. It's where I grew up. They came to Brooklyn from Rudell, Mississippi." Her focus drifted away for a moment, then returned to him. "I usually visit for Sunday dinner." She had a faraway look in her eye and a half smile of remembrance. "My mother used to tell me at least once a year about her first time coming to the 'big city,' as she called it. She and my dad rode the bus all the way from Mississippi. Took three days. That was bad enough, my mother said, but it was her first cab ride that nearly had her running all the way back home in her brand-new pumps and white gloves." She laughed.

"What happened?"

"According to my mother, my dad really couldn't afford the cab ride from Port Authority in Manhattan to Brooklyn, but my mama said she wasn't gettin' in no cars that traveled underground." She laughed and gave Jason the side eye. "'Sides, she'd said, how was she s'posed to see this big ol' city he was bringing her to from under the ground?" Anita ad-libbed in a thick southern drawl. "So they stood in line on a steamy August morning and waited for a taxi along with the other travelers who'd made the three-day bus ride from Mississippi. My mother said she could barely concentrate on the wondrous sights of New York City that sped beyond the grimy cab window because of the ache in her fingers from squeezing Daddy's hand so hard every time the cab lurched across the lanes to tear in front of another car.

"My dad said that for the entire taxi ride, his eyes were fixed on the meter. Sweat kept sliding down from beneath his straw hat as the numbers rose by fifteen cents every few miles. Finally the cab came to a merciful stop in front of three-nine-five Lewis Avenue, and my mother whispered, 'Amen.'

"That was my parents' first apartment. But you'd have to hear my mother tell it. She will have you in stitches."

"That's some story." He chuckled at the vision of the young southern couple experiencing New York for the first time. He could totally understand the wide-eyed wonder. "Why did you move to Harlem?"

She draped her thin arms over her crossed thighs. "Hmm, I wanted to be out on my own, for one, and I wanted to be in the center of Black life. Harlem is like our mecca."

Maybe, he mused as he watched her face light up as she spoke, but Atlanta was the center of the movement.

"The soul of our culture. There's a lot of history there, and it's a great place for an artist and activist." She lightly touched his thigh. "What about you?"

"Grew up in Atlanta. We didn't have a *big old house*," he said, smiling, "but it was big enough for my sister and brother and me. I got involved in the movement about three years ago after hearing Dr. King speak at our church. I started going to meetings, getting to know the people behind the movement and understanding their vision and conviction." He dragged in a breath. "When the opportunity came for someone to come up North to spread the message, I knew it had to be me."

Anita stared at him with such a steady, unwavering look, it was as if she was trying to see beyond flesh and bone to what truly lived and breathed underneath. He shifted his body, drawing in on himself. He wasn't accustomed to this feeling of vulnerability, this level of scrutiny. It was enticing and a bit intimidating all at once.

"I totally get it. I feel the same way about Brother Malcolm. Last year he gave a speech about police brutality and our self-hatred that is crippling us as a people. It put so much in perspective for me. Brother Malcolm asked in his speech in Los Angeles: who taught us to hate ourselves, the color of our skin, the shape of our noses? To hate each other so that we don't want to be around each other? And the only way to overcome all that is to come together against the common enemy. He said we gotta get straight to the root—the cause. And when we get to the root, people think we dealin' in hate."

She shook her head, then met his gaze. "We want the same things, do-gooder, we just coming at it from different directions. I'll get you to come over to my side before it's all said and done," she added with conviction.

• • •

Visit: https://www.youtube.com/watch?v=6_uYWDyYNUg
for the complete speech.
Smithsonian Channel
Published on Feb 16, 2018
*In 1962, a confrontation with the LAPD outside a mosque
resulted in the death of a Nation of Islam member. It was
an event seized on by an outraged Malcolm X, who would
condemn it in an impassioned speech.*

• • •

He angled his body toward her. "That is exactly my point. Can't you see that? What Malcolm X is espousing—for all his good intentions—will do just the opposite. His rhetoric *will* fuel violence. Nonviolence is the way forward." His eyes narrowed. "So much has been accomplished by Dr. King and the movement through nonviolent actions. We are so close to getting civil rights legislations passed," he continued passionately. "All we want is to be treated equally."

"All *we* want is to be treated humanely," she countered. "Why must we want what they have? Why can't we have our own, build our own, support our own, and live in peace? I don't need to go to their schools or live in their neighborhoods or shop in their stores—if we have our own! Self-determination. Don't you get it?" she said, her voice rising with her passion.

Jason was quiet for a moment. "But we are all God's children, Anita. We must all live in harmony, *equally*; love each other unconditionally; pull each other up; and be judged on the content of our character, not the color of our skin."

She slowly shook her head and looked at him as if he were an addled child. "That's a utopia, not the real world. It's not in their interest to let it happen. You'll see."

"You gain more with compromise than with violent rhetoric. Two trains on the same track coming right at each other, heading for the same destination…are bound to collide if someone doesn't hit the brakes—take the high road."

She lifted her chin, stared him in the eye. "I like playing chicken, do-gooder."

She turned to face forward. "Why didn't you call me?" she asked out of the blue.

Jason blinked in confusion. "What?"

"I gave you my number. Why didn't you call me?" She turned those firefly eyes on him, and for a moment he couldn't think.

He swallowed. "Uh, I was going to."

She pursed her lips. "Right."

"*Nostrand Avenue, next stop*," crackled the conductor.

"Come on. That's us." She stood. The train swayed, and she tumbled onto his lap. She grinned at him. "Sorry." Her lips parted ever so slightly.

His face was on fire. Instinctively, his hands had reached out to grab her, and now they were on either side of a very narrow waist. He gritted his teeth to keep from stroking her sides.

She used his shoulders to push up to her feet just as the doors opened, then reached back and grabbed his hand. "Come on."

Jason shook his head to clear it and did as he was instructed.

They ascended the stairs, filing out with the hodgepodge of travelers, and emerged in the midst of what could only be described as a jamboree of vitality. Music blared from open windows. Every inch of concrete was populated with open-door stores that hawked half of their products from racks on the sidewalk; mom-and-pop diners serving up barbecue ribs; pizzerias; pawnshops; and electronics outlets. Street vendors manned their tables with jewelry, clothing, and cassette tapes. The air was thick with the aromas of foods that he could not quite identify even as they taunted his taste buds.

It was a mini version of 125th Street contained in a three-block radius on Nostrand Avenue from Fulton to Atlantic. He tried not to look as if he "just got off the train," but he was totally amazed with the pulse and vibe of the neighborhood.

"Birdel's is down the street. Next block," Anita said, tugging him out of his reverie.

They walked side by side as best they could, dodging around walkers, those standing still, and baby strollers.

"Busy place," Jason said.

She linked her arm through his. "Yep."

They stopped in front of what, from the outside, appeared to be no bigger than a small storefront. But even from the street, he could see through the window that the space was crowded. The Temptations' "You've Got to Earn It" pumped through the speakers that were mounted above the Birdel's signage. Flyers announcing tickets on sale for the James Brown revue at the Apollo Theater and a dance party at the Masonic Temple on Bushwick Avenue were posted in the window.

Anita pulled the door open. The inside was even smaller than he'd imagined, but the amount of inventory was kind of overwhelming. Every inch of the narrow aisles was lined with LPs and 45s held in crates that sat on wooden tables running from the front to the back of the shop. The shelving on the walls was stacked with albums categorized by genre and dating back to the early forties. Any free wall space was covered with flyers signed by recording artists.

"Wow," Jason murmured, taking a slow turn around.

"Pretty cool, right?"

He grinned. Nodded. "Yeah. Pretty cool."

"One of my favorite customers!"

Anita turned, a smile lighting up her face. "Hey, Mr. Mack."

"Whatchu know good?"

She giggled. "I was looking for a gospel album for my mom. Anything new? Oh yeah, and did you get a chance to put together the mix tape for me?"

"Sure did." He lightly rubbed his forehead. "Let me see what I can find for your mother." He turned his attention to Jason. "And what are you in the mood for, young man?"

"I'm sorry, Mr. Mack. This is Jason. Jason, Mr. Mack. He runs the shop with Mr. Long. Where is Mr. Long today?"

"Had to run some errands. He should be back later on." He extended his hand to Jason. "Welcome. What's your flavor?"

Jason gave a slight shrug. "Hmm, R&B and the blues mostly."

"Got plenty of both." He chuckled. "Take your time and look around. I know you'll find something. I'mma get that tape for you. Mr. Long put it aside in back."

"Thanks." Anita sidled up to Jason. "So, what do you think?"

He looked into her smiling face. "It was worth the trip."

She gave him a playful slug in the arm. "See, I told ya. Come on, let's look around."

They spent more than an hour browsing the shelves and stacks. Anita got her mixtape and the Dixie Hummingbirds' *Greatest Hits* for her mom. Jason purchased James Brown's "Please, Please, Please," "I Can't Stop Loving You," by Ray Charles, and Anita insisted that he had to have "Pride and Joy" by Marvin Gaye. He didn't have anything to play them on, so he wasn't sure if he'd made the purchases because he really wanted them or if he really wanted to impress Anita.

"Maybe next time you'll get to meet Mr. Long," Anita said as they squeezed around the customers and out into the street.

"Next time?"

She looked up at him. "Yeah. Next time," she repeated with such conviction, there was no room for him to disagree. "Wanna grab a slice before we head back?"

"Sure. My treat."

She grinned. "No argument from me. Best pizza in the hood is right on the corner of Fulton and Nostrand." She hooked her arm possessively through his. "You want me to put your stuff in my bag?"

He had to get used to her doing that, pulling him into her space, taking possession of him. Girls back home were never so bold.

He held up the plastic bag with his purchases. "I think I can manage."

"Come on, let's cross!" she suddenly shouted and literally pulled him across the street, barely missing getting hit by a yellow cab.

The cry of an ambulance's siren, rumbling trucks, and a steady stream of buses drowned out any meaningful conversation. Beyond the plate glass window of the pizza shop, a bustling world ebbed and flowed. The montage of people, cars, trucks, and cyclists that all intersected at the corner of Fulton and Nostrand was like a pathway to the world. On their side of the glass, the tight quarters of cracked red leather counter stools and three square Formica tables in an indistinguishable color braced by plastic chairs belied how good the pizza was.

Jason wiped his mouth with the tiny paper napkin. "You

were right. This is some good-eatin' pizza," he shouted. He lifted the small clear plastic cup of fountain soda and took a long swallow.

"Guess so by the look of that empty plate. Nothing but crumbs."

"My mama always said, 'Clean your plate, son; don't insult the cook.'"

"Then your mother would be proud."

"Want another slice?" Jason offered.

"No thanks." She checked her watch, a simple Timex with a frayed black leather band. "I need to get back. Work tonight."

"Right. Sure." He lifted his chin toward her wrist. "Had a watch just like that one."

She glanced at her wrist as if intrigued that the watch was there.

"My dad bought it for me for my twenty-first birthday. Thought I'd packed it, but I didn't. Can't seem to find it. Called home—not there, either." He crumpled the napkin and put it on top of the paper plate.

Anita studied him above the rim of her cup. There was a hint of something sad in his voice and a far-off look in his eyes that drew his brows together. She'd been as far from New York as California, but only to spend summers with her aunt Violet, and no further than the next city over for a place to live. Her friends and family were all around her, and she had no idea what it felt like to be alone in a strange city.

The observation made her feel soft inside, and she didn't particularly like the feeling. She finished her cup of soda, crumpled her napkin. "Ready?" She pushed to her feet.

"Yep." He gathered the paper plates and cups and tossed them in the metal trash can by the door.

Anita stepped outside. The tingle in her spine let her know he was behind her. She adjusted her tote on her shoulder.

"You said you grew up around here, right?"

"Yep. Walking distance," she said as they started toward the train. "Next time, I'll take you over to my old neighborhood." She almost blurted out, *And you can meet my mom and dad*, but she caught the wayward thought just in time. She jogged down the subway stairs.

"Don't know if I'll ever get used to this," Jason said as they walked along the sticky gray platform.

"Modern-day version of the underground railroad," Anita quipped. "Freed people on the journey to adventure and discovery at every stop."

"Hmm." He chuckled. "Guess you could stretch the imagination. A lot."

"What are your plans for the rest of the evening?" She glanced at his profile.

He turned his head. "Nothing special."

"You should come down to B-Flat," she said, hoping to sound more disinterested than she felt.

His gaze leveled on her. "Maybe. No promises."

She was relieved to hear the train roaring into the station to camouflage the flash of excitement she felt.

They stepped on board, squeezed among the tightly packed bodies, and found a corner of space by wrapping themselves along a pole.

"Where are all these people going?" Jason asked, truly perplexed.

Anita grinned. "Heading uptown for a night out. Plenty of clubs, bars, restaurants, street life. Harlem on a Friday, Saturday night—nothing like it. What's a Friday night like in Atlanta?"

His brows flicked in amusement. "Hmm, pretty sure nothing like New York, but we have our good times. Plenty of parties, some decent clubs…great food, though."

"Do you miss home?"

He pulled in a breath. "Yeah. Trying to get used to things here."

Anita made every effort not to pay attention to how close they were and the shock that leaped through her every time the train lurched and tossed them together. "How is work at your new office going?" she asked, needing to switch her mind to something other than wanting to touch him.

"Making a lot of progress. Signed up some volunteers."

"Glad to hear it. Won't make a difference, but good for you anyway."

His jaw flexed. "Why are you so sure? What makes you think your way is best?"

She rolled her eyes. "Think about it, do-gooder. For all the marching and passive resistance, what has it gotten our people?"

"How about national attention, the ear of the president."

She scoffed. "Right. And the day after President Kennedy gets on TV to talk about the civil rights that we deserve, Medgar Evers is gunned down in his own damn driveway!" She ignored the eyes that turned in her direction. To do otherwise would validate that she was somehow wrong for her passion. But also that she might have embarrassed Jason. She didn't want to be one of "those women" she'd see on the street or in the club yelling and cussing out a man, neck rolling and finger pointing. "I'm sorry," she murmured. "I get—"

"Passionate. I understand."

He uttered the words so gently that she dared to look at him; the quiet peace in his eyes calmed the storm that swirled inside her. And she believed him.

The corners of his mouth lifted in a half-moon smile. "So, your mom likes gospel," he said, turning them away from the fork in the road that always seemed to separate them.

"Loves it. My dad is the R&B and jazz lover. My mom's gospel collection rivals my dad's," she said, her gaze drifting off to a happy place. "I was always surrounded by music and art. Real bougie," she said, half-joking.

"Sounds like an everyday Black family. Mine is pretty much the same." He adjusted his weight from one foot to the other as the train rocked and rolled into the next station. "My mother is a devout practicing Baptist. Missing church on Sunday was not an option. My dad, on the other hand, hasn't set foot in a church since he and my mom got married. Wore it like a badge of honor. Growing up, my sister and I were always in some kind of trouble or the other with our Sunday school teacher, Sister June Ellen. Either talking out of turn, chewing gum, or messing with the other kids." He shook his head in amusement.

Anita chuckled. "So you were grooming yourself for trouble since you were young."

"Guess so, huh." He looked at her with curiosity. "I know why *I* left home. Why did you?"

She smiled softly. "I guess for both of us, it's like Langston Hughes wrote: 'I am fed up with Jim Crow laws, people who are cruel and afraid, who lynch and run, who are scared of me and me of them. So I pick up my life and take it away on a one-way ticket—gone up North, gone out West. Gone,'" she recited by rote. "We've done what humans seeking freedom and change have done since the beginning of time…we left."

Jason's eyes mirrored his admiration. "Do you always have a poem on the tip of your tongue?"

"There are words for every occasion—of inspiration, admonishment, hope, love, fear. They're one of the most powerful weapons."

"You use them well."

The train screeched to a stop.

Her gaze jumped away from the hypnotic pull of his and toward the window that framed the 125th Street station sign. "This is us." She moved toward the door, thankful for the brief reprieve from being so close to him.

When they emerged, the sun had begun to set over the tips of the towering tenements and office buildings, casting a soft orange glow that bounced off rows of car hoods and apartment windows.

Anita stuck her hands into the back pockets of her jeans and tilted her head to the side to look at him. "Thanks for the company."

"Thanks for the insistent invite," he teased.

She lowered her head and chuckled, then looked up. "Anyway, I need to get home."

"Yep. Me too."

"See you later," she said, as much of a question as a statement.

"Maybe," he said, his tone teasing.

She pressed the tip of her finger against his chest. "Take care, do-gooder." She turned and sashayed down the street, hoping that she was leaving him with an enticing parting image.

Chapter Six

Jason tugged off his jacket and draped it across the back of the one wooden chair in the room and dropped the paper bag with his records in it on the seat. He slowly unbuttoned his shirt, sat on a side of the bed, and took in his surroundings. He suddenly felt the thin walls closing in on him.

Being with Anita was like getting set free to run through a grassy field. And all the color was gone now, as if the world was suddenly in black and white. What he wanted to do was just ask her out on a real date, get to know her over dinner and a movie. But Anita wasn't like the women he'd known. They expected the man to call all the shots, take charge. Anita was nothing like that. In fact, she was the exact opposite.

She already believed he was an unsophisticated country boy, not to mention that their politics and their personalities were polar opposites. It was like she was toying with him all the time. To put it simply, Anita Hopkins threw him off his game, and he had no intention of being made the fool. For now, he should leave things like they were—whatever that was. He flopped back spread-eagled on the bed and stared at the crack that ran across the ceiling until it looked like a piece of artwork.

He sprang up from the bed, took four steps to the other side of the room, and tugged open the top drawer of the wobbly three-drawer chest. He lifted the receipt from B-Flat with Anita's number on it. *Too soon?* He'd just left her. What would she think? She did invite him to the club, and she had asked why he never called. He could find out what was the best time to show up or ask if she was performing. *Yeah, make it casual. No big deal.*

He scooped up some change from the drawer along with the receipt and went out into the hall to the pay phone, thankful that it wasn't in use. On the downside, it didn't give him any excuse to rethink.

Jason lifted the black receiver and dropped a dime into the slot. He checked the receipt and dialed, his finger shaking just a little each time he stuck it in the numbered hole and turned the dial. The shrill ringing jumped his heart. With each sound, he doubted what he was doing and started to hang up.

"Hello?"

The greeting seemed in harmony with the music in the background.

His stomach muscles clenched. "Hello. This is Jason. May I speak with Anita?"

There was a pause. The music stopped. "Hi. Who else did you expect?"

"Old habits, I guess." He could almost hear her smile through the phone, and the thought that he'd put it there did something to his insides that he couldn't explain. He shifted his weight. "Yeah, so I was just wondering what's a good time to come to the club."

"Starts getting crowded around nine. Hard to get a seat after that. You plan on stopping by?"

"I was thinking about it."

"Oh. Cool."

He cleared his throat. "So, uh, maybe I'll come by."

"Okay."

"See you later, then."

"Okay. See you later."

"Goodbye."

"Bye."

Jason hung up the phone and felt as if he'd run around the block, his heart was knocking so hard. He dropped the rest of the change in his pocket, then walked back to his room, grabbed his toiletries caddy, and headed for the bathroom before someone beat him to it. He needed a shower and a shave. There was a pressed white shirt hanging in the narrow closet, and he'd leave the tie. Didn't want to stick out as overdressed like last time. He wanted to blend in with all the other city slickers.

Then maybe tonight she'd call him Jason.

She'd been on duty for an hour already, and each time the front door swung open, her pulse took a leap. *Did he say for sure he was coming?* Not really. "Maybe" didn't mean "yes." *Why are you in knots about some country boy who's never been on a subway before?* She tugged on her bottom lip with her teeth to keep from laughing out loud. The look on his face when they went down in the subway had been worth the price of admission. Now she knew firsthand what "deer in the headlights" really meant.

"What can I get for you?" she asked, stopping at a table in her section.

The single customer angled his head and glanced up. A

wave of yesterday crashed against her, swaying her on her feet. Her lips parted, but no words came out. His endlessly dark eyes framed by outrageously perfect lashes tightened ever so slightly to either question or bring her into focus.

"Anita?"

Her heart slammed in her chest. She swallowed over the knot in her throat.

"Leon."

He stood, still towering over her, still long and muscularly lean. He lowered his head, placed a hand on her shoulder, and kissed her cheek. "You look good, girl." He didn't move his hand.

That same jazz in his voice.

"You too," she managed, finally locating her words.

Those long lashes lowered over his eyes. "Guess I can't buy you a drink," he said with a grin.

"Not while I'm on duty."

"So, this is your thing?" He glanced around.

"Part-time. I do spoken word here some nights, too." *See, I've moved on without your sorry ass. I have a life.*

His eyes widened. "For real." He bobbed his head. "Yeah, yeah, I remember you use to write. Cool."

"I also work for the Action Network with Brother Malcolm X." *Top that.*

"No shit."

She sputtered a laugh.

"I never pictured you as a revolutionary, but it fits you well," he said. He reached toward her 'fro with the tip of his finger. "Looks good on you."

"Hey, baby. Line as usual."

Leon turned halfway and placed his arm around the waist of a woman whose voice sounded like sunshine and brought her fully into view. "Anita, this is my wife, Gail."

Everything played in slow motion. The words pushed through water that sloshed around in her head. *What the fuck did he just say?*

"Gail, baby, this is Anita. We go way back to Bed-Stuy days," he said with the kind of jovial tone that belied what they'd had. What she thought they'd had.

Gail—*hi-yella*, as her grandmother would say—had that "good hair" that never needed a perm or a hot comb. The lighting might be playing tricks on her, but she'd swear this chick had green eyes. Her own gaze traveled down toward Gail's extended hand, and that was when she saw the rounded belly, incubating their child. *Leon is about to be a father with this woman.* Not with her like she had dreamed all those summers ago. Her temple throbbed.

"Hi, nice to meet you, Gail." She forced herself to smile and shake Gail's hand. "When are you due?"

Gail beamed, glanced lovingly at her husband. "Just around Christmas. Feels like any minute," she said over tinkling laughter and a flash of deep dimples.

Anita dragged in a breath. "Well, no alcohol for you," she said, managing to keep her voice light. "Do y'all live in Harlem or just hanging out?" She would pass right out if he said they lived nearby.

"Naw, we live in Philly. Came down to visit Gail's mom."

"Y-your mother-in-law," she mumbled, thrown yet again by the reality that Leon's mother-in-law was some random woman and not her mother, Celia Hopkins. "Well, uh, are you two ready to order?"

"Actually, we were probably going to leave soon," Leon said. "Too much noise and smoke for my babies." He pulled Gail close and kissed her forehead.

In her head she was screaming, *You mutha…* She wasn't sure if she was relieved or disappointed that she wouldn't have much longer to look at him or to cuss him out. "Well, it was really nice to see you again, Leon, and nice to meet you, Gail." She leaned in on tiptoe and placed a kiss on his cheek, longer than a peck, just to remind him that she had been there first.

Then she stepped back, their eyes dancing together to all those summers ago, and then the song ended. "Good luck with the baby."

She turned away before she did or said something she'd regret.

By rote, she took orders and distributed food and drinks, making it a point to keep her eyes and attention away from Leon's table. But when she did dare to look, they were gone, and all she could do was blink away the burn in her eyes and the past that came with it.

J ason swiped his stingy brimmed hat from his head, ran his hand along his clean-shaven jaw, then pushed through the doors of B-Flat. He was met with the sensual pulse of live sax on stage and the Mississippi-like flow of voices rising and falling, gliding above the notes.

And he felt oddly at home.

He made his way around tables and couples on the floor swaying to the music and found a spot at the bar. He ordered his go-to drink of rum and Coke this time and casually looked around in hopes of spotting Anita. He glimpsed the clock above the bar. Anita was right—it was barely nine thirty and the place was packed.

The vibe was the same as the last time he had been there. Everybody was cool and grooving to the music and the company.

The bartender placed his drink in front of him with a bowl of peanuts.

"Thank ya." Jason reached for his drink with one hand and took a scoop of peanuts with the other. He tossed a few nuts into his mouth and washed them down with a swallow of his drink.

The band ended their set and exited the stage to be quickly followed by the DJ, who spun Jackie Wilson's "Baby Workout." Tables emptied as couples jumped onto the small dance floor.

"Hey, you made it."

The instant he saw her, something shifted inside him, tightening his belly. "Hey." He ran his tongue along his bottom lip. "Y-You were right about the crowd," he sputtered, overcome by a bout of awkwardness.

Anita balanced a tray of drinks on her palm. "Yep."

The bite was gone from her voice, along with the flame in her eyes.

"Something wrong? Are you all right?" He watched her nostrils flare and the rapid flutter of her lashes. He got up, ready to slay some dragons.

Her smile appeared forced. She took a step back as if she anticipated what he was about to do. "Fine. A bit of a headache is all. Thanks, though. You need a table?"

"I'm good here. It's just me tonight."

"I'll see if I can get you a table anyway. Then I can sit with you for a bit during my break."

"Oh...sure. In that case. I'd like that."

"Give me a few minutes."

Watching her walk away reminded him of a kid's toy that needed a new battery—still working but with effort.

Admittedly, he didn't know everything about her. Barely

knew her at all, but from the moment they'd met, he'd felt her energy, her passion, and her vitality. He felt a connection that he couldn't quite explain, which was why he knew something was wrong. It wasn't a headache.

But probably none of his business anyway.

He sipped on his drink while the Miracles crooned "You Really Got a Hold on Me." He snorted a laugh at the irony.

By the time the song ended, Anita returned. "I got you a table. Bring your drink." She signaled something to the bartender, then led the way to the table.

It was off to the side in a softly lit corner near the kitchen. Curiously intimate. His first thought was that she'd dragged a table and two chairs from some back room to set them up just for him. Impossible. Or did she know that he'd feel out of place seated alone in the middle of the club and instead found a spot where he could see but not necessarily be seen? If she did, that might mean that she actually cared—at least a little bit.

"Thanks." He pulled out a chair and put his glass on the table.

"You want to order something?"

He'd missed dinner—too busy getting ready to see her again—and his stomach was singing its own tune. He considered the fifteen dollars he had in his pocket. It wouldn't go far. But drinking on an empty stomach wasn't a good move. "Any suggestions?"

"The chicken and waffles are the joint."

His stomach growled in agreement. "Sounds good."

"I'll put the order in right away."

"Are you performing tonight?"

Her gaze darted away, then back. "Was going to." She half shrugged a bit. "Changed my mind."

He noticed how she wouldn't really look at him with that

familiar challenge in her eyes.

He sat, looked up at her. "What time is your break?"

"About an hour. Hopefully." She almost smiled. "Let me get your order in." She hurried away.

Jason settled in his seat, leaned back, and sipped his drink. From his secured spot, he realized he had a bird's-eye view of 90 percent of the club and a clear line of sight to the stage. This was what he and the fellas back home would call a "date table." Hmm. Interesting.

The band returned to the stage, and another waitress showed up at his table with a refill of his drink.

"I didn't order this," he called out over the pulse of the band.

"Nita sent it," she said over her shoulder.

He looked around, beyond heads and between bodies, but he didn't see her. Two drinks and dinner would definitely eat a big hole in his fifteen dollars. He tugged on the inside of his cheek and tapped his foot double time until he spotted Anita coming toward him with a tray raised to chin level. She expertly weaved her way across the room.

"Sorry it took so long." She lowered the tray and placed one loaded plate in front of him and the other in front of the empty seat.

He squinted when she sat and slid the tray under the table.

"Hope you didn't think that second drink was for you," she said. The sparkling snark had returned.

Jason chuckled, held up his hands in surrender. "Guilty." He angled his head to the side and lifted his chin toward the plate in front of her.

"I'm on break—for the rest of the night."

"Oh really?" He slowly bobbed his head. "Sooo, you're joining me for dinner."

"Yep. Looks that way." She reached for the glass bottle of syrup and proceeded to lather her waffles. "Do you mind? You did say you were here by yourself."

"Naw. Just pleasantly surprised, is all." He couldn't tell if she was coming on to him one minute or ready to slice him up like a Sunday ham with that sharp tongue of hers the next.

"Let me know if it was a good choice," she said with a lift of her chin toward his plate, tugging him out of the trance he'd tumbled into.

He gave a quick shake of his head, picked up the golden chicken breast, and took a deep bite. Anita Hopkins was one complex woman.

"**D**on't you usually work until closer to one?" Jason asked as he held the door open for her.

Anita stepped out, looked heavenward. "Mostly."

The door to B-Flat swung closed behind them.

"Nice out," she said. "Want to walk a little bit?" She hooked her arm through his before he could offer it. She felt wobbly and needed something strong to hold on to tonight.

"Any particular direction?"

She pulled in a breath of relief. "Toward the park."

"Lead the way."

They strolled along Lenox to 128th and up to St. Nicholas. *A perfect night for lovers.* Why did that thought pop into her head? She'd been a mess since seeing Leon. How could he still do that to her after all this fucking time? She had been a kid, barely filling out her bra when they first met. But she was a full-blown woman in more ways than one when he'd walked away for the last time.

"If you squeeze my arm any tighter, you're gonna snap all that muscle under my jacket," he teased. He looked at her profile. "Wanna talk?"

"Sorry," she heard herself mumble. They walked some more. "I saw someone tonight from when I used to live in Brooklyn," she blurted out.

"Is that why you don't seem yourself?"

She snapped her head toward him, not sure what she'd expected him to say, but certainly not that he'd actually paid that much attention to notice that she wasn't herself at all.

She loosened her hold on his arm. "Don't know what you mean."

They stopped at the corner and waited for the light to change.

"My mistake." He looked across the intersection, straight ahead.

The light turned green.

"I didn't tell you that I really appreciated you setting me up at the table and having dinner with me," he said as they started across the street.

"I know what it feels like to get settled in a new place, not knowing anybody," she replied.

"Yeah? How's that?"

They reached the entrance to the park and strolled in. "There's a row of benches just down this path," Anita said.

They got to the benches and sat. Anita stretched her legs out in front of her and crossed her hands on her lap. "When I first moved out—"

"How long ago was that?" Jason asked.

"Hmm, going on five, almost six years now."

He nodded.

"When I moved out, I didn't know anybody who lived in

Harlem. My whole life was in Brooklyn. But I knew I had to spread my wings beyond the boundaries of where I lived. Growing up, my friends and I would come to Harlem for the nightlife, the festivals, shopping. It was exciting, exotic. But Harlem has a history for us. It houses our culture, supports our art, and is the northern center for change." She looked at him. "Like Atlanta is for the South."

"I'm kinda starting to get that." He gave her a smile.

"For me, it wasn't too hard to find the artist community, open mic nights and stuff." She shrugged. "And after the first year, my best friend, Liza, moved to Harlem to run a nonprofit. But there were plenty of nights when I ate alone, drank alone, walked around alone. Can be tough when you're used to something different."

"Yeah," he said on a breath. "When I first got here," he said with a chuckle, "I was 'bout ready to turn and hightail it right back to Atlanta. New Yorkers ain't nothing like the folks back home. Everybody's in a hurry. And there's so many of y'all."

Anita laughed—hard. It felt good.

"But I never was totally alone," he added, "'cause I met you."

Her stomach did a somersault.

He continued, "You ever think about how wild it was that we met on the bus and then wound up right here? I do. Figure it's not just coincidence. More like fate."

She snapped her head to look at him and dove headlong into the pillow softness of his eyes. Her heart had somehow pole-vaulted into her throat. "Fate, huh?" She chuckled while trying to reclaim her footing and shifted in her seat, looked around, then looked at him from beneath her lashes. "Maybe," she conceded. "But what does it mean?" Her shoulder rose and fell. "Nothing really. Just two random people meet and then meet up again. Probably happens every day."

"Probably."

Say something to make it matter. To make us meeting matter.

"I believe that people are put in places, in situations, and connected to certain people for a reason," he said. "We may not always know what that reason is, but it will come to light in good time."

"Is that the Baptist in you talking?"

He lowered his head and slowly shook it. "Why is it so hard for you?"

She hitched in a breath. "I don't know what you mean."

"Second time you've said that tonight." He paused, studied her in a sidelong glance. "I think you do."

She uncrossed, then recrossed her legs. "I come here a lot to think, to write…to center myself." She took a breath. "I don't ever bring anyone with me." She dared to raise her gaze to meet his.

Jason pursed his lips. "I have a place back home that's kinda my special place." His mouth curved into a half smile. "It's this spot by the creek. There's this big ol' maple tree." He grinned. "Gives the best shade. That's my spot."

She bent her knees, drew them to her chest, draped her arms across them, and rested her chin. "Solve any real problems under that tree?"

"Don't know about solving them. Done a lot of reconcilin', though."

"Hmm." She ran her tongue across her lips. "That person I saw tonight…meant a lot to me once upon a time. First-boyfriend kinda thing." Her laugh sounded as nervous as she felt. "Changed me. Left a mark that I thought I'd gotten over but guess I never really did."

She tried to stop herself, but the words kept coming

because this was her special place where words flowed from her. She told him how they'd met, how she would sneak away from school to be with him, how her parents warned her over and over to stay away from him.

What she didn't tell him about was the baby that they'd made and lost, afraid of how his religiousness would view her, and for some reason she needed him not to judge, not to lose the look of respect in his eyes. That was a story for another day, maybe.

"It was a shock to see him after all this time, not to mention married with a...a baby on the way."

"I can only imagine," he said gently.

"I suppose you never really understand how people will figure into your life even after they're out of it."

He draped his arm along the back of the bench, and a slight shiver slid down her spine.

"My mama used to always say, 'To each person there is a season. They come and they go. But you can't get to the new season if you're not willin' to leave the old one.'"

She sniffed. "Sounds smart, your mom."

"She has a saying for just about everything." He chuckled. "But that's one of the ones that stuck with me."

At some point, she wasn't even sure when or how, but she was sitting hip to hip with Jason, and his fingers that were dangling on the back of the bench now rested gently on her shoulder. That hurt little girl from the handball court on Decatur Street wanted to jump up and run. But the young woman who'd been in a constant struggle against just about everything needed to stay. To see if she could.

She tipped her head and rested it on his shoulder. Her heart slammed and banged in her chest, her limbs trembling. But then he rested his chin on the top of her head and casually stroked her shoulder, the way one would to calm someone trying to sleep.

And for the first time in longer than she could remember, she felt calm.

"Thanks for walking me home."

"Of course. Couldn't let a lady walk the streets alone. 'Specially these streets," he added with a grin.

Anita looked down at her shoes, then over her shoulder to her front door. "Now you know where I live," she said, as much for information as invitation.

Jason nodded. "That I do."

Her heart pounded so hard, she was sure he could hear it.

They stood there in that space of uncertainty.

"I should be going. I'll wait till you get inside," he finally said.

She took a half step back. "Thanks for tonight, too. For listening."

"Works both ways." His eyes moved in slow motion across her face.

Her fingertips tingled with the need to touch him, but she couldn't move.

His lips parted as if he was going to say something—but didn't.

They were so close. She could see the glow of the streetlight in his eyes and a future that she couldn't name.

She leaned in suddenly, cupped his cheeks in her palms, and kissed him on the lips. The electric contact loosened her knees. She heard a moan, wasn't sure if it was him or her, when his arm slipped around her waist and pulled her to him. *Oh, damn.* The tip of his tongue teased her lips open.

Sweet like maple sugar, sweeter than she imagined. Her fingers splayed across the back of his neck and through the tight coils at his nape. His heat enveloped her. She felt herself slipping away to a point of no return. She wouldn't be *that* girl.

Before this went further than she was ready to go, she pulled away, turned and pushed through the heavy front door that was never locked, and darted inside.

Jason didn't move. Couldn't. He stared at the wood-and-glass door. Slowly he ran his tongue across his bottom lip. Her taste was salty and sweet. His heart was racing as he dragged in a steadying breath. Approaching laughter came in his direction, alerting him to his surroundings.

He shook his head, offered a faint smile to the raucous couple who walked past him. He shoved his hands into the pockets of his slacks and headed in the direction of home.

Anita Hopkins unsettled him. That was the only description he could come up with.

Every time he was in her presence, he felt as if he was an inexperienced roller skater and any minute those skates were going to slide right out from under him...and he was going down hard.

When he got home, he unbuttoned his white shirt and hung it on the back of the chair, unbuckled and unzipped his slacks, folded them along the crease, and hung them in the closet.

The reason he'd come to New York was for a mission for the greater good, to spread the message and the movement of Dr. King, to do his part to recruit new members in the fight for civil rights. It would take time and energy to build a northern coalition. It was a big responsibility, one that the movement expected him to fulfill. He couldn't neglect what he had been sent to do. Too many people were depending on him.

He pressed his fingertip to his lips. *Anita*. He groaned and flopped back on the bed. *A distraction*.

If he were to believe his mother's adage about people coming into one's life for a season, then he'd just have to let this season run its course and move on.

He tucked his hands under his head and closed his eyes. The evening played out in short frames behind his lids. Entering the club. Sitting at the bar. Seeing Anita. Walking to the park. Standing in front of her apartment. What lingered was her voice that had seeped into his veins, was flowing through him now. Listening to her, even in her heartache, was like experiencing music.

If he didn't understand how deeply she was hurt by this fella from her past, he'd have believed he was listening to a lullaby. She had the power of persuasion in her voice, the kind of persuasion that scooped out feelings you didn't know you had and then set them right in front of you to take stock of.

And then there was the kiss.

His eyes slowly opened, and he stared up at the yellowed ceiling. *Anita Hopkins*. Fate, coincidence. It was a thin line between the two, like the one that ran across the length of the ceiling. Who knows? Something brought them together for reasons that neither could see. Where could this possibly go?

He threw an arm across his eyes. *Seasons*.

• • •

S unday was the one day of the week that he didn't go to the office. If he'd been back home, Sunday morning until noon would be spent in church and the rest of the day with family.

Since he'd been in New York, he'd yet to find a church home. He'd tried a couple of local spots that were not more than storefronts, but they didn't feel like home. He'd heard good things about Abyssinian Baptist on 138th Street. Adam Clayton Powell Sr. had served as pastor for decades until his son took over before running for Congress. Michael was a sometime member and said he'd go with him, since he claimed he was overdue for some saving.

He wasn't sure what to expect when they arrived, but not much could have prepared him for the enormity of the cathedral and the massive amount of churchgoers. Out front, cars were double- and triple-parked for several blocks, the attendees arriving in their Sunday finery. A kaleidoscope of color permeated the avenue. Women were decked out in fur stoles and hats in all sizes and shapes, the likes of which rivaled any he'd seen in Atlanta. The men were "casket sharp," as his grandmother would often say. Black folk sure knew how to style.

They found seats near the rear of the massive church.

"Settle in," Michael quipped. "It's gonna be a while."

Jason placed his hat on his lap as the choir processional began and took their places on the bleachers behind the dais. Several moments later, Reverend Adam Clayton Powell Jr. stepped up to the pulpit. He was, in a word, commanding.

A respectful hush fell over the congregation, and the reverend's impassioned voice boomed to the rafters. Jason, like every parishioner, was mesmerized.

• • •

Visit https://www.youtube.com/watch?v=ymMWnclVvlA
for the entire speech.

• • •

"As far as I know here, you're in trouble," the reverend said, looking out on his rapt congregation, Jason included. "Where it says about thirty percent are unemployed. That's why I'm working hard to get this surplus food here. Some of you say to me, 'Well, I'm not like you: I'm not a congressman.' 'I haven't got education.' 'I haven't got work.'"

Jason knew exactly what the reverend meant. Day after day he came face to face with those who didn't have two nickels to rub together, struggling to survive, yet still found the means to make a way out of no way.

"But you're a human being. And you know what you've got? You've got in your hand the power to use your vote and to use even those few cents you get from welfare to spend them only where you want to spend them! Lookit that!"

He held up his hand like an exhibit, and the cheering and applause was deafening to Jason's ears, his own clapping just as loud alongside theirs.

The reverend continued, "A young slave boy stood one day before the greatest ruler of his day. And God said to Moses, 'What's in your hand?' And Moses said, 'LORD, I've only got a stick, that's all.' He said, 'Well, let me use what's in your hand!' And God used that slave boy with a stick in his hand to divide the Red Sea, march through a wilderness, bring water out of rocks, manna from heaven, and bring his people to freedom land! What's in *your* hand?"

The congregation erupted in applause once again. Even as Jason joined in, what shook him to his soul was that the words validated his purpose. It was his time, just like the reverend said. It was up to him to use what he had and make a difference.

"What's in your hand? George Washington Carver! Who was so frail that he was traded for a broken-down horse as a slave boy... And George Washington Carver sitting in the science laboratory at Tuskegee told me, he said, 'Dr. Powell,' he said, 'I just go out into the fields each morning at five o'clock, and I let God guide me...and I bring back these little things and work them with my laboratory.' And that man did more to revolutionize the agricultural science of peanuts and of cotton and sweet potatoes than any other human being in the field of agricultural science.

"What's in your hand? Just let God use you, that's all. What's in your hand?

"Little hunchback sitting in a Roman jail? 'I haven't got anything in my hand but an old quill pen...but...God says, 'Write what I tell ya to write!' And Paul wrote:'I have run my race with patience. I've finished my course.'"

"Yes, Lord! Amen," the gathering shouted.

"I've kept the faith."

"Hallelujah!"

"'What's in your hand, little boy?' 'All I've got is a slingshot, and the enemies of my people are great and big and more numerous than we are!' 'Well, little David, go down to the brook and pick out a few stones and come on back and close your eyes if you want to and pull back that slingshot and let it go!' And David killed the biggest enemy—the leader of the giants, against his people—and his people became free, just letting God guide a stone in his hand. And a few years passed, and David is a king."

Dr. King...? The thought jarred him. Could he have been... sent to rid them of the giants that stepped on their people? *One man. To lead us to freedom.* And Jason had been chosen as well, by Dr. King himself.

His mission and his message were so much clearer to him now.

"What's in your hand? Man Hanging on a Cross? 'I've got two nails in my hands! Father! I stretch my hands to thee! No other help I know. If thou withdraw thyself from me, whither shall I go?' And that man with two nails in his hands split history in half: BC and AD!"

"Amen!" Jason shouted, renewed with purpose.

"And what's in your hands today, people? You've got *God* in your hand, and He'll let you win! Because He's on your side, and one with God's always in the majority. So walk with Him and talk with Him, and work with Him, and stick together, and fight together! And with God's hand in your hand, the victory will be accomplished, here, sooner than you dreamed, sooner than you hoped, sooner than you prayed for, sooner than you imagined."

The church members rose to their feet, stomping, shouting, and praising.

Reverend Powell gazed out across his flock. "God bless you."

"That was some powerful sermon," Jason intoned as he and Michael filed out. "Gave us some things to think about, huh?"

Michael nodded in agreement.

He draped his arm across Michael's shoulders. "We don't have much to work with, but we're gonna use what we got in our hands to make a difference, to bring the message, to enlighten the people and prepare them for the fight."

Michael slid a glance toward him. "Yes, we will, brother." They reached the corner. "I'm going to head home, watch the game."

"Sounds good. Guess I'll see you in the morning."

They shook hands and parted.

He felt more committed than ever to do the work he was sent to do. Every now and then, the message from the pulpit was exactly what you needed to hear. He was destined to be sitting right where he had been this Sunday morning, taking in the word of Reverend Powell. He tugged in a breath of resolve. It was just what he needed to hear.

On his walk back home, he thought about what his Sunday would be like if he were back home. Right about now, he'd be in the passenger seat of his father's ancient Oldsmobile with his mother behind the wheel, humming whatever the last tune was at the church service they'd just left. Patrice and Mason would be in the back, whispering about sister so-and-so "catching the spirit again and again" or the young new deacon who kept eyeing the pastor's daughter Stephanie.

He'd listen in amused silence as they bantered back and forth and had to agree with their take on the shenanigans of the congregants. Their mother would periodically remind them that it was sinful to talk about people behind their backs, even as she bit back her own chuckles.

When they got home, Pops would be exactly where they left him, sitting on his throne in front of the television. His sister would dash off to gossip some more with her friends, and Mason would head to the backyard to shoot some hoops, and he'd promise to join him.

Shouts from football fans would blare from the television, and gospel from the radio would compete in the kitchen.

He turned onto 120th Street and stopped in front of his building, and an overwhelming wave of melancholy swept through him. In this big nonstop city, he could be surrounded by hundreds of people at once and still feel alone.

Maybe he should call his aunt Faye and go by for a visit.

He hadn't seen her since he'd arrived in New York, and if his mother asked about it one more time, he wanted to tell her that he'd done his duty and visited family.

He pulled open the heavy wooden door, walked into the dimly lit ground floor hallway, and climbed the stairs to his room which felt smaller than usual. He took off his jacket and hung it up, then went to his dresser to look for his aunt's number in the drawer.

His aunt Faye wasn't the churchgoing type, which was a bone of contention between her and his mother. Aunt Faye's big gripe with his mother was that she said Mae Ellen was a hypocrite, while Mae Ellen swore that her wayward sister-in-law was going straight to hell in a handbasket for her non-churchgoing self. Meanwhile, Faye contended that Mae Ellen was going to join her in hell for sleeping next to a man who hadn't seen the inside of a church since his wedding day. That was different, his mother insisted. They'd taken vows—for better or for worse.

Jason chuckled as he looked at the slip of paper with her name and number on it. His mother and his aunt talked a good game, but underneath it all, they loved each other. Their monthly phone calls, birthday gifts, and holiday cards overshadowed their differences on the meaning of Sunday.

For his mother, Sunday was a day of thanks and renewal. For Aunt Faye, Sunday was a day of recovery from Saturday night.

He checked for change in his pocket and went out into the hall to the pay phone.

The phone rang about a dozen times with no answer. He hung up, listened for his change to drop into the slot, then called back. Same outcome. He dropped the change back into his pocket and returned to his room.

He flopped across the bed and stared at the ceiling. This

could not be what his life would be like in New York. Work five, six days a week and church on Sunday, then come home alone all seven days. He closed his eyes, and Anita, the evening, and the kiss they'd shared bloomed to life. He jumped up from the bed, got the receipt with her phone number on it, and went back to the pay phone.

. . .

Anita stepped out of the tub, pulled the stopper, and let out the water. She wrapped herself in a towel before padding off to her bedroom. It was nearly two, and she'd promised her folks she'd be there in time for Sunday dinner. Maybe if she hurried, she'd actually make it.

She sat on the side of the bed, dried off, and soothed herself with Jergens lotion. As she massaged the cool cream along her limbs, she thought about all those mornings when her mother would remind her to lotion her ashy knees. *Get the Jergens*, her mother would say.

Anita laughed and rubbed her toes. When she was a little girl, too young to bathe by herself, her mother would lift her out of the tub, wrap her in a towel, and rub her body with lotion until she smelled like sunshine and her skin felt like silk. While her mother smoothed her skin, she would always tell her some childhood story about growing up in Mississippi. How she and her siblings ran barefoot in the dirt and grass, chased squirrels, and didn't have indoor plumbing. Anita couldn't imagine having to bathe in a shed or take a pee in a hole in the ground.

We was always ashy, her mother had reminisced, and all they had to soothe their skin was grease from fat. *You could cook us up for dinner*, she'd say with a laugh. *I promised myself that when I grew up, I'd never smell like bacon grease again.*

So one day, when she was maybe nine or ten, she'd said, she'd fallen and scrapped up her knees. Her teacher, Ms. Jackson, took her into the washroom and cleaned her up, and then she went in her purse and took out a bottle of Jergens lotion and rubbed it all over her legs and knees. *I'd never smelled anything on my body that sweet,* her mama would say. *It was like sunshine in a bottle.*

Hmmm. *Jergens lotion.* One of the few things that Anita and her mother agreed on.

Anita hung up her towel to dry, riffled through her drawer for some underwear just as her phone rang. She groaned. It was definitely her mother wanting to know what time she would be arriving. If she didn't answer, at least her mother would think she was on her way. She let the phone ring until it finally stopped.

Mildly relieved, she put on her underwear, but then the phone started ringing again. What she needed was an answering machine, but there was never enough extra money to get one. Maybe something was wrong. She hesitated, already flinching at what would be her mother's reprimand that she was still in her house. Maybe the ringing would stop. It didn't.

She dragged in a breath of resolve and picked up the handset. "Hello?"

"Hi, Anita. It's Jason Tanner. I hope I'm not disturbing you."

A surge of giddy excitement zipped along her recently lotioned limbs. "Hi. No. Not at all." She glanced at the clock over the refrigerator: 2:15. She cringed. "How are you?"

"I'm fine. Just got in from church."

"Oh. Okay."

"Um. I was wondering if you weren't busy, that maybe I

could take you to supper."

She blinked back her surprise. Was he asking her on a date? "I'd love to," she blurted out.

"You would?"

Sunday dinner. "Yeah. I mean I'd love to on another day. I was getting ready to go to Brooklyn to see my folks for Sunday dinner. It's a regular thing. Ya know."

"Oh, sure. I understand. Maybe another time."

She felt his disappointment through the phone, and it mirrored her own. She didn't want to dwell on or admit to herself what had happened between them the night before — how she felt to have someone to talk with, how the kiss felt. She hadn't allowed room in her head to think about it.

"Hey, why don't you come with me?" The words were out of her mouth before she realized it.

"To Brooklyn?"

She squeezed her eyes shut, tugged on her bottom lip. "Yeah, to Brooklyn. On the train." She giggled, hoping she sounded casual and not too nervous. "My folks won't mind." *Hopefully.* "My mother cooks enough for an army." And if they did mind, she'd deal with it.

"If you're sure…"

"Absolutely. I was getting dressed. Can you meet me at the 125th Street train station in like twenty minutes?"

"I can do that."

"See you then."

"See you then," he repeated.

She hung up the phone. *Anita Hopkins, what are you getting yourself into*?

Chapter Seven

The pastor's sermon came back to Jason as he strolled down the street to meet Anita. *Make use of what is in your hand.* He smiled, looking down at the flowers he'd picked up along the way.

"You really didn't have to bring anything," Anita said later as they were ascending the stairs from the subway.

"My grandmother always said to never visit a person's home for the first time empty-handed. So it was either flowers or a can of tuna."

She stopped short, gave him a sideways glance. "Tuna?"

He chuckled. "Yep. Since there's no cooking and no refrigerator in the rooming house where I stay, I stock up on tuna." He shrugged. "Cheap and easy."

"Wow. Didn't know." She hooked her arm through his. "We'll have to do something about that."

He didn't want to ask her what she meant; he'd rather imagine.

She checked her Timex. "Hey, we better put a pep in our step. My mom is probably pacing the floor by now. She's very particular about Sunday dinner."

"So is mine." He chuckled. "It's a ritual, and you'd better have a darn good reason why you weren't at the table and on time."

"Then this will be just like home," she said with a glance in his direction.

They walked the eight blocks from the Utica Avenue stop along Stuyvesant Avenue in companionable silence as Jason took in the beauty of the neighborhood.

"These houses look like mansions," Jason said.

The tree-lined street boasted row after row of three- and four-story majestic brownstones. Massive stone lion heads stood as sentinels atop the stoops, guarding the double doors. The late-afternoon sun illuminated the stained glass arches above the slender windows, creating rainbows of color to dapple the stone steps.

"Many of them were at one point," Anita said. "That one"— she pointed to an enormous home that sat on the corner of Decatur Street and wrapped around it to the other side—"it's been designated as a landmark. Sometimes they offer tours and have shot a couple of movies there, too."

"Wow." He nodded in admiration.

"This section has been designated as a historic landmark district. So inside, other than updating wiring and plumbing, most of the interior is original, and of course they can't change the outside at all. My folks' house has a lot of the original details."

"Must have been great growing up in a house like that."

She shrugged. "Didn't really think about it. It was just home, ya know?"

They stopped for a light on the corner.

"Two more blocks."

• • •

"This is it." She walked onto the ground-floor entrance and used her key to open the black iron gate. She glanced over her shoulder and flashed Jason a bemused look. "You comin'?"

Jason blinked, took a deep swallow, and trailed Anita inside.

He wasn't sure what to expect, but the inside shook his imagination. The entry hallway was straight out of movies like *Breakfast at Tiffany's* and *Imitation of Life*. Sliding wood doors to his left, a servant's bell built into the wall, a long hallway in front, and a mahogany staircase that led to rooms above.

"Come on." She took his hand and led him down the hall that opened into a kitchen that was the size of the entire first floor of his house back in Atlanta. The house may have had many of the original features and architecture, but the kitchen had been updated with all the latest gadgets: a white six-burner stove, matching double door refrigerator, and enough room for a dining table that easily sat six. Two large windows, decked out in yellow and white lace, looked onto an expansive, well-kept backyard.

"Hey, Ma," Anita greeted. She dropped her tote bag on a chair.

A thin woman was at the stove. She turned toward the sound of her daughter's greeting, and Jason knew on first sight exactly what Anita would look like in later years. They had the same warm coloring; bright, fiery eyes; and enchanting dimples when they smiled.

Anita's mother beamed at her daughter, wiped her hands on a blue-and-white-checkered towel, and drew Anita in for a hug. "'Bout time you got here," she playfully scolded.

Anita kissed her mother's cheek. "Party can't start without me," she tossed back. She turned toward Jason. "Mom, this is my...friend, Jason Tanner. Jason, this is Celia Hopkins. Jason's new to New York and—"

Celia placed her hand on Anita's shoulder. "Since when do you have to explain bringing a friend for dinner?" She crossed over to Jason and extended her hand. "Welcome. I hope you like to eat, young man, 'cause there's plenty."

"Yes, ma'am. Yes, ma'am, I do. Oh, these are for you." He handed over the bouquet of sunflowers and purple daisies.

Celia brought them to her nose. Her eyes fluttered. "These are beautiful; thank you. Very thoughtful. Nice upbringing," she added, waving a finger at him. She spun toward Anita and pushed the flowers toward her. "Get my vase from the china cabinet and put these in some water, sweetheart."

Anita took the flowers and disappeared into an adjoining room.

Celia turned to Jason. "You must be thirsty after that long ride. What can I get you?"

"Water is fine, ma'am."

"Well, wash your hands and have a seat."

"Yes, ma'am." Jason walked over to the kitchen sink. "You have a beautiful home, ma'am." He dried his hands on a towel.

"Thank you." She brought the glass of ice water to the table, then glanced around and drew in a long breath. "When we first got here from Mississippi, I never in all my life imagined that I'd be living in a place like this, have the kind of good life we've built. But my Willie promised my folks that he was going to take care of me, and he sure kept his promise." She absently wiped her hands on her apron. "We hope that Anita will take over the house one day." She slowly shook her head. "But that chile, she's stubborn. Wants to do her own thing," she singsonged. "All that militant craziness."

Anita came back with the vase, tossed an accusing look

from one to the other. "She's been talking about me, hasn't she?"

Jason offered wide-eyed innocence.

"As a matter of fact, yes," her mother said without guilt. "Now, help me set the table. Then you can go wake your daddy from his nap."

Anita made a face at her mother's back.

"I saw that," Celia said with laughter in her voice.

Jason smothered a chuckle. "Do all mothers have X-ray vision and super hearing?"

Celia glanced over her shoulder. "Need 'em with kids and a husband." She opened the oven and checked the contents. "Use the good dishes, sweetheart. And bring out the serving bowls."

"Yes, Mother," she said, dragging out every syllable.

Anita opened a narrow door that led to an anteroom with a closet on one side, a working sink, and built-in drawers and cabinets that reached the ceiling.

Jason jumped up from his seat. "Let me help."

Anita opened the high dark-wood cabinets to display shelves of white china. "The ones with the gold trim or the flowers?" she called out to her mother.

"You choose."

"Lot of dishes," Jason whispered under his breath, awed.

"Mom collects them. But most of them my grandmother sent up years ago. Mom has been adding to them ever since."

"Impressive."

Anita shrugged. She handed him a stack of dishes with a thin gold trim around the circumference of the dinner and dessert plates.

"The serving bowls and the linen are in the pantry," Celia said.

"I know, Ma. I did live here all my life."

"Watch that mouth, girl," Celia gently warned.

Anita threw a look at Jason and rolled her eyes upward, then closed the doors to the cabinets and followed him back out into the kitchen. She went to a second closed door opposite the dinner table and pulled it open to reveal a pantry that was as big as his bedroom in the rooming house. From his vantage point, he noticed that the shutters, when opened, looked into the next room.

"This used to be for the servants to serve food from the kitchen to the main room on the other side," she said while she gathered white linen and serving bowls.

"Servants?"

"Yeah, this house is, hmm, a hundred and ten years old. Right, Mom?"

"Something like that." She chuckled. "When we first moved in, there was an actual pot belly stove, right here," she said, pointing to her stove. "I wanted to keep it. Reminded me of home. But Willie wanted a *real* stove, he'd said." She turned off the oven and took out the roasting pan nearly overflowing with two golden chickens. She placed it on the counter by the stove. "Come on now, get this table ready. You can help, young man. Anita, go get your dad."

Anita placed the bowls on the table. "Be right back."

"So, you grew up in Atlanta," Willie Hopkins said, his Mississippi drawl not dampened by his years in New York.

"Yes, sir, I did."

"What brought you up north?"

"Well." He wiped his mouth with the linen napkin. "I'm here on behalf of Dr. King."

Anita glanced up from beneath her lashes but continued

to chew on her string beans. Celia's eyes widened.

"Is that right? Dr. King. Hmm, so you one of those 'turn the otha cheek' fellas?"

Jason swallowed over the sudden knot in his throat. "I wouldn't quite put it that way, but yes, sir, I believe in the nonviolent way."

Willie mumbled something unintelligible. Celia threw him a warning glance that did no good.

"So you don't have no problem with our people being run over, hosed down, spit on, firebombed. And all we suppose to do is turn the cheek and let them hit us agin?" Willie grumbled.

His entire body tensed. He flashed a quick look at Anita, who kept her gaze on her plate, trying to hide her slight smile. "No. No, not at all, sir. That's not what the nonviolent movement is about. It's about compassion, even for our enemy. Showing love in the face of hatred. Coming together as a people joined by love."

"Humph," Willie scoffed. "We been passive too long," he said, lowering his head full of gray hair. He stabbed a piece of chicken with his fork, and Jason swore he felt it.

"We're making progress with the movement," Jason continued. "We're close to getting the president to sign a civil rights bill."

"And then what? You really think them white folk gonna just welcome us into their world with open arms 'cause a piece of paper said so?" His light-brown eyes had turned dark and stormy. His full lips, the ones that Anita had inherited, drew together in a pucker.

"So, Jason. Where are you staying in Harlem, and how did you and Anita meet?" Celia asked, cutting Willie off before he really got stirred up.

"I'm staying in a rooming house on 120th Street. It's

comfortable." He glanced toward Anita. "We met for the first time on a Greyhound," he said, thankful for the intervention.

"Same day they blew up the church in Birmingham," Anita added. She reached for her glass of iced tea. "Still no word on who did it. Of course." She took a long swallow.

"Civil rights bill ain't gonna fix that," Willie said.

For a while, the only sound was the click of flatware against the china and the polite requests to pass this or that.

"How did you and Mr. Hopkins meet?" Jason finally asked, breaking the stalemate. "If I'm not being too bold."

Celia's expression brightened as she patted Willie's hand. Her eyes looked lovingly at her husband.

"I was barely sixteen years old when I first laid eyes on Willie Hopkins. It was the hottest, driest summer the state of Mississippi had seen in years. I always liked to believe that it was my desperate prayers that finally turned things around that summer for the town and for me.

"See, my daddy was the town preacher. Reverend Isaiah Forster had been telling his weakened and despondent parishioners that they would not be abandoned," she said, settling into her story. "Daddy assured them that God heard their cries, understood their fears, and if they prayed with an open heart, He would deliver them from the wasteland that Rudell had become. So the people prayed. They prayed as they slow walked along the dry, dusty roads with the blistering sun scorching their skin. They prayed at night and they prayed when the sun came up again."

Anita shot Jason an "I'm sorry" look, but he waved it off with a smile. One thing he'd gotten accustomed to growing up was story time. His folks had a story for every occasion. This felt just like home.

"Rudell had gone without water for so long that the land cracked beneath our bare feet," Celia was saying. "Grass turned as brown as the people who tilled the soil, crops gave up the fight, animals fell dead on the road, and the people — the people prayed. They prayed for rain."

"I remember my grandmother telling stories about how bad the drought could be," Jason said.

"Uh-huh, it was something. But I swore I was gonna fix it." She laughed at her own naïveté. "I stood out in the field one Sunday, following my father's sermon, with the crops wilting and turning their heads to the ground, nothing but nothingness as far as I could see. So I looks up, cup my hand over my eyes, and asks the Lord to just stop what He was doing for a minute and take a listen to what I was about to say."

Willie chuckled. "Woman swears she got a direct line to the Lord."

Jason watched Anita stifle a smirk.

"Anyway, I get ta praying. I said, 'See here, Lord, my daddy is the reverend here in Rudell. I'm sure you know that, but maybe what you don't know is that my daddy has been singing your praises, telling folk not to give up, that you were gon deliver us from this drought. That all they had to do was pray.

"'Well, Lord, we been praying. Praying till our knees gone raw and our voices hoarse. And the thing is, Lord,' I said, 'some folks find it hard to believe nowadays with everything being taken from them one after the other — the crops, the animals, their grandmas and babies.'"

She shook her head at the memory. "I knew I was treading on dangerous ground, blaspheming and all, but I had to say out loud what was in my heart, what I kept hidden from the all-seeing eyes of my daddy and the knowing looks of my mama, Belle. So I continued, 'I guess what I'm saying, Lord, is if you could find your way not to make my daddy out to be a liar, I'd be much obliged. Well, that's all I gots to say. And if I offended you, I'm sorry.'"

"That was pretty bold, Mrs. Hopkins," Jason said behind his smile.

"Let me tell you, I was scared silly. Anyways, I tramped back out of the field and returned home. That night, the sound of shouting and banging woke me. I sat up and saw my mother standing in my doorway, lit up by flashes of white light, telling me ta hurry and close the windows. I'd never seen anything like it before. The sky was bloodred. Lightning strikes cracked and zigzagged faster than one could count. The wind howled in agony as it bent the backs of trees, snapping in half those that were not strong enough to fight back, lifting anything that wasn't fixed to the ground and hurling it twisting and turning into the night.

"And then it came. The rain and wind galloped into Mississippi like a herd of wild stallions. It rained. It rained straight down and crossways. It rained all day and all night. It rained in buckets and in sheets. It rained so hard, it turned the dirt roads to mud and dug grooves in the ground. The creeks overflowed, dead chickens floated with their feet straight up in the air, water covered the front steps of some homes and came right on in the kitchens of others. It rained for two solid weeks—and I was sure it was my fault."

The group broke into laughter.

"Well, I was," she said with all sincerity. She held up her hand. "And then on the fifteenth day, it stopped just as suddenly as it had begun." She snapped her fingers for emphasis.

"Maaaa, get to the part where you meet Daddy," Anita pleaded. She flashed her dad a dimpled smile.

"This is my story. I'mma tell it the way I want to tell it." She slid a warning look around the table. "Anyway, as I was saying, the rain stopped, and I was sitting at the window, with my knees pulled to my chest, watching the sky like I'd been doing for the past two weeks and wondering if I should ask for any more favors from the Lord."

Willie chuckled.

"Then there it was, a soft glow of light peeking from behind the flat gray clouds that had been drained dry. The light grew and slowly spread across the horizon. The rain slowed to a shower and then a mist. I ran to the front door, flung it open, sucked in the clean air, and turned my face to the sun. Maybe I wouldn't go to hell after all."

Her shoulders shook with laughter. "At least not right away, which would give me plenty of time to work on Willie Hopkins." She winked at her husband.

"See, her parents had agreed that since she sixteen, she could start taking company," Willie cut in. "Thing was, there wasn't a soul in Rudell who interested her in the least, except this old Mississippi Hopkins boy. Ain't that right, sugar?"

Celia blushed. "But he didn't come to church, and I knew my daddy didn't take kindly to folks who didn't worship on a regular basis. But I figured if my prayers worked before, they would work again, and I prayed my way right into Willie Hopkins's life."

"How did you know…I mean, that he was the right one?" Jason asked.

"I'd see him from time to time, hanging out with his friends in the general store, or fishing down by the creek if I happened to be passing by with some of my girlfriends on the way to church. I just figured if I didn't walk right on up to him and say the first hello, we might never speak, and I would be condemned to be courted by those churchgoing boys who had as much personality as an empty pot."

They all laughed at the analogy.

"So that's just what I decided to do that Saturday afternoon, while my mama was snapping beans at Ms. Corinne's house and my daddy was locked away in his room, preparing his Sunday sermon. I put on my favorite blue-and-white dress and my good black shoes, sprinkled some of my mother's expensive talc power down the inside of the front of my dress, and marched right on over to the creek.

"There were three of them. Willie was the one in the middle. He was taller than the other two, thicker in the body and not as lanky as his friends. Whenever I saw him, it was always the other two who were doing all the talking, and I wondered if he talked at all, and if he did, would his voice sound the way I imagined?" she said in a faraway voice.

"A tree branch musta snapped under my foot, and three dark, accusing faces turned in my direction at once. 'You done scared the fish away,' the one with the wide nose said. Willie stood there looking at me with his head tipped to the side and a little bit of a smile on his mouth. He walked up the slope and came to a stop just below where I stood. I swam for a moment on the waves of his hair and got pulled into the undertow of his eyes," she said wistfully.

Willie chuckled, nodding. "Yeah, I remember I said, 'Your name's Celia.'"

Celia grinned. "And his voice was just like I imagined it would be, thick and slow like molasses. 'And you're Willie Hopkins,'" I said.

His eyes crinkled at the corners when he smiled. "'Yeah, I am' I said and looked her up and down. Asked if your people knew you was down by the creek with three grown men.'"

"I put my hand on my hip and said, 'You not that grown.'"

Celia and Willie laughed at the memory. "She was something from way back then," he said of his wife. "I told her, 'I'm nineteen,' and stood a little taller, right, sugar?"

"Mm-hmm."

"'How old are you?' I asked her. Told me she was seventeen." He made a face. "I knew she was storytellin', and I like to had a fit. 'Plenty of women are married with families at sixteen,' she told me. 'Sides, she'd said, her folks told her she could start takin' company on the porch."

"'And that makes me plenty woman,'" Celia chimed in. "'Member that's what I said."

Willie stared at her, then broke into laughter. "You still 'bout something else."

"I musta been, 'cause I got you to walk me halfway home that afternoon, didn't I?" She turned her attention back to Jason and Anita. "But it took a lot of Saturdays by the creek to get Willie to walk me all the way to my front porch and longer still to get him across the front door."

"Once this woman sets her mind to something, that's it." He held up his large hands in surrender. "I never stood a chance."

Celia waved her hand at Willie.

"You sure can tell a good story, Mrs. Hopkins. Reminds me of home."

Celia reached over and patted his hand. "I got plenty more where that came from, and every bit of it is true."

"Must be where Anita gets her talent."

The gathering grew quiet.

Jason glanced around the table from one to the other. "Did I...say something wrong?"

"It's fine," Anita said. "Mom doesn't agree with what I do."

Celia got up and started clearing the table. "I think Anita is plenty talented. I just think she should be doing something else besides running around, spouting off about how we need to rise up and talking all that Malcolm X mess."

"It's not mess, Ma! It's about self-determination, about

not allowing ourselves to be walked on, disrespected, or discriminated against because of our skin color. I don't need to sit next to the white man in the movies or on a bus or in a diner to feel good. I wanna have my *own* movie theater and diner and buses."

Celia spun from the sink and zeroed in on her daughter. "Chile, you think for one minute you would have the kind of life me and your daddy provided for you if we'd been in the streets stirring up folks' anger and grievances? We're all here on this earth as God's children. And we have to get along."

Anita waited a beat, then walked over to where her mother stood, stoic and dug in. She turned to her father in an appeal for support. *You know your mother*, he mouthed.

Anita leaned forward and gave her mother a noisy kiss on the cheek. "You claim to be so peaceful, but I swear you are the most rebellious person I know. We could use you in the movement," she added with wide-eyed innocence.

"Don't swear in my house," Celia murmured, fighting back a smile.

Anita kissed her again. "Love you, too."

Celia swatted Anita's arm. "Girl, you just love to get me going. Gonna have your company think you don't have any home training. Come help me clean up this kitchen."

Anita rested her head against her mother's for a moment, and Celia slid her arm around Anita's waist. The Polaroid moment ingrained itself in Jason's mind's eye. Watching the exchange between them was both amusing and enlightening. Anita Hopkins knew just what buttons to press and when to approach and when to retreat, and as much as she and her mother might disagree on Anita's politics and choices, the bond between them was unbreakable. It was clear that Anita and her mom were on opposite ends, much like he and Anita were. But looking at the two of them gave him hope that they could meet in the middle of the bridge that separated them.

"Don't mind them," Willie said for Jason's ears only. "They go through this about once a month. I learned long ago to stay out of it." He chuckled and finished off his iced tea. "You like football?"

"To watch it. Not much of a player."

Willie pushed back from the table. "Game's on." He started out of the kitchen.

Jason debated the wisdom of sitting alone with Anita's dad, which in itself presented all kinds of booby traps, especially after his brief monologue on civil rights. Or he could stay in the kitchen with the women and hope that he wouldn't get dragged into any fireworks.

He'd take his chances. He got up and followed Willie down the hall.

"You haven't brought a young man home to Sunday dinner—ever," Celia said while drying a plate. She placed it on the table. "Must be special."

Anita tucked in a smile. "Not sure. I mean, he's really nice and handsome, smart…" She wouldn't dare say *too country* and risk setting her mother off again about her own country roots.

"Does he treat you nice?"

"Always. Polite. Opens doors." She shrugged. "I don't know, Ma. We're just different."

"You should be," Celia said. "Pretty boring life if you agreed about everything. Wasn't nothing about your father that came close to what I was expected to want. I was a preacher's daughter. Your daddy came from the wrong side of town, hadn't finished high school, didn't go to church." She slowly shook her head in amusement. "Humph. But none of that mattered to me."

She looked at Anita with a soft light in her eyes. "He won your grandparents over and promised them that he'd always protect and take care of me, make a home for me. And he did." She cupped Anita's chin. "Then we had you, and every dream I'd ever had came true. I never regretted one day of my life with your father. We have our differences on everything from rice or potatoes for dinner to how we view the world."

She dried the last dish. "You'll figure it out."

Chapter Eight

It was a bit beyond twilight by the time they left Brooklyn, that surreal time of day that held the world in moments of limbo before splashing the sky with pinpoints of stars and moonlight.

Anita was uncharacteristically quiet, subdued on the walk to the train, and the crowded conveyance didn't spark conversation for the ride. The day had been perfect, even the back-and-forth with her mom. Her parents had embraced Jason as if he'd always been around. It felt as if he was part of the family. Her mother was right. She'd never brought anyone home for Sunday dinner, and she was still coming to terms with what that meant. More important, would the end of this night lead to more of the night before?

"I had a good time today," Jason said when they exited at 125th Street. "Thanks for inviting me."

"Sure," she said softly.

"Your parents are really nice people."

"Yeah," she smiled, glanced into his eyes, "they kinda are."

"You look a lot like your mother. Have her fire, but you practice your father's beliefs. Interesting combination."

Anita slid a glance at him. She didn't know anyone who had ever made that observation. Growing up, listening to her mother's preaching about "loving your enemy," she always viewed the woman as passive in comparison to her father's harsh view of the world and the life of Negroes in general. She'd always believed that she aligned herself with her father's vision.

She'd never considered her mother as fiery in the activist sense of the word but rather as the commander in chief of the Hopkins household. She'd listened to her father's stories of horror growing up in segregated Mississippi, of how his father had "disappeared" after a run-in with a white landowner.

That was the story Jason needed to hear. Maybe then he'd understand her passion. But it wasn't a story for tonight.

"I suppose," she finally said. "Not that I agree, but I suppose."

"Are you always so determined to never give an inch?"

"Give 'em an inch, they'll take a yard." She winked. "Gonna walk me home?"

"Is that a question or a command?"

She tilted her head to the side. "You pick." She flashed her dimples at him.

He snorted a laugh. "Come on." He guided her to the inside and took his place of protector beside her. "Our families are a lot alike," Jason said. "My mom—church-going, god-fearing. My pops…" He chuckled. "Not happening." He slid his hands into his pants pockets. "He saw a lot of ugliness growing up—beatings, night riders, lynchings. I've seen 'em, too."

"Lynching?" Her voice rose in alarm.

"No. The riders." His jaw flexed, his voice growing hard and flat. "Used to drive by in trucks and on horseback, carrying torches, hiding behind white sheets." His gaze drifted off into the distance. "One summer, I musta been about ten or eleven, they tormented the whole town—every Negro house in the area, every night for a month. I can still hear my mother crying and begging my father for us to leave." His nostrils flared. "My pop would sit out on the porch from sundown to sunup with a shotgun across his lap. He told us wasn't nobody gonna run us off of our land ever again."

"Ever again?"

"His family barely survived the Red Summer of 1919, saw his house burn to the ground, friends shot on the street. The entire Black section of town destroyed. They ran and wound up in Georgia, only to have my grandfather lynched."

Anita squeezed his upper arm in both shock and to comfort. "Oh my god, Jason…"

He dragged in a breath. Then looked at her with an intensity that drilled down to her soul. "So I get it. I just choose to go after things in a different way."

She pressed her lips together to keep from doing what she always did—toss back something smart-ass. Now wasn't the time. She pressed her body a little closer to his and kept her mouth shut.

"Thanks for walking me home."

"Sure."

"Um, you wanna come up for a minute?" she hedged and hoped he didn't hear the tremor in her voice.

His brows rose. "Okay. Sure."

Her whole self relaxed, then twisted back into a knot. "It's a walk-up," she warned after unlocking the front door. "Three flights," she added, as if perhaps that might be the thing to change his mind.

"I do it every day at the rooming house."

Anita led the way while doing a mental check of how she'd left her apartment before running out and of why in the world she'd invited Jason in the first place.

She stopped in front of her door and took her key out of her tote. Whispering a silent prayer that she'd picked up her discarded bra and panties off the bathroom floor, she opened the door and flipped on the light. "Come on in."

She stepped aside and let him pass, then shut the door behind them, and her eyes went straight to the stack of unfolded laundry she'd left on the back of the couch, the empty cereal bowl on the wobbly kitchen table, and the black plastic bag of garbage that she'd forgotten to take out. At least it hadn't started to smell.

"I was kinda in a rush," she said, darting over to the couch to snatch up the discarded clothes. "Have a seat." She deposited the laundry on her bed and shut the door.

Jason looked around at the artsy space. "Your place is really you," he said and walked over to examine the stacks of books piled in neat rows on the floor and the milk crates of albums. A stereo sat in a place of honor on a table by the window. Every corner seemed to reflect an aspect of Anita's personality. Pictures of Malcolm X and news clippings of protestors being attacked by dogs and police batons were tacked onto the off-white walls. He walked over to a blowup of a woman who looked vaguely like Anita.

"Relative?" he asked.

"No." She giggled. "That's Angela Davis. I met her when I went to visit my aunt Violet in California. She was leading a rally on the campus of Berkeley."

Jason read the paragraph beneath the picture.

• • •

Angela Davis
(c) SPUTNIK / Alamy Stock Photo

Revolution is a serious thing, the most serious thing about a revolutionary's life. When one commits oneself to the struggle, it must be for a lifetime.
     —Angela Davis

She came to stand beside him. "Very serious sister. Powerful speaker. Works with another brother, Fred Hampton, who was totally down for the cause, too. He's working with some young people to launch a community-based organization to start free-lunch programs for kids and a neighborhood watch program. They're all about self-determination, building from within, and protecting what's ours—with weapons if necessary."

     Jason threw her a look of surprise. "And you're good with that—arming ourselves?"

     She lifted her chin. "If that's what it takes."

     "Violence only feeds more violence."

     "If that were true, we'd all be living in harmony like you say, since Dr. King preaches turning the other cheek. Being peaceful and weaponless doesn't stop them from jailing us, beating us, killing us at will, and making up laws to help them do it."

He looked at her with what she could only describe as sympathy, the kind of look you give someone who will never understand an idea no matter how many times it is explained. She didn't need anybody feeling sorry for her. She felt sorry for *him*.

She let out a sigh. "Can I get you something to drink? Soda. Apple juice. Ice water. Think I might have a little wine," she offered instead of apologizing for her rant. She wanted him to understand, not run off.

He turned away from the pictures on the wall. "Water is fine."

"Cool." She took her one good glass from the cabinet and got the water from the fridge.

Her hand shook as she poured the ice water into the glass. Nerves? She had nothing to be nervous about. This wasn't the first time she'd had a guy in her apartment. And unless he suddenly turned into Jack the Ripper, Jason was the definition of a gentleman. After all, *she* gave him her phone number, invited him to B-Flat, took him to her safe space in the park, took him on his first subway ride. *She* kissed *him*, and then brought him home to meet her parents.

She cringed. Could she be any more brazen? *A real floozy*, as her grandmother would say. Meanwhile, he hadn't made a move. She bet if she stripped down to her birthday suit right now, all he would do is take his jacket and put it over her.

She stomped the five feet from the fridge to the couch, stuck the glass out to him. "Do you have a girlfriend or something?"

He winced, then frowned. "Excuse me?" He took the glass of water.

Anita propped her hand on her hip and repeated her question.

"Uh. No. I don't."

"Somebody back home?"

"No." His lips flickered like he wanted to laugh, and that only ticked her off all the more.

"So do you like men?"

Now he did laugh. A deep, no-holding-back belly laugh that lasted long enough to knock the wind out of Anita's self-imposed pissed-off sail.

She plopped down on the couch next to him and petulantly folded her arms.

He placed the glass on the end table and adjusted his body so that he was turned halfway toward her. He slowly wound his finger around a thick shaft of her hair.

Her pulse pounded and roared in her ears. He was so close, and the thrill of anticipation had her nerve endings vibrating under her skin.

"What is it that you want, Anita?"

The question was nearly in her ear. A shiver wiggled down her spine.

She swiveled her head and tumbled into the dusk of his eyes. Her breath hitched as she licked her lips. "I don't want anything." She didn't sound convincing, even to her own ears. Sure, there'd been guys over the years, nothing serious—not since Leon, and she liked it that way. At least, she'd thought she did until Jason tumbled into her life. Now her head was all messed up, and she wasn't too sure about much of anything.

Jason's hand drifted down and around her shoulder. He eased her close until her head rested beneath his chin. "Neither do I." He pressed his face into her hair. "But I will as soon as you want to."

She lifted her head. His lips were a beat away from hers. She could leap into what she knew would be a mess, or she could play it safe and ignore whatever this was between them.

"Want to listen to some music?" she asked. Her voice wobbled out of her throat.

The corner of Jason's mouth lifted. "Maybe another night. Have a long day tomorrow," he said, his voice as low and soothing as a prayer. He pressed his lips to her forehead and pushed to his feet. "Thanks for a really great day, Anita." He started for the door.

Anita walked behind him. She couldn't let him leave. Didn't want him to. Not yet.

He turned to her with his hand on the knob. "Good—"

She looped her arms around his neck and pulled him into the kiss that she'd fantasized about. She felt his moan vibrate against her.

He slid a tentative arm around her. She pressed closer, and he drew her fully to him.

She tingled. Tiny explosions popped behind her lids when the tip of his tongue stroked hers. She heard her own sighs as Jason abandoned any hesitation and took control of their kiss.

He reversed their positions so that he had her back against the door, then stretched her arms above her head and pinned them there while he explored her mouth, placing hot kisses along her neck, then tasting her again. He gently lowered her arms to her sides and took a half step back. He brushed a finger along her bottom lip and exhaled a long breath.

Anita's heart was in her throat, pumping like crazy.

"I'd better go, 'fore things get away from us."

Anita didn't trust her voice. She lowered her head, then nodded and moved aside to open the door.

Jason stepped out into the hallway. "Good night."

"Good night."

He trotted down the stairs, and it took all her willpower not to call him back. She shut the door and locked it. Next time, he wasn't getting away that easy, and there was definitely going to be a next time.

If those were the moves of an ol' country boy, she was ready to change her zip code.

She crossed the room and plopped down on the sofa. *Tuna.* She smiled as she remembered their earlier conversation. She'd have to do some grocery shopping and let him experience some of her other skills.

J ason unlocked the metal gate that covered the doors and windows of the storefront office and slid it upward. The rising metal grated and clanged, echoing into the light chill of the early-morning air. Businesses along the avenue were still shuttered closed save for the corner bodega that stayed open twenty-four hours. It was only seven a.m., but he couldn't stay in that tiny room any longer.

Most of the night, he'd lain in the single bed, staring up at the ceiling, playing over and again the day and evening he'd spent with Anita. Being with her was an exercise in emotional control. She was a button pusher. One minute they were sparring, at philosophical odds; the next, sharing a laugh and common interests, revealing pieces of themselves; then back to the debate, only to end up with a kiss that peeled away the guard he'd put up around himself from the moment they'd met.

He didn't know what she wanted from him or what *he* wanted from her, for that matter. He wished Jeff were around to talk to. He'd say, *Man if you dig her, then tell her. You know women are confusing on purpose.*

He laughed. Yeah, that was probably what Jeff would say.

He flipped on the lights, then went to the desk to check the answering machine and was pleased to hear that six local residents wanted to attend the passive resistance workshop. He jotted down the names and phone numbers.

The list of community members interested in Dr. King's message was growing, slow but steady. The snail's pace was frustrating. There had to be more that he could do. He'd been in New York for nearly two months and felt he should be further along with the job he'd been sent to do. He needed to be out in the street with the people. He wanted everyone to understand the message of peace and love, be part of the process that would bring positive change for the Negro.

And he wanted it now.

Headquarters would ask for an update at the end of the month, and he needed to have a positive report. He exhaled and glanced up at the poster of Dr. King on the wall.

—Martin Luther King, Jr. in 1964.
(c) Dick DeMarsico, World Telegram staff photographer / Public domain

For more than two centuries our forebearers labored in this
country without wages; they made cotton king; they built the
homes of their masters while suffering gross injustice and
shameful humiliation—and yet out of bottomless vitality they
continued to thrive and develop. If the inexpressible cruelties
of slavery could not stop us, the opposition we now face will
surely fail. We will win our freedom because the sacred heritage
of our nation and the eternal will of God are embodied in our
echoing demands.

　　　—Martin Luther King, Jr.

Who was he to complain when all those who came before
him had endured so much? One day at a time. No building
was constructed in a day. Patience.

The bell over the door jingled, making Jason glance up.
Two young men—in their late teens or early twenties, dressed
in dark dungarees and leather jackets—walked in. Black-and-
white bandanas were tied around their heads, knotted in front.

Warning alarms rang in his head. Jason slowly rose.
"Mornin'. What can I do for you?"

One of the two walked toward Jason while the other
stood at the door.

"Yo, we heard about this place. What y'all do here?"

Jason cleared his throat. "I work for Dr. Martin Luther
King. I came up here from Atlanta to help spread the message
of nonviolent resistance, train community organizers, and we
also do voter registration."

"Nonviolent resistance," the young man near the door
sneered. "You kiddin', right?"

"No. Violence only breeds more violence."

"Yeah, so when the po-po roll up on us, throw us around,
beat our asses in dey cars for nuthin', we just s'pose to do
what—smile?"

The two men laughed. The one closer to Jason picked up one of his flyers from the desk. "What's this about?"

"Our next workshop. You're more than welcome to sit in, listen to what we're talking about. Do you live in the area?"

"Yeah. Grew up down the street in the projects."

"My name is Jason Tanner."

"Ronald. That's Marcus."

"So, how can I help?"

"You got jobs? That's what we need—some jobs." He tossed the paper back toward the table, but it floated to the ground.

"I'd be happy to help you find work. You might be interested in working for us after coming to the meeting."

The one closest to Jason angled his head to the side. "How much it pay?"

"How much are you making now?"

He glanced over his shoulder at his friend. "He tryna be funny." He looked back at Jason. "I ain't one to be jokin' wit. You feel me?" He took a step toward Jason.

Jason held up his hands in peace and, on closer inspection, realized the young man was about his age, but his environment had aged him. "That's not what I meant or what I intended. I know that we can't pay much. It would only be part-time, a few dollars a week. But if you're already working"—he gave a slight shrug—"then it might not be worth your while."

Ronald gave him a long, hard look. "What day is this here meetin'?"

"Saturday morning. Eleven."

Ronald glanced back at his friend, who remained at the door like a lookout for a robbery or shakedown. Marcus jerked his chin up in agreement.

"Yeah, all right. We'll come through."

"That's good. I'll look out for you both."

Ronald looked him up and down, smirked, then turned and walked out with Marcus, leaving the door open after them.

He stared at the door. They fit a "type." And for a brief moment, he'd fallen for it. The type that was plastered on the news or in the papers—hoodlums. Those two, they weren't that at all. Just kids trying to look a part they weren't really ready to play. Negro neighborhoods were sprinkled with them on street corners, local hangouts, slouched on porches and stoops, waiting and hoping. The elders would hurry past them or *tsk, tsk* in dismay as the dark eyes reflected a future they didn't want to see.

An idea began to swirl in his gut, gaining strength as it materialized. A slow smile moved across his mouth. He'd talk it over with Michael when he came in. Maybe he'd finally found his true calling.

He pulled out a fresh yellow pad from the desk and began writing down ideas.

Anita locked her apartment door and headed out to the office. It was more than cool for this early in October. She buttoned her sweater and debated for a moment whether she should go back inside and get her jacket. The thought of jogging back up three flights of stairs was a turnoff. She kept walking.

She planned to put in a couple of hours, meet Liza for lunch, and do some grocery shopping. She smiled as she wondered if he liked spaghetti and meatballs or if he'd prefer something more homey like fried chicken with mac and cheese. He seemed to have enjoyed what her mom cooked, and if she had to say so herself, she could give Celia Hopkins a run for her money in the kitchen.

She turned onto Lenox Avenue and stopped at the newsstand to pick up a copy of the *Amsterdam News*. The front page ran a headline about Hurricane Flora, which had torn through Haiti and Cuba, killing more than six thousand. The images of destruction were heartbreaking. The island looked like a war zone. She sighed, flipped the page, and briefly scanned the article about President Kennedy having signed the ratification for a nuclear test ban treaty. At least for now, a man-made disaster was put on hold.

"Hey, Brother Malcolm is on TV," one of the interns called out the moment she walked through the door.

"Turn it up," Anita said and joined the rest of the staff gathered around the television.

• • •

View the interview at:
https://www.youtube.com/watch?v=FZMrti8QcPA
Originally recorded October 11, 1963.

• • •

"Today in our discussion of minority groups, we have with us two guests," the announcer began. "One is Minister Malcolm X Shabazz, one of the top leaders of the Nation of Islam or the so-called Black Muslims, and we also have Mr. Herman Blake, one of the teaching assistants in the course. We will discuss today some of the goals and some of the strategies of the Nation of Islam, and I wonder if Mr. Blake might started off by asking Mr. Shabazz a question."

"Minister Malcolm, the thing that I thought might be good for starting it off is to talk about one of the most pervasive beliefs in the general society about the Nation of Islam, and that is that it is a violent means to attain its goals. The question I have is how true is this? And why do you think it persists in society?"

"Well," Brother Malcolm started, and Anita's heart beat a bit faster to hear his voice, to see him on the screen. "The Muslims that accepted the religion of Islam and follow the religious guidance of the Honorable Elijah Muhammad have never bombed any churches, have never murdered any little girls as was done in Birmingham. They have never lynched anybody, have never at any time been guilty of initiating any aggressive acts of violence during the entire thirty-three years or more that the Honorable Elijah Muhammad has been teaching us."

Yes! Anita thought. *That's right!*

Brother Malcolm continued, "The charge of violence against us actually stems from the guilt complex that exists in the conscious and subconscious minds of most white people in this country. They know that they've been violent in their brutality against Negroes, and they feel that someday the Negro is going to wake up and try and do unto them as the whites have done unto us.

"We are not a violent group. We are taught by the Honorable Elijah Muhammad to obey the law, to respect everyone who respects us. We're taught to display courtesy, to be polite, but we're also taught that at any time anyone in any way inflicts or seeks to inflict violence upon us, we are within our religious rights to retaliate in self-defense to the maximum degree of our ability. We never initiate any violence upon anyone, but if anyone attacks us, we reserve the right to defend ourselves."

The others in the room with Anita clapped and cheered.

"So to accuse us of being violent is like accusing a man who is being lynched, who is being hung on a tree simply because he struggles vigorously against his lyncher; the victim is accused of violence. I only point this out because the various racist groups that are set up in this country by whites and who have actually practiced violence against Blacks for four hundred years are never associated or identified or made synonymous with the term 'violence.' But speak of Muslims almost synonymously with violence whenever Muslims are mentioned by them."

"Amen," someone near Anita called out. Their eyes met, and she smiled.

"Minister Malcolm, let me, on the basis of your remarks, ask a double question," the other guest speaker continued. "One: Is it then your assertion that the laws, with respect to how Negroes are supposed to have equal opportunity and equal rights in this country, are not meaningful or believed by whites? And secondly, what then is your opinion and attitude toward the civil rights movement in general and particularly the Reverend Martin Luther King and his philosophy of nonviolence through direct action?"

The camera passed back to Brother Malcolm. "If the white people really passed meaningful laws, it would not be necessary to pass any more laws. There are already enough laws on the law books to protect an American citizen; you only need additional laws when you're dealing with someone who was not regarded as an American citizen, but whites are so hypocritical, they don't want to admit that this Black man is not a citizen, so they classify him as a second-class citizen to get around making him a real citizen. If he was a real citizen, you'd need no more laws. You'd need no civil rights legislation. When you have civil rights, you have citizenship; it's automatic. White people don't need laws to protect their citizenship because they're citizens."

Anita felt the hair on her arms vibrate as she listened to

the words of Brother Malcolm. He touched on all the things that were wrong in society and put on record for the world to see what the Nation of Islam and the movement was really about.

He was so right. When had any Negro blown up a church and killed four little girls? When had they ever used dogs and hoses on people, hung them by their necks, jailed them?

Who were really the violent ones?

The room broke into spontaneous applause when the interview came to an end. Anita folded her arms and drew in a satisfied breath. She hoped that Jason was watching. Maybe then he could understand where she was coming from.

Chapter Nine

"You took him home with you? To Mom and Pop Hopkins?" Liza asked in disbelief.

"Yeah, I mean it kinda just happened. One minute, we were talking on the phone, the next, I was inviting him to Sunday dinner." She shook her head. Chuckled.

"So what was all *that* like? Did Papa Hopkins grill him?"

Anita laughed. "It wasn't that bad. Actually, it was pretty nice. Natural. Jason fit right in." She relayed some of the highlights of the afternoon, from her mom telling the story of meeting her father to Jason and her dad watching the game together.

"Damn, I woulda paid money to see all that. You know you have a thing for this guy, whether you want to up and admit it or not." She took a long swallow from her glass of Coke.

Anita speared a french fry. "I do like him," she admitted. She looked up from beneath her mascaraed lashes. "We kissed—really kissed—when he brought me home," she quietly confessed.

Liza leaned in. "Say what, now? Well...how was it?"

Anita sighed at the memory. "Mm. Could've gone further, but..."

"But what?"

"He put on the brakes."

"He did? Whoa. That's new. And different."

"I know, right? But in a strange way…I kinda like it. He's not overly aggressive like some guys. Jumping in bed isn't the only thing on his mind when we do spend time together. At least, I don't think so. He doesn't come off that way." She paused a minute. "The truth is it's been me who keeps stepping up to him."

"You? You're always the one on defense. It's been a while since you've had anyone special, Nita."

Anita shrugged, chewed slowly on her french fry. "I know it's been a long time. But that whole thing with Leon really did a number on me."

"Yeah, but y'all were just kids."

"Three years of my life. I guess your first will always have a space, you know?" She took a bite of her cheeseburger, and the words that she'd kept buried bubbled to the surface. "Something I never told you…about Leon and me."

"What?"

"I was pregnant."

Liza's eyes widened as she put down her fork. "Why didn't you ever tell me?" she asked softly.

Anita lowered her head. "Ashamed. Hurt. Confused."

"Did your parents know?" Liza whispered.

She shook her head vigorously. "No."

"So what happened?"

"I was so fuckin' scared." Anita sucked in a breath. "I told Leon, and he said he wasn't ready for any kids." She snorted a laugh. "Like I was, right? It was my last year of high school. Seventeen. I was so naive back then." She looked off into the distance. "You know I never had any boobs to speak of."

They laughed.

"So when I started gaining weight, I kept telling myself I

was finally 'filling out.' Not sure what I was thinking." Anita was quiet for a while. "Leon said he had this friend who could help me."

"Nita…"

"So I went to this lady's house in Queens. She was a nurse. She examined me and said I wasn't very far along, maybe six weeks. She gave me some stuff to drink for a week, and at the end of the week, I should come back. It was the worst, tasted awful and made me so sick — and the cramps." She cringed at the memory. "I wanted to die." She reached for her soda. "But I didn't," she said, her voice hollow. "And it didn't work. That was the summer I went to spend with my aunt Violet in California. I told her. She took me to a real clinic, and we never spoke about it again."

"I'm so sorry, Nita. I wish you would have told me. I would have been there for you. I can't imagine how awful that must have been."

"Haunts me. Makes it real hard for me to even think about being that close to anyone again. I don't even know if I can ever have kids now." She knuckled a tear from the corner of her eye and tugged in a breath, forced a smile. "So besides our philosophical differences, Jason lit a spot in me that I've kept a lid on for a long time, and it scares the hell outta me."

"If there's one thing I know about you, you never back away from a challenge. This time the challenge is your own fears."

Anita wiped her mouth with the paper napkin. "I was planning to invite him to dinner at my place." She tugged on her bottom lip with her teeth.

"That's a start," Liza said with a grin.

"But he doesn't have a phone."

"Hmm. Well, you know where he works, right?"

Anita's brow rose with her smile. "True."

They gave each other a high five.

...

Telling Liza about what really happened between her and Leon was like being released from weights wrapped around her ankles. She felt lighter in spirit and in her step. Now that she'd actually spoken the words out loud for the first time since it happened, maybe she could take a chance again without fear. Maybe.

She approached the storefront where Jason worked. Her pulse began to gallop like it always did whenever she thought of him, talked with him, was with him. She stopped in front of the glass door and peeked inside, caught a glimpse of him in the back of the room, leaning over a desk, talking to another guy, and she felt slightly giddy.

She spun away. What if he didn't want to see her? She took maybe five steps and stopped. *What are you so afraid of? Letting someone in again?* Her heart thumped. Dragging in a breath of resolve, she turned back and pulled the door open.

Several pairs of eyes turned toward the sound of the jingle. She felt totally on display, but still, she lifted her chin and strolled in as if she walked the runway every day.

Jason straightened. A slow smile moved across his mouth as she drew closer until she stopped in front of him.

"Hey." He squinted in question. "Everything okay?"

"Yeah, everything's cool. What you got going on?" she asked, gazing around.

"Preparing for Saturday's workshop."

"Hmm." She shifted on her feet. "Can I talk to you for a minute?"

"Sure." He looked around. "Why don't we go outside?" He placed a hand at the small of her back and led her out front.

"Listen, if this is about last night...I don't want you to

think that I left for any reason other than that I want you to know I respect you." His eyes moved in slow motion across her face. "I'd never do anything you might not want or we might not be ready for, ya know."

Her heart was beating so hard, she swore she heard it pounding. She licked her dry lips. "Sure. I appreciate that." She swallowed.

"Good." He looked relieved.

"Listen, I was wondering, since you only have tuna at your place, if maybe you might like another home-cooked meal." There—she'd gotten it out, and she didn't faint.

His smile lit up his eyes. "Back to Brooklyn?"

She laughed out loud, the tension in her belly releasing. "No, silly. At my place. I was going to fix dinner."

He slid his hands into his pockets. "Who am I to turn down a home-cooked meal? When did you have in mind?"

"Tonight."

His brows rose. "Oh. Tonight. Yeah, sure—what time?"

"Seven?"

"Okay. Sounds good."

"So I'll see you then. You like spaghetti?"

"Love it," he said.

The words dipped down and stroked her insides. "See you at seven." She turned and headed down the street, and it took all her self-control not to skip all the way to the supermarket.

Her nerves sizzled. It was almost six. The sauce was simmering, the salad chilling in the fridge along with a bottle of wine. She needed to take a shower and change, set the table, and put the pasta on to boil.

Her wardrobe consisted of dungarees, T-shirts, a couple of blouses, two pairs of pants, and one dress that her mother had bought for her last birthday. She opted for the dress. She wanted Jason to see her differently tonight, softer. The dress was a deep-orange color—sleeveless, scoop neck, fitted at the waist, and hitting just above her knees. She took a slow turn while trying to see herself in the mirror over her dresser. It would have to do.

She picked out her hair and patted it into a perfect halo around her head, added her signature hoop earrings, lathered on some mascara, and shoved her feet into her flip-flops.

Darting into the kitchen, she turned the water on to boil, added salt and a pinch of oil. She looked around her space, placed her hand on her hip. Then decided to plump her multicolored throw pillows, pushed one of the album crates farther into the corner, and checked the couch cushion for anything that might have disappeared between them, finding two quarters and an Oreo cookie.

She did one more quick scan. This was about as good as it got. Besides, it wasn't like Jason hadn't been here before. She put the pasta into the boiling water, then took out the plates and silverware to set the table.

Just as she finished draining the pasta, the doorbell rang. Her heart jumped. She placed a cover over the pasta pot and went to the intercom. "Yes?"

"It's Jason."

She took a breath. "Come on up," she said over the thud of her heart.

She pressed the buzzer to release the front door and began to pace, then stopped and dashed over to her stereo. She grabbed her Dells album but quickly decided against it. The Dells personified sexy, and she didn't want Jason to get the wrong idea...yet. She grabbed a Marvin Gaye 45, *Can I*

Get a Witness, instead and put it on the turntable just as the knock came on her door.

She pushed out a breath and went to the door. The instant she laid eyes on him, something went soft and gooey inside her.

"Hey," she said soflty.

"You look really nice."

"Thanks." She pretended to shrug it off but relished the look of appreciation that lit his eyes, and she was glad she'd chosen the dress.

He handed her a bouquet of flowers. "For you. Can't come empty-handed," he added with a smile.

She lifted them to her nose. "Mm, beautiful. Thanks. Come on in. Why are we standing in the doorway?" She stepped aside to let him pass. "Dinner is actually ready. Hope you're hungry."

He turned toward her. "Smells great. I'm starved."

She extended her hand toward the small kitchen table. "Have a seat."

"Can I help with anything?"

"No, I got this. But you can line up some music if you want."

"Sure." He walked over to the stereo and stooped down to flip through the crates containing her massive album collection. "I gotta tell you, this rivals the record shop you took me to," he said as Marvin Gaye's hit came to an end.

She emptied the pasta into a bowl at the center of the table. "I know, right?" She laughed. "Between collecting music and books, I'll have to live on top of my kitchen table."

He chuckled. "All for a good cause."

She took the salad out of the fridge and the pitcher of iced tea. She'd save the wine for later. "Next to the music store, my favorite place growing up was the library on Macon Street. Spent every Saturday there. I could sit in the window seat for hours, just reading and imagining faraway places," she said wistfully.

"I can tell," he said. "Extensive jazz collection, too, I see."

"Yeah," she murmured in a tone that sounded as if she was realizing it for the first time. "I think I must have subliminally grown to love jazz because my dad always played it. It was like the soundtrack in the background of my life or something."

"Mind if we listen to some Miles, then?"

"Perfect dinner music."

He put the album on the turntable, and the trumpeter's signature notes filled the space.

"'All of You,'" Anita said. "Great choice."

Jason grinned. "Good ear." He joined her at the table.

"Well, please help yourself. Take as much as you want. Oh, I only have French and Italian dressing for the salad."

"French is fine." He used the tongs to get his helping of spaghetti.

Anita passed him the bowl of pasta sauce.

"Wow, this sauce is almost a meal by itself," he commented, ladling the thick sauce.

"Sausage, ground beef, red and green peppers, fresh tomatoes, and a lotta soul." She grinned. "My specialty." She passed him the salad.

Once they'd filled their plates, Jason steepled his fingers and bowed his head, just as she was ready to dig in.

"Lord, bless this food we are about to receive. May it strengthen and make our bodies good. And bless the chef." He peeked up and winked.

"Amen," she said with a grin.

There was a lot of clinking of forks against plates and murmurs of enjoyment while they ate with music playing softly in the background.

"Tell me about Atlanta. What do you do when you're

not being a do-gooder?" she teased, glancing at him from beneath her lashes.

Jason tipped his head to the side, put down his fork. "We don't live in caves, ya know," he lobbed back. "Plenty of parties, clubs, movies." He gave a light shrug. "I worked as a bookkeeper, actually."

Anita pointed her fork at him. "You look like a bookkeeper."

Jason chuckled. "I'm going to take that as a compliment and let it go."

Anita tugged on her bottom lip to keep from laughing.

"It was steady work," he continued. "Decent pay. Had my own place, too. It was small but it was mine." He pushed out a breath. "I knew I wanted to do something more than push numbers up and down a spreadsheet for the rest of my life, though. And all that changed when Dr. King came to my church and preached. I heard my calling." He took a mouthful of food and chewed slowly. "What about you? Who were you before you turned into a fiery revolutionary?"

Anita tore off a piece of buttered Italian bread and dipped it into the sauce. "A regular bougie Black girl growing up in a big house, Catholic school education, two-parent household, decent part-time jobs." She shrugged and looked across the table at him with such intensity that he shifted in his seat. "The American dream. The Black version." She chewed her piece of bread. "Like you, I felt in my soul that it wasn't enough. Not when I saw what was happening to our people outside of my little comfort zone." She took a long swallow of her iced tea. "So here we are."

"Here we are." He took a long swallow, then sighed contentedly.

"Glad you like it," she said, more pleased than she had a right to be. "Take more if you want."

He leaned back in his seat and patted his stomach. "I think I've reached my limit."

Anita wiped her mouth, quickly got up, and began to clear the table.

"Let me help with that." He collected their dinner plates while Anita transferred the leftovers into plastic bowls and put them in the fridge.

"I'll wash if you dry," Jason offered.

Anita raised a brow. "No complaints from me."

They worked comfortably side by side, as if this was something they always did.

Her nerves were no longer frazzled. Instead, there was a sensation of wholeness—a complete feeling that settled her, made her want to put down her armor and smile from the inside out. Somehow, Jason had made her feel that way from their earliest meeting. There was an aura about him that made her feel secure and protected. He knew nothing about her when they met on the bus, yet the first thing he did when he'd heard what happened in Birmingham was try to comfort her. Even as she railed against him and the world.

Intermittently, she stole side glances at him while they worked. Did that whole "live in peace, turn the other cheek, brotherhood, love your neighbor" philosophy give him that essence of calm that seemed embedded in his every move? What would a day be like for her without the deep-seated sensation of edgy anxiety that often fueled her?

Jason dried his hands on a dish towel. "We work pretty well as a team."

She looked up at him. "Yeah, we do."

An awkward moment of "what to do next" waffled between them.

She pulled open the refrigerator door. "How about a glass of wine?"

"Sure." He put down the towel.

She took out the bottle of wine and got two mismatched wineglasses from the cabinet.

They sat side by side on the couch. She handed him the bottle to open, and he poured for each of them.

"Thank you."

She tipped her glass to his. "Anytime."

He took a sip of his wine. "Now that I know you cook like that, I just might take you up on it."

Her body flushed with heat. "So, how did everything go for you today?"

"There were these two guys who came in this morning—early," he started, his face lighting up. "I was the only one there. Kinda had my guard up, I'm ashamed to say. But after talking with them, an idea started rolling around in my head. A way to really involve the community in the nonviolent movement."

Anita listened intently to Jason's vision of mobilizing the youth of the community through small-job programs and educational workshops.

"I'm pretty sure that the home office in Atlanta would be willing to send funds to help. We'd use the space here to host job training, get the businesses in the community to list openings and be willing to take some of the young people as employees." He shook his head. "When I was talking with those two guys, I realized that when Ronald tossed the flyer aside, it wasn't in dismissal. It was that *he couldn't read it.*" Jason shook his head, his eyes glittering. "How many more guys like that are out there, feeling forgotten and lost?" He dragged in a breath. "We can help them, and in turn, they can help all of us."

She tucked her foot beneath her and took a sip of her wine. "It sounds great. But who's going to do all this training?"

He heaved a sigh. "Don't know yet. Michael and me at first, I suppose."

"You know, what you're promoting is no different from what Brother Malcolm speaks about." She leaned closer, pressing her point. "What Angela Davis and Fred Hampton speak about out in California. Self-determination," she said, feeling that cauldron of passion begin to bubble.

She went on to tell him about the interview she'd seen earlier in the day and the message that Brother Malcolm was conveying. "We're not promoting violence, but we *are* promoting protecting ourselves from the violence perpetuated against us."

Jason's gaze roamed across her face. "You're extraordinary. Do you know that?" he asked softly, steering them away from the debate that always loomed between them.

Her skin tingled, her heart thumped. She ran her tongue across her lip.

Jason reached out and trailed his finger along the line of her jaw, making her breath hitch. His fingers spread and threaded through the back of her hair. He eased her toward him.

When his lips touched hers, tiny bursts of fire ignited, setting her body aflame from the soles of her feet to the top of her head.

Jason drew her close, and she felt her body melt into the comfort, the warmth, and desire that he stoked in her.

Her tongue parried with his, teasing and retreating. She wrapped her arms around his neck, and he lifted her onto his lap as if she were no heavier than an infant. The overwhelming sensation of being cocooned in a blanket of protection, respect, and caring welled inside her, and in that moment, she knew that he would not betray what she wanted to give to him. That he would honor it—and her—no matter what.

Anita eased back, unsealing their lips. She looked into his eyes and believed she saw the sincerity of his soul, and she knew she would be protected and cared for with Jason. "I make a great breakfast," she whispered, her voice shaking with sudden uncertainty. What if he thought she was too forward? What if—

Jason brought his mouth to hers, and whatever doubt may have arisen was crushed in that instant.

She eased off his lap and slowly stood, took his hand, and led him into her bedroom. Then she stood in front of him, her usual bravado nonexistent.

Jason cupped her cheek. "This is what I want. But only if you do."

She hitched in a breath. This was different. He wasn't like any other man she'd been with. She could tumble headlong into real feelings with Jason—get all tied up in emotional knots. This wasn't a Leon-teenage-love thing. Her heart banged in her chest. If she let him in, though, there was no turning back.

His fingers stroked her cheek, making her lids flutter. She nodded, doubting the strength of her voice. Her fingers trembled ever so slightly as she fumbled with the buttons of his shirt, popping one off in the process. They both laughed as it bounced and rolled across the floor, breaking the barrier of uncertainty, seeming to give them permission to let go.

Jason tugged off his shirt as Anita lifted her dress over her head. She backed up toward her bed and sat down on the edge of it, inviting him forward. Jason crossed the short distance and stood above her before lowering himself to his knees. He reached around her, and when he unfastened the snap of her bra, she slipped one strap off and then the other. Jason finished the job and peeled it away.

Anita held her breath as she experienced the heat of his

gaze while it slowly sizzled across her skin.

Jason kissed the insides of her knees, stroked her thighs in a way that made her sigh and shiver. Her eyes slid closed while Jason explored her body with light kisses, tender touches, and murmurs of desire against her flesh.

She gasped when his lips teased and tasted her nipples. Her fingertips dug into his shoulders. She whispered his name.

She unfastened his belt, unzipped him, and reached inside, and suddenly the air caught in her throat. Jason groaned when her fingers wrapped around him, stroked him to a magical rhythm.

They inched and twisted their way up the length of the bed, mouths and limbs entwined. Anita managed, with a little help, to push Jason's slacks down his hips, then he kicked them off the rest of the way. The only thing between them was her white cotton panties which were quickly descarded.

Jason braced himself above her, then rolled over and grabbed his pants from the floor. Rooted around in his pocket for a moment until he found the condom he had in his wallet.

He lay on his back to open it when Anita nipped it from his fingers. "Let me."

His jaw clenched as she rolled the latex down his length.

"Did I do it right?" she said on a ragged whisper.

"Let's see." He rolled her onto her back, then in one quick motion, he was inside her.

Her universe came to a standstill. "Ohhh!" she groaned out as her fingertips dug into his back. Sweet agony pushed and pulsed deep inside her. *Oh God, it's been so long.* She clung to him, dragging in air. It felt like the first time—scary, exciting, new.

She willed herself to relax and give in. By degrees, her body adjusted to him, and those first moments of discomfort gave way to waves of dizzying pleasure.

He was so gentle yet strong and powerful at the same time. He cared for every inch of her with a touch, a kiss, a whisper in her ear—all with a sensitivity that made her soul sing. She floated on a bed of pleasure that continued to escalate, shaking her, leaving her defenseless against the onslaught of sensation that Jason whipped through her.

"Anita," he groaned deep in her ear, repeating her name over and over.

She felt the tightening of his muscles, the deepening of his thrusts, the way his breathing escalated. She slowly raised her legs until they rested high and wide across his back, opening herself completely to him, offering her vulnerability, knowing that he would take it and treat it with care.

And he did, stroking and thrusting and hugging her through the deep throes of release until she was totally spent, weak, and satisfied. And complete.

Chapter Ten

They shared breakfast at daybreak, having been up for most of the night raining pleasure down on each other. Anita padded around in Jason's shirt and he in a towel.

Now, she watched as he slowly chewed on a slice of bacon. "Your breakfast is as good as your dinner."

She'd prepared bacon, perfectly seasoned home fries, grits, and eggs. She poured a glass of orange juice, then sashayed over to him, loosened his towel, and sat on his lap.

Jason nuzzled her breasts that teased him from between the open button-down shirt. "But I'd rather have you for breakfast, lunch, and dinner any day," he said, taking the peak of her nipple into his mouth.

Anita felt her eyes flutter. She moaned softly, then twisted her body to straddle him. "I feel the same way," she said before looping her arms around his neck and dipping her tongue into his mouth.

Jason clasped her hips. She reached for the condom packet on the counter, ripped it open with her teeth, and made an erotic show of sliding it along the length of him, conjuring Jason's groans of desire. She rose up, positioned herself above his thick erection, and slowly eased down until he was buried deep inside her.

She cupped his face in her hands. "I hope you're still hungry."

They faced each other in her doorway, and Anita suddenly felt shy. All the sass and bravado she'd displayed earlier was gone. Now all the misgivings she'd carried around about her and relationships resurfaced with full force.

She wanted him to go and wanted him to hold her at the same time.

"So, uh, I guess we'll talk," she said. "Or whatever." She leaned against the frame of the door with her arms folded protectively around her.

"Are you working tonight?"

She bobbed her head.

"I'll stop by. Walk you home."

She swallowed. "I get off at ten."

He leaned in and kissed her. "See you then."

Jason daydreamed his way through the morning, replaying making love to Anita over and over again. She was like a drug. He felt lightheaded, intoxicated by her scent. He could barely concentrate on what he needed to do in the office as he struggled to jot down his ideas about using the office as a community resource for the young men in the area.

He'd need to have his head screwed on straight when he explained why he was asking for money from the home office to pull it off and still fulfill what he'd been sent to New York to do. But he fully believed that the nonviolent passive resistance training would be an added layer to the services.

He ran through his head how he would appeal to the leaders. He'd use the work that John Lewis was doing as an example.

John Lewis was not much older than he was, and Lewis was heading up SNCC, the Student Nonviolent Coordinating Committee. He was inspired by all that Lewis had accomplished, particularly with his organization of the young people. There was no reason why he couldn't do something similar in New York with his idea that would grow out of the basic mission of the movement.

He stared at his notes. Anita's smile flashed on the page. The last thing he'd planned to do when he'd come to New York was to fall for a revolutionary beauty who stood for all the things he rallied against.

Anita. Just thinking her name flooded him with an excitement that he hadn't felt with anyone in longer than he could remember—if ever. He could easily spend all his time with her, and that was a problem. He was there to do a job, and he couldn't let the tug of her eyes or the tease in her smile or the way her body did things to his distract him. He shook his head, blinked her away, and pulled the heavy black phone toward him. He dialed the long-distance number in Atlanta.

Anita dragged a kitchen chair across the short space, placed it in front of the window, and curled into it. Her notebook rested on the sill, next to an ashtray and her pen. The avenue below vibrated with its everyday activity. Car horns blared, shouts of acknowledgment volleyed from one side of the street to the other, exhaust fumes from rumbling delivery trucks mixed with the aromas of hot dog vendors on the corner. Leaning on her elbow, she rested her chin on her palm as her thoughts swayed in concert with the turning leaves on the tree below her window. Fall was in the air.

She'd crossed her self-imposed line with Jason. It was not in her plan to get involved with anyone, especially physically. Especially now. It frightened her. She knew how vulnerable she'd become with Leon—not only the emotional but the physical toll the relationship took on her.

But with Jason, all her rules and regulations fell apart.

She sighed. Then to compound all that was their total opposite views, and it was a recipe for disaster. But what was she going to do about it? She couldn't very well pretend that nothing had happened between them or that she wasn't feeling all kinds of feelings and just go on about her business.

Her mother's counsel after Sunday dinner replayed in her head. She'd said she and Dad disagreed on just about everything, that they came from two different worlds, but none of that mattered because how they felt about each other was more important.

Anita sighed. Her mother made it sound simple. But she wasn't like her mother in that way.

For her mother, life was one big bowl of soup with all the ingredients in a boiling pot. Mom could separate out the ingredients—vegetables, meat, seasoning—and identify them all, substituting one ingredient for another.

She, on the other hand, was a puzzle. All the pieces had to fit perfectly. She couldn't separate herself from her convictions, her emotions, her writing, her place in the world, her relationships. She couldn't pick them apart or have one without the other. She needed all the pieces to make her complete.

So where did that leave her and Jason?

She opened her notebook to a blank page, started and stopped until the words began to appear on the white space.

Uncertain steps in dark spaces,
Bumping against shapes unseen,
Making sense from the senselessness
Of the everyday unordinary-ness
That has become the here and now.
Uncertain steps in dark spaces
That echo danger ahead,
Unseen but felt,
Raising alarms and hair on arms.
Certainly uncertain steps
Arrive at places before unseen,
Coming clear in the twilight,
Deciding if I might
Glimpse a ray of light around uncertainty
Maybe.

Anita inhaled a breath, coming back from that surreal headspace that consumed her when she wrote. She looked at the scribbled words on the page, amazed. The process always left her stunned that they had come from her, as if she were only a vessel from which the poems flowed out of her control.

She reread the poem, changed a few words, moved some of the lines until she was satisfied with the tone and movement of the final version, then she recopied it onto a clean sheet of paper.

But what was she really saying?

Generally when she shaped a poem, it was in response to what affected her. In looking at what she'd titled "Certainly Uncertain," she realized that her words were a mixture of politics, emotions, and events, all of which defied clarity, even as she struggled to secure it. As much as it cast a light on the state of Black life, it also illuminated her confusion about Jason. *Reflections of each other.*

She pushed open the window and plucked a half-smoked Newport from the ashtray—a bad habit that she had unsuccessfully tried to break. Unfortunately, the nicotine need only rose when she felt overwhelmed, stressed, or *uncertain.*

She smirked at the irony. She didn't think she could plow through the tumble of thoughts roaming in her head without something she could hold on to, something to wrap her lips around, to fill her up inside and simply disappear in a puff of smoke without asking for anything in return.

If only life were that simple.

The sharp flame from the match lit the tip of the cigarette into a bright orange. She dragged in a long, satisfying lungful, then slowly blew it out. The smoke curled around her face before floating away.

A police siren broke through the cool early-evening air. Inadvertently, the hair on her arms rose. *Who did something now? Is it my block? Whose kid? Anybody hear gunshots?* The questions raced around, then disappeared as dark eyes and relieved souls on the street below followed the siren's wail until it grew faint and continued toward another neighborhood of bad news and fractured dreams.

She smoked down to the filter, smashed out the flame, and then lit another cigarette. She sighed, closed her notebook. Held it to her chest. *Maybe.* Yes, maybe.

Chapter Eleven

"…deciding if I might
Glimpse a ray of light around uncertainty
Maybe."

The lights on the stage dimmed as the applause and finger snaps rose. Anita sunbathed in the admiration, her skin warmed under the rays of adulation. The clapping of hands and stomping of feet reverberated in the center of her soul. What happened to her up on a stage was an out-of-body experience. As much as she sought to transport the audience with the journey of her words, she, too, was transported.

"Thank you." She stuck the mic back in the stand and floated off stage.

As she moved past tables, she was slowed repeatedly with appreciative nods, quick clasps of her hands, and light pats of congratulations on her back.

All she wanted was to bring minds along on a ride of revelation—to see, think, and feel something they'd never felt before. She went behind the bar, retrieved her apron, and took a moment to gaze out onto the gathering, and she was reminded of a quote from one of her favorite writers, James Baldwin, who'd said, "You write in order to change the world… if you alter, even but a millimeter, the way people look at reality, then you can change it."

She dragged in a breath and came back from behind the bar. That's all she wanted to do: change realities and minds with her words.

She rounded the tables to check on the customer orders and stopped short. Unbidden, a smile tugged hard at her mouth. There he was. This time looking cool and easy in the space, from the casualness of the open collar of his shirt to the way he angled his body, drink in hand.

"Hey. When did you get here?" she asked. "I didn't see you come in."

Jason ran his tongue along his bottom lip. "I know I'd planned to pick you up after your shift, but I didn't feel like waiting." He set down his glass.

The air stuck in her throat.

"Got here just in time to see you do your thing up there, though. Glad I came when I did."

She grew hot all over. "Cool." She leaned her weight on her right leg, wanting to know what he thought but not about to fish for compliments.

"Powerful stuff," he said, as always seeming to read her mind. He tipped his head to the side. "Uncertain, huh? How should I take that?"

She blinked, shifted her weight, then frowned in defense. "It's up to the individual how they interpret what I say."

His eyes didn't leave her face as he slowly nodded. "Hmm. Okay. Can I get a beer?"

"Sure." She smiled warmly. "Hungry? Burger, wings?"

"Tempting. Umm, yeah, some wings and fries. Will you be able to join me for a minute?"

"I wish. But we're kinda busy, and I want to get out on time tonight."

The corner of his mouth lifted, making her tingle at the memory of what that mouth was capable of. She cleared her throat. "I'll put your order in." She spun away and nearly collided with Henry.

"You did good up there tonight, kid," he said. "Getting better every time."

For an instant, she couldn't respond. She'd always thought Henry let her spit her poems because it was good for business. It never crossed her mind that he actually paid any attention to what she said. Damn, she'd have to take back everything she'd thought about him.

"Wow. Thanks, Henry. That…means a lot."

"Hey, now," he grumbled. "Don't get all warm and fuzzy on me." He lifted his double chin toward a table of four. "We got customers."

She tucked in a smile. "Right." She walked away, pushed through the swinging door to the kitchen, and put in Jason's order. *One millimeter at a time.*

"D id you get to test out your idea with your people in Atlanta?" Anita asked while they strolled down Lenox Avenue toward her apartment.

"Yes! I did."

"And?"

"Well, they want me to give it a try. Start recruiting the young men specifically. Offer job training and get them to understand the mission of our movement and have them train others."

"Each one teach one," she murmured. Her gaze softened. She squeezed his hand. "This is what it's about. The young people are our future." She leaned in and kissed his cheek. "What you're doing is good, J, real good."

His smile cinched the corner of his eyes. "Trying."

She looped her arm through his, looked up at him. "I'm

really glad for you."

"You mean you don't have a problem with a whole lotta do-gooders hanging around Harlem?"

She laughed up at the clouds. "I swear I don't know if I can handle it." Her laughter quieted. She stopped in the middle of the sidewalk and turned to him. "One do-gooder is good enough for me," she softly said.

His jaw tightened. "That's all I want you to need," he replied before leaning in for a long, deep kiss.

She was sinking. She could feel it in the pull of his gaze. The threads of her resistance were unraveling, and soon she would have no choice but to let go and hope that Jason would break her fall.

"I think I still have some wine," she said, the words trembling in her chest.

"Sounds good." He slid his arm around her waist.

She rested her head against his shoulder and let go.

Anita flicked on the light and dropped her tote on the chair as Jason stood in the doorway. "Make yourself comfortable. I'll get the wine and glasses."

Jason meandered into the living room space, which was really an extension of the small kitchen and short entryway.

Once again, the finger of her artistic spirit beckoned him to explore the music, the books, photos, and art that breathed life into the dull walls and wood floors. The apartment, though small, was a minimuseum steeped in Black culture. He lifted the framed photo of her aunt Violet with Angela Davis and a smiling Anita. She could not have been more than sixteen, seventeen in the photo, but already there was more than simple joy in her eyes—the fire was simmering. Yet the girl in the picture was so completely different from the one her parents—at least her mother—apparently had hoped she'd become.

He returned the picture to its place on the square wooden table. What was the moment that changed her from a Catholic school girl, living a simple middle-class life, to a revolutionary?

"Here ya go."

He turned around. "Thanks." He took the glass from her hand.

"Music?"

"Sure."

She walked over to the stereo, turned it on, and let the album, already on the spindle, descend onto the turntable. The first scratch and hiss of the needle on vinyl was soon replaced by the Miracles' "You Really Got a Hold on Me." Anita swayed her hips to the rhythm and sang along in perfect pitch with the lead singer, Smokey Robinson.

When the song reached the chorus, "Ba-baay, I love you…" she raised one arm, then the other in the air before wrapping them around her waist and belting out the lyrics. She ran her hands down along her hips, pouted out the words, "Hold me, hold me, hooooold me."

Jason watched from his front row seat on the couch, as always captured by the raw emotion that she exuded even with something as singular as an R&B song. She was mesmerizing, and he was under her spell.

The song came to an end, and Jason watched as that otherworldly look that she had in her eyes when she performed slowly disappeared.

She blinked, pushed out a breath, and smiled shyly.

He clapped in appreciation. "Your talents are endless. You have a great voice, Anita."

She bit down on her lip, shoved her hands in the back pockets of her dungarees. "Years of singing in the church choir, I suppose."

He chuckled. "You were in the choir?"

"Yep." She came over to the couch and plopped down beside him. "From the time I was about six until my last year of high school."

"Wow. How come you didn't pursue gospel or singing?"

She sighed, got up, and retrieved her glass of wine from the table. She turned to Jason, one arm wrapped around her waist as she took a sip of wine. "Hmm. Too much hypocrisy in the church. Praise the Lord on Sunday and get back to sinning on Monday. I wanted to sing songs like Etta James, Ruth Brown, or Betty Carter, the Shirelles." She snorted a laugh with a jerk of her head. "My mother wasn't having none of that 'devil music' in her house," she said with a wave of her finger back and forth. "She would always tell me that my voice was *anointed*, and I needed to use it for God's work." She leaned against the back of the couch and finished her wine with a faraway look in her eyes. "Humph, so much for that."

Jason reached over and twirled a lock of her hair around his finger. "Might not be what your mama would have wanted for you, but you do use your voice."

She looked down at their linked fingers. "Growing up, I wanted to be in a singing group," she said, the memory softening her tone.

"Yeah?"

"Me and two friends from school. We called ourselves the VIPs." She giggled. "When we got to high school, we used to enter the local talent shows at the PS 35. My folks didn't know. At least, I thought they didn't." She laughed. "One night me and Denise and Laverne came tumbling out of the gym where we'd just performed in the show, and my daddy was standing in front of the school, leaning against his Cadillac. I damn near peed on myself."

Jason sputtered a laugh.

"For real! I ain't never been so scared to see somebody in my life."

"So what happened?"

"My dad may be from the country, but he was cool as ice. Greeting me and my friends like nothing happened and asking did they need a ride home. So we all get in. He drops them off, and lemme tell you, I wanted to get out with them." She chuckled. "But he didn't holler. What he told me was no matter what, nothing was more important than being truthful to yourself and the people you care about. Don't ever forget that. He parked the car in front of the house, but before we went inside he said, 'You three were really good up there.'"

She blinked, looked at Jason. "I never forgot that night or what my father said to me. I told my mother I couldn't sing in the choir anymore. It was the summer I spent with my aunt Violet." The summer that changed who she was and set her on the path to who she was becoming.

"Always the rebel."

She lowered her gaze. "Yeah, I suppose so. I found my voice in another way. Like Baldwin said, 'The point is to get your work done, and your work is to change the world.' At least, I hope that I can." She noticed her empty glass. "More wine?"

"Are you trying to dull my senses and take advantage of this ol' country boy?"

She giggled. "The thought had crossed my mind." She leaned in and kissed him. "Got a problem with that, do-gooder?" she whispered against his lips.

"Not at all." He pulled her into his arms.

...

Jason walked back to his apartment the next morning as the sun was cresting above businesses and towering tenements. It was still quiet save for the neighborhood winos who clustered together on corners or beneath stairwells. This time of day gave him a few moments to think without the onslaught of noise that pulsed like blood through the veins of the city.

This thing with Anita was taking on a life of its own. Started off as a spark that turned into a full-fledged fire. The thing was, he wasn't sure exactly what it was she wanted. Did she want a real relationship or something else—whatever that might be?

Anita was complicated. On one hand, she was this fiery activist who seemed to have no problem taking up a weapon if necessary and who turned her nose up at what he believed in. Then on the other hand, she was this thoughtful, deep-thinking artist—funny, sexy, sensual, great cook, fierce, and shy all at the same time.

What did you make of a woman like that? He had nothing and no one to compare her with.

He opened the door to his building and climbed the three flights of stairs. The house was coming alive. He could hear the deep voices and muffled laughter, water running, doors opening and closing.

"Ain't those the same clothes you had on last night, youngblood?" Randolph asked with a wink. He tossed a towel over his shoulder. "She put you out kinda early." He chuckled and headed for the bathroom at the end of the hall and shut the door behind him.

Jason snorted a laugh of his own as he entered his room.

If he could have stayed with Anita all day and into the next, he would have. But he wasn't sure if that was what she wanted.

He tugged off his jacket, unbuttoned his shirt, and tossed them both on the chair, then sat on the side of the single bed. He flopped back on the mattress. *Every day with Anita?* Was that something that could even be real? He tucked his hands beneath his head.

Challenging would be the least of it.

What would Jeff say if he were here? He'd tell him what he always told him: "Put your cards on the table, man. It's the only way to known what's what." He pushed out a long breath. First, he had to figure out what his cards were.

Chapter Twelve

October turned to November, ushering in shorter days and chilly nights, and Jason and Anita spent as much of that time together as they could. He spent at least two evenings a week at her place and made sure to stop into B-Flat on the nights that she worked. Some days she would pop by his office, and they would head to the park for lunch or just walk the neighborhood and talk. And every parting grew more difficult.

In between, his focus was on building the movement. He and Michael had hosted two Saturday workshops on nonviolent resistance. The first had only five attendees, three of whom had clearly come solely for the free refreshments. But the following workshop, two from the prior session brought several friends.

"Dr. King has six points that support nonviolent resistance," Jason said as the group sat in aluminum chairs in a semicircle around him. "Some of you may think that nonviolent resistance is cowardly. But Dr. King preaches that it's not cowardly at all." He stood, looked each in the eye. "It is resistance; it is passionate." He tapped his temple with his forefinger. "Your mind and your emotions are always active, always ready to see, to persuade your

opponent that they are mistaken in their belief. You don't
need to be aggressive to do that—just firm in your belief
of righteous justice."

He got a few nods of approval, while others seemed
unmoved.

"Dr. King says that the purpose of nonviolent resistance
is not to embarrass or humiliate your opponent but rather to
gain their friendship and understanding."

"How's that gonna work when they're hosing folks and
siccing dogs on us?" one young man wanted to know.

"Yeah. What about that?" several chorused, their voices
rising.

Jason held up his hand. "He preaches thirdly that the
battle is not against any individual but against the forces
of evil. The fight cannot be between the races but between
justice and injustice. That's why we march. That's why we
boycott, to bring injustice to light." He paused. "Together in
our unified faith and conviction, we are a mighty army on
the side of justice."

He went on to outline the rest of Dr. King's platform:
nonviolent resistance required the willingness to suffer,
even go to jail; the universe, Dr. King said, was on the side
of justice, therefore the activist had to have faith that justice
would happen; and finally, nonviolence prevented physical
violence and the "internal violence of the spirit." Dr. King
believed, as opposed to the views of Malcolm, that it was
the responsibility of every citizen to be prepared to defend
the rights of everyone who was faced with injustice, even
when that meant going to war. *Because injustice anywhere
is a threat to justice everywhere.* It was a hard philosophy to
embrace, but he understood.

And if duty called, he would serve.

The group of ten seemed to understand, if not fully

embrace, the philosophy. It would take time, Jason reasoned. They were churchgoers, had deep roots in the community, and wanted to see their people thrive. That was inspiration enough for most of them.

One of the attendees, Mary Waters, wanted to volunteer to help bring in some of the young men from her church for the program that Jason had proposed. And Michael seemed eager to bring her on board—maybe a little *too* eager.

He was feeling somewhat good about the progress they were making, and the home office was pleased as well. It just wasn't moving half as quickly as he would have liked. But in the meantime, he needed to get the training program started, ideally before the beginning of the new year. Michael and Mary had been canvassing some of the local businesses that might be willing to hire a few young men from the community. He'd posted flyers up and down Amsterdam and Lenox Avenues asking for volunteer teachers to help out with the reading and math program. So far, no takers. But he would press on.

Everyone was gone for the evening. Michael and Mary were going to grab a bite to eat at a local diner. Anita was attending a meeting at the community center. He'd promised to meet her there and they'd go to dinner after, since she was off for the night.

On his way to the community center, he was stopped by a young man leaning against the lamppost, smoking a cigarette. Two other men were with him.

"Yo, you the dude from that storefront," the one smoking said, pointing the lighted tip at Jason.

Jason peered into the dimness. It was Ronald, the young man who came into the office weeks earlier and hadn't been back.

"Hey. Ronald, right?"

"Yeah." He unfolded his long arms and legs and took a step toward him. "You still got stuff going on?"

"Yes. I do." He stuck his hands in the pockets of his coat.

Ronald took a short glance over his shoulder while his two friends looked on. He lowered his voice. "Yo, I was in some trouble, you feel me? That's why I ain't been back."

Jason nodded. "Whenever you're ready. How's the trouble?"

Ronald shrugged his narrow shoulder. "I'mma work it out."

"Good."

A cold wind whipped around the corner, caught them in the crosshairs. Jason drew his shoulders to his chin.

Ronald shifted from one foot to the other. "So, look, I was figurin' that I'd come through and maybe hear some more what you was talkin' about. You know, maybe help out or somethin'."

Jason held on to his surprise. "Anytime, my brother. Anytime. Office opens around nine till around six."

"Cool. I'mma come through."

"I'll look for you." He stuck out his hand.

Ronald looked at Jason's hand for a moment and finally shook it. He roll-walked back to his friends.

Jason smiled and crossed the street. *One day at a time.*

Jason arrived at the community center. The meeting was still in progress when he opened the door to the main meeting room and quietly took a seat in the back row. Much to his surprise, Anita was in front, speaking to the gathering.

"Brother Malcolm said very clearly, concerning his position on nonviolence: he said, 'It is criminal to teach a man not to defend himself when he is the constant victim of brutal attacks.'" The audience shouted their approval. "He said, 'It is legal and lawful to own a shotgun or a rifle. We believe in obeying the law.'"

"That's right," a man in the audience shouted.

"The law don't believe in us!" someone else yelled.

The audience erupted into shouts and applause.

Anita held up her hands to quiet the crowd even as she paced in front of them, stirring the pot. "He says," she yelled over the din, "'In areas where our people are the constant victims of brutality and the government seems unable or unwilling to protect them, we should form rifle clubs that can be used to defend our lives and our property in times of emergency, such as happened last year in Birmingham; Plaquemine, Louisiana; Cambridge, Maryland; and Danville, Virginia. When our people are being bitten by dogs, they are within their rights to kill those dogs.'"

"Yes! Yes!"

"But"—she held up her hand—"Brother Malcolm warns us that, 'We should be peaceful, law-abiding—but the time has come for the American Negro to fight back in self-defense whenever and wherever he is being unjustly and unlawfully attacked.'"

The audience rose to their feet and clapped.

"'If the government thinks I am wrong, for saying this,'" she shouted over the noise, "Brother Malcolm says, 'then let the government start doing its job.'"

This was the Anita he'd met on the bus from down South. Fire and fury. Passion and persuasion. The raw energy that flowed from her was contagious.

Although she spoke the words of someone else, they were spoken with such conviction and strength, they could have as easily been her own. He could see Anita leading a march, standing at the head of a massive crowd, swaying the unbeliever to believe.

His heart swelled in admiration and pride, and at the same time, constricted in uncertainty. Watching her, fully engaged, reminded him in no uncertain terms how far apart they were, a bridge that they might never be able to cross. So where did that leave them?

It was the question that turned over in his mind even while he loved her inside and out that night and all the nights that followed.

"I'm thinking of going home for Thanksgiving," Jason said while he helped Anita wash the dinner dishes.

He'd all but unofficially moved into her place, staying more days out of the week than not. So when he was there, he helped out any way he could: cleaning up, cooking, even repainting her bathroom. He'd been saving as much money as he could to be able to get his own little place so that he could have her over. It was still a few months out of reach, and the trip home would cut deep into his savings.

She glanced at him, her hands stopped in the sudsy water. "Oh." She focused on the bubbles. "I didn't know. I guess I should have figured as much." She shrugged her left shoulder.

"It's a pretty big deal with the family."

"Yeah, mine too." She looked over at him. "So maybe we can plan something when you get back."

"Yeah." Before the idea could fully form in his head, he blurted it out. "How 'bout you come home with me? I know your family has its thing...but then we can spend Christmas with your folks." He stared into her stunned expression, and then that soft light hit her eyes, and a slow smile curved her mouth.

"My mother will be upset as hell, but I think she'll understand eventually. Yeah." She grinned broadly. "I'll go."

"You will!" He dropped a damp hand at her waist and pulled her close. "They'll love you." He swallowed. "How could they not…love you," he whispered.

He watched the pulse beat at the base of her throat. Her lips parted while her eyes danced across his face, and she cupped his cheeks in her palms. "Only if you're sure," she murmured before pressing her lips for a moment to his.

She stepped back. They looked everywhere but at each other, Jason understanding in that moment that they'd entered new territory, had offered up a veiled emotional confession that bound them against all the things that would keep them apart.

Anita's lips quivered for an instant before the old bravado returned. She lifted her chin and propped her hand on her hip. "So now what?" she challenged.

Jason slowly exhaled. "Now we really see if we can make us work." He rested his hip against the side of the white porcelain sink. "I had no intention of getting involved with anyone when I came here," he began slowly. "Last thing on my mind." He sighed and shook his head in wonder. "But we was meant to be, Nita. From the moment we met up on that bus."

She placed her hand over his. "We come from opposite sides of the bridge. Believe different things. Are feelings gonna be enough to get us across?"

He brought her hand to his lips and kissed the inside of her palm. Her lids fluttered. "I don't know, sugah. But maybe we should just try to meet in the middle."

Her brow arched. "Deciding if I might"—she stroked his cheek—"glimpse a ray of light around uncertainty. Maybe," she said with a mischievous glint in her eyes.

Jason scooped her up in his arms, and she wrapped her legs around his waist. "Let's see if we can get some light shinin' on any leftover maybes," he said and carried her giggling off to the bedroom.

He laid her gently on the bed. For a moment all he could do was look at her, consumed by a rush of emotion. He reached toward her, brushed her thick bush of hair away from her face, exposing her wide questioning eyes. In that moment before he entered her, he knew that whatever plans he had, Anita had to be part of them. Differences be damned.

"I...love you," he moaned as her wet warmth wrapped tightly around him.

Anita sucked in a breath. The tips of her fingers pressed deep into his back. "I love you, too."

Anita sat in the waiting area at Liza's office, flipping mindlessly through magazines on the table. She'd told Jason how she felt, and she had been second-guessing herself ever since. What was love really? Maybe it was lust or loneliness. Had she only echoed his words because she thought she should? The questions had tumbled around in her head since the other morning in her kitchen. And for the past few days, she'd been making excuses not to see Jason.

"Hey, girl. Ready?" Liza bounced into the waiting room, ready for the weather.

"Damn, girl. You dressed for the North Pole or what?"

Anita stood and slipped on her wool pea coat.

"Listen, we're from the motherland. I don't know what's wrong with you, but I do not like the cold," she said, wrapping a thick white scarf around her neck and pulling a matching wool hat down over her ears.

Anita pursed her lips. "What are you going to do when it really gets cold?" She buttoned her coat and hooked her tote on her shoulder.

"Put on more clothes!"

"Girl, you are too much," she said, laughing. "Come on. I'm starved."

They went to their favorite diner and ordered their usual: burgers and fries.

"So, what are your plans for the holidays? Mama Hopkins throwing down?" Liza took a deep bite of her burger and hummed in delight.

Anita squirted ketchup all over her fries and speared two. "Planning to go to Atlanta with Jason." She scoped out Liza from beneath her lashes and shoved the fries in her mouth.

Liza froze midbite. "Say what?" Her voice rose, sharp enough to cut through the din of lunchtime conversation.

"That's the plan. He asked me to go with him."

"I know your mother musta flipped. What did she say?" Liza asked in a harsh whisper, practically in Anita's lap from her side of the table.

"Haven't told her yet."

"Giiirrl."

"I know. I know. I'll do it soon." She paused. "Jason told me he loves me," she practically whispered.

Liza blinked like something was in her eyes. "He did? When?"

"Last week."

"Wow. Hey, that's a good thing, right?"

She nodded weakly. "Yes." She tugged on her bottom lip. "I told him I love him, too. It just slipped out, ya know." Her brow knotted. Love wasn't just some word of the moment, not for her. It meant something, and she hadn't said it to anyone, not a soul other than her parents, since Leon. Love was a commitment of the soul. Was that what she wanted now? Did Jason even mean it or was it just about good sex?

Liza put down her fork, wiped her mouth with the napkin. "Whoa." She waited a beat. "Big deal for you, sis."

Anita blinked, pushed out a breath. "Yeah, and now I don't even know if I mean it or if I just said it in the moment…"

"You don't know if you mean it?"

Anita frowned. "I mean, I don't really even know him. Do I? It's only been a couple of months. Who falls in love in a couple of months? Nobody with good sense. Not to mention our political differences."

Liza rolled her eyes. "Girl, how long are you gonna hang on to that line? I told you, you had a thing for that man since y'all met on the bus. He all but lives at your place, and I haven't seen that glow in your eyes since who knows when." She lifted her burger to her lips.

Anita bit back a smile. She shoved two sliced pickles in between the bun and burger and took a large bite. "Whatever," she mumbled over a mouthful of food.

"Whatever is right, *and* he's asking you to come home and meet his folks, too," she added. "Girl," she waved her hand, "you hooked."

Anita sputtered a laugh. "No I'm not!"

"Yeah, you are," she retorted, wide-eyed.

Anita sighed. "I'm just not sure."

"About what? Him?"

She nodded.

"Why?"

Anita didn't know how to answer, because she really didn't know why it was still so difficult to embrace the idea of being in a relationship or at the very least allow herself to embrace how she felt. "I don't know," she mumbled. "I guess it just… makes me vulnerable, ya know. Weak. And when you're weak, you can be taken advantage of."

"Every man is not Leon."

Anita propped her chin on her fist. "I know. I mean I know that on the outside, logically. But inside…" She sighed.

"Give yourself a chance. That's all I can tell you. You like the guy. *Really* like him. Enjoy that."

Anita took a long swallow of her soda, then leaned toward her friend. "I'll give you five dollars if you'll tell my mother I'm not coming to Thanksgiving dinner."

Liza's laughter sputtered burger bun onto her plate. "Oh hell no," she managed. "Mama Hopkins will not biblically cuss *me* out!"

The two friends laughed at the truth of the image. Anita was in for it, for sure. And for whatever the reason she was willing to risk the scolding from her mama to be with Jason. Flashes of her parent's warnings years ago tightened her stomach. It was different this time. Jason was different. Jason was no Leon. She bit down on her bottom lip. That realization was settling and thrilling all at once.

"When am I gonna meet this Mr. Wonderful anyway?" Liza asked while they walked back toward her office.

"How about before the holiday? That way you can give me your honest opinion. I'll fix dinner, say, tomorrow night. I'm off. You can come over."

"Sounds like a plan. I'm always down for a free meal. Need me to bring anything?"

"Don't think so. What should I fix?"

"Girl, you can burn. Whatever you decide is fine with me."

"Maybe I'll do ribs," she murmured thoughtfully.

"Ribs! Ooh, don't tease me. Ribs in the middle of the week."

Anita playfully shoved Liza's shoulder, and they both slowed their steps.

"Wonder what's going on," Anita said, scoping out the crowd that had gathered in front of Jimmy's Electronics.

"Giving away something, probably."

They got closer, and that's when they heard the sobs and realized that the crowd was looking at the television screens displayed in the window of an electronics store. They hurried over, peering in between bodies above heads.

"What's going on?" Anita asked one woman who was weeping into her gloved fist.

"They done shot the president," she wailed.

"What! Oh my god."

Anita pushed her way to the front with Liza right behind her. They couldn't hear the words of the obviously shaken newscaster, the revered Walter Cronkite, but across the bottom of the screen, the words said that President John F. Kennedy had been shot in Dallas, Texas.

Anita's breath caught in her chest. She was still trying to make sense of what she was reading when a collective gasp rose from the assembled group. *President Kennedy pronounced dead at Parkland Memorial Hospital*, the words spelled out at the bottom of the screen. Walter Cronkite could be seen fighting back tears.

Liza placed a hand on Anita's shoulder. "Damn," she whispered. "What's going to happen now?"

Anita turned around, feeling numb. "I wish I knew. I have to go see Jason," she said, her voice urgent.

"Yeah, sure. Go. Go. We'll talk later."

They cheek-kissed and hugged. Anita jammed her hands in her coat pockets and hurried off toward Jason's office.

J ason stood in the center of the room, with the ragtag staff gathered around the television as they watched and listened to the unthinkable events unfold in front of them. He could not imagine the utter terror and anguish of Jackie Kennedy and the children.

For days the news would play over and over again of the moment the shot rang out, Jackie Kennedy rising up in her seat, blood splattered across her pink suit. But what would forever be etched in Jason's mind was the stunned look that paled Mrs. Kennedy's face, the horror and disbelief that flattened her lips and rounded her eyes. That moment itself would be covered in the history books, but no one would ever be able to capture or even understand the long-term toll it would take on the family and the country.

"What does this all mean?" Michael quietly asked Jason.

Jason slowly shook his head. "One thing, all the progress that Dr. King made with Kennedy, slim as it was, is gonna come to a standstill. Country is gonna be in upheaval and mourning for a while. Johnson will be sworn in. He's an old diehard Southerner, and there's no telling where he will land on racial issues. We're gonna need prayer for the Kennedy family and the country."

The bell over the door chimed. Jason felt the knot in his throat grow when he saw Anita standing there. He stepped around the bodies and went to her, felt her bury her face in his chest as he wrapped his arms around her.

"You okay?" she asked, looking up at him.

He nodded and kissed her forehead. "Better now. This is just horrible."

"Scary." Her body shuddered.

"Yes. It is." He dragged in a breath. "But we gotta believe we'll all come through this on the other side."

"Always the optimist," she murmured. She looked him straight in the eyes. "Don't you get it? If they could do that to a white man—the *president* of the United States—what chance does the Negro have?"

Jason wanted to snap back with some line of hope, but he just didn't have the energy.

"Hmmm." She finally took a look around. "Lot more people," she commented.

His brows lifted. "Yes," he said on a breath, thankful for the detour in topics. "Couple of the brothers from the neighborhood." He lifted his chin toward Ronald. "That's the young man I was telling you about. Comes in to help hand out flyers about our meetings and does some small jobs around the office, whatever I can find. He brought two of his friends, too. And that's Mary Waters. Met her at church. She volunteers with the typing and filing. Brings lunch from the church some days, and she found us a tutor. We'll be able to start our reading program. Come on, I'll introduce you." He took her hand. "Mary," he said softly, coming up behind her.

She turned. Her doe-brown eyes glistened with unshed tears, and she pressed a tissue to her nose as she forced a smile at Jason.

He placed a comforting hand on Mary's slender shoulder. "I wanted to introduce you to someone. This is Anita Hopkins. Anita, Mary Waters."

"Nice to meet you," Mary said.

"You too."

Mary tilted her head slightly to the side. "You look familiar."

"I live in the neighborhood," Anita offered.

"Hmm." Her eyes suddenly widened in recognition. "It was last summer at Grant's Tomb. You were leading a protest, and it got ugly with the police. It was in the paper."

Anita's lips tightened. Jason watched her carefully.

"Happens sometimes when people are passionate about their rights and their cause, and the white man doesn't want you to have none of it," she shot back.

The room grew suddenly quiet. All eyes turned in their direction.

"I gotta go," she snapped at Jason and whirled away.

But he was right behind her. "Anita!" The door closed behind him.

Anita was practically running down the street. He ran to catch up with her, grabbed her shoulder. "Hold on. Hold on."

She stopped, spun toward him. Her eyes were on fire. "What? You got a *Miss Do-Gooder*, and I'm just a loud-mouth troublemaker, right? *Right?*" she practically shouted. "While y'all are sitting around holding hands and praying for change, *I'm* about the real business of change! I'm in the street fighting the fight for real. And I'll be damned if I'm gonna let anybody knock me down and I'm just gonna stay down!"

He clasped her shoulders. She was shaking. "Anita," he said, his voice low but urgent. "I don't know what you got in that pretty head of yours, but you're wrong." He stared deep into her troubled eyes, willing his words to penetrate his meaning.

"How do you know what I got wrong?" she snapped as a puff of white breath floated ghostlike between them. "What do I have in my head, Jason? Huh? What?"

There was no arguing or reasoning with her when she got all riled up, that much he knew. He cupped her cheeks in his cold palms, leaned in, and kissed her. "I'm freezing. We're gonna talk about this later."

Before she could protest, he turned and hurried back down the street to his office.

For several moments, she stood there, stewing in her own juice, and for the life of her, she didn't know exactly what she was so pissed off about. She licked her lips. Tasted Jason. He'd eaten one of those damn salted pretzels that she liked.

She stopped at the next corner and purchased a pretzel from the hot dog stand. And for a second too long, she wondered if Miss Do-Gooder liked salted pretzels, too. Except the instant the thought entered her head, she realized how ridiculous it was and how ridiculous she'd acted. Fear of falling would do that to you, make you feel wobbly and a little out of sorts.

The president of the United States. Damn it. That big ugly truth made her feel vulnerable, touchable, and painfully aware of how tenuous life could be. She struggled with those emotions, and this American horror only made her more aware of just how deep she'd sunk into her own feelings about Jason.

She sighed heavily. She was going to have to get used to this love thing all over again.

Front page of the Dallas Morning News (replica copy) on November 23rd, 1963, reporting the news of the assassination of John F. Kennedy on Nov 22nd.
(c) Maurice Savage/Alamy

Chapter Thirteen

A pall had settled over the country. It seemed to Anita that everything and everyone moved in some kind of slow motion. Disconnected. Dazed.

The usually vibrant streets that overflowed with people and activity even at the apex of summer heat or the dead of winter cold were all but silent—a reverent silence. Schools dismissed their students early after the news, having parents scrambling to scoop up their confused children and try to explain what "assassination" meant. Most schools did not open the next day. The metal gates of many businesses stayed shuttered, and the church bells from across the city echoed the sadness that so many felt.

The front page of every newspaper and all of the television stations carried the surreal news that President John F. Kennedy had been assassinated as he rode in an open-top car with his wife at his side. It was a miracle that Mrs. Kennedy had not been injured, but the trauma of the moment surely would never go away.

The images caught on camera were terrifying to watch, yet they were played over and over on some kind of macabre loop, narrated by the deep, somber voices of the newscasters reminding people of all the awfulness of the world.

Anita sipped her cup of tea. Her notebook was open on the table. Jason was still in the shower. She'd wanted to be stubborn and difficult when he'd come knocking on her door last night. But truthfully, she didn't want to be alone. She could have gone and spent the night over at Liza's studio apartment, but Liza couldn't give her what she'd discovered only Jason could—making her feel safe and protected. And she'd felt shaken, down to her core.

When she'd opened the door and he was standing there, all she could do was step into the arms he'd extended and let him wrap her in them. She'd closed her eyes, inhaled his familiar scent, and her heart slowed to its normal rhythm.

And while they kissed and hugged and whispered soft, inaudible words, and gave themselves over to each other, there was no need for words of the world, images of solemn faces and places miles away. What mattered was the now, the here, the them together, trying to make sense out of the senselessness of it all. All of it.

Jason came up behind her now and kissed the back of her neck. He ran a towel over his damp hair, which had tightened into close, shiny curls.

"There's some eggs and bacon still warm in the oven," she said, reaching behind her to cup his freshly shaved chin. "Juice in the fridge."

"Thanks. You're not eating?" He took a plate from the cabinet.

"I had some toast with my tea." She lifted her cup in confirmation.

Jason opened the oven and took out the pan, ladled the contents onto his plate, and joined her at the table. "Working on something new?" he asked with a lift of his chin toward her notebook.

She chewed on the tip of the pen. "Mm-hmm." She

looked across at him. "Have to. Ya know. Words are important right now." She fluttered her lashes slowly. "Like Nina Simone said, 'An artist's duty as far as I'm concerned is to reflect the times.'" Her veins tingled with commitment to the words.

He smiled in agreement, then picked up a piece of bacon and chewed slowly. As if signaled, they both looked toward the window.

"Is that snow?" Jason asked, sounding as delighted as a child would be.

Anita grinned. "Yeah. Guess y'all don't get much of the stuff in Atlanta."

"Not at all," he said as he watched the white crystals flutter past the windowpane.

"The first snow of the year is always special. Clears the air. Kinda magical."

"Hmm. I can see that."

She drew in a breath. "Maybe it's a sign."

He stared at her profile. "Of what?"

"Maybe I should clear the air."

Jason frowned. "What are you talking about?"

She lowered her head a moment, then looked at him. "The protest that the woman in your office talked about..." she said quietly. She slowly rose and walked to the window, braced her hands behind her on the sill.

Jason lowered his fork. Didn't say a word. The radiators banged and hissed with anticipation.

"I did lead that protest. A march, actually. I had to." She lowered her head for a moment. "We marched through the streets in response to a brother, Steven Young, being beaten into a coma by the police for drinking a beer on the street!" Her eyes clouded with tears. She turned to Jason, but she didn't really see him. "There were about a hundred of us. Signs raised, voices and fists raised. Folks were pissed. Hurt. I stood on those steps at Grant's Tomb and looked out on their faces—expectant, frightened, angry, restless. All of them needed someone to tell them how to harness everything they felt.

"It was me. My time. I manifested the words of Brother Malcolm: 'We are nonviolent with people who are nonviolent with us.' So when the police decided they'd heard and seen enough, they—" Her voice hitched. "They descended on us like locusts." She folded her arms tightly around her waist. "I got swept up in the arrests, tussling with the police." Suddenly, she lifted her halo of hair away from her temple. "See this?" she asked as she ran her finger along a thin raised scar along her hairline. "Billy club, flashlight? I don't even know. Five stitches."

She sat on the edge of the windowsill, her knees feeling a little weak. "My father came and bailed me out. My mother demanded that I move back to Brooklyn." She all but glared at Jason, her anger renewed. "I fought them! I fought them for my right to exist. They didn't believe that I or anyone out there that day deserved to be there, had the right to speak up on all the things that were wrong, to fight back!" She pushed out a breath. "You see, the thing is, Jason…I'd do it again. And what happened yesterday to the fuckin' president! That just proves that no one is out of the reach of someone who don't give a damn about your life." She huffed.

"Violence against violence is not the way," Jason said, soft as a prayer. Slowly he got up and came to stand in front of her. He pulled her to his chest, held her until their hearts beat in sync.

• • •

Jason squeezed his eyes shut for a second as he started walking down the street after leaving Anita. The idea of her being beaten by police tore at his insides. Anita was a tornado—spinning, gaining in strength, and willing to knock down anything in her path to get to where she needed to go. She was fueled by the same injustices that fueled him, but she met wrongs with fury, while he met them with the fig leaves of peace. But it was the trait that drew him to her, fascinated him, and frightened him about what her unwavering vision would cost her.

Still, he knew he loved her.

When Jason called home after returning to the boarding-house, he would have thought that his mother had lost her best friend. Her tears and broken sobs were real, and he could visualize her staring at the pictures of John Kennedy, which sat alongside pictures of Dr. King and Jesus on the mantel like members of the family.

"What is the world coming to, son?" she sobbed. "I just don't understand the hatefulness. He was such a good man. He wanted to do good things for the Negro." She sniffed.

"I know, Mama," Jason said gently, hoping to console her even as he was trying to come to grips with the devastating setback this would cause for the civil rights movement. "This country has been through worse. We'll get through this."

The weight of her sigh didn't seem to agree. "Dark days, son." She sniffed again and cleared her throat. "How are you? Everything all right? Need me to send you anything? I worry so about you up there in New York."

He smiled. Even at twenty-seven years old, he still had a mother who thought she had to take care of him. "I'm fine, Mama. Really. Actually, I was calling to tell you that I was planning on coming home for Thanksgiving."

"Oh, Jason!"

He felt her smile through the phone. "I, uh, want to bring someone with me."

There was a pause.

His stomach tightened. Anita was nothing like the girls he'd dated back home. But if he knew anything about his parents, they would put on a show of welcome no matter what. They'd save their comments for later.

"Say what, now? Bringing someone home? Someone like who?"

"I told you about the young lady I met—Anita."

"Uh-huh. What about her family?"

"Well, we talked about it," he hedged, "and we decided that we'd spend Thanksgiving with my family and stay here for Christmas with hers."

He felt his mother's sharp intake of breath.

"You won't be here for Christmas?" Her voice hitched up a notch.

"Anita and I talked it over and came to a compromise."

"Humph. You and Anita. Must be special," she groused.

He leaned against the wall. "She is." A flood of warmth ran through him. Yeah, she really was special in ways that he hadn't expected. He'd fallen for her. Hard. Fast. Even as their philosophies differed, it didn't matter to him more than being with her.

Whoa. The sudden acceptance came out of nowhere—just like Anita that day on the bus.

His mother sighed heavily. "Well then, we'll have to make her feel special when she gets here. I'll fix up the guest room for her," she conceded.

Jason bit back a smile. Of course. Sleeping together and being unmarried would never fly under the Tanner roof. "We're looking at making the arrangements to come down."

"Well, you just let me know so your dad can be available

to pick you up—and your guest."

"As soon as we know for sure, I'll call and let you know."

"You do that. Can't wait to see you," she said, her tone softening.

"Me too."

"And…your young lady, Anita."

"I think you'll like her."

"We'll make her feel right at home."

"*Please deposit five cents for the next ten minutes*," the recorded voice said, breaking into the call.

"Hang on a second, Mama." He dug in his pocket for change.

"You go 'head. Call me when you settle on your plans."

"Okay. I will. By the end of the week."

"You take care of yourself up there."

"Of course. Send my love to everyone."

They ended the call, and Jason returned to his room. Bringing someone home for the holidays was a pretty big deal—not something that his folks took lightly. At the Tanner household, holidays were strictly a time for family, reconnecting with each other, and anyone included in that circle had to be someone special.

With that hurdle out of the way, he prepared for work at the office. He knew it would be a tough day for everyone, and he would need all his focus to be able to keep the calm and reassure his people.

His people. The idea sent a jolt through him. When had that happened? When did he realize or accept that he was actually a leader, a leader who was building a coalition? A surge of something he could not define flooded his chest as he adjusted his tie.

His hazy image reflected back at him from the worn dresser mirror. For the first time, he allowed himself to acknowledge that not only was he pressing forward Dr. King's message but also carving a place for himself in the landscape of history. He firmly believed in the biblical saying that the children shall lead us. He was grooming a new generation of leaders. Maybe not to lead marches or boycotts, but rather to lead their communities and their families.

He finished dressing, put on his coat that he'd had to get from a used-clothing store, wrapped a scarf around his neck, grabbed his hat, and left for the office. When he stepped outside, a light sprinkling of snow greeted him. Dealing with the cold weather and now snow was going to take some getting used to. He'd be more than grateful to return to the warmth of Atlanta for a few days.

Being with friends and family during this tumultuous time was more important than ever. Coming together in grief and solidarity was a means to heal and fight against all the news outlets, and every conversation on the street and in shops that swirled around the murder of the American president. There was a shift in the air, a heavy blanket of uncertainty—especially among the Negro residents of the country. Would newly installed President Johnson champion their cause or roll back any advances already achieved?

Anita planned dinner for her best friend and her best man. She wanted Liza and Jason to like each other. Next to her parents, they were the most important people in her life. It was important to her that they got along.

She'd splurged on a slab of ribs that she'd promised Liza

she would fix. She opted for potato salad instead of mac and cheese. Liza would be disappointed, but she'd get over it, and she employed her mother's recipe for spicy collard greens and her daddy's not-so-secret barbecue sauce for the ribs.

Her apartment smelled like back home on Saturday nights when her mom and dad would try to outdo each other in the kitchen with their specialties and compel her to choose whose dish was best that week with bribes, from more money in her allowance to an extra half hour of television time. All done to the backdrop of trumpeter Miles Davis mixed with the gospel sounds of the Blind Boys of Alabama. She'd learned early that there was no easy way out, so she simply either alternated between the two of them from one week to the next or landed on whoever was offering the best deal.

Tonight, instead of Miles Davis, she pulled out some Martha Reeves and the Vandellas, Marvelettes, and Little Stevie Wonder to lighten the mood.

"Girl, girl, he is some kinda special, and cute too," Liza whispered while she and Anita worked side by side, clearing the remnants of dinner. "I like him."

Anita beamed. "You do? For real?"

"Yeah, for real." Her expression softened. "He really cares about you, Nita. It's all over his face every time he looks at you."

Anita's chest filled. She glanced over her shoulder to where Jason was flipping through her album collection, bobbing his head to the music. She breathed a sigh of relief. "I needed you to like him. That was important to me."

"Are you finally starting to feel better about your political differences? Do you think you can keep them out of the relationship?"

Anita leaned against the sink. "I want to…" she hedged. "And I'll try."

Liza pursed her lips. "At some point, my dear friend, you're going to have to come to terms with what is more important—an idea or happiness."

Chapter Fourteen

"We coulda took the bus," Jason said for the umpteenth time since they'd arrived at the packed airport.

Anita looped her arm through Jason's and snuggled close against a blast of cold air that swept through the departing flights' entryway. "We coulda stay our asses right in Harlem, too. But we're not." She leaned up and kissed his cheek. "Relax. It will be fine, and we'll be in Atlanta in a little over two hours." She gave his arm a comforting squeeze.

He murmured something deep in his throat about how if people were meant to fly, God woulda given them wings. Anita giggled.

They entered the terminal, their small suitcases banging against their thighs as they joined the check-in line of travelers and their luggage of every size and shape that snaked around the terminal.

Jason was clearly struggling to disguise his terror beneath a veneer of discontent. He hadn't liked the cab ride from Harlem to JFK airport. The cabbie drove too fast, he'd complained, took too many risks. Then it was the cold. Too cold to fly. The crowds and the bags and the noise. All his pseudocomplaints escalated to what amounted to outright terror when they boarded the plane, inched down the narrow aisle, and found their seats. Anita opted to let Jason have the window seat.

When the pilot announced, "Prepare for takeoff," he gripped Anita's hand so hard, she yelped. She turned to look at him, and his face was a frozen mask of fear: wide eyes, sweaty brow. She watched the pulse beat in the hollow of his throat.

"Why didn't you tell me you've never flown before?" Anita asked in a tight whisper over the stewardess's reminder that "all seat belts must be fastened." She witnessed his face go gray when the stewardess stood in the middle of the aisle to explain how to evacuate in the event of an emergency.

Jason dragged in short breaths. He gripped the armrest as the plane started off down the runway.

"We probably should have had a drink before we left," she said in his ear. "I won't let anything happen to you." She kissed him on the cheek. "Promise. Just put your head back, close your eyes, and we'll be there before you know it."

She closed her eyes and pulled in a long breath. Jason's anxiety might have risen to the surface, but hers tumbled and swirled like a toy sailboat tossed into a storm. She'd had maybe one decent hour of sleep, tormented by the prospect of meeting Jason's whole family. Each time she thought about it, the storm intensified—her stomach knotted, and her pulse beat so hard in her temples that her eyes popped open.

What would she say to them? What if they didn't like her, or, worse, they didn't like her for Jason? No one had ever taken her home to "meet the parents." Not that she had a long list of past relationships—none that mattered that much, anyway. That was part of the angst—Jason mattered.

She'd let her guard down, or maybe it simply came down when she was too deep in those persuasive eyes or captured by lips that mesmerized her with sweet words that undressed the protective film around her heart.

She wasn't even sure when she'd tumbled into the pull of his embrace so fully. But here she was, and as certain as she was about so many other things, Jason was the one thing she remained uncertain about. Not because she doubted him—but herself.

The taxi pulled to a stop in front of a modest blue-and-white house with an inviting porch and a picture-perfect front yard, complete with emerald-green grass and a riot of potted flowers. Anita could almost see Jason as a child running across the yard.

He paid the driver and got their suitcases from the trunk.

"Hey there Jason," Mrs. C called out.

Jason shut the trunk of the cab.

"Afternoon Mrs. C. How you doing?"

"Can't complain. Knee acting up." She lifted her chin. "Bringing company home for the holidays I see."

"Yes, ma'am. This is Anita Hopkins. Anita, Mrs. C. My mama's best friend and lifelong neighbor."

"Hello." Anita finger waved.

Jason picked up the suitcases. "Take care Mrs. C."

"Must be mighty special to come all the ways up here for the holidays," she said.

"She is," Jason replied and shot a look at Anita.

Her heart thumped. If she thought the idea of going home with him scared her before, she'd had no idea what the real thing would feel like.

Before they reached the front gate, the door opened. His mother and father stood on the threshold.

"Oh boy," Anita murmured.

"It'll be fine." He took her hand and gently squeezed it. "Remember? If I survived my first plane ride, you can do this." He winked. "Come on."

"Jason!" His mother beamed and wrapped him in a long, tight hug over Jason's chuckles. She stepped back, cupped his chin in her hand. Her eyes were misty with happiness. "So glad you're home."

"Hello, son." His father clapped him heartily on the back.

"Mom, Dad, this is Anita Hopkins. Anita, this is Mae Ellen and Ralph."

"Welcome. Welcome," Mae Ellen said.

"Thank you for having me," she said, smiling her thanks.

"Jason said you was a friend of his, so you a friend of ours," Ralph said.

Maybe this won't be that bad after all.

"Y'all come on inside, get out of those heavy coats," Mae Ellen instructed. She hooked her arm possessively through Jason's.

Ralph took Anita's suitcase and leaned close. "That boy ain't nevah been on a plane before. Hope he wasn't too much trouble," he said with a twinkle in his eyes and the inkling of a smile on his lips.

Anita grinned. "He got through it."

"Good. Good." He placed a light hand on her shoulder, and they all piled inside.

They were immediately greeted by squeals and shouts from Jason's sister and brother.

Jason's face lit up. "Hey, hey." He grabbed the two siblings in a hug, then turned behind him and waved Anita over. "This here is Patrice and Mason. This is Anita."

"Hey!" they chorused.

"Hi. Nice to meet you. Jason talks about you both all the time."

"Lies, all lies," Patrice teased. "Except the good stuff!"

"You wish," Jason retorted, then turned his attention to his brother. "You look like you done grown a whole foot since I seen you last."

Mason laughed. "Coach says I'll be a starter next season. Might get a full ride for college."

Jason clasped his brother's hand in a tight grip and brought it to his chest. "Proud of you, little bro." He ruffled his hair, much to Mason's delighted embarrassment.

"Hope you have a big appetite," Mae Ellen said to Anita. "You a little bitty thing, with all that hair."

Anita felt her cheeks heat. Instinctively she patted her fro. "I can work my way around a dinner table," she said, hoping her tone remained lighter than she felt.

"Well, we gonna sit down to eat in about a half hour. Patrice will show you where to put your things. Then you come on and get some refreshment before supper."

"Yes, ma'am," Anita whispered, the word feeling foreign on her tongue but appropriate for the setting.

She wondered if she'd ever get this right. But for Jason, it was worth it.

"Jason, you can start taking out the good china. Your sister was supposed to set the table, but she was too busy worryin' 'bout when you were gonna get here," she said, the chords of happiness playing in her voice.

After making sure Anita was settled, Jason followed his mother into the kitchen.

"She seems nice," his mother murmured while she stirred the pitcher of sweet tea. She looked at Jason from beneath her lashes.

"She is nice, Mama."

Mom wiped her hands on her apron and checked the fresh string beans simmering in seasonings and smoked turkey neck. The macaroni and cheese was done. The ham, adorned with pineapple and maraschino cherries, was cooked and ready to be sliced. Dad would do the honors of cutting up the turkey, a tradition that would not be altered save for an act of God.

There were other things that Jason knew were ingrained into the DNA of the Tanner family: God first in all things, family before friends, honesty, and hard work. His parents knew all those ideals to be true. Their faith in God had seen them through more storms than Jason could ever imagine: barely escaping the wrath of the Klan; working the land for next to no money; turned down for jobs simply because they were Black; kept out of schools, stores, theaters, and neighborhoods—Jim Crow's foot constantly on their necks. But together and by faith, they'd endured, rose to the surface of the water, and the tide of perseverance brought them to shore.

Those life lessons of never letting go of faith, standing up for what is right, putting in an honest day's work were the examples they set for their children. Tradition carried the legacy from one generation to the next. From something as symbolic as a wedding gown from mother to daughter to a father teaching his son how to change a tire and from sharing the secret ingredients to the perfect peach cobbler to the prayers of thanks over every meal—they were all part and parcel of the Tanner family legacy.

All this was what Jason saw flash across his mother's face as she checked the good glasses for smudges. They had a tradition of *just* family for the holiday meal. Family before friends.

He swallowed hard. It could be a long night.

. . .

In response to Mae Ellen's summons that dinner was ready, Anita followed Patrice out of the bedroom that they would share. At least for a while, she'd kept her fears about Jason's parents at bay while she entertained Patrice with life in New York.

"You ever been to the Apollo?" Patrice had asked.

"Sure. Quite a few times. It's walking distance from my apartment."

Patrice's eyes widened. "You have your own apartment?"

"Yeah. My folks weren't too thrilled about it at first, but they got used to it."

Patrice looked awestruck. "My folks would have a natural fit. They want me to be married when I leave the house unless I'm going away to college."

Anita reserved her comments, believing that was such a handicap for a woman—to live with her parents, then get married and live with a man. When would she ever have space for herself? First, someone's daughter. Next, someone's wife. "I'm sure they only want what's best for you," she'd said instead.

When they entered the dining room, the long table that easily sat eight was covered with a winter-white lace tablecloth topped from one end to the next with bowls and platters of food. Anita experienced a sweep of melancholy so sharp and sudden that her eyes watered, knowing that her parents' table would look much the same but her seat would be empty. She blinked the image away. She was glad to be here with Jason, really.

Jason held out a seat for her between him and his brother. Patrice sat next to her mother, and Ralph presided over the head of the table.

"Let's join hands and bow our heads," Ralph said. "Jason, you give the blessing."

Jason subtly lifted his head. His eyes darted toward his father, whose head was bowed and waiting. He cleared his throat. "Heavenly Father," he began.

When he was finished, they all said "Amen," in unison.

Jason looked to his father, and a halo of pride sparked in Ralph's eyes.

"Let's eat!" Mason announced.

There was a flurry of "pass this" and "pass that," followed by the clicking of forks and knives against plates and warnings about manners from Mae Ellen. Ralph made a ceremonial showing of carving up the turkey, and Mae Ellen glowed with pride from the compliments about her cooking.

"Do y'all eat like this at your people's house?" Mae Ellen asked Anita.

"We sure do." She scanned the table. "The only thing my mom always has is collard greens." She chuckled. "She has to have her collards."

"There's a reason why we don't serve collards," Mae Ellen said. She slid a glance at Ralph.

Ralph shuffled in his seat. "Pass the potatoes," he said.

"Daddy, you should tell Anita what happened. My dad was a real hotshot in his day," Patrice said.

"Mm-hmm, Jason gets it honest," Mason added.

All eyes turned to Ralph. He slowly chewed on a slice of ham. Then he wiped his mouth with the embroidered linen napkin and cleared his throat. He sat back in his seat.

"Might as well," Mae Ellen coaxed.

"Well…it all started when I was about twelve and my daddy found out from Mr. Jackson up the road that me and a bunch of my friends ran through his collards and trampled them. It was Mike's idea. Mike never did like Mr. Jackson." He pursed his lips and slowly shook his head with the memory.

"So anyhow, I knew something was wrong the minute I hit the door. My daddy was sittin' at the kitchen table, Mama at the sink. Daddy was never home in the middle of the day. He was a hard worker. He always told me that's what a real man did. Didn't matter what kind of job a man had, long as it was honest and you did it with dignity and dressed like you respected yourself even if nobody else did."

He paused and took a long swallow of sweet tea. The sound of forks and knives clicking against plates had ceased.

Anita stopped chewing and slowly lowered her fork.

"Every morning, my daddy would put on a crisp white shirt. I'd sit in the kitchen chair and watch my mother use that heavy iron that she heated on the stove, and she'd press creases so sharp in Daddy's sleeves and collar that they could cut glass.

"Daddy would wear his white shirt and brown slacks with a kind of pride that made me stand up straight and stick out my chest when I watched him walk out the door, down the dirt path, and up the road to his job."

His gaze drifted off for a moment. The room held its collective breath.

Ralph's jaw clenched. "Daddy was a school janitor. He was about the only colored person in the school. Negroes weren't allowed to attend, not back then, but Daddy walked the halls same as the white folk every day.

"That's why I knew I was in trouble, 'cause nothing could pull my daddy away from what he did every day to take care of his family—except trouble. Humph. He still had on his starched white shirt and his brown slacks. Mama turned from the sink when she heard me come in, and I didn't know whose face shook me up the most—the hurt look in my mama's eyes or the disappointment in my daddy's.

"Lawd, my heart was beatin' so fast, I knew they could hear it. Daddy said how disappointed he was in me, that doing what I did to Mr. Jackson was not how I was raised. He said Negroes was struggling every day to get respect and to be respected, so how could I disrespect someone else by destroying what was important to them? How could I disrespect the family's good name? That's not what a man is. That is a coward."

Ralph took a long breath. His voice dropped an octave. "Negroes still disappeared in Mississippi in the 1920s. Taken out of their houses, out of school, out of church, out of the woods, and never seen again. Until they found them in a creek or hanging from a tree or behind the trash or not at all. Daddy didn't want them to come for us. For him.

"Daddy put on his hat and Mama got her purse and her white gloves that she always wore to church. The mile walk to Mr. Jackson's house under the beat of the Mississippi sun in August seemed to take longer than forever. I remember not being able to breathe too good. Not because of the heat but the fear that was squeezing the air right out of me until I was panting just like my dog Buster.

"Mr. Jackson's house all of sudden appeared, and we were walking up the three raggedy steps to his front door. I remember thinking how raggedy his house was for a white man and how bright and fixed up our house was. Daddy knocked. Mama twisted the straps of her purse. They both stood tall and straight. I had to pee. The door pulled open and let out an old smell, and Mr. Jackson stood there. His face was pink and full of a bunch of hard wrinkles, like someone had squeezed his face in their hand until they couldn't squeeze no more. His hair was off white, like it would be white if it was clean. His suspenders were black over a dingy white shirt. Daddy was taller and bigger than him, but when Mr. Jackson looked at us with his hard, watery blue eyes, he made us feel small. Made Daddy look down at his feet and Mama down at hers.

"Daddy told Mr. Jackson that I had come to apologize for what I'd done. I said how sorry I was. Really sorry and would never do it again. Ever."

Ralph's eyes grew dark. His expression hardened. "Mr. Jackson hitched up his pants and spit right on that raggedy step. Right at the tip of Daddy's work shoes. His eyes just about disappeared when he looked at us, said that was the problem with niggah parents, they didn't know how to raise no kids. Raised 'em like wild animals. He turned his pink face at Mama. That was why they shouldn't have 'em, he'd said. Mama squeezed my hand. Mr. Jackson turned back to Daddy. He hooked his fingers around his black suspenders, told Daddy he would forget all about it on the condition that he come by his house every day after cleaning the toilets and the floors and the windows up at the school and replant his garden and run some errands and such.

"I saw Mama look at Daddy. My eyes jumped back and forth between the two of them. Daddy's back wasn't so straight. 'Yessir,' Daddy said in a voice I barely recognized. Was this the same Daddy who had come home injured from the war but proud in his uniform? 'It's kind of you, sir,' he'd said. 'I 'spec to see you here first thing after work tomorrow, *boy*,' Mr. Jackson told Daddy before he slammed the door.

"We could hear him laughing as we walked down those raggedy steps. We walked back home. Daddy was on one side, Mama on the other, and I was in the middle. No one spoke a word, but I caught Mama and Daddy talking to each other with their eyes.

"They never spoke a word about that day. It wasn't as if they acted like it didn't happen. It did. It changed everything. Especially Daddy. Instead of him setting at the table with us at supper, most nights he didn't get home until I was in bed and half-asleep. I'd try to stay up so I could hear him come in. Hear him drop his work shoes at the back door and Mama whispering to him while she fixed his plate. Then I could sleep, comforted in knowing that they wasn't gonna come for us. Daddy fixed it.

"Daddy worked for Mr. Jackson for almost three years. No way it took that long to replant some collards and run errands. Mr. Jackson just got pleasure out of it, that's all. Then one day they heard that Mr. Jackson got run over by his own tractor. Fell off when he was tilling the collard field and the darn thing kept rolling right over him. Ain't that something? That was the end of Daddy working for Mr. Jackson." He chuckled.

"Well, things went back to the way they were. Daddy was home for dinner every night. He still made me help him fix things around the house and clean up after Buster. But ever since then, I never had much taste for collards.

"That's what I was thinking when I was grown, courting Mae Ellen and looking up at her house right in front of me. A brick house on Red Creek Lane. I stood there for a minute, thinking about collard greens and white shirts, when the door got pulled open, and it was Mr. Jackson but it wasn't. It was Mr. Woods, and he asked me whether I was planning on coming in or did I expect Mrs. Woods to bring my plate to me on the steps. He was like that. He would ask questions that made you do what you set out to do in the first place. After dinner I finally got the nerve to ask for her hand." He looked across the table at Mae Ellen.

"Funny that asking to marry Mae Ellen reminded me how scared I'd been all those years earlier on Mr. Jackson's steps. But I ain't had a mouthful of collards ever since." He slapped his palm on the table to punctuate the end of his tale.

Everyone released the breath they'd held, the magic of

storytelling finally letting them loose.

"Collards might scare you, but nothing scared me more than you following in your daddy's footsteps and going off to war." Mae Ellen pressed her hand to her heart. "Lawd."

Ralph reached out and squeezed her free hand. "Man gotta do his duty for his family and his country."

Mae Ellen offered him the light in her eyes. Anita sent a soft smile out to Jason.

In this, they were the same. They were both born of the deep seeds of struggle that ran through their veins. Birthed through the resilience of their parents and grand- and great-grandparents.

It was only fitting that they continued to wage war against all who would try to silence their story.

After dinner, Anita insisted on helping clean up the dining room and the dishes. Much like her own mother, the kitchen and the dining room were Mae Ellen's domains, and she didn't particularly want anyone fiddling around unless they were invited.

"I wouldn't feel right if I didn't help. It's the least I can do after that wonderful meal," Anita said to Mae Ellen. "And for welcoming me into your home."

"Well," Mae Ellen said on a breath, "I suppose you can dry while I wash."

"Not a problem."

Mae Ellen handed her a towel. "Just set them on the table when you dry. I'll get Patrice to put them away."

"Yes, ma'am." The word was getting easier to say.

"So, your folks didn't miss you for the holidays?"

"Yes. But they understood."

"They met Jason?"

Anita smiled. "Yes. I took him with me to Brooklyn one Sunday."

"Oh, so you don't live with your folks."

"No, I have an apartment in Harlem. My parents live in Brooklyn—in the same house I grew up in."

"Hmmm," she murmured. "So what kind of work do you do to take care of yourself?"

"I'm a waitress."

"Oh." She washed and rinsed and washed a plate then rinsed it again. "Is that enough to live on in New York?"

"It's difficult sometimes, but I manage."

"Mm-hmm." She rinsed a glass. "What's your home church up there? Jason told me he really likes Abyssinian. Is that where you go?"

"I don't...actually go to church."

A plate slipped from Mae Ellen's hand back into the sudsy water with a splash. "You don't *actually* go to church. What do you mean, chile?"

She'd really stepped in it this time. Clearly this was a churchgoing woman—just like Anita's mother. Mom had grown used to her blasphemous attitude about church and simply put in extra prayers for her "lost child." Anita wanted Jason's mother to like her, to accept her, but she didn't want to lie in the process.

"Well, to be honest, Mrs. Tanner, I went to Catholic school for twelve years. All through elementary and four years of high school. Church every single solitary Sunday. The nuns would take attendance, and if you were absent, you had to stay after school and write one hundred times, 'I will attend nine o'clock mass.'" She gave a little shiver. "But I guess one of the things that began to really turn me off was when I was in the fourth grade. They used to let us outside for lunch. It was winter, and the streets were still slick with ice. I was walking with my friends, and I slipped on the ice." Her eyes narrowed. "I heard my thigh bone when it broke."

"Oh my."

"One of the older boys picked me up and carried me into the school auditorium. The nuns"—she shook her head slowly—"I guess they didn't believe me or really believed that some *power* was going to come down and magically fix me, so they told me to walk the length of the auditorium, which to a fourth grader felt and looked like a football field, and to say Hail Marys and I would be all right." She swallowed. The muscle memory thumped in her thigh.

"Oh, chile. I can't imagine…"

"By the time they finally called my mom to come and get me, my thigh was bigger than me. Was in the hospital in traction for weeks before I could leave and spent the rest of the school year at home." She shrugged. "That part wasn't too bad," she said with a half grin. "Got a tutor."

Mae Ellen handed her a dish.

"And when my grandma got ill—she'd been a devout parishioner of Our Lady of Victory, paid her tithes—and couldn't attend service, the priest wouldn't even come to see her." She blinked back her still-simmering fury. "Between those two things, I pretty much lost my faith in church."

Mae Ellen pressed her hand on Anita's shoulder. "The church is only a place; faith is bigger than that. Don't lose your faith, chile. 'Cause when all else fails, faith in something greater than ourselves is all we got. 'Faith is confidence in what we hope for and assurance about what we do not see.' Hebrews 11:1."

Anita felt herself pulled in by the commanding power of Mae Ellen's soft-brown eyes, the same mesmerizing eyes that Jason possessed. Something inside her shifted, shook her, then settled.

The warmth of Mae Ellen's hand on her shoulder remained long after it was lifted.

J ason was feeling really good about the trip home. Thankfully, his and Anita's battling ideologies hadn't come up in conversation. Minus some minor glitches, Anita seemed to fit right in, laughing and joking with his siblings and finding an easy passage with his parents, and she'd definitely charmed his father when they found common ground discussing the history of jazz and blues. If he'd had any doubts about Anita fitting in with his family, they were evaporating. Maybe this "thing" they had really would work.

They'd planned to head back to New York on Saturday, but he'd made arrangements to meet the committee members at Paschal's for the Friday-afternoon gathering, and he wanted Anita to come with him. John had mentioned that Dr. King was in town and would stop in before he left Atlanta, as he was eager to hear of the progress in New York. Maybe if Anita saw the faces and heard the conviction in the voices of the members, she would have a change of heart, or at the very least be more open to acceptance.

I 've heard about this restaurant," Anita said as she slipped on a sweater and stepped out onto the porch with Jason. "It's more than a restaurant, really."

She hooked her arm through his and drew him into her space, as she was accustomed to doing.

"How's that?"

"Well, it's owned by two brothers, James and Robert Paschal. Story goes that they loved cooking so much and their customers started growing so fast that their home kitchen got too small. So they invested their money and went from a home business to a ninety-seat coffee shop dining area. Humph, you ain't had real fried chicken till you wrapped those luscious lips around their signature fried chicken or their 'slap yo mama good' peach cobbler."

"Now you got me all hungry," she said over her laughter.

He laughed along with her. "I'm tellin' you it's true. But besides being restaurateurs, the brothers are diehard supporters of the movement. Sometimes they post bond for jailed protesters, serve complimentary meals, and extend their hours of operation to accommodate families who need to reconnect with their loved ones released from jail." He turned to look at Anita, lowered his voice almost reverently. "Most important, the restaurant is a gathering spot for Dr. King and the supporters of his nonviolent resistance movement. A whole lotta planning happens at those tables."

"Hmm," she murmured softly. "Sounds larger than life."

"I just got a feelin' that when these days are looked back on in the history books, they gon' talk about Paschal's and all the people who came through there."

They crossed to the next street and turned left onto Hunter, passing rows of neat homes with garnet lawns and peach trees, barbershops, and mom-and-pop diners, serving up everything from bacon and eggs to fried fish and barbecue. She was miles away from home yet home at the same time. The comfort in the voices, the rich laughter, and faces that looked so much like her own, the familiar. There was a singular vibrating thread that knitted them all together across cities, countries, oceans, time. Family—not by blood but bound by a shared history. A surge of pride flowed through her, lifted her chin, lit her eyes, and curved her mouth.

"It's right across the street," Jason said, pointing to the restaurant. He took her hand.

The early lunch-goers had lingered, and the late arrivals were filing in. Paschal's boasted a ninety-seat counter in addition to its main dining room that could easily host more than one hundred. All but a few seats were left at the lunch counter.

Robert, one of the owners, spotted Jason and signaled to him that the setup was in the back. "They're just getting started."

"Thanks! That's Robert, one of the owners," he said to Anita.

They walked to the back of the restaurant to a section that was set off from the rest with a fifteen-seat table, which was already half full with members from the movement, plates of food, and pitchers of sweet tea.

"Hey!" John wiped his mouth and rose to his feet upon seeing Jason. "Welcome home."

A round of heartfelt greetings, back slaps, and handshakes from the assembled group not only reminded Jason of how much he missed home but also reinforced his commitment to the cause.

"And who is this young lady?" Andy asked.

"Everyone, this is Anita Hopkins. She's visiting here with me. Lives in New York."

"Welcome, Ms. Hopkins. Please have a seat," John said. "Hope you're hungry."

"Thank you. I am."

The men introduced themselves. Bayard Rustin, Andrew Young, John Lewis, Fred Shuttlesworth, Whitney Young, and Roy Wilkins all offered effusive welcomes, and Anita was a bit overwhelmed by the concentrated power in one space. She'd seen their faces on the television and read about most of them in the newspapers following a protest, sit-in, or a march. They, like Malcolm, were real flesh-and-blood people, determined to make a difference the best way they knew how.

Jason helped Anita into a seat and sat next to her. "Order whatever you want," he said and handed her a menu.

"So bring us up to speed, young brother. How are things going in New York?" Bayard asked.

Before Jason had a chance to respond, they all turned toward the shift in energy at the entrance. Dr. King had just arrived with Jesse at his side and was causing a bit of a stir with customers who wanted a word or to shake his hand.

As was his way, King took his time and spoke to each and every one and shook every hand that was extended.

Anita watched the scene unfold as if in slow motion. She could not put words to what she was feeling and experiencing. All she was sure of was that a presence was in the room, an aura that radiated outward to everyone in its path. Whether or not their ideologies matched, she felt his magnetism in every fiber of her being.

Her throat clenched and her pulse raced. Her entire body warmed even under the whirr of the overhead fans.

Several of the men stood when Dr. King finally reached their table.

"Martin," Bayard greeted. "It's about time!" He chuckled and gave him a tight hug.

"There's work to do everywhere," King intoned and flashed his often-photographed smile. He shook the hands of his group, the centerpieces of the movement.

He stopped with Jason, smiled broadly, and clasped Jason's shoulders. "Welcome home. I've been hearing good things about your work."

"Yes, sir. Things are going very well." He quickly turned toward Anita. "I want to introduce you to Anita Hopkins."

Anita felt a bit weak in the knees, but she managed to stand. "Dr. King. It's an honor to meet you."

He gave a short nod. "Martin. We're all friends here." He patted her shoulder, then moved to his seat at the head of the table.

Before long, the members were deep into discussions about the progress of the movement and plans for a major march to Selma. It was agreed that it would take a massive amount of planning, perhaps a year—if not more—if they wanted to ensure its success. Voting rights were at the top of the agenda, and now that President Kennedy had been murdered and Johnson was in office, they would have to intensify their proposals for civil and voting rights legislation.

Jason had his opportunity to talk about the progress he was making in New York with the recruitment of young men and the nonviolent resistance training sessions that were drawing more people from the community, along with the tutoring program.

Dr. King assured Jason that he would continue to receive whatever funding the committee could afford to make sure that his initiative continued.

John turned to Anita. "Are you helping out with Jason at the New York office?"

Anita swallowed, shot Jason a quick look. "I, uh, no. I don't work there. I actually work with Brother Malcolm."

Even though she only spoke to John, conversation around the table slowed, and many eyes turned toward her.

"You work with Brother Malcolm?" Dr. King asked, his preacher tone in full effect, and now every eye in the place was on her.

She swallowed, looked him square in the face, trying for bravado. "Yes. I do. I've been working with his cause for almost two years now."

"I see," Dr. King intoned. "Well, we are all entitled to our beliefs," he said, in the slow purposeful way of his, "and our purpose in this world. I may not agree with the methods of Brother Malcolm, but I respect his passion for the cause that we both serve."

Anita pressed her lips into a tight smile of gratitude, feeling as if she'd been somehow anointed, and with the tacit acceptance from their leader, conversation quickly returned to the issues at hand.

She watched and listened in respectful silence, understanding that no matter her choices going forward, she was, at that moment, in the center of an unstoppable tide of change.

"Thank you so much for having me," Anita said to Ralph and Mae Ellen as she and Jason walked to the door. "I had a wonderful time."

"You're always welcome to come back," Ralph said. "I'll make sure I have some more music we can listen to."

"You mean argue about," Mae Ellen playfully chided.

Anita smiled. "I'm going to hold you to that, Mr. Tanner."

Mae Ellen stepped forward and lightly kissed her cheek. "Don't forget what I said, chile," she whispered in her ear. "Faith." She stepped back. "You keep an eye on my son," she added, her eyes suddenly clouding with tears as she wrapped Jason in her arms. "You take care of yourself, you hear me?" She kissed both his cheeks, then sniffed hard.

"Of course. Don't worry." He turned to his father. "Dad."

Ralph embraced him. "Proud of you, son." He held him tight against his chest.

"So what are we, chopped liver?" Patrice teased, her eyes sparkling with unshed tears.

Jason chuckled. "Kinda." He wrapped her in a hug and kissed her cheek before bear hugging his brother. "You look out for them," he said in his brother's ear.

"I will."

Jason and Anita piled into the sea-green-and-white "the Brothers Johnson" taxicab and waved and waved until the Tanner family was out of sight.

Jason fared much better on the return trip and actually looked out the window, made comments on the flight, and seemed to forget about his death grip on the armrest. Anita, on the other hand, was much more reserved, her spirit sobered by her trip to Atlanta. Meeting the members who Jason worked with and for had begun to test her own ideologies. Having Dr. King reconfirm that no matter the approach, the goal was the same, led her to feel that the self-made wall she'd constructed between her and Jason was minor in the bigger picture.

She rested her head on his shoulder and closed her eyes. All the excuses she'd conjured to keep just enough distance between her heart and Jason's were no more than emotional morning mist—dissipating under the warmth of his love.

"I love you," he whispered into her hair, as if instinctively knowing those were the words she needed to hear.

She lifted her head and kissed him. "I love you, too, Jason Tanner." And once the words slipped from her lips, she felt her spirit soar free.

"I probably should head on over to my place," Jason said once Anita had put down her suitcase. "Let you get settled." He stood in the doorway. "Thank you for coming with me. It meant a lot."

Anita dragged in a breath, batted around all the things that could go wrong against all the things that could go right.

She shoved her hands into the back pockets of her dungarees, looked down at her Converse sneakers and then into his eyes. Her heart skittered in her chest. "Um, why don't you stay here?"

He frowned. "For tonight?"

"For...every night."

Surprise widened his eyes and he took a step across the threshold. "What are you saying?"

She swallowed. "I'm saying that you live in that little room and...we spend most evenings and weekends here anyway and...well, I think it might be nice. Me and you." She lifted and raised her right shoulder. "I mean, if *you* think it's cool."

Jason rested his suitcase on the floor but didn't come a step farther, as if doing so would commit him to a circumstance he was not quite prepared to engage in. At least, he didn't think so. But maybe he was. When his head wasn't buried in the details of his mission, it was Anita who was on his mind.

She filled all his spaces, challenged him at every opportunity, yet for whatever differences they might have, from where and how they grew up to which side of the movement they were on, he couldn't see himself with anyone besides her. But living with someone and not being married tugged against the last threads of his moral fiber. Plenty of couples were doing it these days, but if he was going to commit, he wanted to commit fully, and he knew he wasn't ready for marriage. Not yet.

She held up her hand. "You don't have to say it—I can read your thoughts. They're splashed all over your face. It's cool, though. Really."

"Nita…"

"No, really. It's cool. Just an idea. No big deal," she said, and it looked as if she were forcing a wobbly smile. "Hey, I'm really beat. Gonna take a shower and probably turn in early."

He studied her for a moment, wanted to reel back in the thoughts that he'd blindly cast out only for Anita to catch. He cleared his throat. "Uh, yeah. I'm kinda tired, too. Call you tomorrow?"

"Sure."

He reached down and picked up his suitcase. Anita walked to the door, put her hand on the knob. Waited.

Jason leaned in to kiss her and caught her cheek instead. He straightened. "Good night. Rest well."

"You too." She pushed the door closed with a *thud*.

Chapter Fifteen

"Why buy the cow when you can get the milk for free?" Liza quipped. "I'm not sayin' you're a cow—"

"Very damn funny." Anita rolled her eyes and brought the glass of rum and Coke to her lips. It was the first time she and Liza had gotten together since her return from Atlanta and Liza's business trip to Chicago. "I don't know what I was thinking."

"You were thinking you wanted to be with your man."

"Well, clearly he doesn't feel the same way."

"Have you even talked to him about it, asked him why not?"

"Haven't spoken to him since we got back from Atlanta."

"Nita! That was almost two weeks ago!"

Liza was right. She usually was. Between the two of them, it was Liza who was levelheaded and practical, and Anita was the one always ready to jump off the proverbial cliff. She studied the brown liquid and floating ice in her glass. Since she was off for the evening, she didn't want to stay in her apartment or hang out at her place of employment, so they decided to try the Lenox Lounge and lucked out on coming on a night with a live band.

Plus, she didn't want to run the risk of Jason turning up at

B-Flat in the hopes of seeing her. He'd left several messages on her answering machine asking to stop by, asking her to stop by his office, asking that she call the pay phone at the rooming house. She'd ignored all of them.

At least, she'd tried to.

"I don't need scolding. I'm just not ready to talk to him."

"You ladies want to order?" A waitress had stopped at their table.

"How about sharing a plate of wings?" Liza asked.

"Sure. And could you add some fries and coleslaw?"

"And two rum and Cokes," Liza added.

"No problem. Coming right up." She collected the menus and walked away.

"You need to talk to him, Nita—tell him how you feel. He may have a real good reason why he doesn't want to live with you. Could be a man thing. But you'll never know if you keep avoiding him."

The waitress retuned with their drinks and set them in the table.

"Thanks," Anita murmured absently. "Telling him how I feel is why I'm in this mess!" She took a long swallow of her drink, then blew out a sigh. "I knew I should have kept it casual."

"He loves you, Nita."

"Yeah, right."

Liza leaned in. "You don't believe him?"

Anita glanced away. "I don't know," she mumbled.

"Girl. Put on your big girl pants and talk to him. Lay it on the table one way or the other."

Their food arrived.

"Tried that…and here we are." She snatched a wing from the platter and tore off a piece, grinding the meat into a memory between her teeth.

...

J ason stared off at nothing in particular, perhaps in the hope that something would catch his eye and lift his spirit. His gaze finally landed on the calendar on his desk. It had been exactly two weeks since he'd seen or spoken to Anita. He'd actually prayed on it, prayed to get a sign as to what to do. He'd lost count of the nickels and dimes he'd dropped into the pay phone and the number of messages he'd left. If she would only give him a chance to explain his reasoning, he could get her to understand.

Humph. But knowing Anita, she would find some chink in his rationale that would have him second-guessing his own beliefs. That was Anita, filled with fire and brimstone and ready for the good fight.

It was why he loved her.

"Hey, man."

Jason blinked the room into focus, and Ronald was standing in front of his desk.

"You cool?"

Jason straightened in his chair, adjusted his tie, and forced a tepid smile. "Yeah. I'm fine."

"I ain't tryin' to get in your business or nothin', but you ain't seem like yourself lately." He half shrugged. "Everything cool with the organization?"

"Yes. Everything is fine, really. Like I said when I got back from Atlanta, we have the full support of the movement."

"Mind if I sit?"

An instant of concern knitted his brow when he saw the serious expression on Ronald's face. "Uh, sure. Pull up a chair."

Ronald dragged the aluminum chair close to the side of Jason's metal desk. He linked his long, dark fingers together and rested his arms on his thighs. "Look, man, I know we don't hang out. And you ain't gotta tell me nothin' but... Look, when I rolled up in here a few months ago, you coulda did what most people do when they see a dude like me—call the pigs or get aggressive. You didn't do none a' that. You mighta wanted to," he added with a knowing grin. "That meant something to me. Still does. You gave me an ear and a chance. And I'm feeling good about myself. Real good. I'm doing shit—sorry, doing stuff I'm proud of, for me and for my community." He ran his tongue across his lip. "So what I'm saying is maybe I can be a friend if you need to talk. And from the looks of things, if it ain't this place," he said with a wave of his hand around the room, "then it gotta be a woman. That's the only thing to put that kinda look on a man's face."

Jason huffed a chuckle. "Is that right?"

"For real," he said with conviction. "I can definitely testify to that," he said with a laugh.

"Yeah, women can be something..." he hedged. He snatched a glance at Ronald. "Can't read 'em sometime."

"True. True." He paused a beat. "Your lady is the one who stops by from time to time. Right?"

Jason swallowed down the excuse that tried to slip by his tongue. "She is...or was. Not really sure, to be honest." He studied the pencil on his desk.

"She's a real fox. No disrespect," Ronald quickly added. "Probably only need to take her to dinner, buy her some flowers, and beg forgiveness," he said around light laughter. "Works for me every time."

"I would if she'd answer my calls," he blurted out in frustration. And once the dam was broken, the river flowed.

"You really dig her, huh?" Ronald quietly asked when Jason's confession ended.

"Yeah."

"Look, you gotta suck up your pride, man, and go see her. I wouldn't try her spot, though, but to the club. You said she works at B-Flat."

"Yeah."

"At least if she blows you off, no one'll notice."

They both chuckled at the truth in that.

Jason pushed out a breath. "Hmm, I don't know—"

"I'll go with you. Two dudes hanging out."

"Yeah?"

"Sure. I ain't been to B-Flat in a minute. You know what nights she works?"

"Tonight for sure. She always works on Fridays."

"Cool. So we go tonight."

Jason ran the scenario over in his head. Things couldn't be worse than they already were between him and Anita. And it would be a lot harder for her to ignore him in person.

"Okay," he finally agreed. "Say nine?"

Ronald pushed to his feet. "Meet you out front."

Jason nodded. "Gimme five."

They slapped palms, and Ronald swaggered away.

Jason leaned back in his seat. In a million years, he would have never thought the sign he'd asked for would be Ronald.

Chapter Sixteen

Jason's father's story of white shirts and collard greens ran through his head as he walked down Lenox to B-Flat, which could have just as easily been Mr. Jackson's house back in Mississippi. He was straight-up scared. This was his last-ditch effort to explain and get them back to where they were.

If she turned him away again…

He stepped around a couple too hugged up to notice him. That was what he was afraid of—that she would shut the door for good. He drew his shoulders to his ears to ward off the whip of icy December wind.

Jason spotted Ronald out front, leaning on the hood of a white Cadillac, and he wondered for a minute if it was Ronald's ride and if so, where did a young kid with no real job to speak of get the money to pay for it? He wasn't going to entertain the idea.

"Hey, man," he greeted Ronald.

They slapped palms, then gripped.

Okay, he had to ask. "This your ride?"

Ronald glanced behind him to the Caddy, tossed his head back, and laughed from deep in his gut. "Naw, man. Wish it was." He leaned in, lowered his voice. "It's a prop. Women see me chillin' on a Caddy…" He shrugged his shoulder and winked. "Might get lucky."

"And when they find out it's not yours?"

"By that time, my charm woulda kicked in."

Jason snorted a laugh, shook his head in amusement, and pulled open the club door.

A blast of warm air mingled with Friday-night perfumes, colognes, and the thump of the bass playing in time to conversation and laughter that beckoned them inside.

Jason shrugged out of his overcoat and draped it on his arm.

Ronald gave him a quick once over. "You here to hang at the club or a business meeting, my man?"

Perplexed, Jason looked down at his three-piece cedar-brown suit, brown-and-beige-striped tie, and brown spit-shined Stacy Adams shoes. "What's wrong with what I got on?"

"Lose the tie *and* the vest. Unbutton that top button. Try to look like you're here to relax and have a good time, not write insurance policies."

Jason huffed, started to argue, but realized Ronald was probably right. When he looked around at the club-goers, he was definitely overdressed again. Even the fellas who had on suits, they were only two-piece and were a lot more stylish than his. He loosened his tie, took it off, and shoved it into the pocket to his coat. So much for trying to impress Anita tonight.

He walked two steps behind Ronald as they made their way around the tightly packed tables to the bar.

"You see her?" Ronald shouted over the din while sliding onto an empty stool.

Jason tried to act casual. "No. Not yet." He lifted a hand to get the bartender's attention. "Beer," he called out. "What do you want? First one's on me."

"Beer is cool."

"Make that two!" He eased in next to Ronald.

"You know what you want to say when you see her?"

"Not really. I'm hoping a miracle of words happens."

The bartender plopped a bottle of beer and a glass in front of each of them.

"Buck fifty for both," the bartender said. He slapped a white towel over his shoulder.

Jason dug in his jacket pocket, took out his billfold, and handed over a five. "Hey, you know if Anita is working tonight?"

The bartender, for the first time, actually focused on Jason. He braced large hands with thick knuckles—the kind of knuckles that connected with hard objects—on the bar top. His dark face pressed forward. "Who wants to know?"

"A friend. Jason."

He studied Jason for a moment. "If you were a real friend, you'd know all that." He wiped the counter in front of Jason.

"I haven't spoken to her in a couple of weeks. Okay? Is she around or isn't she?"

The bartender chuckled. "Right over there, my man." He lifted his chin toward the far side of the club. Anita was coming out from behind the swinging door, carrying a tray on her palm.

Ronald nudged Jason in the side. "Watchchu gonna do?" he asked over the neck of his beer bottle.

"Figure what tables she's working and get a seat in her section."

They slapped palms.

Seeing her again was a punch to the gut. He knew he missed her, but actually seeing her face reinforced just how empty he'd been with her gone from his day-to-day. His work was important. Seeing the progress that was being made with the organization and the support from the community was great. But at the end of the day, he went home to an empty room, and even surrounded by the business of daily living, he felt alone without her.

Here goes nothing.

Anita took an order from a table of four, looked quickly around at her section of eight tables, and knew that it was going to be a hectic evening. A full house had its ups and downs. On the one hand, she worked until her feet ached—on the other, the tips were great, and she loved performing in front of a packed room.

And then—she felt him before she saw him. It was that same shivery tingle that made her heart race and her body overheat. Jason was here, and there was nothing she could do about it—and honestly? She didn't want to.

She inched over to her customers' table and placed their orders in front of them. The shiver grew more intense.

When she straightened, the group that had blocked her line of sight across the room had found seats, and Jason was right in front of her. Her heart actually sang, and that dark spot in the center of her chest made way for the light.

He was coming toward her. She should hightail it away, but she couldn't get her feet to move. He crossed between the tables and chairs with panther-like grace until the only thing that separated them was excuses.

"Hi." He fixed his gaze on her face.

Anita rested her weight on her right leg, tucked the empty tray under her arm. "Hey," she said, feeling as if the word was a strain. "What are you doing here?"

"Heard the wings were excellent and the service even better."

She pursed her lips. "You got a table?" she asked, knowing that her question sounded more like an accusation than an inquiry. But she couldn't help it. Whenever she was rattled, her defenses went into high gear. And she was totally rattled.

"No." He flicked his head. "Came with Ronald. We were hanging out at the bar until we got a table."

She propped her hand on her hip. "We're really busy, but I'll see if I can get you one. You might have to wait a while."

"That's fine. I'm willing to wait for as long as it takes."

She couldn't breathe, not when he looked at her like he knew her secrets. She jutted her chin. "I gotta get back to work." She whirled around, then right into the table behind her. She mumbled apologies and hurried off.

"Damn, girl. What is wrong with you?" Liza asked when Anita stopped at her table in the front of the club. "You're either mad as hell or scared shitless." She lifted her glass of rum and Coke to her lips and waited.

"Jason is here," she hissed, as if passing government secrets.

"Where?"

"He's sitting at the bar with that guy from his office."

Liza lifted her butt up out of the chair, high enough to see over heads to the bar. "Humph, looking good, too. Friend's not a slouch either."

"Liza!"

"What? What did I say that's a lie? You've been silently moaning for two whole weeks over that man. Now that he's here, you're acting like a twelve-year-old."

Anita rolled her eyes so hard, she thought her grandmother's warning that they would stick to the back of her head might come true. *Dammit. Maybe I am acting like a twelve-year-old.*

"Clearly you have lost your mojo." Liza pushed her chair back away from the table and got up. "I'll take it from here." She sashayed across the congested space in her body-hugging leopard print minidress, drawing the appreciative stares of more than a few men, all of whom she ignored.

Anita watched as Liza made her way up to Jason. She had no idea what her friend was going to say, but suddenly, it all felt like too much. She ducked into the employee restroom. This was unbelievable.

Anita turned on the faucets and splashed cold water on her face. She looked up at her reflection. *You know you're happy to see him. You know you've missed the heck out of him. Stop trying to act like you don't give a damn. Listen to what he has to say. Be nice.*

She pushed out a long breath of resolve, snatched some paper towels from the dispenser, and dabbed the water away. *You got this.*

She picked up her tray from the sink and went to the kitchen, dropped the tray on the stack to be washed, then went to check on her customers and get her mind right before she had to get up on stage—with Jason sitting right in front of her.

At some point, she was going to have to kill her best friend.

"**J**ason."

Anita's friend Liza tapped him lightly on the shoulder, and he turned around on his stool. "Liza. Hello."

She leaned in and kissed his cheek. "How are you?"

"Been better," he admitted. "Oh." He turned to Ronald and made introductions. "Ronald helps out at the office."

Ronald's gaze did a slow walk along Liza's curves before landing on her face. He hopped off the stool. "Nice to meet you."

Liza offered a flirty smile. "You guys waiting on a table?"

"Yes," Jason said.

"I already have one. Up front. Plenty of room for two more."

Jason placed his beer bottle on the bar top. "You sure?"

"Of course. No problem. Plus you'll have perfect seats when Nita goes on later." She winked and led the way to her table.

Jason worked hard at pretending that he wasn't tracking Anita's every move as they walked over and sat down. When she came to take their orders, she barely looked at him. But one thing was certain—her indifference was getting to him. Maybe he'd made a mistake in listening to Ronald's advice about coming to B-Flat.

He might have his doubts, but Ronald was definitely making the most of his night, as he was practically nose to nose in conversation with Liza.

Jason nursed his drink but was disappointed when another waitress brought their food orders. Ronald and Liza didn't even notice. But his disappointment was short-lived when Henry stepped on stage to introduce Anita. The club erupted into shouts, clapping, and whoops of welcome.

The lights on the stage dimmed, and Anita moved in front of the microphone. "What's happening?" she called out.

"You. You," someone shouted from the back.

Anita grinned. She cupped the mic in her palms. "A lot

of mess done happened. Bunch of hopes and dreams for our people might be put on pause, 'cause if they can gun down a white president, you know what they can do to us," she said, her gaze burning across the faces of the audience.

Another round of applause, whoops, and foot stomping.

Anita, clearly feeling her power, held up her hands to quiet the crowd. "It's why we have to be in control of our own destinies, our own communities, families, schools…our lives." The impassioned rise of her voice filled the room.

"Preach!"

Anita smiled. "So I wrote a little something to remind us what we're up against and how much we need one another." She turned to the four-piece band behind her, lifted her hand ever so slightly, and the bass player began a slow, bluesy strumming that held up and carried her words.

"I call this piece 'If They Knew.'"

> *"Nothin' is what they say,*
> *Spinnin' tales of make-believin'*
> *In people not meant to be*
> *Here.*
> *Where from this place do*
> *We fit in, sit in, silently*
> *Beaten back into submission.*
> *No.*
> *If they knew*
> *Not this time again will they win*
> *Against our right to exist,*
> *To resist.*
> *The march toward our extinction*
> *Will not overcome*
> *Our conviction*
> *To survive another day*

In the presence of this reality.
'Cause if they knew
That by any means necessary,
We realize that over and again
We rise."

Anita lowered her head, closed her eyes, and basked in the adulation from the crowd, many of whom were on their feet. She pressed her hands to her thumping heart in homage to her audience. She felt electrified, experienced a pure adrenaline rush. When she opened her eyes, her gaze landed right on Jason, whose expression she couldn't read, and she wondered if he'd listened between the lines to find the two of them strolling there.

She waved to the audience and walked off stage. Every time she performed, it was often akin to an out-of-body experience. She was there. She could see and hear, but from a distance.

By degrees she slowly descended from her creative high and softly landed on her feet. She pushed through the swinging door of the kitchen and picked up two trays designated for her sections, still hearing the applause ringing in her ears.

What did Jason think? How much did he realize, if at all, that the poem, much like the life that swirled around them, was a metaphor for their relationship?

If she'd known that day on the bus where she would be now, would she have done things differently? Would she have allowed herself to become a victim of emotional circumstance, who struggled every day against all the whys and wherefores that defined and separated them?

She checked the order slip on the tray, dragged in a breath, and walked to the table where Jason sat. She expertly removed the drinks from the tray and placed them on the table.

"You were fabulous up there," Jason said, covering her hand with his.

A flash of heat raced up her arm. Her breath hitched. "Thanks." She eased her hand away.

"You killed it," Liza added. "Proud of you, girl."

She put Liza's drink in front of her, then Ronald's. "Need anything else?" she asked as she looked from one to the other.

Ronald's face was already buried in his glass.

"I'm good," Liza said. She eyed Anita from beneath her lashes while a smile flickered around her lips.

"You can't ignore me forever, sugah."

Her glance darted toward him, then away. She made busy work of checking her order pad. She could ignore him if she put her mind to it. But...she didn't want to. She wanted to hear about his day and tell him about hers. She wanted to debate the rights and wrongs of their positions, listen to some jazz, and make some love. But she wouldn't make it easy, because not only did they see the world differently, they saw relationships differently as well.

At the end of the day, she didn't want to be the milk.

"What time do you get off? I really want us to talk," Jason said, just loud enough for her ears.

"Midnight."

"I'll be here."

Her throat was too dry to swallow. "Fine," she managed without choking and hurried away.

Ronald had somehow convinced Liza that he should walk her home, leaving Jason to wait alone for Anita. He stood outside of B-Flat as the minutes past midnight ticked by and wondered if he'd missed her.

Then the door swung open, and Anita stepped out. She tossed her scarf around her neck, then froze when her gaze landed on him.

He straightened from his lean against a light pole and walked over to her. "Told you I'd wait."

"What do you want to talk about, Jason?"

"Us."

"What about us?"

"I need to explain."

She shoved her hands into the pockets of her coat. "No need. My superpower is reading between the lines."

"Can you just for one minute stop working so hard to push me away?"

Her nostrils flared. She stared at him hard. "Fine. I'm listening."

"Can we walk and talk? Keep the blood flowing," he said, half in jest.

She tugged in a breath. "Fine."

He was getting the distinct impression that when Anita said, "fine," it wasn't really fine at all.

"I love you," he began. "From the bottom of my heart. And it may seem corny or square, but I have some lines that I don't want to cross. One of them is living with a woman I'm not married to."

Anita's heart beat in her throat. She couldn't let sweet words distract her, no matter how much she wanted to tell him that she missed him all the time, that she hadn't been the same since they'd been apart, that her day-to-day was just an endless list of things to do without him at the end of it.

They walked for a block in silence until she turned the conversation back on asking him what he thought about the club and her performance. Listening to the ease of his voice calmed her, gave her room to breathe, to think.

"So what are you saying? From before," she asked, switching topics, and caught the questioning look in his expression. "About us…being together."

He stopped walking, turned to stand in front of her. He clasped her arms. "I'm saying that when we live together, it will be as husband and wife and only when I'm in a position to take care of you like a husband should. And if you don't or can't agree with that"—he released her, stepped back, and held up his hands—"I'll leave you alone. It'll hurt, but I'll do it."

Would he really walk away from her? Had she pushed him too far? "What makes you think I need taking care of?" she challenged, trying to regain her footing.

He reached out and tenderly stroked her cheek. Her lids fluttered, and she knew she wanted him to wrap her up in his protection even as she fought for her independence.

"We all need someone to be by our side. Even you, sugah."

She wouldn't let him melt her with endearments. "Why is your way the only way? You're all rules and regulation and traditions. Step out of your box, J. Come on. Let's be for real. I'm the last person you would have thought to be with, and the same goes for me. We took a chance on each other." Her eyes ran over his face. "You say you love me, and in the next breath, you're willing to walk away if our relationship can't be a Hallmark card."

They stopped in front of her building. She shoved her hands into the pockets of her coat and turned to face him. "So are you coming up?" She knew if he walked away now, it was over.

• • •

Anita unlocked the door to her fourth-floor apartment. The old radiators hissed and banged in greeting.

Jason stepped in behind her and closed the door.

"Want some tea?" she asked, getting out of her coat and shaking off a shiver.

"Sure." He hung up his coat and followed her into the kitchen.

"You know where everything is. I'll be right back." She walked off to her bedroom.

Jason moved comfortably around the familiar kitchen, taking two mugs from the overhead cabinet, then filling a pot with water to boil. He checked the shelves for the box of tea bags and dropped one in each mug.

He supposed this was Anita's version of a truce, inviting him to come up to her apartment. After he'd made his confession, of sorts, she'd been oddly quiet, then turned the conversation to B-Flat and the crowd that evening. She touched on the poem she'd presented, saying that the events of her world and in her life had inspired it.

She made loving her so hard. She fought him at every turn, but he was up for the challenge. And she was worth it. Anita Hopkins was unlike any woman he'd ever known. The women he'd been accustomed to perfected the art of the damsel in distress, the sweet southern belle who needed a man to rescue her from the cold, cruel world. Anita was the total opposite. And as infuriating as she could be, he relished it.

The water had come to a boil just as Anita returned. She'd changed out of her work clothes into her terry robe and fluffy baby-blue slippers. She tightened the belt on her robe.

Jason turned off the flame beneath the pot and poured

the boiling water over the tea bags. He'd taken lemons out of the fridge for Anita. He preferred milk.

Anita sat down. "Thanks." She squeezed the sliced lemon into her cup.

Jason fixed his tea and sat opposite her. "Did you get what I was saying, Anita?" he quietly asked.

Everything hinged on her answer.

Anita focused all her attention on adding a teaspoon of sugar to her tea while her thoughts swirled in concert with the turning of her spoon. She lifted the cup to her lips. "I suppose," she murmured, then suddenly put down the cup, sloshing the contents over the top. She flattened her palms on the table and leaned toward Jason. "I get that you have all these values and principles up the wazoo, but this is 1963, not 1943! Things are different. We don't have to do what our parents and grandparents did. Couples shack up every day."

"I don't want us to be an everyday kind of couple. I want more than that for us." He gave a slight shrug. "Call me old fashioned, but that's what I feel, and I feel that way because I love and respect you."

She tilted her head to the side and looked at him long and hard. "But you don't have a problem spending the night in my bed? Premarital sex? That part is cool."

Anita watched the muscle under his eye twitch. She could almost see the wheels turning in his head to come up with an answer but had no idea why she was pushing him, prodding and goading him. Diminishing his beliefs. Challenging his view of their relationship. She heaved a breath. She didn't want them to fight. She wanted him to give up and throw in the towel. She wanted it to be *his* fault if they didn't work out.

"You're right," he finally conceded.

Her heart banged in her chest.

Jason looked into her eyes. "Can't have it both ways."

His voice took on that lazy-river tone that soothed her even when she didn't want to be soothed. She folded her arms, pouted, prepared to steel herself against the sweet talk.

"I know that I don't want to lose you, Anita. But I want to be able to take care of you like a man should. Right now I can't, but I'm getting there." His eyes cinched. "I believe that we should work toward making us permanent. Married. Totally committed. But it's a process. I want what my parents have, what your parents have. Don't you?"

She blinked away the sting in her eyes, didn't dare yet speak over the tightness in her throat. No one had ever come even this close to committing to her, to testifying to what they could be together. She'd had a couple of lovers in her life, ones she'd always compared to Leon, who'd tainted her heart and made it damn near impossible for anyone to penetrate the bricks and mortar that she'd built around it. Until now.

She could hear the facade crumbling, and she was scared shitless.

"So what do we do now?" Her voice cracked.

"We work on forever."

Anita got to her feet, came around to his side of the table, and lowered herself onto his lap. Jason looped an arm around her waist. She looked into his eyes, seeing endless possibilities hovering there, waiting for her to truly take a leap of faith and dive in with him.

Faith. Again, his mother's parting words resurfaced.

"I'll go along with this...moralistic plan of yours." She traced his bottom lip with her finger. "But only if we leave out the part about not making love until we're married. That's a deal breaker for me."

Jason looked at her and then tossed his head back, laughing from deep in his gut. "Anita Hopkins, what am I going to do with you?"

She unfastened the sash on her robe, pulled the cloth down off one shoulder and then the other to tease at her nakedness. "Take me to bed and show me just how much this whole future thing with us is going to work."

He groaned and slid his fingers through the cotton softness of her thick hair and urged her toward him. "I only have so much willpower," he said before pulling her into a deep and long-overdue kiss.

Her needy, naked body was on fire. Flames of lust shot through her veins, ignited by each touch, every kiss, and whispered word that Jason plied upon her. She'd fallen under some spell that left her unable to control her own body. She was completely at his mercy, a willing supplicant to the passion that he willed from her body.

"I've missed you," he groaned in her ear before running hot lips along her neck and across her collarbone until her body trembled. His head drifted downward along the rise of her breasts, between the honeyed valley until his tongue flicked across a peaked nipple and took one into his mouth.

"Ohhhh." Her fingers pressed into his shoulders, and her back instinctively arched, offering her breasts more fully for his consumption.

His long fingers danced across her sizzling flesh, teasing, coaxing her body to higher heights. He seemed to be everywhere at once, leaving her weak, tremulous, and wanting, and then she felt the stroke of his tongue between her legs setting off explosions that erupted behind her lids. Her hips lifted. She gripped handfuls of sheet in her fists even as the muscles in her neck constricted the cry that rose from the soles of her feet.

Jason gripped her thighs, held them apart, allowing him to savor her essence until she begged for mercy.

By degrees, he inched up her body, dropping petals of kisses along the way until he was able to look into her eyes.

"Jase," she whispered against his lips.

He eased up a bit further. The swollen head of his erection pressed urgently against her opening.

Her breath hitched as her body curved around him. His mouth covered hers an instant before he pushed deep inside her and swallowed her moan.

"I love you, Nita," he groaned while he moved within her, fast, slow, faster, deeper.

Her fingers dug into his shoulders. She draped her legs across his back, lifting and grinding her pelvis against him, meeting him stroke for stroke. "Yes. Yes," she whimpered. "God, yes."

Everything seemed to spin. Her pulse pounded loudly, her temples blurring her vision behind the lights that exploded like fireworks. Desperately she wanted to come, and at the same time didn't want the thrill to end. Even the hairs on her head felt electrified.

Jason slid his hands beneath her hips, pulled her tight against him, and ground his hips against her until her body shook.

The sizzle ran up the insides of her legs. She nearly leaped off the bed when the first wave of release crashed against her, but Jason held her in place, worked her over and into a frenzy of escalating desire. The second wave hit her, shook her, released her, and shook her again and again until she was weak but thoroughly satisfied.

Jason tenderly kissed her lips and the tears that spilled from the corners of her eyes. He cooed in her ear while he continued to slowly stroke her, gathering her shuddering body into the cocoon of his arms before his rose up, and draped her legs over the bend of his arms.

Anita held her breath when she looked up at him kneeling above her, her body fully open for him, vulnerable and exposed.

He thrust deep inside her, shoving the air out of her lungs. Again. Her eyes slammed shut. Again. She cried out. Again.

Anita whimpered, moaned. Words would not form. She was on the verge of exploding.

"Look at me," Jason said, his voice raw and nearly unrecognizable. "Look at me," he repeated.

Anita's lids fluttered open. Her lips parted. She sank into the dark depths of his gaze and was carried away with him into a bed of utter ecstasy.

Anita curled her body against Jason, wanted to burrow under his skin. She was still shaking. Her head was spinning.

The neon light from the corner liquor store bathed them in sporadic red and blue.

"That was… I don't know what that was," Anita managed.

Jason kissed her forehead, appeared to be trying to catch his breath. "It was mind blowing." He pulled the sheet up over them.

"Think it can always be this way with us?" Anita tentatively asked into the rainbowed night.

He gave her a wry grin. "If it doesn't kill us first."

. . .

The sizzling aroma of bacon tickled Jason's nose, seducing him out of a satisfying sleep. He blinked against the bright-white light that filtered in from the window.

Moaning softly, he sat up, rubbed his eyes, and drew in a deep breath. Anita's scent clung to him and drew a smile to his lips.

He tossed the sheets and blanket aside and flinched just a little when his feet hit the cold floor. He'd have to invest in some slippers. The idea gave him a moment of pause. Up to now, he hadn't left anything personal in Anita's space beyond a toothbrush. He'd climbed up on his high horse about his moralistic stand on living together. So if he believed that, the last thing he'd do was begin leaving clothes and slippers at her home—carving out a space that he had no right to.

It was already hypocritical enough that they slept together minus marriage. A flash of Anita wrapped around him exploded in his head. He supposed his red line only went so far. He had every intention of righting that indiscretion as soon as possible.

He pulled on his underwear, went into the bathroom to freshen up. He lifted the bottle of Jergens lotion from the sink counter and brought it to his nose. His eyes closed for a moment. *Anita.* He returned the bottle to the countertop and wrapped a towel around his waist.

When he walked into the kitchen, Anita was humming and mouthing words, but not to any piece of music that sounded familiar to him. She was creating.

"Morning."

She grinned, kept bobbing her head to her inner beat while she put the plates of bacon, eggs, and cheese grits on the table.

He watched her, fascinated. She was totally in a different space yet there with him at the same time. He'd never met anyone like her, and he would do whatever it took for him to get to a place in his life to be able to share that life with her.

He'd been checking the classifieds for available apartments, and the cost was steep. They didn't need more than a one-bedroom, but even that could run them at least two hundred dollars per month before expenses. What he truly wanted for them was a house, like the one he grew up in, but even a decent apartment would take more than his stipend from the movement and Anita's wages from B-Flat. He was going to have to get a real paying job if he ever hoped to turn Anita Hopkins into Anita Tanner.

Chapter Seventeen

"Thank you for an amazing Christmas dinner, Mrs. Hopkins," Jason said. He patted his stomach and smiled. "The food, the tree, the decorations, the gift…made not being home not as hard."

"You're always welcome here," Mom said to him. "I know how difficult it is to be away from family, holiday or not." She slid a subtle look of accusation toward Anita.

Frustration burned in her gut. "I've been working, Ma. And we would stay longer, but I told you we have tickets to the Apollo."

"Mm-hmm."

Dad cleared his throat. "So, Jason, how is the job hunt going? Understand from Anita that you were lookin' for work."

"Uh, yes, sir. As a matter of fact, I start right after the new year at an office supply company in the Bronx. I'll be working on their books."

"It's what Jason did back in Georgia," Anita piped in. She flashed Jason a smile. "An accountant."

"Not quite," he admitted, "but close. Bookkeeper. I want to go back to school at some point and get my CPA license. With that, I can make a really good living."

Her father nodded in agreement, then pointed a finger in Jason's direction. "Now that's a plan."

"I want to be able to take care of Anita." Everyone froze. "When the time comes."

Anita reached for her glass of sweet tea and wished it were a rum and Coke. Her heart was running a sudden marathon in her chest. What the hell had gotten into him to make him say something like that? Since they'd gotten back together, the topic of permanence was not discussed. They'd danced around it in unspoken terms, but mostly they'd fallen into a comfortable pattern.

During the week, they spent the night in their respective beds. On the weekends, Jason would often stay at her place. That was the extent of it. Sure, she knew that his goal was to be able to take care of her the "right way," as he put it, but never in a zillion years did she expect that he would blurt out what he just had to her parents.

Dad pursed his lips, wiped them with a napkin. Slowly he nodded. "I like to hear that, young man. Good knowing that you have my daughter's best interest at heart and you understand the importance of being a man and a provider."

"Yes, sir."

Her mother heaved a breath. "Well, I sure hope you have time and some room for dessert. Sweet potato or apple pie?"

"Your folks are some kinda special," Jason said as they hustled to the train station. It had begun to snow again, and Anita clung to his arm to avoid landing on her butt.

The show started in a little over an hour, and it would take about that long to get back to Harlem, with the trains running on a holiday schedule. She didn't want to miss one minute. It was just as much a Christmas present to herself as it was for Jason.

It would be his first time at the Apollo. The Motortown Revue had a lineup of all the major Motown artists in one place. They were on a countrywide bus tour, and this was the only stop in New York. But she couldn't run out on her family early. Her mother would have never let her hear the end of it.

Jason tugged the bright-blue wool scarf, which Anita's parents have given him as a gift, up around his face to block off the swirling snow.

"So are yours. What's it even like in Atlanta at Christmas with no snow?" she asked as they descended the stairs into the subway.

He chuckled and dropped his token into the turnstile slot. "Pretty much like this. Decorations. Carolers. Presents. Smell of evergreens. Plenty of food, parties. Just no snow."

"Humph. Bizarre." She pushed through the turnstile. "Like my aunt Vi in California. Just strange."

They walked onto the platform. The swirl of wind and the low rumble beneath their feet signaled the arriving train.

"Just in time," Anita said as she peered down the semidark tunnel. "No telling what time we would have gotten to the city if we'd missed this one."

The train roared into the station, and as usual, to Jason's amazement, even on a holiday the car was packed with people. Every one of them seemed loaded down with shopping bags brimming with wrapped gifts.

They squeezed in, finding a space in the corner.

Anita stood in front of Jason and looped her arms around his waist. "You're gonna love this show. I'm so excited."

Jason chuckled. "I can see. But, sugah, you didn't have to spend all that money on me. Two tickets. That's twenty dollars we could have used for a bill."

She leaned in and kissed him. "You deserve it," she said against his mouth. "Plus, it's my present to myself, too." She grinned.

Jason's eyes did a slow stroll over her smiling face. "I love you."

Her face lit from within. "I love you, too."

By the time they reached 125th Street, they had ten minutes to spare before showtime. They eagerly joined the line that snaked down the snow-covered street.

The Apollo marquee lit up with the names of the Motown entertainers. They inched along with the line that wound down the street until finally they were inside the famed halls.

Anita squeezed Jason's hand, reached up and kissed his cheek. "Let's party," she said, and led the way down the aisle to their seats.

Apollo Theater in Harlem, New York City.
(c) Felix Lipov/Alamy

• • •

Anita and Jason tumbled out of the theater, laughing, hollering, stomping their feet, totally overwhelmed by the performances they'd witnessed.

"Damn. Damn. Damn!" Anita gushed. "That was a show! Marvin, Smokey Robinson, Martha Reeves!"

"I'm still blown away by Stevie Wonder. Twelve years old," Jason said.

"I know! Wow."

"Thanks, sugah. This was the best Christmas present."

She kissed his cheek. "Glad you liked it. You planning to stay over tonight?" she asked.

"If it's cool with you."

She snuggled closer. "Very. I have the rest of your Christmas present."

"Can't wait to unwrap it," he said before leaning down to kiss her.

Jason and Anita celebrated the New Year with Liza and Ronald, who to everyone's surprise had become a real couple. Jason and Ronald had splurged for tickets to the Cotton Club, and they rang in the New Year in style.

Jason started his new job at Anderson Office Supplies. The train ride wasn't too bad, but it didn't leave him any time during the week to get work done at the office. He turned over the daily operations to Michael, and Ronald had really stepped up as well. The nonviolent resistance training, reading and math classes, and voter-registration drives were all coming along better than expected. More folks from the community were stopping in to see what services were offered, and many joined in the movement.

On the opposite end, Anita continued her work with Malcolm's organization, promoting self-determination and separation. She was still a staunch advocate of facing down the enemy, and she continued to vocalize her beliefs during her spotlights at B-Flat.

Together Jason and Anita fell into an easy rhythm. They both loved to eat and taught each other how to prepare some of their favorite dishes. Jason shared with Anita his mother's secret fried fish recipe, which Anita all but perfected. And she guided him through the intricate steps of the perfect sweet potato pie—or at least as close to perfect as they could get. He even got her to enjoy a glass of Georgia sweet tea from time to time.

Then there were those other moments, those times when they clashed like gladiators.

A week earlier, a young Negro man had been wrongfully arrested, according to the community, and the police had refused to allow anyone in to see him. Word got to Malcolm X.

Jason was adamant about Anita not participating in the walk to the precinct. "I just…I don't want you to go."

She checked her tote for her keys and identification. Then looked up at him, her eyes flamed in passion. "This is what I do. It's what we do. Why can't you understand that?"

"You're intentionally going to incite the police. Do you have any idea what they can do to you?"

Her nostrils flared, and her chest rose and fell as if she'd been running. "If Dr. King asked you to 'peacefully' march for a cause that he said was important, would you say no because the march might upset the powers that be? Or is it only okay when it's you and what *you* believe in?"

"That's not fair." He reached out for her arm, but she stepped away from his grasp. "I don't want anything to happen to you. I don't want you to get hurt."

Her tone softened. She cupped his cheek in her palm. "I know," she conceded. "I'll be fine. Promise." She leaned up and kissed him lightly on the lips. "But just in case, there's a couple hundred dollars in the nightstand in a Newport cigarette box—in case you need to bail me out."

"Nita!"

She flashed a smile, whirled away, and was out the door.

For the next five hours he paced, checked the news on television, paced some more, went out on the street and back inside to pace even more. It was nearly midnight when he heard her key in the door.

He jumped up from his spot on the couch, and before she was halfway into the apartment, he'd swooped her up in his arms and held her tightly against him.

"Been nonstop worrying, sugah," he said into the soft cotton of her hair.

She wrapped her arms around his waist. "I'm okay. Told you I would be okay." She tipped her head back and looked into his eyes. "Gonna have to get used to it," she said softly. "There'll be more times when I'm going to be out there. Just like you will."

He pressed his lips tightly together and nodded. "I know, sugah. I know."

They were good together. They'd make it work. And he was happier than he'd ever been or expected to be.

• • •

"You are glowing, girl," Liza said. She bit down on her burger.

"Yeah? I guess 'cause I feel good, ya know. Things with me and Jason…" Her voice drifted, and she was sure her expression had grown dreamy. "Are really great." She looked across the table at her friend. "Really in love."

"I can tell. I'm happy for you, girl. You deserve it."

Anita wrapped her hands around her glass of soda. "I'm finally beyond Leon and what happened." She turned her gaze away from the past. "It was a hard lesson, and it changed me. That much is true. But I'm finally better for it. I know I can deal with anything, and I know that I can love someone and get to be loved right back. For real."

Liza lifted her glass. "To the future and kicking the past in the butt."

"Yes, ma'am," she agreed and tapped her glass against Liza's. "And you and Ronald have been at it for a minute now, too."

"I know." She frowned in confusion. "I would have never thought in a million years that I'd wind up with someone like Ronald. But, Nita, he's really special. I mean, I know I have him beat by a few years and he didn't go to college, but…he's a great guy, works hard. We like the same things. He's a little rough around the edges, but I dig it." She flashed a shy smile.

"You seem happy."

"I am."

"Guess we both found exactly what we weren't looking for, with the last people on our radar. Funny how things work out." She pushed her french fries around on her plate. "When I met Jason on the bus last summer, I never figured he'd be the one. But it was like fate or something. Can't believe it's almost been a year."

"Yeah, a lot has gone down."

"Hmm." She took a bite of her burger. "It sure has."

...

J ason climbed the steps toward fresh air. As he drew closer to the top, the fading evening sun could be seen over the arch of trees. The sounds of rumbling train engines and the stifling heat of the enclosed metal boxes were replaced by the hum of car motors and the humid breeze of early July. He cleared the last step of the 125th Street subway station, spewed out of the underground womb with so many others onto the banks of Lenox Avenue.

His starched light-blue shirt that Anita had lovingly pressed perfect creases into clung to his back. He pulled a damp handkerchief from the pocket of his navy-blue khaki pants and wiped his wet face and the back of his neck, then began his slow walk to Anita's place. It was like an oasis after his hour-long journey on the train.

He continued along Lenox, caught glimpses of the everyday transactions that he'd grown accustomed to: the number runners carrying the hopes of the dreamers on little slips of paper. Excitement buzzed on the faces and lips of the people he passed as they stood together in twos and threes, huddled over newspapers reading the big headline of the day.

Change had come to America—or so they believed.

He reached Anita's front door and could almost smell her cooking calling out to him on the tufts of hot air. Living in an apartment building with folks coming and going was not what he envisioned for him and Anita in the long term, but he was working hard to change that. And for now, it was comfortable.

The neighbors were nosy but friendly, and Anita had turned her one-bedroom apartment into space for two. He wasn't sure how she managed it, but the small yet cozy space was neat. On the evenings that he came by, she usually cooked some or they'd order from the local pizza shop. But best of all, whenever he came through the door, there was a loving woman waiting for him at night.

Since he didn't work on the weekends and with him being the only stable male in the building, old Ms. Levin, the building owner, had given him superintendent duties and cut Anita's rent in half for his services. There was always somebody with something that needed patching or painting or plugging, and Jason tucked away every extra dollar.

He used the key she'd insisted he have and let himself in.

Anita was putting his plate on the table when he came up behind her and hugged her tight around the waist.

He kissed the back of her neck. "How's my best girl?" he whispered in her ear.

She giggled and tried to wiggle away. "Jason Tanner, I've been sweating over a hot stove, and you gonna make me spill it all over my freshly washed floor," she said with a dramatic hand to her head.

He kissed her again. "And I would get down on bended knee and pick up every drop," he said, all the while sliding down her body until his lips were at the back of her knees.

"Jason…now…don't start no mess," she said, a little breathless.

"Don't know what mess you talkin' 'bout, sugah." He scooped her up in his arms and carried her off to her bedroom.

They propped themselves up in the double bed, finishing off the last of the smothered pork chops, snap peas, and Uncle Ben's rice that Anita had reheated.

The whole meal had waited patiently on the table until the

two finally untangled themselves from each other, laughing, breathing hard, sweaty, and filled up with love.

Anita took his plate, placed it on top of hers, and put both on the nightstand.

"Ain't it something about President Johnson signing that civil rights bill?" he said, his eyes lit with excitement. "I listened to it on the radio today. Almost couldn't believe it." He chuckled, shook his head. "Finally making some progress after a lot of long, hard work."

"Hmmm." She wiped her mouth with a paper napkin. "Sounds good, but no telling how things are really gonna turn out for Negroes. Is it gonna mean higher pay and better jobs, decent places to live, not getting beat by the police?"

"It's gonna mean Negroes—by law—got to be treated just like the white folks."

She slowly shook her head and sighed deeply.

Jason reached for her hand. "I got a feeling things will change for the better. Dr. King said he had a dream that one day we'd all be judged by the content of our character and not the color of our skin. I think the dream has come true."

Anita made a noise in her throat, then wrapped her fingers around his. "They still haven't found those three missing civil rights boys in Mississippi, and as long as there are folks like J. Edgar, Governor Wallace in Alabama, and Strom Thurmond in the Senate, I don't see how things are going to change. At least, not for a very long time."

"Have some faith, sugah." He leaned over and kissed her cheek.

"We'll see." She flipped onto her side to face him. "Now back to our agreement." She slid the tip of her finger along the bridge of his nose.

"Agree to disagree," they chorused in unison, then tumbled into each other's arms.

• • •

NEW YORK—(UPI)—Screaming rock- and bottle-throwing rioters battled police in Brooklyn Wednesday night and looters took over Thursday in this city's fifth consecutive night of disturbances.

Three suspected looters, all colored, were wounded by police, and two policemen battling the mobs were injured.

There were indications some of the rioters were organized. One detective said a few of the looters were equipped with walkie-talkies, over which they received information about the location of police units. Some police units were sent on wild goose chases resulting from false telephone tips.

For the first time since the disorders began in Harlem last Saturday night, police used horses to disperse the Brooklyn mobs.

An estimated 1,000 angry, jeering youths mounted two major charges against the helmeted riot police in defiance of Mayor Robert Wagner's broadcast warning that "mob rule" would not be tolerated.

Mayor Wagner addressing New Yorkers in the wake of four nights of uprisings, declared that "mob rule" in the nation's largest city would not be tolerated "at any time."

The mayor, speaking on a citywide radio and television hookup, said "the mandate to maintain law and order is absolute" and the city would not "bow or surrender to pressure."

"Without law and order, colored and civil rights programs would be set back one half century," Wagner said in his speech to the people. "Law and order are the colored citizen's best freedom—make no mistake about that."

The mayor's office said it has received hundreds of telephone calls and telegrams, the overwhelming majority of them supporting the mayor.

In Cairo, where he attended an African Conference, Black Nationalist leader Malcolm X predicted the city's racial troubles "will probably get much worse."

Rep. Adam Clayton Powell said in Washington on Wednesday that only immediate action by Mayor Wagner to reform police procedures can stop further violence. The Harlem Democrat urged the mayor to replace white policemen with more colored ones and bar the use of live ammunition in dealing with rioters.

Confrontation between African Americans and police with billysticks at Fulton Street and Nostrand Avenue during the Bedford–Stuyvesant riot of 1964, an extension of the Harlem riot. (c) FLCH 18/Alamy

. . .

The summer of '64 had been a series of highs and lows. The civil rights bill had passed, right on the heels of the disappearance and murder of Chaney and Goodman, and then there was the riots that stretched from Harlem to Brooklyn.

Anita wanted to go to Brooklyn to be with her parents, but her parents wouldn't hear of it, even if Jason came with her. *Too dangerous*, her father insisted. They were fine. They were staying indoors, and the rioting and looting had been contained to the stores and businesses on Broadway, which ran beneath the elevated train line about a mile away from where they lived.

The best Anita could do was check on them by phone until things got back to some semblance of normal.

"I just don't understand people," Mom was saying.

"Don't understand what people?" Anita asked.

"*Our* people. What kind of sense does it make to tear up your own neighborhoods, where you live? What are people going to do when it all dies down? Where are they going to go?"

"Frustration will make you do all kinds of things, Ma. James Powell was only fifteen years old, and the cop shot him dead in the street in front of his friends!" Anita gazed out the window at the overturned trash cans and boarded-up store windows. "When people get tired of being mistreated and stepped on and pushed around—they rise up."

A black-and-white police car slowly cruised through the block, and she wished she had a brick to throw. She sipped her glass of lemonade instead and let the pulp sit for a moment on her tongue.

"Shooting that boy up here in Harlem was probably the

last straw for some of them, and the others just needed an excuse," she added.

"I s'pose you're right. It's a God-honest shame."

"That so-called civil rights bill that President Johnson signed two weeks ago didn't do that young boy one bit of good. Gets kind of exhausting to try to stand upright when you always have a foot on your neck."

Her mother sighed heavily. "I just pray this will all be over soon and no more lives are lost."

"Yeah, me too, Ma," she murmured, even if she didn't see how.

Chapter Eighteen

The war in Vietnam began to dominate the evening news and the headlines of all the papers. The United States had been, over the years, sending young American soldiers halfway across the world to fight "the enemy." A year earlier, Malcolm X had given a speech in Detroit calling out the hypocrisy of the United States in sending Negroes into battle to fight an enemy, yet America was not willing to fight the enemy of racism for the Negro.

Anita felt the same way. Why should her brothers go to war to fight for a country that showed no humanity toward their own? Like James Baldwin said, "We can disagree and still love each other, unless your disagreement is rooted in my oppression and denial of my humanity and right to exist… To be a Negro in this country and to be relatively conscious is to be in a rage almost all the time."

Anita's fury grew as she watched President Johnson on the six o'clock news announce to the country that he'd just signed the Tonkin Resolution on August 7, which would officially engage the United States in the Vietnam War and send thousands of young men to fight for a cause that remained unclear.

US President Lyndon B. Johnson signs the 1964 Civil Rights Act
as Martin Luther King, Jr. and others look on in the East Room of
the White House, July 2, 1964 in Washington, DC.
(c) White House Photo/Alamy

When Jason finally got Anita on the phone line, she'd clearly already worked herself into a major huff, launching into a rant about the war, Malcolm's position, her fury that so many young men would go to war and possibly lose their lives for a conflict that was not theirs.

Jason listened patiently, torn between his love for Anita and his commitment to what was right.

"Nita!" he finally cut in. He could almost see her mind coming to a screeching halt.

"Yes. What? Hey, I'm sorry, I'm running my mouth. But you know this kind of mess makes me angry."

"I, uh, wanted to stop by. If that's okay."

She paused a moment. "Since when do you ask if it's okay? What's wrong?"

"Nothing."

"Don't lie to me. I know you, remember?"

He cleared his throat. "I'll tell you all about it when I get there. Okay?"

"Fine."

He flinched at the word, knowing that wasn't what it meant at all.

Anita was parked on the small sofa in front of the television. The fire in her eyes that had attracted him that first day on the bus flashed like lightning bugs when she threw a look in his direction.

"Hey," she murmured and turned her attention back to the news.

"Hey." He softly closed the door behind him and came to sit beside her. He kissed her cheek.

She pointed an accusing finger at the television. "You see this shit? Unreal." She shook her head, the fluff of her hair as furious as she was. "I mean, Brother Malcolm said it right. 'How are you going to be nonviolent in Mississippi, as violent as you were in Korea? How can you justify being nonviolent in Mississippi and Alabama when your churches are being bombed and your little girls are being murdered, and at the same time you are going to get violent with Hitler and Tojo and somebody else you don't even know?'"

She took a breath and picked right back up, her skill as a miracle word worker evident as she recited line by line what Malcolm had said more than a year earlier. "'If violence is wrong in America, violence is wrong abroad. If it is wrong to be violent defending Black women and Black children and Black babies and Black men, then it is wrong for America to draft us and make us violent abroad in defense of her. And if it is right for America to draft us, and teach us how to be violent in defense of her, then it is right for you and me to do whatever is necessary to defend our own people right here in this country.'"

She turned to Jason and folded her arms defiantly.

"You have a look on your face," she said suddenly. "Did something happen at work?"

"I don't know how to tell you this."

She sat up straighter. "Tell me what? You're scaring me."

He lowered his head for a moment, turned to her, and took her hands in his. "I enlisted today."

She blinked in confusion. "Stop playing."

"I'm serious, Nita. I enlisted this afternoon."

She stared at him like she would a stranger who'd suddenly walked up on her. Then suddenly, she snatched her hands away. "What the hell are you telling me, Jason? You enlisted! In the fucking army!" She jumped up from the sofa, stomped halfway across the room, then whirled back around. Her chest heaved. "What is wrong with you? Why?" Her voice cracked. "Why would you do this?"

Jason got up and came to stand in front of her. She held up her hands and stepped back. "Don't." The skin across her face was tight as a drum. She backed up to the sink and folded her arms.

"I know this is hard to accept. I understand your position on all this, but I need you to understand mine as well." He pressed a hand to his chest. "I believe in and love this country, and I believe it's my duty to fight for it. Like my father and my grandfather did, in tougher times for Negroes in this country than now."

"Fight for it! Do you even hear yourself? What have the Vietnamese ever done to you?"

"It's not that simple, Nita, and you know it. If we want freedom and rights in our country, we need to be able to support the fight for freedom and the rights of others when they are threatened to be taken away."

She hung her head, her body deflated. When she looked back up at him, her eyes were clouded with unshed tears, dimming the fire but leaving them smoldering.

"What about us, Jason? What about our plans, our life? Did you think about that when you were busy signing up to fight for 'the man'? Huh? Huh?"

"Of course I did," he said slowly. "You may not believe me, but I did." His brows tightened. "I'm going to fight as much for the Vietnamese as I am for our people."

"So what happened to all that nonviolent bullshit you've been spewing?" She swiped at her eyes.

"This is different. Dr. King clearly said that 'Injustice anywhere is a threat to justice everywhere… Whatever affects one directly, affects all indirectly.'"

Anita looked at him and snorted a laugh of disgust. She waved her hand. "Make yourself believe that." She turned her back to him, braced her palms on the edge of the sink. "We always were too far apart, saw things too differently. You should probably leave before we—before I say something that can't be taken back."

He took a step toward her and watched her body flinch. He dropped his hands to his sides. "I'll call you."

"Don't."

"Nita—"

"Just go. Now, Jason. And leave your key on the table."

His mouth opened to protest, but no words would form. His chest tightened as he dug in the pocket of his slacks and took her two keys from his ring. He placed them on the kitchen table, and when he looked at her stiff back once more before walking out, he was no longer sure of right and wrong.

Chapter Nineteen

Anita wiped her eyes, sniffed hard.

"I don't even know what to say, Nita," Liza said softly.

Anita shook her head, still shaken with disbelief more than two weeks after Jason's enlistment bombshell—and her own shocking discovery afterward.

"Did you try to talk to him?"

"And say what? He made it clear that this was his 'duty.'" She cussed under her breath. "He leaves for basic training next week. I should have known that our differences would screw things up." She pounded her fist against the arm of Liza's leather couch. "I should have never let myself fall for somebody like that."

"You can't help who you love. And if you really love him, you'll stand by him and his decision. I thought you said y'all's motto was 'Agree to disagree.'"

Anita rolled her eyes.

"And you need to tell him. It's not fair that you keep this from him. You can't let him go over there and not know."

Anita's lips tightened. "I'm not going to do that to Jason," she said over the hard knot in her throat.

For more than a week, she'd been in a state of denial, euphoria, and terror after getting the news from her doctor.

Six weeks pregnant, she'd told her. After what happened with Leon, she hadn't been sure if she'd ever be able to have children. To find out that she was carrying her and Jason's child was a blessing and a curse. She would have wanted things to be different, and she thought she and Jason were so close to securing their financial goals and then marriage, *then* kids.

"I'm not going to use being pregnant to trap him or keep him from focusing on staying alive…" Her voice broke into a million pieces while the tears of hurt and confusion slid down her cheeks, dripping onto her blouse.

Liza reached over and covered Anita's hand. "Those sound like the words of a woman who loves a man."

"Whatever." She looked Liza directly in the eye. "I'm not going to tell him—because I *do* love him. And you're not gonna tell him, either. Do not say a word to Ronald."

"Nita!"

"Promise me."

Liza pushed out a breath of defeat. "I promise," she managed. "So what are you going to do? You ready to be a single mother? Have you told your parents?"

"I'll figure it out. I will. I'll figure it out."

"I'm gonna be real. I don't agree with what you're doing, but I got your back. No matter what."

Anita's lips thinned. She blinked back a new round of tears. "I know," she whispered.

Jason had turned in his notice to his accounting job the day after he enlisted. Now he sat down with the members of the committee to outline how things would move forward without him.

The transition, he knew, would be relatively easy, as Michael, Ronald, and Mary knew the ins and outs and took care of the day-to-day operations.

"This is a big move, man," Michael said. "I tried to enlist; they wouldn't take me. Heart murmur."

Jason nodded. "We couldn't have both of us on the battlefield. Need someone to hold it down over here," he said, trying to make light of the moment. He drew in a breath and looked out at the ragtag group of volunteers. "So, Michael will run the office. All decisions go through him. He will be the contact between this office and the headquarters in Atlanta. Ronald is Michael's backup and will continue to work on recruitment and training. Mary will continue to run the classes."

He cleared his throat, suddenly feeling choked up. They'd come so far since he'd arrived to an empty storefront and big ideas more than a year ago. His National Action office had become an oasis for the community, even more so following the riots that tore through their community. He had much to be proud of.

Jason pushed to his feet. "So I expect y'all to hold it down for me till I get back." He forced a smile.

"We got this," Ronald announced for the group. "You make sure you hold up your end, brother. And get back here safe."

"I will."

Jason listlessly emptied the drawers of the dresser, neatly folded his clothes, and placed them in his suitcase. He was scheduled to ship out in two days. In the morning he had a flight to Atlanta to see his parents before he left for basic training in Dover, Maryland. He was scared, but this was something he had to do. If only he could hear Nita's voice, see her face, and hold her one last time before he had to leave.

Anita refused his calls, and it was like a knife twisting in his gut. He'd lost count of the number of messages he'd left her. He shoved a new package of boxers into the suitcase. He'd stopped by her office and was told she had not been in for the past two weeks, and was politely reminded that volunteers came and went.

Henry at B-Flat informed him that she'd taken a few weeks off. Long overdue vacation, he'd said, but somehow Jason didn't believe him. He didn't believe anyone. He was in a state of paranoia and was feeling as if the world was conspiring against him to keep him from seeing Anita.

Was he really doing the right thing? Were his convictions worth losing the woman he loved and hurting her the way he did? He would be gone for at least four years. Would she wait for him? Would she even care if he came back?

He plopped down on the side of the bed. His shoulders shuddered as he dropped his head into his palms.

Anita pressed her fist against her lips as she listened to Jason's message on her answering machine.

The hurt in his voice nearly broke her. But if she ever had to be strong, it was now. She loved him with all her heart, but she would not put the weight of their child on top of all that he would have to carry in the months ahead.

Tears slid from her eyes. She pressed her palms against the gentle rise in her stomach. She'd finally told her parents

about the pregnancy and that she had no intention of telling
Jason until he returned. Once her mother stopped praying and
sobbing, and her father stopped cussing, they both testified
that they loved her no matter what. Her mother insisted and
her father cosigned that she return home so they could look
after her. They didn't agree with her decision, but the baby
was innocent and must have everything it needed, especially
grandparents.

"Moving back to Brooklyn—with your mother and
father?" Liza asked incredulously a few weeks later.
"You?"

"I know. Never thought you'd see the day, right?"

They walked along Amsterdam Avenue. Every other
storefront window hung posters about how *Uncle Sam Wants
You*.

"Guess I'll be catching the iron horse to Brooklyn," Liza
said.

"You better."

"When are you moving?"

"After the new year. Closer to my date."

"What about your work at the center?"

"I'll work a couple more months, until I really start to show.
Same thing with B-Flat. I gotta do that as long as possible. I
need the money."

"You know whatever you need, all you have to do is let
me know."

"Thanks, girl."

"Still haven't changed your mind about telling Jason, huh?"

"I have no idea how to reach him." She would not allow

herself to imagine never talking to or seeing him again. She wouldn't. "I should have told him." Her eyes filled. "I told myself I was being noble, but I was being selfish because a part of me wanted to hurt him for leaving me." She sniffed hard and lowered her head. "Now…" Her voice cracked. "It's too late. What if he…" Tears dropped onto her cheeks.

Liza grabbed her hand and squeezed it. "Don't go there, Nita. Jason will come home and you'll tell him about the baby and you two will be a family with your child."

Anita swiped at her eyes. "I love him Liza. So much."

"I know, sweetie."

"I need to be able to tell him how much I love him and how sorry I am."

"You will. Believe that. You will."

Chapter Twenty

October 15, 1964
   Dear Anita,
      I wanted to let you know that I arrived safely in Dong Ha after basic training. I would have written to you earlier, but I wanted to honor the space that you needed to have. I do wish that we had parted on different terms, but I have to respect your reasons.

I'm one of the lucky ones. I got a desk job working in an office—well, sort of an office. It's a big tent with makeshift walls, desks, files, and rifles and ammunition. I take care of inventory, making sure that all the units have the supplies they need and check what comes in and what goes out.

We are pretty close to the DMZ, but we are well behind the enemy lines. Of all the places I could be, so far it's pretty safe here. Every now and then, there is incoming artillery fire and we have to dive into the trenches, but it's still safer than being out on the combat field.

I got pretty used to living in a small space in my room in Harlem and sharing facilities with other guys. I guess I was getting prepared to live with four other guys in a tent. It's not the best of circumstances but better than most.

I think of you every day, all day, and hope that you are

well and still raising hell. I bought a jar of Jergens lotion and packed it in my bag. I use it sparingly so as to not run out and when I do, it puts a smile on my face because I can smell you. Reminds me of us being together. Makes me feel connected.

Anyway, they're serving dinner. I won't even tell you what we eat. Definitely not home cooked!

I love you. I pray for you. Please take care of yourself.

I will write again when I can.

Always,

Jason

· · ·

November 15, 1964

Dear Anita,

I pray that you are well. Sorry it has been a while since I've written. Our unit was moved several times because it wasn't safe. I guess that's why I haven't gotten a letter from you. But don't worry. I'm okay. We took on a great deal of enemy fire, and one of my bunkmates was injured. He was medevaced out. I hope he will be okay.

It has been raining here nonstop for the past three weeks. Mud comes above our ankles. The canopy of trees is so thick that even when the sun comes out, you can barely see it.

The holidays are coming up. First time I have been away from my family and friends for the holidays. But it is for a good cause.

Have you written any new poems? Please send me one when you get a chance.

I heard from my folks. They are doing well and asked about you.

Well, I have to go. I hope that you write. I am going to rub some Jergens on my hands!

Always,
Jason

. . .

December 2, 1964
I finally got your letter today. You have no idea how happy it made me to read your words. I could almost hear your voice. Good to know that you are doing well. I had Michael and Ronald check over at B-Flat and the office for you, but no one has seen you. Is everything okay? I have to go. I have watch duty tonight. Please write soon.

Always,
Jason

. . .

December 25, 1964
Dear Anita,
Merry Christmas. I hope you got to spend time with your folks. Please tell them I asked after them.

Not sure when you will get this letter or when I will get a chance to write again. Our unit is being moved again. We will be closer to Laos.

We cooked up a pretty good holiday dinner, and it was nice to relax and laugh and joke with the guys.

Anyway, I am doing well. Since I don't work in the office anymore, I'm in the fields with my unit. Getting some muscles with all the heavy lifting of equipment and climbing the hills.

You wouldn't recognize me!
Well, you take care of yourself, Anita.
Always,
Jason
P.S. Happy New Year (just in case I don't get to write again).

• • •

Anita wiped her eyes. His last letter was written Christmas day, and more than a month later, it had finally arrived. She gently folded the letters into their envelopes, some with the forwarded address of her parents' home. She put them in the shoebox where she kept all the others.

She jumped at the sudden kick to her tummy. Instinctively she massaged her belly, cooing softly to the budding, wiggling life inside.

"It's okay, sweetheart. Mommy was just a little sad for a minute. Don't you worry, though. We're gonna be okay. I get to meet you in one more month, so hang on till then. And when you get here, we'll tell your daddy all about you. I promise." She huffed as she inched to the edge of the bed and gingerly pushed to her feet that had begun to swell as they did every afternoon.

She caught a glimpse of her profile in the full-length mirror that hung on the door of her childhood bedroom. Since she'd returned home after Thanksgiving, she'd added her adult touches to the room, from the books on the shelves to the quilt on her bed, from the clothes that hung in the closet to the box of letters from her child's father that she now kept in her dresser drawer instead of her teenage diary.

Her doctor told her that she and the baby were coming along just fine, and although she might feel like a whale, her weight gain was quite normal.

Anita ran her palm along the beach ball that her tummy had become. A soft smile curved her mouth. Everything about her was bigger. Her lips and nose were fuller, her breasts belonged on a *Playboy* cover, and her hair was close to cocooning her. She had to keep it controlled in a big puff on top of her head.

But her skin glowed like a brand-new penny, her eyes literally sparkled, even her usual raging spirit had found a kind of glowing peace that radiated from her—or at least, that was what her mother kept telling her.

The baby was changing her in good ways, Mom had said. *Always do if you let 'em. Soothes the soul*, she'd said. While she massaged Anita's swollen feet, she'd told her what it was like when she found out she was pregnant. *Never thought it would happen*, Celia told her with a faraway look in her eyes. *Prayed on having a baby for years. Watched all my church friends and their children, and my heart would just break. We'd all but given up, me and your dad.*

She looked into Anita's eyes then, and Anita felt the deep power of a mother's love.

Anita blinked and realized that tears were sliding down her cheeks. She did a lot of that lately, crying at the drop of a hat. Being all emotional was totally foreign to her, and that made her cry, too.

She opened the top drawer of her dresser and took out the small gift-wrapped box. She should have taken it to the post office days ago if she'd wanted it to reach Jason by Christmas. But up until his last letter, she didn't know where he was. If she hurried she could catch the post office before they closed early for Saturday hours, and with any luck, he'd have his Christmas present before spring.

• • •

It was getting harder to move around, but staying in the house was making her lose it. Her mom was gone most days, and her dad was busy doing whatever he and the locals did during the week.

Liza had called and promised to meet her in front of Birdel's at two. They were going downtown to A&S department store to do some baby clothes shopping. Liza wanted to host a baby shower, but Anita's one real friend was Liza. That realization made her cry, too.

By the time she'd reached Nostrand and Fulton, it had started to snow again, and she hoped that Liza wasn't running late.

She inched her way down the street, careful of any patches of ice, hunching her shoulders against the cold. Her lower back was aching more than usual, and her nipples kept tingling. The misadventures of pregnancy. She turned onto Nostrand and waddled down the street.

Liza was pacing back and forth in front of Birdel's. She stopped and waved when she saw Anita and hurried toward her. "Hey, you," Liza greeted. She wrapped her arms around her friend as best she could, then stepped back and grinned. "Girl, you 'bout to bust!"

"Sis, I sure feel like it." She grimaced.

"You okay?"

"Hmm. Back is hurting. Thought the walk would help but seems to make it worse."

"Look, let's get you home. Weather is shitty anyway, and you don't feel well. We can shop some other time."

Anita gritted her teeth, squeezed her eyes shut for a minute, then dragged in a breath. "Yeah, I think you're right.

I want to go home."

"Lemme see if I can get us a cab." She hurried to the curb and stuck her arm out to hail a taxi.

Anita wobbled into the house with Liza right by her side.

"Maybe you should go lay down, get off your feet," Liza said as they walked down the hallway to the kitchen.

They could hear the television playing in the living room.

"Oh my god," her father shouted.

"Daddy?" Anita slid open the pocket door to the living room.

Mom walked in front the kitchen. "What's wrong?"

"They done shot Malcolm X at the Audubon Ballroom up in Harlem." Dad slowly shook his head.

Anita felt faint. Her heart began to race and the world around was receding into the background. She'd heard the words, but they couldn't be true.

Not Brother Malcolm. Anyone but him.

"Doesn't look good," Dad said somberly.

Everyone gathered in front of the television. Liza put her arm around Anita's shoulders. "You okay?" she whispered.

"I don't know. I...I just saw him at the offices last week." Anita's nostrils flared as she sucked in air. "He wished me blessings for the baby."

The images were surreal. There he was. Brother Malcolm on a gurney, police, crowds, sirens...

• • •

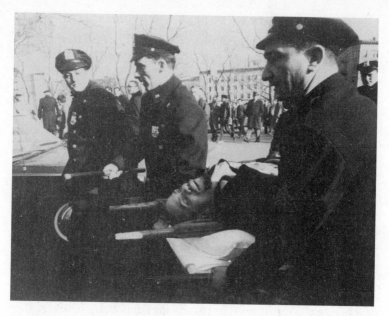

Malcolm X (1925-1965), on stretcher carried by New York policemen following his assassination at a rally in a Harlem, February 1965.
(c) Everett Collection Historical/Alamy

How could this be happening? What about Betty and the girls?
"Is he... Is he...?" Anita stuttered.

"Don't know yet," her father said.

A pain ripped through her belly. Her knees wobbled. "Ohhh!" She gripped Liza's arm to keep from going down.

"Nita!" Mom ushered her to the couch.

Everyone hovered around her.

"It's time, baby," Mom said.

Anita was still trying to catch her breath. "Not yet. Not for another few weeks," she managed.

"Babies come when they're ready. Willie, get the car. Liza, run up to Nita's room. In her closet is her bag. Bring it down and meet us in the car." She gently rubbed Anita's back.

"You're gonna be a mama," she said, her voice soft with love.

"Ohhh!" Anita cried out in pain.

"Hurry up, y'all!" her mother ordered. "Come on, baby. Let's get you in the car."

A few minutes later, Anita leaned her head back against the leather of the car. Tears slipped from between her closed lids as she listened to the newscaster declare that Malcolm X was gone. Her heart was breaking. How could the two most life-altering moments happen on the same day?

She wanted to only bathe in the joy of the life she would bring into the world, but at the same time, she mourned the loss of another who meant so much to her. She gripped her mother's hand as another pain gripped her belly. And she mourned the absence of the one who should have been there with her but wasn't.

She should have told Jason about their baby. She should have told him.

"She is a beauty," Mom cooed. She gripped Dad's hand as they stood around Anita's bed.

Her father pushed out a breath. "Looks just like you when you was a baby," he said to Anita, his usually husky voice uncharacteristically soft.

Her mother rested her head on her father's broad shoulder.

"She's soooo tiny," Liza said in awe.

Anita could barely take her eyes off her daughter. She held her protectively against her breasts, inhaled her baby scent, and her heart filled with something inexplicably joyful. It was like a dream, this soft little brown bundle with a head full of tight black curls, eyes and fists squeezed tight. She was perfect.

She had Jason's mouth and his nose. She was the outpouring of their love. *An angel.* On the same day that the world lost a warrior, an angel was born. The unspoken magnitude of that did not escape Anita.

A nurse came in. "I know how much you all want to be with the newest member of the family, but visiting hours are over, and our new mom needs some rest." She pushed the bassinet next to Anita's bed and gently lifted the baby from her reluctant arms. "Mommy, you can see your baby anytime in the nursery." She offered an assuring smile to soothe the look of angst that must have colored Anita's expression.

Anita pressed her lips tightly together and nodded. She leaned back against the pillows and released a long breath, then looked from one loving face to another. "I still can't believe it," she said in awe. "I have a baby. A real human being."

She looked at her mother, whose gaze telegraphed her total understanding. Her mother's wise counsel when she shared the story of Anita's conception and birth settled within her in a new way. The swollen feet, backaches, unexplained tears, painful breasts, fear, loneliness, excitement, and uncertainty no longer mattered. That little ball of human life was the product of love.

Jason. Jason. It was time.

She had no idea how he would take learning that he was a father and, more importantly, that she'd kept it from him all these months, and how she would live her life without him until he came back home. Then Jason's mother's words to her last Thanksgiving seeped in her head: *Faith is confidence in what we hope for and assurance about what we do not see.*

Her heart thumped. She looked around at her family circle. "I'm going to name her Faith."

. . .

March 10, 1965
Dearest Jason,

I pray that this letter reaches you and that you are safe and well. Hopefully, you have not been moved again. It was so good to get your last letter. The fact that it took so long to reach me made receiving it that much better. But it has been a while since I've heard from you. Did you get my Christmas present? I hope you like it and will keep it with you.

I have some news to share with you. I should have told you long ago, but I thought at the time that it was best not to so that you could focus on being safe and not worry about what was going on back here.

We have a daughter, Jason. I named her Faith Angela. She was born on February 25. Six pounds. Six ounces. I have enclosed a picture of her. She is healthy and beautiful and amazing.

I know now that I should have told you. I hope that you will one day forgive me for keeping this kind of secret. A combination of my arrogance in figuring what was best for you and being scared that you would feel trapped kept me from telling. It has been so hard keeping this from you. I worried about it every day. But she is here, Jason. And I can't wait for you to return so she can meet her daddy.

Please stay safe and know that you have a new member of your family waiting for you to come home.

Love
Anita and Faith

Her next letter was to Jason's parents. She wished she had a number to call, but a letter would have to do. She invited them to come and visit their granddaughter and asked for their forgiveness as well. She enclosed a picture of Faith and her home phone number and address.

The inklings of spring tried valiantly to push the chill of winter to an afterthought. Spring still had work to do, but the sun was bright and warm, and the wind was manageable.

"It's early to be taking that baby out," Mom said as she sat at the kitchen table snapping green beans for dinner. "Barely two weeks old." She got up from the table and went to the sink to wash her hands, then came over to the stroller and peeked deep inside to check that little Faith was bundled against the elements. She adjusted the pink blanket and pulled her fluffy pink hat a bit farther down onto her tiny forehead. "There." She straightened and beamed. "Where are you headed?"

"Just a short walk. I want to drop these two letters in the box."

Mom lifted her chin and hummed in her throat. "That letter telling Jason about his daughter, I hope."

"Yes."

"Good. Good. Should never keep something like this from a father."

"I wrote to his parents, too."

Her mother squeezed her shoulder. "As you should." She leaned in and kissed Anita's cheek. "Well, go on now while the sun is high."

Anita stepped outside into the early-afternoon sunshine. She turned her face up to the warmth, glanced down to make sure that Faith was properly covered, then began their stroll.

She started down Lewis Avenue toward Fulton Street,

thinking that she'd walk through Fulton Park. The air sparkled. The sun dropped pinpoints of light on the tiny buds that dared to pop their heads up, giving the world an inkling of newness and possibility.

When she approached Decatur Street, she started to walk by, but the old days, the days of playing handball, learning how to smoke her first cigarette, leaning up against Leon in the shadows of the basketball court, drew her beyond the metal gates.

School was in session. She could hear the cacophony of children's voices drifting out from the partially opened windows. She pushed Faith's stroller across the handball court, then the basketball courts, remembering how young she was back then, how full of expectations.

Young *and* naive.

She sighed and glanced up at the classroom windows, wishing she knew then what she knew now—how young boys from Chauncey Street could make you feel like a woman when you were still a girl. How lazy smiles and secret touches could awaken a body in ways they'd never experienced. She wished that she could share with those young voices behind those windows all that she'd learned.

Anita glanced down at Faith, whose wide brown eyes gazed right into her own, and knew that in the months and years to come, she would have many life lessons to share with her daughter.

She pushed the stroller out of the school's gate and continued on her walk toward the park. Since Faith's birth, she hadn't had time or the desire to really process the loss of Brother Malcolm, what it meant to his movement, and what her role could or should be going forward, especially with a baby. But she knew she would return, continue his work.

She took a seat on the park bench, checked Faith again.

She was fast asleep. Anita adjusted her blankets. At some point, she wanted to get back up to Harlem, stop in the office, and see for herself how everyone was doing. Henry had sent her a card of congratulations with fifty bucks inside from the staff at B-Flat, with an open invitation to come back whenever she was ready. Her audience, Henry had written, was missing her. She smiled at that, knowing it was Henry's way of saying that *he* missed her.

Before she made any more decisions in her life, though, she would wait to hear from Jason.

Anita was lulling Faith to sleep in the rocking chair her dad had brought down from the attic—the same chair her mom used to rock her in—when the phone rang. Her mother was at her part-time job at the Macon Branch library, and her dad was on Halsey Street playing cards, which he regularly did on Saturday afternoons.

She started to let the phone ring and go to the answering machine, but somehow she felt there was an insistence about the ringing that elevated her pulse.

She cradled an almost-sleeping infant, lowered her into the crib, and inched over to the phone on her nightstand before the ringing eliminated any chance of an afternoon nap.

"Hello?"

"Can I speak to Anita?"

"This is Anita." She caught the slight southern drawl, and the hairs on her arms tingled. "Mrs. Tanner?"

"Yes. Anita. Oh, Anita…"

"Mrs. Tanner, I'm so sorry. I know I should have told Jason, told you and Mr. Tanner—"

"It's not that." Mae Ellen's voice cracked in a million pieces. "Jason is missing."

Anita stopped breathing. She reached behind her for the edge of the bed and sat. "Wh— What are you saying?"

"We got a visit from the army—the same day you wrote that Faith was born," she said.

Anita felt Mae Ellen's struggle not to cry.

"They said that Jason's unit was on maneuvers; somehow they crossed over into enemy territory. There was gunfire." Her voice hitched. "Several bodies were recovered, but not Jason."

The room slowly spun. "Oh God." She pressed her fist to her mouth. Her stomach roiled.

"A baby," Mae Ellen barely whispered. "Faith." Her voice broke. Her sobs vibrated in Anita's chest to mix with her own. "Oh my Lord," she cried.

Anita was shaking all over by the time she hung up. She couldn't think. Her heart was racing so fast, it was hard to breathe.

She sat curled in the rocker, in the dark. That was where her mother found her.

Mom flipped on the light. Anita didn't move.

"Nita, why are you sitting in the dark?" She quietly crossed the room so as not to wake Faith. "Nita?"

Slowly, Anita looked up into her mother's concerned face.

Her mother's breath caught, and she got to her knees to look Anita straight in the eyes. She pressed her palms on Anita's thighs. "Chile, what is it? What happened? Is the baby okay?" Her head snapped toward the crib.

"They. Can't. Find. Jason." Her gaze drifted off to some distant place.

"Sweet Lord. Nita, baby. How? What do you know?"

In fits and starts, between tears and her mind simply

wandering, she finally relayed what Mae Ellen had told her about the visit from the army and what they knew up to this point.

"They believe he may still be alive." She swallowed. "And has been taken captive." A tear slid down her cheek. She swiped it away. "Mr. and Mrs. Tanner want to come see Faith, but they don't want to leave home in case… He went missing the same day Faith…was born." She covered her face with her hands and wept.

Anita stayed in touch with Jason's parents by phone on a weekly basis. But as the days turned to weeks and weeks into months, there was no word on Jason. The army assured the Tanner family that they were doing everything they could to try to find the missing servicemen.

None of that mattered. Not one damned bit when she looked into her daughter's face and didn't know what kind of future she would have without her father.

Constant waves of guilt swept through her, weakened her. She should have told him the moment she found out about Faith. Jason deserved to know. What right did she have to take the decision away from him? And now…

Most nights she cried herself to sleep, and between that and waking every three hours to feed Faith, she moved through her days like a zombie. Her mother had convinced her that what she needed in her life more than anything was church and prayer. She needed to bend her knees to the Lord and ask Him to bring peace to her heart and Jason back to his family. And she needed to have *faith*.

• • •

I t was the first Sunday in August and at least ninety degrees in the shade. Congregants poured out of Cornerstone Baptist Church, fanning church fans and mopping brows with embroidered handkerchiefs and crumpled tissue.

Her mother walked down the steps of the church. "That was some sermon Reverend Harvey preached." She whipped out the fan from her purse and proceeded to create some cool air.

"Yes, it was," Anita agreed. She hoisted Faith up on her hip and adjusted the bonnet on her head.

Mom cupped her hand over her eyes to block the glare. "This is that Mississippi kinda heat, wrap around you like a damp sheet and won't let go. Make sure you have that hat down good over Faith's eyes."

"I did."

They strolled between the throng of churchgoers down Madison Street and turned onto Lewis Avenue before curving onto their street.

"I haven't seen you do any of your writing lately," her mother said. She glanced at Anita's profile.

Anita's brows rose and fell. She adjusted Faith's weight. "I've written a few things. Bits and pieces. Nothing is really finished."

"You know, I'd be happy to watch Faith some night if you want to…go to the place where you worked and read your poetry."

Anita's neck jerked back in surprise. Her mother had never really been a supporter of her living in Harlem, working with Malcolm X, or working in a bar and reading her poetry. "Seriously?"

Mom beamed. "Yes, Nita, seriously." She patted her shoulder. "I think it'll be good for you. To get out. See friends. Read your work."

Anita drew in a quick breath. Since Faith had been born, she'd devoted all her time and attention to her daughter, hadn't allowed herself room to think about anything else. It was too painful.

Her mother unlocked the wrought iron gate to the front door of their house, and they went inside.

Anita wasn't even sure she had what it took to stand on stage and bare her soul—again. "Thank you. I'll think about it."

Chapter Twenty-One

Anita changed her outfit three different times, put on lipstick, wiped it off, then put it back on. She used her pick to fluff her hair, put on her hoop earrings, took them off, and put on the silver teardrops instead. She stood in front of the full-length mirror, turned left, then right, and looked over her shoulder at her newfound very round behind.

She walked over to the window, sat in the rocking chair, and picked up her notebook. She flipped it open.

Since coming home from church three weeks earlier, she'd spent Faith's nap time working on finishing some of her poems that she'd left undone in her notebook and even writing new ones. She had one that she'd finally perfected, and she dragged up enough nerve to give Henry a call. He was more than happy to have her come in and do a set. He'd even put up a flyer in the window, he'd said, to let the clientele know she was back.

Well, tonight was the night. Her mother was going to watch Faith. Liza would meet her at B-Flat at eight. She'd finally settled on an outfit—maybe—and the piece that she'd written took her to a new place. She wanted to bring the audience along with her.

She closed the notebook, looked out at the twilight

that had begun to descend upon the city, and mouthed the prayer that she'd prayed every day for the past seven months: *Wherever he is, Lord, keep Jason safe and bring him back home to us. Amen.*

When she ascended the steps of the train station and stepped out onto 125th Street, she felt the jolt of electric energy that flowed up from the concrete, bounced off the neon signs, and danced like showgirls at the Cotton Club.

The tingle of excitement in her limbs was fueled by the street corner guys who hollered at her to give them just a minute of her time. Her smile remained inside with only a lift of her brow in response and an extra sway of her hips. Damn, it felt good to be out again, to feel like her old self again. At least for a few hours.

She turned onto Lenox. A crowd of Saturday nightclub hoppers was in front of the Lenox Lounge. Thumping music slid out every time a door opened and joined the parade of the night. She kept walking, passing couples and singles and groups laughing and talking loud or soft or something in between. B-Flat was up ahead.

Anita spotted Liza first, and when their gazes met, Liza waved above the heads and padded shoulders in the rainbows of shapes and colors on the street.

"Hey," Anita greeted on a breath of excitement. She hugged her friend.

"Saturday night in Harlem," Liza singsonged. She hooked her arm through Anita's. "You ready for your return to the spotlight?" she asked with a note of grandeur in her voice.

Anita's giggle wobbled. "I sure as hell hope so." She pulled open the door to B-Flat and instantly felt that she had come home.

The first thing she did was look for Henry, who she found behind the bar. When he spotted her standing there with her hand on her hip, he actually smiled like he was glad to see her.

He tossed the white cloth onto the bar top and came around to where she stood next to Liza. "Well, well. Look what the fabled A train done dragged in." He smiled for real this time.

Anita broke all protocols and kissed him solidly on the cheek. "Good to see you, Henry. Real good." She glanced around. "Busy as usual."

"Folks heard you was coming back tonight. You have fans, young lady. Matter of fact, I'm not even gonna ask you to start working your station. Find a seat. Whatever you want is on the house. You go on at ten."

"Your generosity is almost more than I can stand," she said over the giddy laughter in her belly.

"How's that pretty ole baby girl of yours?"

Anita's felt her face light up like it could take away the dimness of the club. "Growing like a weed. She's incredible. A happy baby, and we're both finally sleeping through the night!"

Henry chuckled. "I remember those days."

Anita frowned. "You have kids?"

"Two. Girl and boy. All grown up, pretty much."

"I had no idea."

Henry winked. "Lot you don't know." He lifted his chin. "Go find yourself a table, order what you want. I got a business to run." He turned back to the bar.

Anita and Liza settled themselves at a table in the center of the room. Little Stevie Wonder's "Fingertips" was playing.

"Last thing Jason and me did together," Anita said.

"Huh?"

"Took Jason to his first Apollo show. Motortown Revue. Stevie Wonder brought down the house with that song." Her throat tightened.

Liza covered Anita's clenched fist. "When's the last time you had a rum and Coke?" she gently teased.

Anita managed a smile. "Too long."

Liza raised her hand to get the waitress's attention and ordered two rum and Cokes.

"She's new," Anita commented absently. "Guess she took my place."

They were quiet for a moment, then Liza said, "Jason is gonna come home, Nita. He will."

Anita's gaze drifted around the room. "I have to believe that."

Henry hopped up on stage, and the music quieted until it stopped. The spotlight separated him from the band behind him.

He tapped the stand-up microphone. "Evening. Hope y'all are enjoying yourselves tonight. Eating and drinking," he added with a chuckle in his voice. "We have a special treat tonight—one of B-Flat's favorites. Our prodigal sister has come back. Let's give a warm welcome to Anita Hopkins."

The room rose in applause and shouts of welcome. Anita absorbed the energy as she took her place beneath the lights.

She clasped the head of the microphone in her hands, drew in a calming breath to slow the racing beat of her heart.

"I call this piece, 'The Storm.'"

"Forever we stand
against the winds
that seek to sweep

and bend and twist
the body and words yet
cannot break the man,
the message, the movement,
or the backs that stand tall.
Turn your faces toward the storm
with defiance and purpose.
Stand in form and spirit,
deeply together,
holding hands
and hearts for him;
gone now
but never forgotten
what you taught us about us,
Brother Malcolm.
Gone home,
still here in us;
against the storm
We stand."

For several moments, there was a silence that settled like a blanket on the room and then slowly the audience began to stand and celebrated in a unified, singular applause.

Anita's throat clenched over the thundering of her heart. She blinked back tears of relief, realizing that she still loved this, could still do this, and that her messages mattered.

"Thank you." She looked over the still applauding crowd. "Thank you." She held up her hand, and the room slowly quieted. "It's been a minute since I've been up here."

"Welcome back!" someone shouted.

Anita laughed. "Thanks. And it feels real good!"

More applause.

"Since I've been gone, I had a little girl. I named her Faith."

She paused for a moment to collect her thoughts. "Her dad is captured somewhere in 'Nam."

A hum-like wave rolled through the room.

"Faith was born the same day that Brother Malcolm was taken and I found out later that it was the same day that her father was captured." She cleared her throat. "This next piece is for her dad, Jason. I call it 'Confessions.'"

"We parted
in harsh words and silence,
divided by our devised
rights and wrongs,
forgetting that our
two sides of the road
met in the middle,
and discovered us together
were stronger than one
Idea
That longs to sing the same song.
You're gone
Now
but never lost, ever;
I must believe that
Faith will…
Bring you back to her
And us, and the words and space
Will never separate
us
Again.
In these things, I confess,
I cannot see;
It is faith that will
Bring you home to me."

Anita released the microphone, blinked back tears, and walked off stage to another round of rousing applause. She returned to her table.

"Girl. Girl," Liza said and lifted her glass in salute. "You okay?"

Anita offered a tight-lipped smile. "Yeah. I am." She nodded. "I am. I have Faith."

Anita was scanning the want ads in the *New York Daily News* in hopes of finding a part-time job close to her parents' home so she could start saving her money and get back out on her own.

Faith was nine months old, sleeping through the night, trying to crawl, and Anita was actually beginning to feel like a human being again. Since her mom assured her that she would be more than happy to look after Faith, now was a good time for job hunting.

She circled a few possibilities. There was a new soul food restaurant opening on Bedford Avenue, and they were looking for waitresses. That was definitely something she was good at, and maybe she'd even be able to do some open mics. Working would do her good in general. It would give her an outlet from the news, the waiting, the not knowing. Every day that passed with no word on Jason tested her faith.

"Nita! Nita!"

She jerked at the frantic call of her name. She darted to her bedroom door, hoping not to wake Faith from her nap.

She stood at the top of the stairs. "Ma. What's wrong?" she asked in a harsh whisper, trying to keep her voice low.

"Jason's mama's on the phone. They found him!"

Her breath caught. On the phone? Didn't make sense. She glanced at the phone on her nightstand and remembered she'd unplugged it so the ringing wouldn't wake up Faith. A wave of heat roared through her, and she found herself running down two flights of stairs to the kitchen. She snatched up the yellow receiver from its perch on top of the wall-mounted base.

"Hello! Mrs. Tanner?" She slid down into the chair as she listened to the joyful sobs of Jason's mom telling her that the army had conducted a search-and-rescue mission, and among the soldiers recovered, Jason was one of them.

"Do we know how he is? Is he hurt? When will he be home? Can we talk to him? Oh God. Oh God."

Her mother stood beside her, gripped her shoulder.

"Yes. Of course. Okay." Tears streamed down her face. "Thank you. Thank you for calling. Yes. I'll be right by the phone."

In a daze, she absently handed the phone to her mother.

Dad walked in after a day of fishing out in Sheepshead Bay. He snatched his hat from his head, dropped his tackle kit on the floor, looked from one stricken face to another. "What happened? What's wrong?"

Anita lifted her head to look at her father through tear-filled eyes. "They found Jason. He's hurt, but they found him."

The next few weeks were a flurry of phone calls, updates, delays, frustration, and hope. Mae Ellen called pretty much every day whether she had news or not. The army wouldn't tell her much more than what they had originally. The process was long and arduous.

Once the injured were stabilized, they were shipped to the closest medical facility in South Vietnam. Then they were flown to the US base in Germany, where they were evaluated and debriefed before being flown back to the States.

After more than a month since the rescue, Jason was finally on a flight bound for America. He was being sent to the VA Hospital in Arlington, Virginia, and would arrive before Thanksgiving.

Her parents insisted on flying to Virginia with Anita, and Anita was more than happy for the company and the support, especially during the flight over when her mother was the only one who could get Faith to sleep on the plane.

When they landed, Mae Ellen, Ralph, and Jason's brother and sister were already in the waiting area, having just arrived as well.

Mae Ellen spotted Anita and the baby and rushed over.

"Anita!" She hugged her long and hard. Kissed her cheek, then finally took a step back.

Anita put her arm around Mae Ellen's shoulder. Her heart thudded. "Mrs. and Mr. Tanner, this is my mom, Celia, and my dad, Willie Hopkins." She lifted a sleepy Faith from her mother's arms. "And this is your granddaughter, Faith." She beamed with love and pride as she handed over her daughter to her grandparents. Her heart thumped as she watched the awed expressions and listened to the oohs and ahhs. Her baby girl. Her and Jason's baby girl. She would make it up to all of them for depriving them of even one moment with the miracle that she and Jason created.

There was a flurry of hugs and kisses and introductions of Patrice and Mason.

Ralph finally settled the tumbling conversations, relieved

laughter, and passing of Faith from one newfound family member to the next and reminded them that they needed to look for the army representative who was to pick them up and take them to the VA hospital.

"Yes, yes!" Anita blurted, suddenly frantic that they'd missed their contact. She could barely contain her excitement, which bordered on a panic attack.

"We need to meet over by baggage claim," Mae Ellen advised.

The entourage trooped across the terminal to baggage claim, where drivers and family members were lined up, awaiting their passengers.

Anita spotted the army sergeant first. "Over here," she announced to the family.

The sergeant held up a sign with the Tanner name on it.

Ralph walked up to him. "I'm Ralph Tanner—my wife, Mae Ellen, and my other children." He turned to Anita and her family. "This is our son's daughter, Faith, and Faith's mother and grandparents."

Sergeant Abrams's blue eyes accessed the assemblage. "Good thing I drove the Humvee." He smiled. "Follow me please."

The army Humvee pulled to a stop in front of the Virginia Hospital Center. Sergeant Abrams jumped out and opened the doors.

"I'll escort you. You'll need to sign in. Of course, everyone cannot go in to see him at once." He shut the doors and led the way.

They took the elevator to the fourth floor, then down a

long corridor to the family reception room.

"Please make yourselves comfortable. I'll have someone come to get you and take you to see Private First Class Tanner." He nodded to the family, turned on his heels, and walked out.

The next fifteen minutes felt like a lifetime. While Anita paced, alternating Faith on her hip or sharing her with her parents and grandparents, her thoughts twisted and curled around all the times she and Jason shared, the time they lost, and what the future would be. Would he understand and forgive her for not telling him about Faith? And his injuries: how severe were they? Would they change his life, their life? Would he go back to Atlanta with his family? What would that mean for her and Faith? Would she relocate, or maybe he would return to New—

"Hello. I'm Dr. Madison."

Everyone leaped from their seats at once.

He smiled at each one in turn. "It will be very good for Private Tanner's recovery to have the support of his family," he began. "His left arm was broken in several places, and he had a broken tibia and shrapnel in his left thigh. But his recovery is as much mental as it is physical."

Mae Ellen gasped. Ralph put his arm around her. Anita froze, terrified of what words would come next, but needing to hear them.

"Our soldiers have seen and endured things most of us only read about. Coming home will be an adjustment for everyone. He will need a lot of patience." He shoved his hands into the wide pockets of his white lab coat, dragged in a breath, and exhaled. "I know everyone is anxious to see him, but not all at once. Two to three at a time. You all can decide, and I'll take you to see him."

"As long as we know our son is home, we can wait a while longer," Ralph said. "You and Faith should see him first."

Mae Ellen nodded vigorously in agreement. She patted Anita's shoulder. "Go. Let him meet his daughter," she said gently.

"Are you sure?"

"Yes," she answered.

Anita followed Dr. Madison past room after room of soldiers in various states of injury. The path in front of her grew filmy. She drew in a breath to clear her head and vision. What if he really didn't want to see her after what she'd done?

Dr. Madison stopped in front of a room with Jason's name and another soldier's name on the door.

Her heart thumped. Suddenly, it was unbearably hot. She couldn't breathe. Faith squirmed in her arms.

Dr. Madison pushed the door open and stepped to the side to let her pass. "He's at the end," he said, lifting his chin toward Jason.

She patted her hair, tugged at the collar of her blouse that was suddenly itchy. She gave Faith a quick kiss, adjusted her pink-and-white headband, and crossed the spotless white-tiled floor, thankful that she'd chosen her trusty sneakers. The sound of shoe heels popping against the tiles would have sent her over the edge for sure.

Her breath caught in her chest, slowed her movement. Even with his leg in traction and his body covered in a white sheet up to his waist, she would know Jason anywhere. Her spirit would know him. She blinked back the sudden burn in her eyes. He was alive. She could touch him again. Love him again—if he let her.

If he forgave her.

Jason turned his head in her direction. He blinked slowly

as if the effort was more than he could handle, and then he smiled, and the knot in her chest burst and she could almost breathe again.

She reached the side of his bed. His eyes were wiser, and the scar above his brow gave him a rugged look.

"Hey do-gooder…" It came out like a whispered prayer. "Jason, oh God, I didn't… They found you, they found you. I'm so sorry. About everything." The words tumbled out of her mouth. She wanted to spill out her heart and soul before he told her to leave.

Instead, he reached up with his good arm and caressed her cheek the way he used to. "I had to come home to you and…"

Tears sprang to her eyes. Her lips trembled. "Jason. Jason." She leaned down and kissed him, nearly dumping Faith on his chest. "This is your daddy, Faith. Your dad."

She could never put to words the range of emotions that passed across Jason's face, finally settling on awed wonder as he gently touched every exposed part of his daughter. Faith wrapped her fingers around his, and Anita knew those were tears in Jason's eyes. He stared at their daughter in utter amazement. "We did this?" he whispered.

"Yeah, we did this," she said, her voice trembling with joy.

He looked up at her. "I didn't get your letter about Faith until I was in the hospital in Germany." He shifted a bit and winced. "Don't know how the letter finally found me. Guess it was meant to be, huh?" He stared into Anita's eyes, which had filled with tears. "I would have stayed if I'd known," he said softly while he gazed with awe at his daughter.

Anita sniffed hard and wiped her damp cheeks. "I know," she whispered. "I know that *now*, but I couldn't do that to you *then*. I didn't want you to feel obligated to go against what you believed you needed to do." She implored him with her eyes.

"You shoulda let me decide that for myself, Nita. Wasn't

right. Man has a right to know."

She lowered her head. Tears spilled onto Faith. "I'm sorry, J. You gotta forgive me." She blinked hard and looked at him. "It was wrong of me, I admit that. It was selfish. I'm so sorry, J. But we're here now. We're here now," she said, her voice a soft plea.

"Had plenty of time to think it over." He paused. "Much as I didn't like it" — he dragged in a long breath — "it was typical Anita Hopkins."

Her lips opened to spout a retort but stopped when she saw the light of a smile tugging at the corners of his mouth.

"The fierce, fiery, independent, loving woman I fell for the first time I laid eyes on her on that long-ass bus ride."

A giggle bubbled up from her throat. She tugged on her bottom lip. Sniffed.

"I shoulda married you like I really wanted to do. I shouldn't have worried so hard about 'doing the right thing.' The right thing is *us* being together, sugah." It was as much a statement as a question.

Anita nodded vigorously. "I shoulda let you have your say instead of not listening, not taking your calls…"

"I've seen things, Nita," he said, his voice low, almost distant. He looked away. "There's nights when I can't sleep, days that I want to forget. Doctors said that it will take time, patience, and therapy." He snorted a laugh and angled his head to look at her. "I'm not the same man I was when I left."

Anita dragged in a breath. Was he telling her that he didn't think they could make it?

"It's not going to be easy. I have rehab, have to learn to walk again, get my strength back. Visits to the psychologist…" He feigned a smile.

"What are you trying to tell me, Jason?" Her heart raced.

He reached up and stroked her cheek. She gripped his hand and held it to her face.

"How 'bout we make an agreement?" he asked.

"Okay."

"From here on out, no secrets between us. No more thinking we know what's best for the other one." His eyes crinkled in the corners. "We talk about things even when it might hurt."

She bobbed her head.

"Since we're gonna be a family, we're gonna need some place to live."

A giddy sensation bubbled in her stomach.

"It'll be a while before I can get back to work, but the veterans' benefits will be coming in soon, and they have a program for homeownership."

"When you get out of here, you can come stay at my folks' house, or if you want to go back to Atlanta…I'll go. We'll go with you. Long as we're together," she said in a rush.

Jason grinned. "Your people are 'bout as traditional as mine. I don't think they'd look too favorably on us 'living together' under their roof. Even though we done already skipped the 'I dos' with this little beauty here." He leaned down and kissed the forehead of his sleeping daughter.

"So what should we do? I can't be without you, Jason. I won't. Not another minute."

"Then you have to say yes."

Her brows knitted in question.

"Marry me, Anita Hopkins. Drag me kicking and screaming on the subways, introduce me to New York life—buying food and clothes off the street—show me what it was like growing up in a big ole brownstone in Brooklyn, help me to understand your passions even when I don't agree. Help me to raise our daughter to be as fierce and independent as her mama, and sons who love their women like I love you," he added with a smile. "Say yes to this 'do-gooder,' and we can take on the world together—even when we don't agree."

Tears flowed from her eyes, so fast and heavy that everything other than Jason's words blurred. "Yes, yes," she managed over her laughter and the banging of her heart, before leaning over Faith and sealing her lips to Jason's.

In that moment, they fully understood that the passion of their kiss was more than a kiss. It was an "I apologize and I accept." It symbolized the start of a new life, the beginning of healing, a closing off of the past, and an open doorway to their futures.

Slowly, Anita eased back when Faith began to squirm. She gazed at the man who had entered her life and turned it on its head. Who would have thought that this "country boy do-gooder" would have captured and tamed her northern-rebel heart?

She fully realized, from a place deep in her soul, that their love was more powerful than an idea, and what she wanted more than anything was for them to share their life together in whatever shape it took. Working for their ideas and making a home together at the same time.

"Guess we have some plans to make," Jason said with a wide grin.

Anita giggled with joy. "Yep. We sure do." She swiped at her eyes, which just kept spilling over with happiness. She sat on the side of Jason's bed while he held Faith with his one good arm. That was when she noticed. "You're wearing the watch," she said, surprised.

"Yeah. A Timex," he grinned. "Just like the one I'd lost. Somehow I managed to keep it, and it was the one thing that I was able to hold onto, gave me hope that one day I'd get back home to you." He cupped her chin. His eyes danced over her face. "We have all the time in the world now. The three of us."

Anita looked into the eyes of the man who was made for her. "Yes. We do."

Epilogue

One Year Later

Anita was just finishing a piece she planned to perform at B-Flat on Saturday night when she heard the front doorbell.

"Oh, Mrs. Tannnnneeer," Jason shouted out from the ground floor moments later.

Anita laughed. She loved when her husband called her *Mrs. Tanner.* "Yes, Mr. Tanner," she called back. She left the room they'd set up as a study and came to the top of the stairs.

Jason peeked his head around. "Got a delivery, sugah."

Her eyes widened in delight as she darted down the stairs. She hurried down the hall that led into the kitchen. Jason's VA benefits had kicked in, and they had closed on their house two months earlier. As much as her parents gave the newlywed couple their space and privacy when Jason was released from the hospital, there was nothing like having your own home.

The layout of their new house on Stuyvesant Avenue was almost identical to her parents' home, except that hers and Jason's was three stories and her folks' was four. The fact that her parents were only four blocks away was an added benefit when it came to having someone they trusted look after Faith on the days that Jason went to the new space he'd set up on Fulton Street and she went uptown to help out with the movement to continue Brother Malcolm's message of self-reliance.

Jason had used some of his monthly VA benefits to pay the rent on a storefront that he'd converted into a community space called Faith's Place. Several times a month, he hosted a guest speaker from the community, ranging from housing issues to voting, food shortages, and school services. It was slowly becoming a hub for community resources. In between, he still did monthly recruitment and training for nonviolent resistance.

Now that she was a mother, she curtailed her protests and steered away from the mass rallies. But she still answered phones and passed out literature. She might be on the sidelines, but her passion for self-determination never wavered.

Once a month, she performed at B-Flat. She and Jason dubbed that their date night when they visited their old Harlem haunts and hung out with friends.

"Did my pots come?" she asked excitedly as she hurried to the huge box on the table.

"No telling, sugah. Boxes been coming just about every week since we moved in," he teased as he fed Faith a spoonful of the spaghetti that she loved.

"Very funny. You want us to have a home, right? Then I have to get all the things to make it one," she said and tore open the top of the box. "Towels, linens, curtains, furniture..."

"Mm-hmm. Well, if you can't find me and Faith one of these days, just look for us under some of these boxes." He chuckled, and Faith seemed to get the joke, too, and broke out in giggles.

Anita planted her hand on her hip. "Oh, a daddy's girl.

That's how it's gonna be, huh?" She sashayed over to Jason, putting a seductive gleam in her eye, and sat on his good thigh. "You slept totally through the night. That makes three nights in a row." She kissed his forehead.

Jason grinned, slowly bobbed his head. "Feels good. Group is helping, ya know. Listening to other vets share their stories and how they deal with things."

"You can talk to me, you know."

"I know I can, but there are things that I wouldn't put on you. I won't do that."

She stroked his cheek, released a slow breath. "I can handle it."

He chuckled. "You know what — you probably could, strong woman like you. But not on my watch."

She gave him a mock salute, followed by a kiss. She cradled her body against his.

The doctors and physical therapists said that he'd probably always have a slight limp that would get worse during cold weather, but most days it was barely noticeable.

"How do we feel about a *mama's boy*?" she whispered, looking Jason deep in his eyes.

His head jerked back. "Wait. What are you sayin', sugah?" He looped an arm around her waist.

"I'm sayin' that you're going to need to get rid of some of these boxes 'cause we have to make way for another crib." She kissed him lightly on the mouth. "We have a baby coming. About seven months from now."

Jason's eyes moved slowly over her face, her body, in wonder. "For real?"

"For real."

His skin lit from beneath. He pulled her close, threaded his fingers through the cotton softness of her halo of hair. "God, I love you, Anita Tanner," he said against her lips.

"I love you more, Jason Tanner," she whispered and sank into the sweetness of his mouth.

Faith giggled and banged her spoon until Jason and Anita gathered her into their unbreakable circle of love that would always have room for more.

Acknowledgments

Wow. Just wow. This novel was truly a labor of love and determination. It was a story that was no more than a seed nearly a decade ago (the title even older than that), took shape during my graduate thesis, then shifted some more over the years. After submitting to several publishers in its original "thesis" form, they were all mesmerized by the exquisite language and images but... There was always a but.

However, the genesis for a contemporary Romeo and Juliet story line still hovered in the back of my mind, and I played with the elements of my thesis and transplanted my characters into the turbulent sixties. By degrees, *Confessions In B-Flat* budded and bloomed. Unfortunately, this reenvisioned tale still did not have a home until my friend and former college chum Mia Siegert told me about Entangled and put me in the capable hands of Kate Brauning, who got the go-ahead from Liz Pelletier, and I got to work with Stacy Abrams and Jessica Turner. They didn't say "but"—they said "yes."

My heartfelt thanks to Mia, Kate, Liz, Stacy, Jen, and Jessica. Thank you for believing in this story and in me to deliver it. And thanks to the amazing editors who helped to make my words shine, and special thanks to Bree Archer for my incredible cover.

It seems so appropriate that this novel enters the world at the time that it does. While *Confessions* spotlights the civil unrest of the sixties, we are again at an unprecedented turning point in our history that will invariably be chronicled by novelists and scholars alike. As I am able to look back on the sixties and reimagine them, I hope to be able to craft a tale, one day in the future, that illuminates this remarkable time in our history.

As always, my sincere thanks go to the readers who have continued to support me for the past thirty years! I would not be where I am today as an author without each of you.

Thank you all.

Turn the page to start reading the
novel that InTouch Magazine *calls*
*"[H]aunting, heartbreaking and ultimately
inspirational..."*

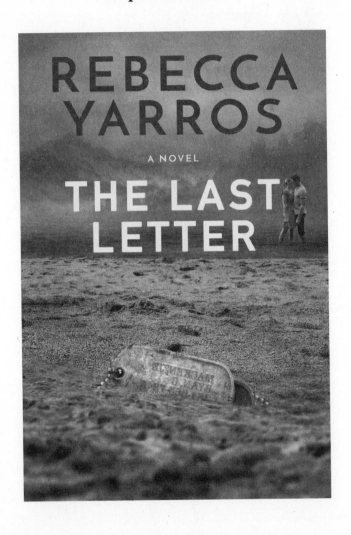

Chapter One

Beckett

#1

Dear Chaos,

At least that's what my brother says they call you. I asked him if any of his buddies needed a little extra mail, and yours was the name I was given.

So hi, I'm Ella. I know the whole no-real-names-in-correspondence rule. I've been writing these letters just as long as he's been doing what he does...which I guess is what you do.

Now, before you put this letter aside and mumble an awkward "Thanks, but no thanks," like guys do, know that this is just as much for me as it is for you. Considering that I'd be able to have a safe place to vent away from the curious eyes of this tiny, nosy town, it would almost be like I'm using you.

So, if you'd like to be my ear, I'd be grateful, and in return, I'd be happy to be yours. Also, I make pretty awesome peanut butter cookies. If cookies didn't come with this letter, then go beat my brother, because he's stolen your cookies.

Where do I start? How do I introduce myself without it sounding like a singles ad? Let me assure you, I'm not looking for anything more than a pen pal—a very faraway pen pal—I promise. Military guys don't do it for me. Guys in general don't. Not that I don't like guys. I just don't have time for them. You know what I do have? Profound regret for writing this letter in pen.

I'm the little sister, but I'm sure my brother already told you that. He's got a pretty big mouth, which means you probably know that I have two kids, too. Yes, I'm a single mom, and no, I don't regret my choices. Man, I get sick of everyone asking me that, or simply giving me the look that implies the question.

I almost erased that last line, but it's true. Also, I'm just too lazy to rewrite the whole thing.

I'm twenty-four and was married to the twins' sperm donor all of about three seconds. Just long enough for the lines to turn pink, the doctor to say there were two heartbeats, and him to pack in the quiet of the night. Kids were never his thing, and honestly, we're probably better for it.

If pen pal kids aren't your thing, I won't take offense. But no cookies. Cookies are for pen pals only.

If you're good with single parenthood in a pen pal, read on.

My twins are five, which, if you did the math correctly, means they were born when I was nineteen. After shocking our little town by deciding to raise them on my own, I just about gave it a coronary when I took over Solitude when my grandmother died. I was only twenty, the twins were still babies, and that B&B was where she'd raised us, so it seemed like a good place to raise my kids. It still is.

Let's see...Maisie and Colt are pretty much my life. In a good way, of course. I'm ridiculously overprotective of them, but I recognize it. I tend to overreact, to build a fortress around them, which keeps me kind of isolated, but hey, there are worse flaws to have, right? Maisie's the quiet one, and I can usually find her hiding with a book. Colt...well, he's usually somewhere he isn't supposed to be, doing something he isn't supposed to be doing. Twins can be crazy, but they'll tell you that they're twice the awesome.

Me? I'm always doing what I have to, and never what I really should be, or what I want to. But I think that's the nature *of being a mom and running a business. Speaking of which, the place is waking up, so I'd better get this box sealed up and shipped.*

Write back if you want. If you don't, I understand. Just know that there's someone in Colorado sending warm thoughts your way.

~ Ella

Today would have been a perfect time for my second curse word.

Usually, when we were on full-blown deployments, it got really *Groundhog Day*. Same crap, different day. There was almost a predictable, welcoming pattern to the monotony.

Not going to lie, I was a big fan of monotony.

Routine was predictable. Safe, or as safe as it was going to get out here. We were a month into another undisclosed location in another country we were never *in*, and routine was about the only thing comfortable about the place.

Today had been anything but routine.

Mission accomplished, as usual, but at a price. There was always a price, and lately, it was getting steep.

I glanced down at my hand, flexing my fingers because I could. Ramirez? He'd lost that ability today. Guy was going to be holding that new baby of his with a prosthetic.

My arm flew, releasing the Kong, and the dog toy streaked across the sky, a flash of red against pristine blue. The sky was the only clean thing about this place. Or maybe today just felt dirty.

Havoc raced across the ground, her strides sure, her focus narrowed to her target until—

"Damn, she's good," Mac said, coming up behind me.

"She's the best." I glanced over my shoulder at him before training my eyes on Havoc as she ran back to me. She had to be the best to get to where we were, on a tier-one team that operated without technically existing. She was a spec op dog, which was about a million miles above any other military working dog.

She was also mine, which automatically made her the best.

My girl was seventy pounds of perfect Labrador retriever. Her black coat stood out against the sand as she stopped just short of my legs. Her rump hit the ground, and she held the Kong out to me, her eyes dancing. "Last time," I said softly as I took it from her mouth.

She was gone before I even retracted my arm to throw.

"Word on Ramirez?" I asked, watching for Havoc to get far enough away.

"Lost his arm. Elbow down."

"Fffff—" I threw the toy as far as I could.

"You could let it slip. Seems appropriate today." Mac scratched the month of beard he was rocking and adjusted his sunglasses.

"His family?"

"Christine will meet him at Landstuhl. They're sending in fresh blood. Forty-eight hours until arrival."

"That soon?" We really were that expendable.

"We're on the move. Meeting is in five."

"Gotcha." Looked like it was on to the next undisclosed location.

Mac glanced down at my arm. "You get that looked at?"

"Doc stitched it up. Just a graze, nothing to get your panties in a twist over." Another scar to add to the dozens that already marked my skin.

"Maybe you need someone to get her panties in a twist over you in general."

I sent a healthy shot of side-eye to my best friend.

"What?" he asked with an exaggerated shrug before

nodding toward Havoc, who pulled up again, just as excited as the first time I threw the Kong, or the thirty-sixth time. "She can't be the only woman in your life, Gentry."

"She's loyal, gorgeous, can seek out explosives, or take out someone trying to kill you. What exactly is she missing?" I took the Kong and rubbed Havoc behind her ear.

"If I have to tell you that, you're too far gone for my help."

We headed back into the small compound, which was really nothing more than a few buildings surrounding a courtyard. Everything was brown. The buildings, the vehicles, the ground, even the sky seemed to be taking on that hue.

Great. A dust storm.

"You don't need to worry about me. I've got no trouble when we're in garrison," I told him.

"Oh, I'm well aware, you Chris Pratt-looking asshole. But man"—he put his hand on my arm, stopping us before we could enter the courtyard where the guys had gathered—"you're not...attached to anyone."

"Neither are you."

"No, I'm not currently in a relationship. That doesn't mean I don't have attachments, people I care about and who care about me."

I knew what he was getting at, and this wasn't the time, the place, or the *ever*. Before he could take it any deeper, I slapped him on the back.

"Look, we can call in Dr. Phil, or we can get the hell out of here and move on to the next mission." Move on, that was always what came easiest to me. I didn't form attachments because I didn't want to, not because I wasn't capable. Attachments—to people, places, or things—were inconvenient or screwed you over. Because there was only one thing certain, and it was change.

"I'm serious." His eyes narrowed into a look I'd seen too

many times in our ten years of friendship.

"Yeah, well I am, too. I'm fine. Besides, I'm attached to you and Havoc. Everyone else is just icing."

"Mac! Gentry!" Williams called from the door on the north building. "Let's go!"

"We're coming!" I yelled back.

"Look, before we go in, I left you something on your bed." Mac rubbed his hand over his beard—his nervous tell.

"Yeah, whatever it is, after this conversation I'm not interested." Havoc and I started walking toward the meeting. Already I felt the itch in my blood for movement, to leave this place behind and see what was waiting for us.

"It's a letter."

"From who? Everyone I know is in that room." I pointed to the door as we crossed the empty courtyard. That's what happened when you grew up bouncing from foster home to foster home and then enlisted the day you turned eighteen. The collection of people you considered worthy of knowing was a group small enough to fit in a Blackhawk, and today we were already missing Ramirez.

Like I said. Attachments were inconvenient.

"My sister."

"I'm sorry?" My hand froze on the rusted-out door handle.

"You heard me. My little sister, Ella."

My brain flipped through its mental Rolodex. Ella. Blond, killer smile, soft, kind eyes that were bluer than any sky I'd ever seen. He'd been waving around pictures of her for the last decade.

"Gentry, come on. Do you need a picture?"

"I know who Ella is. Why the hell is there a letter from her on my bed?"

"Just thought you might need a pen pal." His gaze dropped to his dirty boots.

"A pen pal? Like I'm some fifth-grade project with a sister school?"

Havoc slid closer, her body resting against my leg. She was attuned to my every move, even the slightest changes in my mood. That's what made us an unstoppable team.

"No, not…" He shook his head. "I was just trying to help. She asked if there was anyone who might need a little mail and, since you don't have any family—"

Scoffing, I threw open the door and left his ass standing outside. Maybe some of that sand would fill up his gaping mouth. I hated the *F* word. People bitched about theirs all the time, constantly, really. But the minute they realized you didn't have one, it was like you were an aberration who had to be fixed, a problem that needed to be solved, or worse—pitied.

I was so far beyond anyone's pity that it was almost funny.

"All right, guys." Captain Donahue called our ten-member team—minus one—around the conference table. "Sorry to tell you that we're not headed home. We've got a new mission."

All those guys groaning—no doubt missing their wives, their kids—just reaffirmed my position on the attachment subject.

• • •

"Seriously, New Kid?" I growled as the newbie scrambled to clean up the crap he'd knocked off the footlocker that served as my nightstand.

"Sorry, Gentry," he mumbled as he gathered up the papers. Typical All-American boy fresh out of operator training with no business being on this team yet. He needed another few years and way steadier hands, which meant he was related to someone with some pull.

Havoc tilted her head at him and then glanced up at me.

"He's new," I said softly, scratching behind her ears.

"Here," the kid said, handing me a stack of stuff, his eyes wide like I was going to kick him out of the unit for being clumsy.

God, I hoped he was better with his weapon than he was with my nightstand.

I put the stack on the spare inches of the bed that Havoc wasn't currently consuming. Sorting it took only a couple of minutes. Journal articles I was in the middle of reading on various topics, and— "Crap."

Ella's letter. I'd had the thing almost two weeks, and I hadn't opened it.

I hadn't thrown it away, either.

"Gonna open that?" Mac asked with the timing of an expert shit-giver.

"Why don't you ever swear?" New Kid asked at the same time.

Glaring at Mac, I slid the letter to the bottom of the stack and grabbed the journal article on top. It was on new techniques in search and rescue.

"Fine. Answer the new kid." Mac rolled his eyes and lay back on his bunk, hands behind his head.

"Yeah, my name is Johnson—"

"No, it's New Kid. Haven't earned a name yet," Mac corrected him.

The kid looked like we'd just kicked his damn puppy, so I relented.

"Someone once told me that swearing is a poor excuse for a crap vocabulary. It makes you look low class and uneducated. So I stopped." God knew I had enough going against me. I didn't need to sound like the shit I'd been through.

"Never?" New Kid asked, leaning forward like we were at a slumber party.

"Only in my head," I said, flipping to a new article in the journal.

"She really a working dog? She looks too…sweet," New Kid said, reaching toward Havoc.

Her head snapped up, and she bared her teeth in his direction.

"Yeah, she is, and yes, she'll kill you on command. So do us both a favor and don't ever try to touch her again. She's not a pet." I let her growl for a second to make her point.

"Relax," I told Havoc, running my hand down the side of her neck. Tension immediately drained out of her body, and she collapsed on my leg, blinking up at me like it had never happened.

"Damn," he whispered.

"Don't take it personally, New Kid," Mac said. "Havoc's a one-man woman, and you sure as hell aren't the guy."

"Loyal and deadly," I said with a grin, petting her.

"One day," Mac said, pointing to the letter, which had slid onto the bed next to my thigh.

"Today is not that day."

"The day you crack it open, you're going to kick yourself for not doing it sooner." He leaned over his bunk and came back up with a tub of peanut butter cookies, eating one with the sound effects of a porn.

"Seriously."

"Seriously," he moaned. "So good."

I laughed and slid the letter back under the pile.

"Get some sleep, New Kid. We're all action tomorrow."

The kid nodded. "This is everything I ever wanted."

Mac and I shared a knowing look.

"Say that tomorrow night. Now get some shut-eye and stop knocking over my stuff or your call sign becomes Butterfinger."

His eyes widened, and he sank into his bunk.

...

Three nights later, New Kid was dead.

Johnson. He'd earned his name and lost his life saving Doc's ass.

I lay awake while everyone else slept, my eyes drifting to the empty bunk. He hadn't belonged here, and we'd all known it—expressed our concerns. He hadn't been ready. Not ready for the mission, the pace of our unit, or death.

Not that death cared.

The clock turned over, and I was twenty-eight.

Happy birthday to me.

Deaths always struck me differently when we were out on deployment. They usually fell into two categories. Either I brushed it off and we moved on, or my mortality was a sudden, tangible thing. Maybe it was my birthday, or that New Kid was little more than a baby, but this was the second type.

Hey, Mortality, it's me, Beckett Gentry.

Logically, I knew that with the mission over, we'd head home in the next couple of days, or on to the next hellhole. But in that moment, a raw need for connection gripped me in a way that felt like a physical pressure in my chest.

Not attachment, I told myself. That shit was trouble.

But to be connected to another human in a way that wasn't reserved for the brothers I served with, or even my friendship with Mac, which was the closest I'd ever gotten to family.

In a move of sheer impulsivity, I grabbed my flashlight and the letter from where I'd tucked it into a journal on mountaineering.

Balancing the flashlight on my shoulder, I ripped open the letter and unfolded the lined notebook paper full of neat, feminine scroll.

I read the letter once, twice…a dozen times, placing her words with the pictures of her face I'd seen over the years. I imagined her sneaking a few moments in the early morning to get the letter written, wondered what her day had been like. What kind of guy walked out on his pregnant wife? *An asshole.*

What kind of woman took on twins and a business when she was still a kid herself? *A really damn strong one.*

A strong, capable woman who I needed to know. The yearning that grabbed ahold of me was uncomfortable and undeniable.

Keeping as quiet as possible, I took out a notebook and pen.

A half hour later, I sealed the envelope and then hit Mac in the shoulder with it.

"What the hell?" he snapped at me, rolling over.

"I want my cookies." I enunciated every word with the seriousness I usually reserved for Havoc's commands.

He laughed.

"Ryan, I'm serious." Whipping out the first name meant business.

"Yeah, well, you snooze, you lose your cookies." He smirked and settled back into his bunk, his breathing deep and even a few seconds later.

"Thank you," I said quietly, knowing he couldn't hear me. "Thank you for her."

ꙅIDEWAYS